The Ember Room

CONNELL NISBET

1

Published by Connell Nisbet
Copyright © Connell Nisbet, 2019
The moral right of the author has been asserted.
First published 2019

Cover design and photography by Connell Nisbet

ISBN 9780648394716

Other titles by Connell Nisbet

A Willing Executioner

For my parents,
Robert and Dian

PROLOGUE

It had been a long night. Abdullah had spent most of it lying on the bed in the corner of the brick hut, in the dark, waiting. Occasionally the strip of hessian that hung over the window lifted slightly on a cold breeze, only to settle again. Abdullah would get out of bed to stand in the doorway, listening. The distant dull clunking of a goat's bell somewhere down the mountain – one of his herd searching for thistles. Much further away, perhaps the pulsing thud of helicopter rotors, but Abdullah's ears could have been playing tricks on him. There were nights when he was sure he had heard the deep thunderous crack of heavy artillery from the neighbouring province, but he could never be sure. So far, the fighting had been elsewhere.

Abdullah would return to his bed, which was little more than a bundle of cloth. He would lie back and again put his hand behind his head to stare at the crooked beams that held the roof. It was all he could do to still his feverish mind. Closing his eyes only brought them closer. He would turn on his side, and without warning the tears would come, burning his eyes in the dark. He would sniffle and scrape at his top lip with the sleeve of his *perahan*. He would sit up again and stare out the door, waiting.

Eventually, the 12-year-old shepherd boy stood up. He took the single-barrel rifle from the corner of the hut, slung the leather strap over one shoulder and stepped outside. The palest tinge of dark blue over the plains to the east was just beginning to rob the night sky of its depth. He set off along a well-trodden but seemingly invisible path down the side of the mountain, his sandals slapping softly against the jagged stones. He moved purposefully, questioning the darkness for signs of movement. Years of watching the surrounding hills had accustomed his eyes to the stillness of bandits and the stealth of grey wolves.

Within the hour he was making his way around the foot of the mountain to the west. It was still dark, but he could just see the now familiar glow of the British military base across the border into Helmand province. Beyond an uneven ridge, the ground fell away to form a vast hollow, where the British had set up a temporary outpost seventh months ago. It gave them a clear view over the plain that stretched out towards the city of Sangin. Abdullah followed the descending line of the ridge, as he had done so many times before, to the point where it petered out to level ground. Here it met the only road into the base. The same road which led back around the mountains to Ghorak, the Kandahar village where Abdullah had lived with his family his entire life.

He slipped the rifle from his shoulder as he approached a tree. He leaned the weapon against the trunk, then continued walking unarmed along the edge of the road towards the blazing lights that marked the perimeter of the compound. He could now see the canvas walls of the mess hall, the barracks and prefabricated utility sheds. Further to the north large diesel trucks, six of them, parked neatly in a row. It was a village of sorts, all contained within a cyclone fence topped with razor wire. Through the fence he recognised several men from his village. They were up before the soldiers, moving between the sheds, carrying tins of fuel. These men were to be the new security forces for the region. When the British had arrived in the previous spring, they had announced through a translator that they had come to northern Helmand on the invitation of the tribal leaders to train the men, to give them the arms and the means to crush the Taliban. Abdullah had always thought it odd. He knew that at least three of the villagers working on the compound were former Taliban and one of them was still

6

connected through his cousin. The British soldiers didn't seem to care about this. It was more important that they were 'seen' to be helping the people of Afghanistan.

Abdullah walked past the sentry's post as he did most mornings. The soldier inside the wooden hut, a stocky young man with hair the colour of the desert and a broad flat face, called out to him in English, "Hey there, little man. Where do you think you're going?"

Abdullah stopped and waited. The sentry emerged from his post, his movements stifled by his multi-terrain combat gear, helmet and body armour. An assault rifle was strapped over one shoulder. He could have tried to speak to the boy in Pashto or Dari but it was too early in the morning for that. The kid knew the routine.

Abdullah lifted his arms as the soldier squatted down and patted the boy's clothing for weapons.

"Not selling anything today?" he asked.

The boy stared past him into the compound. The sentry wasn't bothered; the kids out here only ever got excited when there was something to be gained.

"Must be here to collect then," he muttered to himself.

Satisfied, he ruffled the boy's dark hair. "Go on, get on with it."

The young soldier returned to his hut, to continue staring into the darkness of the desert.

Further along the fence one of the trucks roared to life, pulling out from the line. With a loud thunk the floodlights were shut down, and for a moment the base was a tangle of stretching shadows and sweeping headlights. Abdullah headed directly towards the second barracks from the mess hall.

Inside the narrow canvas hut were two lines of low beds interspersed with lockers. The third platoon of a long-standing infantry brigade had just been given the call to get up. Sixteen young men, most of them no older than 19, were going through the motions of another day in

Afghanistan. They sat on the edge of their bunks, wrestling their heels into combat boots and drawing in the belts on their trousers, their once-youthful faces hardened with fatigue. No one spoke. Lockers were opened and shut, beds were made. They were immersed in the muted noises of 16 individuals steeling themselves once again to think and operate as a collective.

Abdullah moved among them unnoticed. He was just one of several kids from the surrounding villages who spent their days ingratiating themselves with the soldiers, offering to run small errands in the hope of receiving some Western snacks or, better still, US dollars they could exchange on the black market in Sangin. Officially, the British saw it as part of their dual aim to crush the Taliban and win hearts and minds, to work directly with the villagers, helping them to help themselves. Other bases were stricter, they had to be. But out here, they needed to let the villagers in, or they would be shut out from the local knowledge that was crucial to their operations. And for the most part, the kids were easier to deal with than their fathers and uncles.

Three beds in from the entrance, a wiry young soldier with ginger hair and cold blue eyes was sitting in his combat pants and boots. Private Barnes' chest and arms were mottled with scar tissue, burns from a roadside bomb on a previous tour. He was about to pull his t-shirt over his head when he stopped and looked up at the lanky blonde soldier who bunked beside him.

"What the fuck do you think you're doing?" Barnes asked, his accent drawn from the damp back streets of Newcastle.

Private Winstone stood over Barnes with a comb in his hand. He was a poster boy for the shortcomings of public education, well-bred and confident but essentially immature. He was already dressed in full fatigues and had been fixing his hair when Barnes had pulled him up.

"What?" he asked, holding the comb in front of Barnes's face. "This?"

Barnes went to grab it back, but Winstone was too quick. He whipped his hand away, grinning at the high-strung gunner who was now breathing heavily through his nose. Out there beyond the cyclone fence, they thought as one unit, their camaraderie keeping them sane, fluid and febrile, but in the barracks fissures appeared where the pent-up steam would threaten to rip them apart.

Barnes stood up, nose to nose with Winstone. The one thing he hated more than people touching his stuff, was entitled toffs taking the piss. "Don't be touching my shit, Winstone. I've warned you."

"For fuck's sake, Barnes. It's just a fucking comb, you Geordie lunatic."

He tossed it on the bed, no longer entertained by the idea, but Barnes wouldn't let him pass. "It's my fucking comb," Barnes said. "You got that, you dopey fucking cunt. My. Fucking. Comb." He emphasised the last three words by poking his index finger into Winstone's chest.

"Fuck you, Bell End," Winstone spat back.

The other soldiers were watching warily now. This had been brewing for days. Someone called out for the two of them to take it easy; it wasn't worth fighting over, but Barnes wasn't listening. He'd had a bad night and was struggling to hold it together.

"I've told this cunt a thousand times not to touch my fucking stuff."

Winstone may have been entitled, but he wasn't one to take an insult lying down. "Call me a cunt one more time, Barnes."

Barnes's chest filled with air as he clenched his fists. "You're not even a cunt. You're worse than a..." before the words could escape from his lips, Winstone head-butted him in the nose, causing the soldier to fall down between the beds.

9

"Oh crap," someone said from a nearby locker, as everyone in the tent leapt over their bunks to reach the two soldiers before they could do anymore damage. But it was too late. Barnes had wrapped his scarred arms around Winstone's legs, tipping him off balance. The two men sprawled on the floor, trying to land punches while grappling one another. Like pit bulls in a backyard match, they unleashed all their pent-up anger and frustration, wild eyed and growling. They had lived on the edge of their nerves for seven months, continually hardwired for combat but unable to engage the enemy. It had only been a matter of time before they turned on one another. Barnes bared his bloody teeth, pulling Winstone's head close to his mouth in an attempt to bite his ear, as Winstone continually drove his fist into Barnes' exposed kidneys – the scar tissue there reddened then split in several places.

Without waiting for instructions, four other soldiers did their best to pull the men apart. Fists were thrown blindly, some connected, loosening teeth. At one moment the attempts to break up the fight threatened to descend into an all-in brawl.

"Enough!" barked First Lieutenant Peel from the entrance to the tent. The platoon leader had left the barracks not five minutes earlier to get the day's orders only to return to find his highly trained soldiers behaving like animals. Hearing their immediate commander's voice, the young soldiers stepped back, leaving Barnes and Winstone glaring at one another, both still seething with hatred.

Peel, taller and wider than both men, stepped between them. "I've had just about enough of this shit from you two."

He was about to lay into them with a fury he usually reserved for new recruits when he noticed something odd past the shoulders of his men. Down at the other end of the tent Private Horace, the company mechanic, was standing stock still, staring straight ahead, oblivious to the fight that had consumed the rest of the platoon. Peel couldn't see what Horace was looking at, but something wasn't right. The private stood like a sentry on duty, but he was only wearing a towel around his waist and his head was still dripping with water. He'd obviously just come in from the shower block. Slowly the other soldiers turned to follow Peel's gaze.

Horace still didn't move. He couldn't. A few feet in front of him an Afghan shepherd boy stood with his arms raised in front of him. In the chaos of the fight, the child had managed to get a hold of a service revolver, and was aiming it at Horace's stomach.

Someone muttered, "Christ." But nobody moved. Barnes was no longer aware of the blood dripping from his broken nose. The fight was already forgotten. They had lowered their guard and the horrors of the war outside had crept into their barracks unseen.

Horace stared at the boy with a look of contempt, a resentment in his eyes that his fellow soldiers had grown used to over their months together. The mechanic from the West Midlands was a difficult son of a bitch: cold, cynical, and reserved to the point of being unnerving. Some put it down to the fact he was several years older than everyone else. His pale, lean torso was scrawled with homemade tattoos that brought to mind a toilet wall, but no one would dare say as much to his face. He possessed a calculated diffidence that warned off any attempts at familiarity. But for all his faults no one for a moment felt that he deserved this.

Abdullah's hands were now shaking and the sniffling had started again. He knew what he had wanted to say at this point but the few words he had learned in English couldn't form through the sobs that were overwhelming him. He took a deep breath to compose himself.

"You no stop them. Why you no stop them?"

Horace made no attempt to respond.

The boy fired the weapon twice. The private was thrown back against his locker and quickly slid to the floor clutching at his crotch. For a fleeting moment there was a flicker of relief in the boy's eyes before the side of his face erupted in ragged flaps of torn skin and shattered skull fragments. One of the other soldiers stood in a well-rehearsed firing stance from 12 feet away, squeezing the trigger of his revolver two more times as the boy collapsed to the ground. The rest of the platoon moved towards Horace who was going into shock.

A blonde soldier who was normally the joker among them, the type to diffuse heated situations with a loose comment, had finally had enough. He stepped over two beds and screamed at the boy on the ground, "What the fuck is wrong with you people?" His usually lilting voice came out as a petulant scream. "You fucking animals!"

He slipped awkwardly in the boy's blood, which only enraged him more. A mate grabbed him and pulled him away as he continued to scream, "We're only trying to help you."

The tent quickly filled with armed soldiers from the adjoining barracks. By the time the medics could push their way through, Private Horace had turned grey and was on the point of passing out. His crotch continued bleeding profusely through his fingers as the First Lieutenant crouched beside him using the private's towel as a compress. Peel told him everything was going to be okay, but Horace just stared at the dead boy with the same unmasked look of contempt. Then his eyes glazed over and he slipped into unconsciousness.

CHAPTER ONE

The thin wire ran through the pulley, lifting the weights smoothly. The load rose up, hovered momentarily then descended with barely a sound. Seven metal bars of five kilograms each moving as one block, up and down. Thirty-five kilograms – the weight of a young child lifted to safety, or plummeting out of reach.

Birgitte Vestergaard, Senior Detective with the Danish National Police, pulled the metal bar down towards her shoulders, the action causing the muscles within her back to burn steadily. She released the tension and took a deep breath as the bar lifted and the weights descended. Adjusting her grip, she pulled down again, an involuntary grunt escaping through her teeth.

Sunlight shone through floor-to-ceiling windows, bathing the small but well-equipped gym in natural light. Birgitte was straddling the bench of the universal machine, midway through an intentionally gruelling session. Her dark hair was tied back from her face. Her pale skin glistened and her chest was burning red. There was a bottle of water at her feet, but she had no intention of reaching for it until she had completed another six reps.

As her shoulders burned, her mind filled with the images that had plagued her sleep. The tortured face of an elderly man dragging himself up the bank of a dry creek bed in outback Australia, his legs torn off at the thigh. A young woman on a steel trolley, bloated grey-blue and littered with weed and mud, her skin bruised and split, her eyes staring with horror. The sun-charred skin of a student in his 20s, his corpse lifted from the emerald-green waters of Sydney Harbour. The images came faster now as she gritted her teeth and used all her mental strength to compel her arms to keep pulling the cold metal bar. Images of Detective Tony Kingsmill – standing up to greet her in the foyer of the East Wind Hotel in Sydney, crouching by the motel pool in Alice Springs, his lop-sided grin softening his features.

Birgitte arched her back and shuffled back on the bench-seat to keep her spine straight. Now her lower back was aching and she couldn't feel her feet. Her fingers struggled to hold on to the steel as the sweat ran from her palms down her wrists. She tried with all her strength to push Tony from her mind but couldn't. They lay in her hotel bed together, exhausted, spent, laughing. Him, standing naked by the window, looking down at the ferries in Circular Quay, the line of his broad shoulders, tapered waist, her fingers tracing the length of his thighs. The scent of his skin.

What bothered her most was the inevitable associations that came with these memories. She couldn't think of Tony without being reminded of Zachary de Graff – the sick sociopath whose willingness to execute innocent strangers had sent her to Australia in the first place. The case had only lasted three weeks, but the fallout had continued to linger like a stain beneath her skin.

As the anger welled within her, she began to breathe more heavily. She jerked at the bar and gave a low guttural scream until the metal touched the nape of her neck. She couldn't clear her mind of de Graff's fine South African features and cruel, soulless eyes. Nor could she stop his face slowly morphing into that of another monster from earlier in her career – Max Anders, the Danish child killer who was now serving multiple life sentences in Copenhagen. With him came the muffled cries of the Svedbo children as they slowly perished because of a choice that she had made. The bar slipped from her fingers and the weights behind her came down with a resounding crash.

Birgitte looked around the gym, startled, desperately trying to catch her breath. Thankfully, the room was still empty. She slumped over her thighs, her lungs expanding and collapsing in her chest. Checking her watch, she realised she must have done several more reps than she'd intended. She was getting physically stronger with every session. But she couldn't say the same for her mind. Most detectives could talk of a particular case that defined their career; Birgitte was on the lighter side of 40, still rising through the ranks, and had already experienced two such cases, both of which continued to haunt her. She stood up gingerly, grabbed her water bottle and draped her towel over her shoulders as she headed for the glass door onto the terrace.

The air outside was thick with humidity and the grating cacophony of distant city traffic. Hong Kong's Victoria Harbour stretched out before her. She drank greedily from her bottle until it was drained. Forty four floors below, the tiny wharves of Kowloon were busy with mid-morning ferry traffic, shunting office workers and tourists back and forth between the mainland and Hong Kong Island. Shipping liners moved steadily between the smaller islands to the south-east, dwarfed by the skyscrapers that lined the far shore and the steep slope up to The Peak.

Somewhere beyond the ramparts of glass-and-steel skyscrapers lining the shore was a narrow moving walkway, expediting local workers up and down the western face of Hong Kong Island. Halfway up the Mid-Levels Escalator, where the streets were narrow and winding and cut by steep stairways, was a popular pocket of restaurants and cafes known as Lan Kwai Fong.

It was hard to believe that a year had passed since Birgitte had sat in the back of a crowded bar, waiting with grim determination to give the signal for the Hong Kong Police to burst in and take down Zachary de Graff. It was a textbook international arrest, a swift, professional denouement to a horrific case that had baffled the authorities in Australia.

15

Her decision to pursue the killer to Hong Kong should have convinced her superiors back in Copenhagen of her restored capabilities as a senior homicide detective. Despite being cleared of any wrong-doing, the Anders Inquest had done much to undermine their faith in her. The arrest of de Graff, at the very least, should have provided her with a sense of redemption. Instead, it all went to hell minutes later with two shots fired in the back of a police van by a corrupt local officer.

Birgitte had returned to her life in Denmark, her position tentatively restored. But she felt like an understudy for own position. The original lead was still disgraced; management were merely suffering the presence of her replacement only so long as it was deemed necessary. Sven had assured that was not the case, but she wasn't convinced. In her usual fashion she responded to uncertainty by going on the front foot. When the Minister for Police had announced the plans for a comprehensive restructure of upper management, she applied for a promotion to the position of Vice Commissioner. Sven was guarded in his opinion of her decision but when he saw how committed she was, he promised her his full support.

At the end of September, he had mentioned an international police conference taking place the following month in Hanoi. It would be a good opportunity for her to network with her potential equals, he said. The focus was to be on psychological profiling and lone-wolf terror attacks. She could tack on two weeks of annual leave. When she resisted the idea of the holiday, he reminded her the decision about her promotion would be finalised within those two weeks. "It's going to be a stressful few days, Birgitte. I've been there. You'll handle it better if you're somewhere else."

She hadn't known how to take this but thanked him for the opportunity, then spent the rest of the afternoon weighing up whether she should just go to the conference or take Sven's advice.

For the past 12 months she had handled a challenging case-load of domestic murders, gangland executions, questionable instances of manslaughter and one mercy killing that would hopefully end in an acquittal. During that time, she would occasionally find herself recalling random images of Hong Kong – sights she barely remembered seeing because she had been so consumed with catching de Graff. The neon lights of a street in Mong Kok, restaurant windows steaming with bamboo baskets laden with dumplings, the surrounding islands resting so peacefully beyond Victoria Harbour. It was as if the city had been sending subliminal messages for her to return. She didn't believe in that sort of thing. But come the first week in October when she was standing in the torrential rain in Skovlunde, pointing a torchlight into a shallow grave where the bound and gagged corpse of a teenage girl had been unearthed by a curious Labrador, she knew it was time to get away.

What she hadn't banked on was her parents joining her. She had mentioned the conference in passing to her mother, Loll, who couldn't believe their luck. Birgitte had forgotten her parents had already booked a 10-day trip to China at around the same time. Loll was adamant – they simply had to catch up with her for a day or two when she started her holiday. Birgitte feigned enthusiasm but inwardly kicked herself for opening her mouth.

The complexities of Birgitte's relationship with her father weren't exactly a family secret. He was a brilliant but difficult man, more at ease in the company of government ministers than with his own child. Loll had always joked that it was Jan and Birgitte's similarities that so often set them at odds with one another. It was all very well to be single-minded at work but there was no place for it in the home. Loll had spent the past 30 years playing the role of peacemaker when one or both of them was out of sorts. As Birgitte had matured she accepted more responsibility for her own reactions to her father's attitudes, but there were still days when he could wound her pride with a little more than thinly veiled criticism.

Birgitte knew she needed to rise above it, especially now that her father was in his 70s. Still, the thought of spending three days listening to him condescend to her mother in that oh-so-subtle way of his, and his continual remarks about Birgitte's choice of career had been almost enough to make her cancel the trip. But she wanted to spend time with Loll. Since Birgitte had learned her estranged husband, Tomas, was due to have a child with a woman he barely knew, she felt in genuine need of her mother's calming influence. She was also now in two minds about her decision to apply for the promotion. If she hadn't had to deal with the Anders Inquest, then Zachary de Graff, she was right on schedule to be considered for a Vice Commissionership. She obviously had Sven's support but sometimes wondered if his view of her as a detective was biased. Loll had always provided sound counsel when Birgitte needed it most. Putting up with her father for three days was just the price she would have to pay.

Birgitte had flown into Lantau the day before, giving her enough time to settle into the city and get her bearings. It wasn't as if she had to spend that much time with him – Loll and Jan were heading back to Denmark the day after next. They could do a bit of sight-seeing, some shopping and try a few restaurants. It might just provide Birgitte a momentary respite from her problems before she would be alone again. As she stepped back into the gym and made her way to the elevator, she did her best not to preempt the arguments she was going to have with Jan. Loll would simply have to do her usual job of keeping the peace between them. Birgitte took a deep breath and told herself it was going to be okay.

The lobby of the Conran Hotel was decidedly European in flavour, white marble flooring inlaid with bold black lines, polished stone columns and a vaulted ceiling with gold-gilt frescoes that drew the eye to three magnificent chandeliers. It was spacious and elegant, catering to the needs of high-net-worth Continental clients – a far cry from the budget hotel in Hanoi where she had stayed for the international policing conference. Jan had insisted on paying for Birgitte's accommodation in Hong Kong before they had all left Denmark, otherwise she would have booked into a more affordable hotel elsewhere in Kowloon. It wasn't worth the argument. If it made her mother happy for them to be all together at the Conran, Birgitte was willing to play along.

She had showered quickly and changed into a pair of light pants and a cotton shirt she had bought in Vietnam. After seven days in Asia she was finally getting used to the humidity. She paused for a moment at the entrance to the elevator bay to collect herself, then stepped out into the lobby.

Her father was standing to one side of the long reception desk, looking every bit the elder statesman in his dark suit pants and tailored shirt, his thick white hair combed back from his long face. He was a few inches taller than most and had always stooped slightly to lessen the impact of his own physical stature, which could be unintentionally intimidating. It was just one of the many methods, Birgitte had realised over the years, he used to ingratiate himself to people – to appear obsequious when in fact he was all too aware of his superior intelligence. Even as he stood there appearing to be not looking at anything in particular, Birgitte knew he was studying his surroundings, the state of the interior, the other guests as they moved past. He was making thousands of tiny judgements to continually ascertain his place at the centre of it all. During his career it had been a conscious choice, a skill he had honed to precision out of necessity. Now, in his retirement, it was as unconscious as breathing.

Jan's face softened when he recognised his daughter walking across the lobby. Birgitte managed to smile in return.

He took her by the shoulders and kissed her forehead as he had done since she was 14 years old. "How was the conference?" he asked in Danish.

"It went well, thanks," she said. "I'm glad I decided to go. How was your time in China?"

He shrugged and smiled. "It's still China."

Birgitte didn't know what that meant. She peered around the lobby for her mother. "Has Loll already gone up to the room?"

"She couldn't make it," he said, his face giving no indication as to his thoughts on the matter.

Birgitte stepped back. "Is everything okay?"

"Your Aunt Carol had a fall. Nothing too serious but Loll felt obliged to fly home from Beijing."

Birgitte stared at him in disbelief. "Why didn't you go with her?"

He returned her gaze with a reassuring look. "She didn't want to disappoint you by altering the arrangements last minute. You know what she's like."

Birgitte bit the inside of her cheek. If it was just the two of them, she couldn't afford to clash with him from the outset. "Was it a bad fall?" she asked with genuine concern. "Will Carol be okay?"

"She'll outlive us all," he said in a tone designed to end the questions. "Now, I've checked in and I'm famished. If you're hungry we can get something to eat, otherwise I can meet up with you later, if you'd prefer."

"There's a place I went to yesterday, in a laneway behind the hotel, that you might like."

"Lead the way."

They walked in silence through the lobby and out into the street. The humidity and the noise hit them both. Leaving the air-conditioned confines of the Conran was like stepping into another country. Birgitte guided him around one side of the hotel. He kept pace with her but she could tell he was struggling with the heat so she slowed down. Within a matter of minutes they were behind the hotel in a shaded laneway lined with colourful restaurants. She pointed across the way to a non-descript shopfront where she had enjoyed a peaceful dinner of handmade noodles on her first night in Hong Kong.

"I hope you brought your appetite, she said. "The food is exceptional."

He held the door open for her. Inside, the restaurant was more crowded, humid and frenetic than out on the street. The room felt narrow and was cluttered with too many settings, every one of them filled with local Chinese shouting at one another across platters of sizzling beef and steamed fish. Harried wait staff moved sideways between tables. If anyone stood up, several people had to move their seats. Birgitte suggested they try somewhere else, but Jan couldn't hear her above the noise. A waiter waved to them from the back of the room. A setting had become free by the kitchen door.

Birgitte negotiated her way between the tables. As soon as he sat down, Jan immersed himself in the menu. He ordered for both of them without consulting her then began to talk dismissively about the smog in China, the traffic and poor service in the hotels. She did her best to listen, but as she predicted, his criticisms merely served as a launching point for detailed reminiscences about his previous trips to Beijing when he worked as a diplomat for the Danish Ministry of Foreign Affairs. It was not that his stories were boring by any means. His contribution to international relations was well documented in the media and academic circles back home. It was that he spoke as if the trip with Loll was of little consequence now that he was retired. It couldn't be easy for him, she reasoned. Loll had warned her that he wasn't coping so well with his newfound freedom. Every year out of the service of the state he talked more vociferously of the issues that he once had a hand in shaping.

Several dishes came out of the kitchen one after the other and all of them were as she had hoped. Jan ate and spoke steadily but Birgitte noticed his concentration would occasionally waver. It might have been the chaos of the restaurant, she thought at first, or the trial of the flight from Beijing, the altered plans. But it was more than that, she realised. His train of thought drifted or stopped abruptly. She would wait for him to continue but he would suddenly raise an unrelated topic, then press on, expecting her to keep up. It became more overt as the meal went on, then it occurred to Birgitte that if Loll had been there, she would have covered for him. She wondered how long had this been going on. She thought back over the past 18 months to all the times her mother would bridge the gaps in Jan's conversation or subtly correct facts crucial to a story. Sometimes she did this at her own peril. Jan could be scathing in his criticism if he thought his acumen was being questioned. But now, without his wife there to guide him, he faltered. At one point he brushed over the fact he couldn't recall the name of his executive assistant of 13 years with a wave of his hand but Birgitte could tell he was confused, self-conscious. She wasn't game to fill her mother's absence. When the conversation fell flat, she attempted to bring him up to date on her career, but he suddenly showed more interest in the dumplings on the end of his chopsticks. She persisted a few more times then brought up a local trade deal she had seen being discussed on TV in the past few days. It worked. His face brightened, and he launched into a long a detailed history of agricultural development in Asia.

As he talked, she found herself thinking of the long lunches they had shared while holidaying in Skagen in the far north of Jutland when she was still a young teenager. They would sit for hours eating and chatting, debating world affairs and the state of the Danish economy, subjects on which Loll was more than capable of challenging her husband given her own academic qualifications. Birgitte would struggle to keep up with the depth of their knowledge but felt very mature just being included. Her attempts at contributing to the conversation usually ended with her petulantly yelling at her father for not listening to her point of view. He'd persist in lecturing her until Loll would interject to keep the peace. When it all got too much they would sit back and watch the light and colours change on the Skagerrak Sea until her mother would shiver with the cold and suggest it was time to go back inside.

They were memories Birgitte held dear, perhaps because she had so few to draw upon. Jan had been an absent father to say the least. His commitments with the Ministry provided the perfect cover for a man who wasn't entirely comfortable in the role of father. Birgitte had often wondered if he would have preferred a son, but she couldn't picture him being any less involved in his career just because his child could play football. Still, as he reached across the table to top up their tea cups, Birgitte found herself wishing to relive more of those moments at Skagen.

"What is it?" she asked him. He was staring intently at a stain on the table.

"Sorry?" he replied, startled by the interruption.

"What were you thinking about just then. You seemed deep in thought."

"Did I?" He stared at his daughter, his eyes were a clear blue but slightly vacant, then with an involuntary blink, the depth returned. "Is the reshuffle going to affect you?"

"What?"

"The reshuffle. I saw the Minister plans to shake up the top order."

Birgitte managed a bewildered smile. "I didn't realise you were interested."

"He's a snivelling toad of a man," he said almost bitterly. "Met him at some conference or other. He was much further down the chain of command back then, but you could see he was going to make his way eventually."

"I haven't actually met him," she said. "But I am going for a promotion."

Perhaps he'd pay attention this time, she hoped.

"Don't give him an inch," he said. "I've seen his type a thousand times over."

"A Vice Commissionership."

"It was some conference in Vesterbro…"

"For Christ's sake, Jan," she said firmly. "Will you just listen for once."

His eyes darkened. "I know full well you are going for a promotion. Your mother hasn't shut up about it for weeks."

"Then why couldn't you say something. Every time I bring it up you change the subject or pretend you didn't hear me."

He looked over her head as if something had caught his attention across the room. He took a deep breath, clearly trying to control his own temper. He waved to a waiter and motioned for the bill. "I'll get this."

He stood up, drew a wad of notes from his pocket, not bothering to check the amount before placing them on the table and walking out. Birgitte stared at the dirty plates and shook her head. It was Skagen all over again.

She caught up to him further down the street but he didn't slow down for her.

"I'm going back to my room," he muttered, then said something about the heat she couldn't catch. She slowed down and watched him walk away from her as if she didn't exist.

The face in the mirror was haggard, familiar but somehow strange, more aged than he remembered – mid 50s, maybe younger, his skin sagging slightly on his jowls, the complexion slightly jaundiced, but that could have been the fluorescent lighting. He pulled down on his cheeks and rolled his eyeballs in their sockets, momentarily transfixed by the broken blood vessels that splayed out from his irises. He could hear muffled conversations through the walls – foreign voices, TVs, radios – and the traffic outside on Nathan Road.

He suddenly gripped the edge of the basin and began dry retching. Nothing. He gasped for breath and spat into the drain. He turned on the tap under the mirror and waited. With a deep chortle, a gush of rusty water shot out of the faucet then slowed to a steady dribble, which eventually ran clear. He splashed his face several times.

When he was able to stand up properly, he began looking for his phone. It was later in the day than he realised. He slowly got dressed, pulling on a pair of brown trousers and a cream cotton shirt, his pale arms jutting through the sleeves. He slipped his shoes on, then swept his lank hair back from his face. Even upright his spine never entirely straightened. His posture had always been rounded, the pirate jibes of his childhood a dull memory, but of late it seemed his sunken chest was sinking beyond reprieve. He stepped out of the cramped, windowless hotel room onto the narrow walkway that lined the interior of the 'courtyard'. Several young Indian men pushed past him to their own rooms further along. He placed a cigarette between his wet lips and leaned on the railing.

Hanjin Mansion was a crumbling office block in the heart of Kowloon that had once housed hundreds of artisan businesses – jewellers, watchmakers, seamstresses. Over the years Indian entrepreneurs saw the chance to convert some of the floors into budget accommodation for the thousands of itinerant workers and travellers who couldn't afford even the mid-priced hotels. Each floor comprised several "Hotels", each consisting of several rooms – porcelain lined coffins that could barely hold a bed. It was crowded, noisy and airless. The Blue Diamond was on the 15th floor. Merrick Cripps didn't care where he stayed so long as it didn't cost much and there was a lock on the door. He lit his cigarette and peered down the courtyard, exhaling smoke with a chesty cough. Below him were floor after floor of similar hotels. It smelt of damp earth and body odour. The concrete walls seeped water that would gather in corners to trickle out into the void over bare electrical wires. The only real colour came from tiny fishbone ferns which sprouted from gaps in the rendering, searching desperately for natural light.

There were mostly Indians on this floor: drivers, labourers, hawkers, a few Chinese. It was hard to tell if they were short-term or permanent residents. From the corner of his eye he could see through the crack in the door of the adjoining room. An Indian man on a bed was masturbating to American porn on a handheld DVD player. Cripps flicked his unfinished cigarette butt down into the void. He returned to his room, grabbed a small backpack then stepped back out onto the landing. It was 2pm. He still had time. He locked the door shut and made his way to the elevator.

The subway train out to the northern suburbs of Kowloon was crowded. Cripps hung onto the handle from the ceiling. The Chinese passengers ignored him, but there was a white family in his carriage – a couple and their young teenage daughter. Cripps could tell they were British by the way they dressed and held themselves. The daughter stared at him, making no attempt to hide the physical disgust she felt. Cripps was not an attractive man. He never had been. It was as if each of his features were slightly out of alignment and didn't comply with accepted measurements. His eyes were too far apart, his nose too long, even his teeth seemed to work against each other. They were subtle anomalies that amounted to an overall appearance of neglect and self-loathing. He stared back at the girl. There was a rawness to her pretty features that was more than just youth. She knew she was attractive to men. Eventually she looked away and refused to look at him again.

He got off the train at Kowloon Tong and emerged from the underground in a tree-lined street, grateful to be able to light up another cigarette. He then pulled a map form his bag, got his bearings and headed south. A few minutes later he arrived outside an international primary school. He looked about to be sure that no one had noticed him. Satisfied he was alone, he rested his bag on the ground at his feet and pulled his cigarettes out of his top pocket again. He leaned against a tree and drew the acrid smoke into his lungs, staring across the street into the windows of the classrooms where scores of children were doing their final lessons for the day. He watched the empty playgrounds and waited.

"Do you remember Albert Canningvale?" Jan asked.

Birgitte shook her head, unsure what he might ask next. They were both looking out across the harbour that was glittering with the neon colours of the city. The evening

27

lightshow had finished more than an hour before. The rooftop bar was quieter now. There was a stillness that Birgitte found soothing. It might have been the bottle of red they had shared.

Jan sat across from her. He was in a surprisingly effusive mood. He had called her room just after 6pm sounding refreshed, inviting her up to the bar to enjoy the lights. She almost yelled at him but realised he may have forgotten his earlier behaviour. There was no point bringing it up again, so she just sighed and told him that she'd love to.

The man who had greeted her at the entrance to the bar was relaxed and well rested. He must have slept for most of the afternoon. He was dressed in a dark suit, with the collar of his shirt open at the neck. His hair was combed back from his face, still slightly wet from his shower. He could have passed for early 60s not mid 70s.

"Feel better?" she had asked, offering her cheek.

He kissed her warmly and squeezed her shoulders. "I thought we might skip dinner and order a couple of desserts with a bottle of your choosing."

Was this his way of apologising, she wondered, or had he completely forgotten their awkward lunch?

He spent the next hour sharing anecdotes about his courtship of her mother. It was as if he had suddenly become aware of Loll's absence and wanted to relive the key aspects of their relationship from the very beginning. Birgitte was unsettled by his shift in behaviour but had to admit to herself that she was thoroughly enjoying his company.

When the wine was finished, they ordered coffees. Birgitte could sense the evening was drawing to a close and it saddened her a little. Surprisingly Jan seemed to pick up on this.

"Did your mother tell you we were invited to a soiree tomorrow night at Government House?"

"I haven't spoken to her yet," she said.

"Do you remember a gentleman by the name of Albert Canningvale?" he asked again, "when we were living in London?"

She thought for a moment but nobody of that name came to mind.

Jan pressed on. "He worked for the UK Department of Trade and Industry – as it was known back then. Large man. Apparently, some of the kids of the other diplomats called him 'Cunning Whale' behind his back."

She shook her head. She couldn't recall spending much time with the kids of other diplomats.

"You were too young, I guess," he said. "He was a former Lieutenant Colonel from memory, did some time in the Middle East."

He peered out the window towards Hong Kong Island as he spoke. "He's Sir Albert Canningvale now. Apparently, he's been living out here for the past 20 years. Made quite a name for himself, and a mountain of money in the local property market. He's seen as a bit of a bridge between the old world of Hong Kong as a British colony and the new world of Chinese capitalism. Anyway, the British Consulate General is throwing a party in his honour at Government House tomorrow night. And we're invited."

Birgitte wanted to remind him that Loll wasn't there, but she let him continue without interruption. He nestled his shoulders back into his seat as if he was riding in a diplomatic convoy. "We got chatting to a former colleague of mine in Beijing. He was the one who suggested it when we told him we were coming to Hong Kong."

"Sounds fascinating," Birgitte said to be polite.

"I mentioned that we were here to visit you, and he insisted you come along too."

Birgitte suddenly realised he was inviting her to a diplomatic function. "Wouldn't you rather catch up with your colleagues on your own?"

He looked at her almost expectantly. "I thought you might like to see Government House while you're here. It's been the residence of the Chief Executive of the Hong Kong SAR for some time now, which means it's not open to the public as much as it once was."

Birgitte couldn't come up with a convincing excuse so she agreed to go along.

With that settled, Jan asked for the bill.

As they walked through the bar to the elevators he recalled their time together in London. She was only eight at the time. He had been sent across for 18 months as part of The Trade Council, working on a deal that would have a significant impact on Denmark's agricultural sector. Loll and Birgitte had joined him shortly after.

Birgitte had only distant memories of that short chapter of her life: an apartment with high ceilings and cold floorboards, white houses on long streets, nasty girls who wouldn't talk to her because she spoke differently to them. But try as she might, she couldn't picture the distinguished Englishman her father had been talking about.

By midnight the main street of Wan Chai was bustling with drunken American sailors on R 'n' R, staggering from one bar to another. Loose groups of fresh-faced boys in their crisp whites, jostled one another, laughing hysterically as they were approached every few metres by heavy-set middle-aged Chinese women out the front of strip clubs promising hot young girls if they came inside. It only took one guy to succumb to his own curiosity before the others would follow, out of drunken bravado or animal need. The rest continued on up the street looking for the next watering hole. The popular bars on the corners were overflowing with ex-pats and tourists. It was bright, colourful, noisy – the forced joyousness and gaudy glamour of commercial sex and late-night humidity.

Merrick Cripps was in a basement bar filled with silver-haired white men who were dancing with young Filipino girls. He had taken a seat up the back where he could watch the girls dancing without drawing too much attention to himself. The music was blaring the latest American R 'n' B tracks. The girls danced to one another, almost ignoring the men. Tiny denim skirts were in, and shoe-string tops. They swayed seductively, admiring themselves in the dark mirrors that lined the walls as if they were each the star of their own music videos. The men ogled them, dancing with their hands. They were sweating profusely, waddling about out of beat to the music. They savoured the youthful flesh of the girls, groping bare thighs and slapping tight buttocks whenever they got the chance. The girls would slip out of their grasp then sidle back up to them and whisper in their ears. Eventually the men would shuffle off the dance floor and return to the bar for another round of drinks. That was the deal.

A dark-skinned Filipino girl approached Cripps. Her tiny denim skirt had ridden high on her thighs. Her loose singlet top allowed her untethered breasts to move freely against the cloth. Cripps eyed her warily. It was customary for the guys to approach the girls, to offer them a drink before dancing. It wasn't until she was up close that he noticed the long birthmark down one side of her face, which she tried to hide behind her hair. He muttered something into her ear. She nodded. He went to the bar and came back with two scotches. When he sat down she slipped onto his knee, put her arm around his neck and then pretended to be shy, turning her cheek away from him. The smell of her – lemongrass and damp cloth – was earthy and alluring. She ran her fingers through his

31

thinning hair. The music was too loud for them to talk so she simply bobbed her head to the beat. He rested one hand on her bare hip and squeezed her flesh gently.

Before he knew it she had finished her drink. She stood up and began to sway seductively, beckoning him on to the dance floor, which was now virtually empty. He shook his head and laughed, his teeth catching the swirling lights from the ceiling so that they glowed like broken gyprock. He motioned to her glass and she nodded. He stood and checked his wallet. It was empty. He shrugged at the girl, who was no longer swaying. She pulled her hair down to hide her cheek and made her way back into the crowd of girls on the edge of the dance floor to wait for a better option.

Cripps sat back down and drank his scotch. He pulled out his hotel key and laughed bitterly to himself. It wasn't like he could have taken her back there anyway. The last drink hit him hard. He was about to leave when he noticed an oafish German in shorts and thongs getting rough with one of the other girls. The girl was smiling nervously as she tried to pull her arm out the German's grip. He lifted his other arm to show her the back of his hand. It was enough to settle the girl down, but it lit a fire inside Cripps. He struggled to get out of his seat but once he was up he was determined to show that Kraut a thing or two. On the way to the dance floor he grabbed an empty beer bottle by the neck. He tried to smash it on the base of a pylon but it just made a loud clanging sound and vibrated in his hand. He staggered towards his opponent, but before he could do anything a white bouncer gripped his shoulder so tightly he could feel his knees buckling.

"I fucking warned you last time," the bouncer yelled over the music. He picked Cripps up by the collar and the belt and dragged him up the stairs to the street. "If I see you in here again, the cops won't get here fast enough to help you."

The bouncer threw him against a car and watched as he slid down the duco, onto one knee, then collapse in the gutter. The last thing Cripps remembered seeing was the girl with the birth mark leaving the club with a guy half his age. She was laughing sweetly and it sounded like music.

CHAPTER TWO

The limousine turned into the sweeping drive of Government House shortly after 7pm, joining a cavalcade of several other official vehicles dropping guests at the door. Birgitte stepped out into the warm night air, wearing a black dress she'd brought for the final night of the conference in Hanoi. She wore her hair up, two delicate earrings accentuating the fine line of her neck. From beyond the trees that surrounded the property, she could hear the warbling call of singing gibbons, a sweet reminder that the Hong Kong Zoo was just across the road. Jan closed the car door behind her.

On the drive across the harbour and up into the hills above Central, Birgitte had noticed once again her father was preoccupied. She had tried to engage him in conversation about the history of Government House, how it had served as the residence for several British governors dating back to the 1850s but beyond arching an eyebrow, he didn't respond. She politely persisted with her one-way conversation, admitting she'd had no idea the Japanese had occupied Hong Kong during the war. Apparently, they'd pared back the architecture quite severely during their stay. Jan said nothing. She brought the conversation closer to home asking him, when was the last time he was there. He muttered that it was back in the 1990s for the close of a tech deal. He continued to peer out the window, deep in thought. Eventually, she had given up and they spent the rest of the ride in uncomfortable silence.

Birgitte looked up at the Victorian facade which still commanded an air of imperial authority. As they walked through the uninviting portico, she suggested the Japanese had certainly made their presence felt. Jan looked up at the surrounding architecture but didn't respond.

They were greeted at the front door by an attractive British woman in her 30s, who introduced herself as Sir Albert Canningvale's aide. She apologised for the need for a security check prior to entering the building but promised it would be painless. Once they had passed through the scanners they were to turn right and follow the staff through to the residence at the back of Government House. Poe-faced police ran hand scanners across their bodies prior to directing them past a check point. Birgitte had observed more security patrolling the grounds out front. The aide had mentioned that the Chief Executive was out of the country, but he was more than happy to provide his residence for the occasion. Apparently, the two men went back many years.

The guests were ushered along several corridors, past office spaces where staff continued to work at their desks. The entrance to the Chief Executive's residence was heralded by a string quartet of Chinese musicians in formal attire playing Sibelius. Attractive waiters presented the new arrivals with flutes of Champagne. Jan walked beside his daughter, nodding towards the Living Room.

"It's through there from memory," he said.

They entered a spacious, stately room, sensibly decorated in soft cream. Ornate crystal chandeliers hung from a distant ceiling, bathing the room in a soft white light, and a series of French doors dressed in box curtains lined one wall. The room was already filling with guests, who moved about the upholstered furniture to admire the artworks on the walls. Birgitte figured most of them were diplomats, politicians and business people with their wives and husbands. It was an even mix of British, European and Chinese couples, mostly over 40. However, she did notice a few elderly local men with stunning young Chinese girls on their arms. She was going to joke that they had obviously brought their daughters as well, but she didn't want to risk upsetting Jan by pointing out the escorts too early in the evening.

She turned to her father, who had appeared disconcerted with his surroundings since they'd arrived. But with a short cough into one hand, his preoccupations seemingly vanished, his shoulders straightened and he looked about the room with a knowing eye. Her ageing father had suddenly given way to the former diplomat who had a job to do. Birgitte was bewildered by the subtle but telling transformation she'd just witnessed. He adopted a warm smile and led Birgitte across the room, introducing her to a few couples he hadn't seen in years, all of whom were pleased to see their old friend. His command of the English language was as strong as Birgitte's. Polite conversation ensued. Birgitte smiled warmly at the comments on her dress and earrings by the elderly wives of retired diplomats. Jan proceeded to hold court. His colleagues clearly enjoyed his company. As baffled as Birgitte was by her father's mood swings, she couldn't help but admire him at times like these. He had always possessed the ability to win people over, either through his engaging warmth or his impressive intellect. As his daughter, she just had to accept he reserved his cool detachment and air of disappointment for her. He was wise enough to keep that behind closed doors. Tonight, he appeared only too proud to have her by his side.

As they moved about the room from group to group, Birgitte thought of her mother. A lifetime of cocktail parties just like this, where she had been expected to maintain a flawless facade. Birgitte tried to keep smiling at each person she met but her heels were conspiring against her and her dress was threatening to bruise her ribs. She suddenly felt a large hand on her bare shoulder accompanied by a smooth deep voice. "And don't tell me this is little Birgitte?"

Jan laughed and held out his hands. "Birgitte... Sir Albert Canningvale."

Canningvale was at least six foot five. He was pushing 70 years of age, but was still clearly a strong man. His shoulders were broad and his neck thick, but his features were soft and rounded. He reminded Birgitte of a Hollywood actor who was once described as having the body of a giant and the face of a child. Canningvale cut an imposing figure but was saved from corpulence by the brilliance of his eyes, which were playful and clear. He stepped back to take in Birgitte.

"The last time I saw you, dear lady, you were giving the boys a hard time for not letting the girls play cricket. Jan has not done you justice in saying what a lovely woman you've become."

Birgitte tried to remember him as a child but couldn't. He turned and shook Jan's hand, then greeted the rest of the small circle of guests in turn. If Jan could hold a crowd, Canningvale could command a room. He possessed a rare presence that was at once inclusive and uplifting. It was as if the energy around them was suddenly more vibrant. He proceeded to tell an hilarious anecdote about Jan when they were both in London as if the party was being held in Jan's honour not his. They all laughed uproariously, causing the surrounding guests to turn their heads and look enviously at the group. Then, as smoothly as a US primary candidate, Canningvale excused himself from the circle to greet other guests, but not before saying to Jan, "Would you mind if I borrow your daughter? I feel like my stock in the room will be somewhat elevated with her on my arm."

Jan gave Birgitte an enquiring glance. She smiled and offered her arm to the guest of honour, feeling slightly ridiculous humouring the old men. Canningvale guided her between the shoulders of his guests, nodding acknowledgement to several faces through the crowd.

"Let's get some tongues wagging, shall we?"

"I'm sure you've had more attractive women on your arm in the past, Sir Albert. Perhaps what I should be asking is if there is a Lady Canningvale?"

"Call me Bertie, and no, there isn't a Lady Canningvale either." He turned to her with smile. "Not yet, anyway. It's Saturday night, anything can happen. How are you finding Hong Kong?"

"Remarkable," she said. "Has it changed much for you since the handover?"

"Considerably," he said, nodding to particular guests as they passed. "In some ways it's better for someone like myself."

"How is that?"

"Beijing is showing a lot of interest in London at the moment, in terms of foreign investment. I am called upon to provide advice, make introductions, smooth the waters culturally, so to speak. It works both ways. My friends in the UK are very keen to get acquainted with the decision makers, learn their ways of doing business. It's an exciting time."

"So long as you're in the middle."

"Exactly." He smiled graciously. "I like the way the Chinese think. Between you and me, they're the shrewdest little beggars outside of the UK."

They had arrived at their destination. Canningvale introduced Birgitte to two elderly British couples. The men were visiting Parliamentarians, one with a background in investment banking, the other in international shipping. Birgitte couldn't quite catch their full titles but she got the feeling their wives would remind her at the slightest prompting. They peered over her shoulder at the other guests as she shook their husbands' hands.

"Birgitte is Jan Sorenson's daughter – former diplomat in Danish Foreign Affairs," Canningvale said by way of introduction. "We worked together in London back in the 80s when she was just a wee little thing."

One of the wives, an imperious woman in her late 60s made the effort to be polite. "And what do you do, Brigeet?"

"It's Birgitte," she responded with a smile. The woman nodded but made no effort to correct herself. Birgitte stared her down. "I'm a detective with the Danish National Police."

One of the men coughed and looked up at the ceiling, the other continued to stare at her, only now he was no doubt picturing her in a skimpy police outfit waving a baton around. The imperious woman's face didn't budge an inch.

"Spectacular," said Canningvale, grinning broadly. "Jan kept that little gem to himself."

"And what sort of detective work do you do?" asked the imperious woman, determined to not lose face.

"Homicide."

The more diminutive of the two men, the one with a recalcitrant comb-over, said, "You must have seen some things."

"I have."

He was obviously about to ask for details when his wife cut him off. "What makes one pursue a line of work with the police?" she asked as if Birgitte was somehow mentally deficient or perhaps a rabid feminist.

"I felt my legal training would be put to better use serving the Danish community, on the front line."

At the mention of her degree the woman's eyebrows raised ever so slightly. Birgitte resisted the temptation to ask what line of work she may be in.

Her husband asked expectantly, "Are you here in an official capacity?"

Birgitte shook her head. "Holidays, with my father. Although he heads back to Denmark on Monday. I'll be here for another week or so."

"Splendid," said Canningvale. "If Reginald here gets out of line, you have my permission to beat him senseless with a telephone book. I'm sure Lady Catherine wouldn't object."

The joke broke the tension. Canningvale directed the conversation towards the current strained relations between Britain and the EU to keep everyone on even ground.

Eventually, they were distracted by the chiming of steel against crystal. The guests turned to the corner of the room where a distinguished-looking gentleman was calling for their attention. It was the Consulate General. Despite the formality of the occasion he wanted the speeches to be casual to denote the level of friendship between the two men. Canningvale politely excused himself and moved forward through the crowd.

The Consulate General spoke confidently for several minutes, outlining the arc of Canningvale's distinguished career, including his time with the British Army. He paid particular attention to the ties Canningvale had built between the British business community, the Hong Kong Government and Beijing. Birgitte made a note to ask her father later how difficult that may have been. Canningvale was obviously very adept at reading the wind. Like the British imperialists before him, he had an uncanny knack for knowing where real power lay and then ensuring his services could be rendered in such a way as to make his ongoing presence in the region indispensable. The Consulate General was profoundly grateful. Canningvale stepped up to the microphone and gave a short reply, thanking the Consulate General and his own former colleagues for helping shape what he referred to as a rewarding career. He facetiously quoted Kierkegaard in an effort to share his personal opinion of his somewhat formidable public image. It was a humble self-effacing performance that further elevated his stature in the room.

The speeches concluded with energetic applause. Waiters appeared with more trays of wine as the crowd mingled once again. The night slipped into longwinded reminiscences – elderly men competing with one another to relive their time in the sun. By 10pm Jan was looking tired and a little distracted. Birgitte suggested it might be time to head back to the hotel.

As they began to say good night to the many guests they had met, Birgitte looked about the room for Canningvale. She spotted him through a pair of closed French doors that faced onto a balcony. He was talking intently to someone, but it was too dark for Birgitte to see who, and they were also obscured by a palm. If she had to guess she would have said it was a woman, something about the line of the silhouette, but she couldn't be sure. She didn't think it was Canningvale's aide. Then the former officer turned away and started talking on his phone. The other person had left. At that angle Birgitte could see Canningvale's face. It was as if a dark cloud had descended over his soul. Gone was the social congeniality, in its place, a stern look of barely concealed wrath. She couldn't hear through the glass but she could tell he was resisting the urge to shout. When he ended the call, he swept his hands through his hair in exasperation. He took a deep breath and stood before the French doors. For a moment it looked as if he was staring directly at Birgitte, until he adjusted his tie in the reflection, then adopted his air of bonhomie and re-entered the room as if nothing had happened.

Jan crossed the floor and shook his hand.

"Thank you for inviting us on such short notice. It was good to see so many old faces again."

41

Canningvale squeezed Jan's upper arm. "Don't be a stranger for so long."

"Give me a call if you're ever in Copenhagen."

"I will. And please allow me the pleasure of looking after your daughter while she is in Hong Kong." He drew a business card from his pocket and handed it to Birgitte. For a moment his attention was diverted to the far side of the room. Birgitte quickly followed his eyes and noticed one of the young escorts she had almost pointed out earlier to Jan in conversation with a woman whom she couldn't quite see. She wondered if it was the woman from the balcony. Canningvale quickly looked back at Birgitte as if it was nothing. "If there is anything at all you need during your stay, call that number on the bottom, dear, and my staff will have a hold of me in a jiffy. Perhaps I can take you to dinner one night and you can meet some more of the people who make this city so exciting."

Birgitte, no longer so enamoured, politely took the card and thanked him for his generous hospitality. She looked back to the far side of the room but the escort had returned to the arm of one of the elderly Chinese guests, and the woman she'd been speaking to was nowhere to be seen. Birgitte found the scene quite intriguing and wondered how well her father knew this Albert Canningvale.

CHAPTER THREE

Jan made his way across the lobby of the Conran Hotel, carrying his hand luggage for the flight back to Europe. Close behind him, a porter pulled a trolley that held his suitcase. Birgitte was waiting for him at the entrance.

They had spent the previous morning wandering through the markets in Stanley on the far side of Hong Kong Island, before catching a bus up to The Peak for lunch. Then they had relaxed with an afternoon Star Ferry cruise around Victoria Harbour. It was a wonderful way to wrap up their holiday together, and Birgitte realised it was probably the nicest time she had spent with her father in many years. The despondency that had marred Jan's mood on the Saturday evening was nowhere to be seen.

A taxi pulled in and the porter began loading Jan's luggage into the boot.

Birgitte hugged her father and kissed him on the cheek. "It was really lovely to see you."

"You too. Be sure to get to the Museum of History."

"I promise. In the next day or two. And you be sure to tell Loll to email me if she needs to talk. And ask after Aunty Carol – I hope she's recovering."

He pressed her hands. "I will."

Impulsively she hugged him again. When she was done, he pressed her shoulders. "Enjoy the rest of your holiday."

Without thinking she said, "I'll let you know about the promotion."

He got into the back of the taxi as if he hadn't heard. She laughed to herself mirthlessly. Things had improved between them, but not that much.

She watched as the taxi pull away from the hotel and waved until it had disappeared down the street. She'd done it – survived three days with her father. It was bittersweet to see him go but it felt good to finally be alone. Her holiday had officially started.

She walked to the Star Ferry Pier and boarded a ferry for Hong Kong Island with a loose plan to explore the antique stores up on Hollywood Road. But even as she watched the larger jet boats cut their way west to Macau and mused to herself that a day trip to see the Portuguese ruins and the outlandish casinos might be enjoyable, she could feel the impulses that had driven her to Hong Kong begin to stir.

When she disembarked at Central Ferry Pier, she caught an escalator up to the elevated walkways and made her way through the complex networks of retail spaces that filled the lower floors of the harbourside skyscrapers, a temperature-controlled world of luxury brands – designer handbags, watches, jewellery and haute couture. Within a matter of minutes, she had crossed several main roads and reached the base of the steep hill that rose up to form The Peak.

The Mid-Levels Escalator carried her upwards, past cafes, restaurants, galleries, narrow cross streets, corner bars and even narrower laneways. She stepped off at Hollywood Road but rather than turn right for the antique shops as planned, she went left towards Lan Kwai Fong. She didn't know exactly what she was looking for; she only knew she wanted to go back, perhaps in the hope of gaining some clarity, or closure, anything that would stop what had been eating away at her for the past 12 months. And perhaps it was just morbid curiosity.

The narrow laneways in this part of Central were quiet mid-morning. The restaurants and cafes were preparing for the impending lunchtime crowds. Before she knew it, she had turned into the cluster of bars and nightclubs that drew in thousands of locals and tourists every night. There were only a handful of staff there now, mopping outdoor areas and putting out bags of rubbish from the night before. She made her way from memory through a dog leg of an alley into a cul de sac. And there it was – the bar where she had waited for de Graff. She stopped and stared at the closed bi-fold doors, confronted only with her own reflection. She didn't know what she expected to see but this wasn't it.

She stood there for several minutes, recalling the events of that night and the weeks leading up to it. It didn't seem right, to have travelled so far against her own better judgement to feel so empty. There was no sense of triumph at facing her fears, no vindication for her actions in removing a killer from the streets. What did she expect, she wondered. Should she have flown to Australia instead? Driven across the desert again? In search of what? The hope of being able to do it all again, differently? To tell Tony how she had felt about him?

Eventually, Birgitte turned away and made her way back through the narrow streets. She found a café by the Mid-Levels Escalator. She ordered a cappuccino and took a seat outside. As she sat watching the people of Central busily moving back and forth her thoughts shifted back to her father. Three days was the most time she had spent with him in her entire adult life. It saddened her to think of the time she'd lost. But what disturbed her more was his state of mind. Despite the mood swings and his decaying ability to concentrate, she felt there was something preying on his mind, particularly on their way to Government House. She thought about the evening in more detail and found herself dwelling on the moment she spotted Sir Albert outside on the balcony. Her instincts had been rankled. Something wasn't right.

She paid for her coffee and dismissed her own concerns about her father and her visit to Lan Kwai Fong – she was looking for drama unnecessarily. Surely, it was a sign that she needed a holiday. Her hectic caseload back in Copenhagen had her chasing chimeras. The fact was she'd had a surprisingly pleasant time with Jan and she couldn't wait to tell Loll all about it.

She spent the next hour or so wandering along the southern end of Hollywood Road, peering through the windows of antiques stores. Occasionally, when one took her interest, she'd step inside and carefully peruse the glass displays of bronze horses, stone warriors and intricate ships of jade. If she'd had the money, there were several items she would have loved to have shipped back to Denmark. Instead, she waited until she found a less imposing store at the quiet end of the street to buy several small pieces of jade – polished symbols of simple design which she could give as presents over the coming year. The purchase pleased her. It felt good to finally be a tourist.

Back out on the street, Birgitte checked her watch. She began to consider the idea of lunch, perhaps back near the Mid-Levels Escalator. There were several restaurants there that had piqued her interest earlier.

She was about to set off, when something caught her eye further down Hollywood Road. A small Chinese boy of seven or eight was watching her expectantly from the top of a stairwell about 20 metres away. He was wearing a navy t-shirt and red shorts. There was something curious about his gaze. As she turned to get a better look at him, his smooth placid face curled into an impish grin, revealing two rows of tiny teeth. He smiled at her knowingly as if they were a playing a made-up game for which she didn't know the rules. Birgitte wanted to ask him what he wanted, but figured he was just doing it for attention. She started to walk back the way she had come, deciding on Japanese for lunch. There was a sushi restaurant several minutes' walk away.

She had only walked a few metres, when she heard the boy call out to her in a bright voice, "Will you save me?"

She stopped suddenly and turned. The little boy jiggled with excitement. Birgitte looked around to see if he was talking to anyone else. There were a few people further up the street window-shopping, but no one close enough for her to be mistaken about who the boy was addressing. Maybe she had misheard him, Birgitte reasoned with herself, so she turned back to ask him what he meant. There could have been a simple explanation. But when she looked down the street the boy had vanished. She peered around to see if anyone had witnessed where he went but no one was paying her any mind.

Birgitte approached the top of the stairs, which led down steeply between the buildings to the next parallel street. There were more shopfronts and a few cafes but no child. She turned and looked at the stairs that continued up the hill. He wasn't there either. The boy's words continued to play in her mind: "Will you save me?" As if he was singling her out for an impending failure of duty. It was a little unsettling, but probably a silly prank, she decided. The boy could have learned the line from TV and was having a laugh at tourists' expense or it was some sort of local game he was used to playing with friends.

She changed her mind about lunch. It had been a busy few days. The conference in Vietnam and the time with her father had caught up with her. She just wanted to go back to the hotel to rest. She walked to the Mid-Levels Escalator and made her way back down to Central Ferry Pier.

The wharves were now crowded with tourists and day-trippers. Birgitte arrived at the turnstiles as a ferry for Kowloon was about to pull out. She searched through her purse for her transport card. As she was about to step through the turnstile a thin white woman in her mid 30s, with dark ginger hair and wide cat-like eyes, stepped in front of her.

"Don't be so ambitious," the woman said firmly in English, her accent distinctly British.

Birgitte didn't respond, unsure of why she was being reprimanded but the interaction distracted her enough that she dropped her purse. Surprisingly, the woman stopped to help her.

Birgitte found the woman's behaviour off-putting, so she made a point of gathering up her things herself, then thanked her without looking up. By the time she moved through the turnstiles the woman had disappeared into the crowd boarding the ferry in front of her.

Birgitte moved with the other passengers and found a spare seat inside the ferry. As it pulled out from the wharf, she sat back and closed her eyes, trying to forget the altercation with the woman and the odd little boy at the top of the stairs.

Several feet away the woman with ginger hair watched Birgitte intently. Her skin was bloodless; her eyes flat and cold. A thin smile pulled at the corners of her lips.

The traffic on Nathan Road in Kowloon was thick with buses and trucks, exhaust fumes plumed from vertical pipes, horns bleated with irritation. There was a restless energy to the street. Merrick Cripps was on a mobile out the front of Hanjin Mansion, surrounded by Indian hawkers. He was struggling to hear over the noise of the street.

"I need more time...." he said in a South London accent, his voice nasal and weak. He stared at the passing buses absently as he listened. "I know I said that, but it's just that I gotta work through this list..."

He drew heavily on his cigarette and exhaled the smoke. "You know I'm good for it, for Christ's sake... two more weeks... it's all I ask, is two more weeks."

He checked his watch – it looked new. He slapped it violently then checked it again. He shook his head in disbelief. He looked around then glared at the hawker who sold him the watch. The Indian man quickly turned away, ignoring him.

Cripps said out loud to himself, "In a city of fucking watches and I get sold a bracelet."

He looked up into the street and saw the time displayed out the front of a watch shop.

"Listen, I have to go but I promise you, you won't be disappointed... but you have to give me more time... hello? ... hello?" He stared at his phone in disbelief. "You fucking wanker."

He checked the time again and began to run towards a train station.

Twenty minutes later he was running down Waterloo Road from Kowloon Tong station, past the school where he had waited outside on Friday, then on towards St Martins International Primary School. He stopped at a bus shelter across the street as scores of children filed out the front door to be collected by their parents and nannies. He looked about desperately. The last children left and no one else emerged. He drew a scrap of paper out of his pocket and scratched another name off the list then cursed under his breath in bitter frustration.

Birgitte awoke mid-morning, the sun streaming through her window. She had rested on her bed for most of the previous afternoon then taken a sleeping pill in the early evening to ensure she would sleep through the night.

She got out of bed and took a long hot shower. As the water rained over her, she thought about the boy who had called out to her in Central. It was the way he had spoken to her which she found unsettling, as if he knew she'd be there. She turned off the taps and stepped out of the shower. It wasn't worth dwelling over, she thought as she dried herself. She got dressed, grabbed her bag and left the room.

After a light breakfast in the Executive Lounge, Birgitte decided to take her father's advice and walk to the Museum of History, which was only a few blocks away in Tsim Sha Tsui East.

It was a humid morning. The thick air embraced her as she stepped out of the climate-controlled environment of the Conran Hotel. Taxis were pulling away from the entrance as others arrived, new guests were being greeted by porters holding trolleys. Birgitte made her way between the other tourists, intent on getting her bearings for the shortest route to the Museum.

Several metres away, on a bench among a copse of mango trees, a thin white woman slowly stood up. She wore a plain white dress and a summer hat, which shielded her face when she kept her head lowered. She watched Birgitte walk along the drive, out onto the street then head east towards Nathan Road, as she had watched her on the ferry the day before. Her wide-set eyes moved quickly, assessing the distance between herself and her target. She stood up and set off at a comfortable pace. When Birgitte waited at a set of lights, the woman slowed her pace and paused to look in shop windows.

Birgitte arrived at the Museum 20 minutes later. For a modern building, it was surprisingly understated, appearing more like a research centre than a cultural institution. She bought a ticket from a fresh-faced young woman at the front desk, who offered her a fold-out map then pointed her towards the entrance to the first gallery.

Birgitte entered a dimly lit room devoted to the prehistoric era. The only light available was cast on the exhibits that lined the walls. She waited a moment for her eyes to adjust. The displays were well set out, with short texts providing context on every scene. She took her time with each topic, consulting the map then moving deeper into the museum. She particularly enjoyed the dioramas on the rise of dynastic power on the mainland – from the

Han to the Qin, before moving into galleries devoted to the folk culture of Hong Kong. Within an hour the museum was filling up with more and more people, tourists like herself, school groups and locals. She had to wait patiently to look at some exhibits. At one point she found herself studying the faces of the people directly around her, prompted by an unsettling feeling that she was being watched. It was only momentary, like a cloud passing over the sun. She put it down to the eerie lighting.

When she reached the section covering the First Opium War, she took more time with each display. As she read the text on how the British imperialists managed to bluster their way into the region, she couldn't help but think of Sir Albert Canningvale – a curious relic of a faded empire. It had always amused her how people of his class continued to display the airs and graces of a bygone era, refusing to accept their real power had diminished – not unlike the retired diplomats with whom her father kept company.

She looked up from the diorama to realise the room had filled with 30 or so school girls wearing blue uniforms, giggling and talking excitedly in Cantonese. They were about seven or eight years old. The darkness of the room excited them. They called out to one another, laughing; one girl squealed, which made several others squeal instinctively. Their teachers were trying to herd them towards a particular display, reminding them to keep answering the questions on their worksheets. It was a pleasant chaos, which Birgitte found quite enjoyable. It reminded her of museum visits when she was there age. Some of the little girls looked up at her as if she was a part of the exhibition. She smiled at them and pointed back to the diorama. They giggled and waved.

She thought of her estranged husband, Tomas. Despite the awkwardness of the situation, she honestly believed he would make a good father. Of course, she was still hurt by what had happened or at least that it had happened so quickly after their own break up, but she was coming to terms with it as best as she could. She only hoped the new woman in his life would do the right thing by him. For all his flaws, he deserved that much.

As she moved towards the next display, a replica of the Bogue Forts, another class of school girls entered the room. For a moment it was just too crowded. The teachers were struggling to maintain control. Birgitte tried to move out of the way but she was pretty much surrounded by children. Somewhere among the melee she heard a little girl's voice behind her say in English, "Will you save me?"

Birgitte's limbs ran cold as she turned around to see who had spoken to her. It was too dark. She was confronted by scores of girls who were now jostling one another, excited to be in such a crowd. Several other tourists had entered the room as well, including a few families with children of their own. One of the teachers suddenly lost her temper with her unruly students. She scolded them in no uncertain terms. They all stared up at her with their mouths open. No one paid Birgitte any mind, yet she was sure someone had just spoken directly to her – asking her exactly the same question as the boy in Central had done only the day before. The girl's tone had been playful, taunting – the question this time posed more as a challenge, as if it was a child's game and Birgitte had been tagged in some way and was now "it". Birgitte did her best to search the children's faces – of the ones she could see, none of them showed any interest in her at all. But she couldn't have been mistaken. One of the children had definitely spoken to her.

Birgitte moved through the group to address one of the teachers, a thin dowdy woman in her 40s wearing thick glasses.

"Excuse me," Birgitte said in English, "One of your students just spoke to me? Did you know who it was?"

The teacher stared at her blankly.

Birgitte asked, "Do you speak English?"

The woman ignored Birgitte, choosing instead to continue guiding the children out of the room. Birgitte called out to all of them, "Who just asked me if I could save them?"

They clearly didn't understand her question, some of the children laughed warmly at her, but soon the concerned look on her face began to alarm them. The room fell silent.

"Please, one of you called out to me. Who was it? I'm not angry," she insisted, trying to force a smile. The teachers glared at Birgitte for being a nuisance. They ushered the children into the next room. Birgitte considered dismissing it, just getting on with her visit, but her instinct told her that her concerns were justified. Something wasn't right, so she followed them, determined to get answers. She thought again of the boy in Central. If someone was playing a joke on her, she wanted to know why. She looked at each of the young students carefully in the hope that one might give themselves away.

A few minutes later, having called out to them several more times, Birgitte was approached by a large Chinese security guard in his 50s who spoke a little English. One of the other teachers must have asked for his assistance.

He said, "Please, leave the children alone."

Birgitte tried to explain. She didn't want to cause a scene but something wasn't right. The security guard was barely listening. "It no good, Madam. You bother children. You must leave now."

He put her hand at her lower back and began to guide her towards an exit. Birgitte turned once more to the children. One of the girls, with a round, sweet face and pig tails, looked up at her knowingly. Birgitte called out to her, "Was it you? Did you call out to me? What do you want?"

A teacher quickly stepped in front of the girl, shielding her from Birgitte, as the security guard roughly grabbed her arm and pulled her towards a side exit. There was nothing Birgitte could do. She allowed the security guard to escort her out of the gallery. The other patrons stared at her as she passed, curious to know what she had done to be hauled out of a cultural institution in the middle of the morning. She scanned their faces. Someone had to be behind what was obviously a mean-spirited joke, designed to unnerve or embarrass her. But no one looked out of place. The security guard held open a black door under a sign marked 'Exit'.

From across the gallery, behind a glass display cabinet, the woman in the plain white dress watched Birgitte pause a final time before leaving the museum. The woman, who held her wide brimmed hat in one hand, lowered her head and veiled a thin smile. Her eyes shone with excitement. She reached into her bag and drew out her phone.

Outside, Birgitte was trying to collect her thoughts. Two children in two days, both asking for her help, but not really wanting it. It didn't make any sense. She headed back to the hotel.

After a gruelling session at the gym she took a long shower, but still felt no less concerned by the events of the past two days. But what could she do? She told herself to let it go. There was no explaining it, but worrying about what it all meant threatened to spoil her time in Hong Kong. She lay on her bed in her bathrobe and closed her eyes, hoping a nap would still her mind.

In the evening the clouds that had lingered for most of the afternoon finally broke, releasing a steady deluge that lasted for half an hour. Birgitte left the hotel as the rains eased to a light drizzle. She cut up through the narrow streets between the hotel and Kowloon Park, looking for a suitable restaurant for dinner. Even in the back streets Hong Kong at night was a riot of colour and light – the brilliant yellows, vibrant greens and Coca-Cola reds of backlit signs and neon advertising now bled across the wet bitumen, the camber of the road shimmering as the rain continued to fall.

Birgitte spotted a northern Chinese restaurant, where young men in white shirts were stretching noodles in the window. She ran across the street, stepping lightly but still managing to soak her shoes. She opened the door and shook the rain from her hair, signalling to a waiter a table for one. He led her to a seat by a fish tank and took her order for a seafood noodle dish she liked the sight of from a nearby table.

The meal was delicious, one of best dishes on her trip so far, but she had to admit that she was struggling to relax. Part of her mind was still at her desk in the Politivoret, sifting through case files and considering possible leads – a forward defence to the possibility of being knocked back for promotion. The two children who had called out to her were also on her mind, but she couldn't think for the life of her of how to resolve the problem.

She paid the bill and stepped out into the rain. There was a hole-in-the-wall bar across the street. She decided to stop giving herself a hard time – if the detective inside her didn't want to switch off then perhaps it was time she took her for a drink for all the hard work she was doing.

The interior of the bar was littered with American baseball regalia – a gaudy theme that meant little to the regulars. It was just a local watering hole for the surrounding businesses and passing tourists. Birgitte took a seat at the bar. The other patrons were all Hong Kong Chinese, two women in their 30s in tailored suits, an elderly man in a peaked cap and three business men who were laughing loudly down the far end. She ordered a glass of red from a plump faced young barman and settled back into her chair. The Eagles were playing on the stereo, and the TV, braced in the corner of the ceiling over the storeroom door, was showing some frenetic game show. It wasn't the sort of bar Birgitte would step foot in back home, which is what made it kind of pleasant to be in. She could see Sven getting drunk in a place like this once a week – if his wife would let him. For a few minutes she imagined him sitting beside her with a beer in his hand bemoaning the politics of senior management. And when he got really hammered, he'd get all serious and tell her what an amazing detective she was and that she would probably end up running the joint one day. She'd brush it off as she'd done so many times before but she really appreciated having Sven in her corner.

By the time she was on to her third wine she felt better about the promotion. She began to think of what cultural changes she would like to implement when her eye was drawn to the TV. It was now on a local news channel delivering an update in Cantonese. She forgot about work and was trying to determine the crux of each news story with only the footage as a reference – something about politicians at a conference, then a story on a blaze in an industrial region. The third story showed the image of a high-rise apartment block, part of a housing estate for low-income earners. The camera zoomed in on a particular apartment where an air-conditioning unit was bent downwards away from the wall as if it had held something heavy. The window behind it was open. The camera then panned back to show the 12-storey drop to the concrete below where a police cordon had been set up, shielding passers-by from what lay behind the screen. Birgitte was beginning to realise the gravity of the story. Then the photo of a young boy was shown in the top left corner and Birgitte almost broke the glass in her hand.

It was the boy from the stairway in Central the day before.

Birgitte called out to the barman in English to turn up the TV. He gave her an odd look but complied. The journalist continued talking in Cantonese. Birgitte grabbed the arm of the elderly man on the stool beside her, who was by now quite drunk.

Birgitte pointed at the TV. "What is she saying?" she asked.

He looked at the TV then back at Birgitte but didn't know how to respond. She turned to the women on her left. They both tried answering at once in broken English. All she could pick up were bits and pieces. "Child out the window"... "on air-conditioner"... "police too late".... "he slip and fall".... "should never be out there in the first place". Then it descended into moral judgements: "Where were the parents?" and "Should be laws for high-rises like that."

Eventually the novelty wore off and the patrons returned to their drinks. It wasn't the only child to fall out of a window, they decided. It happened in China more often than you'd think. They shook their heads and began to talk of other things in Cantonese.

Birgitte couldn't believe what she had just seen. It couldn't have been a coincidence. The child had asked her if she could save him, and now he was dead. She immediately thought of the school girls in the museum. One of them was in grave danger.

CHAPTER FOUR

"I'm concerned for the safety of a girl who spoke to me in the museum," Birgitte said for the third time. She was doing her best to control her tone as she relayed what she knew so far to the middle-aged desk sergeant of the Tsim Sha Tsui Police Station. She checked the clock on the wall in the waiting area. It was almost 10pm.

The station was clean, clinical and brilliantly lit, like the perfume section of a department store. It lacked the subtle sense of chaos she was used to in the stations in Copenhagen, where no one had time to straighten chairs or tidy up notice boards. This station didn't even seem to have notice boards.

The officer looked tired but that could have just been due to his sallow lean face and beleaguered demeanour. Fortunately, his English was passable but Birgitte could tell he wasn't taking her seriously. Like a bureaucrat days from retirement, he kept pointing to the form in front of her, asking her to make a written statement. She told him she knew the routine and was willing to comply but she needed to speak to someone involved with the case. He made it clear that no would be listening to her until her statement was formalised – on the form in front of her.

She sighed and continued to write.

"So you do know about the boy who fell from the 12th-storey window?" she asked.

"I do," he replied, reading an unrelated matter on his computer screen. "It's being handled by the appropriate officers."

"Can I speak to one of them?"

"When you have filled out the form, it will be processed. If your statement is relevant, we will be in touch."

"And you understand that the boy – the boy who fell from the apartment building – approached me only yesterday, asking me to save him?"

58

The desk sergeant was getting tired of the European woman's persistence. "Have you been drinking tonight?"

Birgitte looked at him with contempt and refused to answer.

He didn't say anything else. His point was made.

Birgitte drew her police ID out of her purse. "I am with the Danish National Police."

"You said you were here on holiday."

"I am on holiday, but I am also with the Danish National Police."

He scrutinised the ID more out of personal curiosity, checking it for differences with his own. Birgitte controlled her tone. "The point is I am not trying to waste your time. As one police officer to another, I think someone should take this more seriously than you are doing."

"Detective Vestergaard, is it?"

She nodded.

"Please, fill out the form as I asked earlier, provide all the details of where we can reach you and if we have any questions, we will contact you."

Birgitte wondered if this was how people experienced desk sergeants in Copenhagen. She left the station frustrated.

Back at the hotel she emailed a colleague in Copenhagen to get the contact details of the senior superintendent of the Hong Kong Police who she had worked with when Zachary de Graff was arrested, Harold Leung. There wasn't anything more she could do that night but first thing in the morning she would go back to the Museum of History. Someone there must know the name of the primary school whose students had been in the Opium Wars display with her that morning. Birgitte needed to find the girl who spoke to her as quickly as possible.

The next morning, when Birgitte arrived back at the Museum of History she was wearing her hair up in a ponytail under a baseball cap she'd picked up along the way and a pair of sunglasses. She waited for a large group of tourists to amble past the front desk to slip through the main lobby unnoticed.

After some very subtle questioning of visitors and low-grade staff, Birgitte found a volunteer who remembered the school children who were there the day before. Birgitte concocted a story about being a costume designer in films. The woman was very helpful. She told Birgitte they were from the Xin Lan Primary School in Sham Shui Po, north-west of Kowloon. Birgitte thanked her and slipped out of the museum without encountering the security guard who had ejected her the previous day. She headed back to Tsim Sha Tsui Station.

Overnight, her colleague in Copenhagen had emailed her the details of Senior Superintendent Harold Leung. Before leaving the hotel that morning, Birgitte had sent the detective a polite message explaining her situation as briefly as possible. She received an automatic response, stating that Harold Leung had retired in January of that year. If she had any further enquiries, she should contact his replacement. She thought about it for a moment then decided it was too early to attempt pulling rank with officers she didn't know. She filed the email for later reference, hoping she wouldn't have to draw on it.

Sham Shui Po was an overcrowded, rundown part of Hong Kong. Where the streets of Tsim Sha Tsui blazed like daylight during the night, here the reverse was true. It felt dark and claustrophobic to be outside. The neglected buildings seemed to lean over the street, threatening to collapse under the weight of rusted signs, electrical cables and illegal extensions. It was no less crowded and noisy than the harbour-side suburbs but it clearly lacked the affluence. And it smelled of dirty dishwater and diesel.

Birgitte considered her options as she negotiated her way through the crowds. She could confront the principal, but given the way the teachers had reacted at the museum, and the desk sergeant, she didn't like her chances of being well received. The best she could hope for was wait till the lessons finished and try to find the girl who looked at her. If she was in any immediate danger, the least she could do was alert her family.

Birgitte found the Xin Lan Primary School after about 15 minutes. It was a heavy-looking architectural monstrosity from the 1960s – all concrete, and aluminium shutters, enclosed in a high black metal fence. It backed onto a courtyard devoid of plant-life where the children played in their lunch hour.

When the final bell chimed the students filed out of several blocks and headed for the main gate. Birgitte recognised the uniform and felt a sense of relief that she was in the right place. Now she just hoped the girl who had looked at her in the museum didn't leave by some other exit which she couldn't see.

Eventually, she spotted the child as she approached a teenage girl, who was probably a sister, an aunt or a nanny. Either way Birgitte knew she was too young to be warned or even approached so she followed them at a safe distance as they walked down the street.

Half an hour later they turned onto a cluttered street and entered a doorway three businesses down from the corner. No sooner had they disappeared inside than a Chinese man in his 50s emerged, wearing only a loose pair of shorts, his hairless bony body reminded Birgitte of an exotic cat. He stared at Birgitte then approached her directly. The older girl had obviously spotted Birgitte at some point and alerted the man as soon as she got home.

"What you want?" he said abrasively.

Birgitte attempted a warm, professional smile. "My name is Birgitte Vestergaard. I'm a police officer from

Denmark. I was in the Museum of History yesterday morning. Your daughter was there, with her school – something strange happened and I just wanted to ask her a few questions."

"Not my daughter. But you no belong here."

"I'm concerned for the safety of your child."

"Not my child. My sister's child. Why she no safe?" he asked with a wary look on his face.

"I don't know. A boy called out to me a few days ago at Central and now he is dead. He fell from a window." It sounded ridiculous even as she said each word. She pressed on. "Your niece – she was at the Museum of History yesterday. You can ask her? I need to know if she called out to me."

He stared at her, unmoving. "She call to you?"

"She asked if I could save her."

The look of confusion on his face made him look nasty. "Save her from what?"

"I don't know."

"You crazy. She no speak English" he said, turning back to the doorway. "Stay away from my family."

"Can I just talk to the girl?"

"No. Go or I call the police."

"I've already spoken to them."

"They know you crazy, then."

"Yes. That's what everyone thinks. Please keep a close eye on the girl. Perhaps keep her from school for a few days."

"You go. Leave us alone."

He disappeared inside the building.

The following day Birgitte was at a loss for what to do next. She moved restlessly about her hotel room. A child was dead and another was most certainly at risk and there wasn't a thing she could do about it but wait. She had kept the TV on a local channel all day in the hope of catching a news report but there had been no further development on the boy who had fallen from the apartment block. She considered calling Sven in Copenhagen to get his advice but didn't want to alarm him with a seemingly fanciful story about children who had called out to her to save them. It was now Thursday. She decided it was time to go back to the police station in Tsim Sha Tsui. Hopefully there might be someone else on the front desk who would be more willing to help, or at least she could see if her statement had been read by someone working on the case.

She was about to leave when she noticed the news channel she had been following had cut to a live cross from a helicopter over the north-eastern end of Victoria Harbour. Birgitte went to the window and could see the helicopter in the distance hovering over the water. Another helicopter was approaching from over Kowloon. She turned back to the TV and tried to work out was happening. The live cross now showed of a young female reporter on the mainland talking seriously to the camera and occasionally motioning over her shoulder. She was on the edge of a hastily formed police cordon down by the harbour's edge. Two uniformed officers held their hands up for the camera to stay back. The camera zoomed in and out between cars and buildings in the hope of getting a clear shot of what was going on. There was a lengthy pause where the reporter stared at the camera. She'd run out of information and didn't know what to say. When she spoke again Birgitte could tell that she was just repeating herself. Mid-sentence the footage cut back to the helicopter.

Birgitte sat heavily on her bed as she watched the body of a young girl being lifted out of the harbour. At that distance Birgitte couldn't see they child's face but the uniform looked very familiar, like that worn by the children in the Museum of History on Tuesday. She was sure it was the girl she had followed to Sham Shui Po. She

63

went back to the window, where there were now three helicopters hovering over the scene like vultures. She stared hard at the city and tried to think. Two children. Both had approached her. Both were dead. This couldn't be happening. On instinct she grabbed her bag and ran out of the room.

It took her 20 minutes to get to that part of the Hung Hom Promenade. She had recognised a few of the buildings in the background so she knew where to go. When she arrived the police cordon had been moved outward a further 200 metres. Camera crews shuffled about anxiously, trying to find an angle that would give their program the edge. Reporters yelled at their crews as they took phone calls from their producers. It was hectic and ugly. Birgitte searched the scene for an ambulance in the hope of confirming the identity of the girl but it looked as though the body had already been removed.

She approached one of the young uniformed officers guarding the perimeter of the scene. He seemed oblivious to the drama taking place around him. He'd obviously been on the force long enough to detach himself from crime scenes that weren't his complete responsibility. Birgitte asked him if he knew what had happened. He told her a girl had slipped and fallen into the water and she couldn't swim. It was just an accident. She asked him where they would be taking her and he gave her an odd look.

"Do you at least know which station will be responsible for investigating her death?"

"She slipped."

"But which station will do the report?"

He shrugged then gave it some thought. "Probably Tsim Sha Tsui." The conversation no longer interested him so without another word he moved to another part of the perimeter.

64

Birgitte weighed her options. She could go back to the station and risk being treated like a crazy woman. Or she could use the contact details she had for the senior superintendent who had replaced Harold Leung. Even if they did take her enquiry seriously, it would be a matter of days before anything happened. She knew it was inappropriate to approach the girl's family so soon after she was found. But the child must have known something. Someone had told her to talk to Birgitte at the Museum of History. The child might have confided in the older girl who walked her home, or mentioned it to her mother or uncle. She must have said something.

It was no use. Her involvement at this stage would only cause confusion. She would have to wait until the police had spoken to the families themselves. Hopefully, they would interview the older girl. As the helicopters pulled away from the scene, Birgitte made her way slowly back to Kowloon.

CHAPTER FIVE

On Friday morning Birgitte returned to Tsim Sha Tsui Police Station in the hope of speaking to someone directly involved in the investigations to the children's deaths. Instead she was dealing with another desk sergeant, an officious-looking young woman with steel-framed glasses and severe pony tail. Birgitte had introduced herself as a Danish detective from the outset, explained that two children had died in the past few days in murders that were made to look like accidents and both victims had approached her the day before they were killed. The desk sergeant listened, took notes then handed Birgitte a familiar form. Before Birgitte could protest, the officer told her that while Birgitte was filling it out she would determine the progress of the original forms and get someone to listen to her story in full. Finally, Birgitte thought, she was getting somewhere.

About 10 minutes later a Chinese plain-clothes detective emerged from the main office carrying a copy of both her statements and two manila folders. He was in his mid 50s, with a slender frame and a wide face. Dressed neatly in a collared shirt, dark trousers and blue suit jacket, he introduced himself as Inspector Peter Wong. He led Birgitte passed the front desk, through the main office to a grey windowless interview room.

Inspector Wong asked if she would like a cup of coffee but Birgitte preferred just to get on with it, so he took a seat opposite, calmly studying her face as she did the same to him. There was a solemnity to his demeanour that could be taken as passivity, but his dark eyes suggested a watchful curiosity, which compelled Birgitte to reserve her judgment.

She ran through the order of events, keeping her explanation clinical and rational. Inspector Wong listened, and wrote notes of his own in a small pad he had drawn from his jacket pocket. Occasionally he held up his hand for her to pause so he could check her facts against her original statements. At one point he opened both manila folders – case files on each of the children – then closed them again, preventing Birgitte from getting any sense of where the investigation was up to. She carried on nonetheless. By the time she had finished she had no idea what Inspector Wong was thinking.

"So do you think I'm crazy or is someone killing these children and involving me in some way?"

"Your statements are concerning to me."

"How so?"

He looked down at his pad. "The fact that neither child could speak any English. The fact that you never saw either of them actually speaking. And that both deaths look like plausible accidents."

Birgitte went to defend herself when the inspector calmly held up his hand. "I didn't say I didn't believe you. I'm simply stating my concerns about the facts."

"It wasn't just what they said, it was the way they said it."

"How do you mean?"

"I'm Danish, Inspector, English is my second language. I know how people speak when English is foreign to them. Both children spoke with that sort of intonation, particularly the boy. I remember thinking at the time he was just repeating something he'd heard on TV, which was why I didn't give it that much thought. It now makes me think they were reciting the line."

The Inspector sighed, trying to process what she was saying. "So two complete strangers approach you to recite the same line? To what end?"

"I don't know," she said.

"Did you see them with anyone else at any point? An adult?"

She shook her head.

"What about just someone looking out of place nearby?"

"I did feel like I was being watched at the museum at one point. It felt strange but I couldn't see anyone staring at me so I tried not to think about it."

"Has anyone been following you?"

"I don't think so but I haven't been exactly looking, if you know what I mean."

"Who knows you're here?"

"It's not a secret," she said. "I was at a policing conference in Vietnam then I flew here to Hong Kong to met up with my parents for a few days. They left on Monday to fly back to Denmark."

"The day the first child approached you?"

"Yes. My colleagues know I'm here, but outside of that I don't know who would be interested."

The inspector stared at her carefully, his face unmoved by everything she had told him.

"I know that it must sound strange," she said. "But is it possible they didn't die in accidents? That someone could have killed them?"

He paused a long time before answering. "I think it is worth investigating further."

"So currently neither death is being investigated as a murder?"

"I'd rather not say at this point, but I will speak to the teams dealing with each case and advise they take the time to read through your statements carefully."

"Is that it?"

"At this stage, that is enough. We are thorough here, Detective Vestergaard. I assure you the matter is being taken as seriously as if it happened in Copenhagen. Two children are dead. We appreciate the gravity of the matter."

"If you need to look into my background at all, I was here a year ago. I worked with a Senior Superintendent

Harold Leung on an international matter. I believe he's retired now."

The inspector eyes offered a glint of recognition. "The Senior Superintendent retired in January."

"I'm sure if you called him, he could vouch for me."

"I don't think that will be necessary."

"So what do you want me to do now?"

He pulled a business card from his pocket. "Call me if anyone approaches you again."

Birgitte took the card almost reluctantly. She believed him when he said he was taking it seriously but didn't like the fact the case was now in his hands and not her own.

"I'm staying at the Conran Hotel, room 3616," she said as she stood up. "Please contact me if there are any developments. If someone is trying to taunt me with these murders, I want to do everything I can to help."

"I understand," said the inspector, jotting down the details on a pad by his keyboard. "Do you have a mobile number here in Hong Kong?"

"I do." She had to go to her phone to find it. He wrote it down.

She thanked him for his time and headed for the front desk. The desk sergeant asked her if Goong had been helpful. Birgitte gave her a querulous look. The officer apologised, explaining that most of the officers called Inspector Wong "Goong" – a shortened version of "Goong Goong", which meant "grandfather" in Cantonese. Birgitte wondered if the officer was being derisive but her tone suggested she actually held Inspector Wong in high regard.

"I don't know," Birgitte replied to her original question. "At least he listened to me. Thank you for your help."

The desk sergeant nodded and returned to her computer.

Birgitte stepped out into the humid air and wondered what she should do next. She looked about at the faces in the street, wondering if the killer had been watching her as she went back and forth to the police station. Was he out there now, laughing at her as she floundered? The thought made her angry and slightly paranoid. A long session at the gym would clear her head then she'd give some serious thought as to how to proceed. As far as she was concerned, she was no longer on holidays.

The final school bell chimed. Cripps could feel his shoulders tensing at the sound. He checked the list which was now tissue-paper thin with all his handling. The names of several schools had been crossed out, only one remained. This was it. It had to be. He'd almost run out of time. As the children came out to meet their parents and nannies, he peered through the foliage at each and every one of them until he found his target. He made sure no one was watching him as he set off across the street with his backpack over one shoulder. Twenty feet ahead of him a small school boy, no more than six, dwarfed by his own school bag, was walking beside his nanny. Cripps kept an even distance. When the boy stopped and crouched to do up his shoelace, Cripps stopped and pretended to play with his phone. They reached a corner, turned left and disappeared. Cripps broke into an awkward unnatural jog, the bag continually slipping from his rounded shoulder. He got to the corner, short of breath and fell back into a brisk walk when he spotted them again. He decided to cross the street and follow them from an angle. At the next corner they turned right. At one point he thought the nanny had noticed him, so he dropped right back but then caught up to them again on the next corner.

As they approached a busy intersection Cripps could see that the child and the nanny stopped at the lights. He couldn't help but catch up to them. The nanny turned and stared at him directly. Cripps knew exactly what she must be thinking.

The lights changed. The nanny grabbed the child's hand and virtually dragged him across the street to the right, looking over her shoulder nervously as they went.

Cripps turned to the left, grateful that the nanny and her charge had provided cover from his target for the last four blocks. He saw the woman move down the street, now 40 metres away. She turned into a shopfront and was gone.

Cripps crossed the street several doors back and entered a cafe, which gave him a clear view into the building she had entered. It was a wide dark-brick facade with double shutter doors opening onto a grimy workshop, where two cars were elevated on hydraulic lifts. Over the arch it said "Mason's Garage" in faded paint, under which were logos for several British car brands, such as Jaguar and TVR. It was mechanic's shop specialising in antique sports cars.

Cripps ordered a coffee at the counter and took a seat down the back, using the mirrors on the wall to see what went on across the road without drawing attention to himself.

About half an hour later, as he was beginning to get nervous that something may have gone wrong, he spotted a white guy in dirty coveralls emerging from the back of the garage, wiping his hands on a rag. The man was in his mid 30s but could have passed for much older; his face was hard and his features were tight and pinched. His dark hair was trimmed short on the sides but kept longer on top, combed back from his face in a style reminiscent of the German Friekorps of the 1920s – neat and efficient, but only a ruffling breeze away from losing control. He stepped toward the entrance of the garage with a pained limp, which he had obviously learned to minimise by restricting the movement of his left leg and internalising the discomfort. There was a curious fluidity to the awkwardness of his gait, like a contemporary dancer – restrained and powerful.

Cripps couldn't help but smile. He almost broke into laughter. But when the mechanic tossed the rag on a bench and set out slowly across the street towards the cafe, Cripps suddenly realised he had no means of escape. He ducked under the table and played with his shoe, watching the young man as he ordered a coffee. Cripps could barely breathe. He couldn't afford for it to all go to shit now that he was so close.

Eventually the mechanic collected his coffee, paid without a word and hobbled back across the street. Cripps grabbed his phone and started typing furiously: "I've found him!"

Maestri Tower rose up from Tung Lung Road like a sheer cliff face pocked with square cavities. It was one of a cluster of housing estates on the east side of Kowloon City, clumped between Walled City Park and Kai Tak River; cheap accommodation for thousands of residents who couldn't afford better. What the high-rise apartment block lacked in gleaming glass and steel was made up for in reinforced concrete.

Inspector Wong stood at the entrance with a case file bound in leather in his hands. To any passer-by he would have looked like a superintendent or an engineer on site doing a late-afternoon inspection. He noted the building had a secured entrance, but even as he looked around, he watched a resident who had arrived holding the door open for a delivery guy whose arms were full, so clearly it wouldn't be difficult for anyone to get in.

The inspector walked along Tung Lung Road to the next corner and turned left onto a pedestrian walkway that led between a run of retail business to the back of the estate. About 100 metres down he found a gap between two restaurants that gave him a clear view of the back of Maestri Tower from the fourth floor upwards. The inspector recognised the angle from news footage. He counted the air-conditioning units that marked each floor. When he reached the 12th, he realised the unit that had given way under the child's weight had already been replaced. He pictured the young boy, whose name was Ming Gao, clinging to the metal box, terrified. How long was he out there before he fell?

The inspector cast his eye across the vacant space east towards the Kai Tak River. It was a good few hundred metres before there was another building that could have provided a clear view of the 12th floor of Maestri Tower. So unless one of the other residents in the block happened to be looking out their bathroom windows, which were frosted, the incident would have gone unnoticed. If the boy was too frightened to call out and was only there for a minute or two or perhaps even less, there was a chance no one would have seen anything.

So why was he out there? And what was he doing in Maestri Tower in the first place? From memory, the child lived with his parents a few blocks to the south. The inspector quickly opened his leather folder to check their statement – when they were asked why they thought he would be in this particular building they had no idea. They didn't know anyone who lived there and Ming didn't have many friends. When questioned as to why the boy wasn't at school, they had said he'd fallen ill the previous day, on the Monday, but as they both had to go to work, he had to stay home alone. According to the statement, they had both showed genuine remorse at not watching him more closely. The inspector thought about what Detective Vestergaard had said – she had been approached by a boy matching his appearance in Central on the Monday afternoon.

As expected, it took no more than a few minutes to get past the security door. The inspector simply waited for a resident, a teenage boy, to emerge from the elevator bay on his way out of the building. The guy even held the door open for him.

As with most housing estates, the foyer was a dour, practical space where residents collected their mail before heading up to their apartments. He walked over to the fire door at the back of the block. It opened easily enough and wasn't alarmed. He then caught the elevator to the 12th floor. The corridor was wide and unkempt. It smelled of mildew. As he moved east towards the far end of the building, he could hear the muffled lives of the residents playing out through each front door. Occasionally someone would emerge, an elderly woman or a lonely young student. The kept their eyes down as they passed him.

He followed the corridor round to the fire exit which led down to the lobby. The door opened easily enough. It provided a second entry point to the floor. He looked north along the corridor. Twenty metres ahead was an air-conditioning unit housed between two windows. There were two doors either side of the corridor – four apartments, the residents of which said they hadn't heard anything because they weren't even there. According to statements in his file, on the Tuesday the boy had died, the floor had been cleared for a routine fumigation by pest experts. The inspector made a note to check with the building manager and the pest company for verification. He made his way down the corridor, still no wiser as to why a seven-year old boy would come to this particular floor of Maestri Tower.

The window at the far end was very basic – rusting steel frames holding thin panes – but there were chain holds on the locks so the window could be opened only so far. And the chain locks were brand new. Both windows had been repaired very recently. He unlocked the window on the left and rotated the handle so the metal frame opened slowly outward. It stopped within six inches, barely enough for a boy even as small as Ming Gao to climb out onto the unit. The inspector forced his head through and looked down, there were several windows below where the original locks had rusted open at varying angles, some as far as 20 inches. He checked the photos from his files. The locks had definitely been replaced by building management since the boy's death.

He looked at the height of the window ledge from the floor. A seven year old could climb up if he held onto the frame, but it wouldn't have been easy. He might have had something to stand on, the inspector wondered, looking back along the corridor. From this angle he realised that if the apartments were empty there were only two ways the boy could have left – back along the corridor or out through the window. Unless, of course, the corridor was blocked by someone. If the boy was frightened enough, would adrenalin have propelled him up the window frame and out onto the air-conditioning unit? What could be so terrifying as to make him think that out there was the safer option? He peered across the Kai Tak River, then looked up at the frosted windows of the neighbouring apartments within the tower. No one had seen the boy in his last terrified moments.

He got the impression from the parents' statement that Ming was a bit of a handful – didn't like to be told what he could or couldn't do, tended to go off on his own a lot, possibly because he didn't have many friends. Maybe, thought the inspector, he was just an adventurous child looking for trouble and his games got out of hand.

He closed the window and locked it. Without more evidence he couldn't say either way why the child had climbed out onto the air-conditioning unit but, even putting Detective Vestergaard's statements to one side, death by misadventure didn't sit well with his instincts.

An hour later he was on the northern foreshore of Victoria Harbour, walking along the edge of a large construction site under the Hung Hom Bypass. The peak hour traffic was rolling steadily overhead as he peered through the cyclone fence towards the water. The site was part of a proposed extension of the MTR train line, from Shatin to Central. It was also the nearest landmark to where the body of the young girl, Jenny Liew, had been retrieved the day before. She had only been in the water a few hours but it was long enough to complicate their efforts to determine where she may have entered. As unlikely as it was, some officers had suggested she may have slipped unnoticed from one of the Star ferries – hit her head on the way down. The inspector had checked the autopsy. The girl had simply drowned; there was no trauma to her head or scratches on her body. Her finger nails were even clean of any debris. So somehow she had ended up in the harbour, possibly of her own volition.

Her parents, who lived a few blocks to the north-east, said Jenny had never had swimming lessons, because they couldn't afford it, but she knew the water was dangerous. The inspector had thought it odd that her school bag hadn't been found either. Perhaps it had sunk to the bottom of the harbour, or floated out to sea. Jenny had attended a local school in Hung Hom, which complicated Detective Vestergaard's theory that the girl who had approached her in the Museum of History on the Tuesday was from a school in Sham Shui Po. Was Jenny Lieuw in the Museum on that day?

As with Ming Gao, Jenny had apparently told her parents she wasn't feeling up to going to school on the Tuesday. They had left her in the care of her aunt who was only a teenager herself. In her statement the aunt said she was preoccupied with a fight she was having with her boyfriend and hadn't bothered to even check if Jenny was still in the apartment for most of the day. By the time the parents came home in the evening they had no idea how long Jenny had been gone or where she was headed. Had she just gone for a walk along the foreshore and fallen into the water at some point?

He walked around the perimeter of the construction site to the western side then followed the line of the fence to the harbour's edge. There was a good two-metre drop into the water with no means of climbing back out, but it was also quite visible to the surrounding buildings. He pulled the statements from his leather folder – none of the construction workers who had been canvassed that day saw a young girl in the area. It placed a question mark over her point of entry. He made a note to chase up the harbour authorities who were yet to provide a report detailing the movement of tides and currents on the Tuesday. How far should they be looking from where the girl was found?

He peered towards Kowloon. Twilight was approaching. The lights on Hong Kong Island slowly flickered to life on the other side of the harbour. He cast his eye across the water, just making out the Tsim Sha Tsui East Ferry Pier off in the distance. A thought occurred to him.

He pulled out his phone and brought up a map of the area, scanning the streets near to the foreshore for a two kilometre stretch either side of the construction site. He soon spotted a narrow alleyway down towards the pier. It took a few minutes to get there but it was worthwhile. When he looked up the alley it reminded him of the corridor in Maestri Tower. There were only two points of exit, the city at one end and the harbour at the other. If Jenny's exit to the city was blocked and she was frightened enough, she may have felt she had no choice but to jump into the dark water below. Fear was a powerful but irrational motivator.

The alley wasn't yet lit, making it increasingly difficult to see. The inspector used the torch on his phone to cast a short bright beam over ground at his feet. He couldn't be certain this area had even been searched as part of the initial investigation into the child's death. He had hoped to find the child's school bag but there was nothing so obvious. However, after several minutes of scouring the alley, he spotted a shiny length of jewellery on the ground near one wall. He crouched down. It was a cheap silver-plated bracelet, the type he might expect to see on a girl of Jenny's age. He took a couple of quick photos of the alley and the bracelet in situ, then drew out an evidence bag from his pocket. He lifted the piece of jewellery up with the tip of his pen. If it belonged to the girl, then he'd possibly found where she had gone into the harbour. This immediately raised questions of why she was here and how she ended up in the water. Again, as with Ming Gao, there could be a very simple explanation of misadventure. As isolated cases, that cause of death couldn't be ruled out, but the fact they were both playing truant from school and had found themselves in situations that were incredibly dangerous stretched the misadventure theory almost to breaking point. Add Detective Vestergaard's statements and the inspector had to consider the possibility there was a child-killer in Hong Kong going to great lengths to make their deaths look like accidents. He made a note to speak to the Museum of History to access CCTV footage to see if Jenny Lieuw was in the gallery with the Danish detective. If so, was she with anyone else?

The stairway that ran either side of Hollywood Road was a thoroughfare like any other on the island, designed out of need rather than any aesthetic value, it was direct but uneven. Both sides were lined with shops whose owners stacked their wares on the front stoop so that passers-by would be tempted to enter, giving the steep laneway a pleasantly cluttered, ramshackle feel. It was Saturday afternoon. Birgitte was standing where the first child had called out to her on the previous Monday.

She had retraced her steps in the slim hope she may see something she had been too panicked to see the first time. Since she'd left the hotel at 10am that morning she had the distinct feeling she was being watched, stronger than the sensation she had felt at the museum. It wasn't paranoia, more an attempt to understand the mindset of the killer who was taunting her. If another child attempted to talk to her, this time she would be ready. She had kept herself out in the open and moved slowly, pretending to window-shop as she had been doing the first time she was approached. She had stopped for lunch just after 1pm at a restaurant west of the Mid-Levels Escalator and made a point of eating outside to give her a clear view in both directions. Fortunately, the streets were narrow and winding so she could monitor every passing person's movements adequately. Her surveillance was tiring, because she didn't know who she was looking for.

She'd had one false alarm, when she passed an emporium of Chinese kitsch, a small shop littered with memorabilia from the Cultural Revolution. She had had no intention of stopping when she noticed a dinner plate that caught her eye. In the reflection of the window she saw the figure of a woman standing across the street behind her. The woman had emerged from a shop and stopped stock still and appeared to be looking in Birgitte's direction. Birgitte turned as the woman approached.

"I thought I recognised you," she said with a distinct British accent, not smiling but with an openness that allayed Birgitte's concerns. It was the strange woman who had criticised her at the Central Ferry Pier and then offered to help her pick up her purse. She was wearing pale trousers and light shirt. Birgitte remembered the curious appeal of her wide-set eyes but they were hidden behind a pair of thick black sunglasses.

"I didn't get a chance to thank you," Birgitte said, to be polite.

"Not at all. I was a bit short with you. Still not used to the humidity."

The two women looked at one another, neither sure what to say next. Birgitte went to ask if she'd been in Hong Kong long when the woman said, "I won't hold you up. I need to be getting on myself. Enjoy the rest of your day."

Birgitte had watched as the woman headed back along Hollywood Road towards the Mid-Levels Escalator, slightly bemused at the randomness of their interactions. Perhaps under other circumstances they could have struck up an acquaintance, at least for the duration of the holiday. She had turned to walk down towards the antique shop, unaware that the woman had stopped herself. She moved into the doorway of a boutique and stared back at Birgitte, breathing heavily. That had been way too close. She grabbed her phone and dialled, staring impatiently down the street to see if Birgitte was still walking in the opposite direction.

"Where are you? ... stay there ... then buy him an ice-cream ... it won't be much longer. I'll phone you again when I know where she's going."

Birgitte now climbed up one flight of stairs and looked down on Hollywood Road, trying to picture what the boy would have seen had he come from this way. She could see herself emerging from the antique shop. This section of the stairway was devoted to paper lanterns, the gaudy red orbs were stacked shoulder high. It would have been easy for him to slip in or out of view. Had the killer been there, goading him on? The boy hadn't seemed reluctant to engage with Birgitte. Or had some sort of deal been made? She descended the stairs to Hollywood Road then went down another flight. Peering back up the hill from among the trestle tables of fresh fruit and vegetables, it felt too crowded and more unlikely the boy would have come from this angle. There was no view of the street.

But logic seemed to play very little in this killer's MO. She made a mental note to ask Detective Wong if she could read the transcripts of interviews with the shop owners had been questioned. They had to eliminate the alternative possibilities.

That was her thinking when she had texted Sven the previous evening. She had asked him to get in touch with the relevant authorities in Australia to confirm that the South African contract killer Zachary de Graff was still locked up and wasn't in any position to conduct criminal activities from within the prison, such as organising the abduction and murder of two children in Hong Kong. The disturbing thought had occurred to her when the little girl was fished out of Victoria Harbour.

When Birgitte had been driving back and forth across Australia with Tony Kingsmill, trying to solve the murder of the Danish national Hans Thostrup, de Graff had abducted a student from Melbourne University. He broke the young man's ankle before leaving him in the middle of a desert to slowly perish under the blazing Australian sun. He returned days later to collect the body, which he then drove across the state into Sydney. Birgitte had been taking a much-needed break from the case and was waiting for an old friend at a harbourside restaurant when the badly burned corpse appeared floating beneath a jetty only 50 metres away. Like the girl in Victoria Harbour, the body was a message sent directly to Birgitte.

She had spent an hour or so challenging her own thinking before contacting Sven. She knew how it would look and she had to admit that it bothered her deeply that de Graff still held a lingering power over her a year after his arrest, but she needed to be sure.

Sven had responded immediately, asking what it was all about and whether she was okay. She wrote back to say she was fine and that she would explain in greater detail in the coming days. For a moment she had considered asking

Sven to pursue more senior channels within the Hong Kong Police but decided against it. Inspector Wong was an unknown quantity. She wanted to give him the chance to act on her information. If he proved to be as bureaucratic as the desk sergeants she'd dealt with, only then would she bring more weight to bear from above.

She climbed back up to Hollywood Road. Disheartened, she checked her watch. It was just before 3pm. There was nothing more she could do and skulking around Central all afternoon was pointless. She made her way down the hill with a loose plan of heading to Mong Kok. There was an English-language cinema there. Perhaps a film would help take her mind off things.

Down in the subway of Hong Kong Station she realised there was no direct line to Mong Kok. She should have caught the Mid-Levels Escalator down to Central Station. It was only a few hundred metres away, but now she was underground, she decided to just make do. She checked a Mass Transit Railway (MTR) map and worked out that from Hong Kong Station she could catch a train across the harbour to Lai King then change onto a Central Line to get back to Mong Kok. It was minor nuisance but she was in no hurry.

The platform was crowded with passengers carrying luggage. She checked the noticeboard. There was an Airport Express train due in two minutes. The train she wanted was arriving after that in four minutes.

By the time the Airport Express arrived through the tunnel, Birgitte was shoulder to shoulder with scores of people eager to catch their flights. The train slowed to a stop and the doors opened. A few passengers negotiated their way out of the carriage, then the cumbersome crowd ambled forward to board. Birgitte mused that the seemingly endless flow of humanity in Hong Kong had a curious pulse dictated by electronic doors and mechanical walkways. People moved in and out of trains, up and down escalators, in and out of buildings, up and down elevators. It was a city that stopped and started a million times a day in order to flow more efficiently.

She had been so lost in her own thoughts she'd stopped scanning the crowd for the first time all day. It only took her a moment to realise her mistake. At her elbow came the plaintive voice of a young boy as he stepped past her onto the train.

"Will you save me?"

All she could see of him was the top of his baseball cap and the shoulders of his striped t-shirt, before he slipped through crowd deeper into the carriage.

Birgitte went to lunge forward to get on, but an elderly man who hadn't been paying attention had decided to get off at the last minute, stepping directly in her path. She tried to move round him but they both side-stepped in the same direction two or three times – long enough for the doors to close behind him. She peered through the windows, desperately searching for the boy with the baseball cap. After several agonising seconds, as the train began to pull away, she spotted him. He was staring at her with a mild look of curiosity. There was no fear in his eyes or even the slightest sense that he was in any danger, but Birgitte knew the boy was travelling to his death. She had to stop it somehow.

The noticeboard details had already changed to list the intended stations for the next train. Birgitte hadn't been paying attention to where the Airport Express actually stopped because it hadn't been relevant. She began asking the people around her. They stared at her blankly. A businessman told her it was going to the airport on Lantau Island. She pressed him to tell her where it stopped along the way. He told her it only stopped at Kowloon and Tsing Yi. She looked quickly at the noticeboard again. The next train took in both those stations and all the ones in between – another three stations that would slow her down considerably. But the next express wasn't for another 24 minutes. In that time the boy could be anywhere.

The Tung Chung train she was originally waiting for pulled in and she waited an interminably long time for the doors to open. As passengers shuffled off, she felt as if the pauses in movement that defined the city were now conspiring to seal the child's fate. She pushed her way on to the train, the other passengers scowling at her impatience. She didn't care. Eventually the doors slid shut and the train moved away.

The first stop was Kowloon Station. She leapt out of the train and looked quickly about the platform, checked the escalators, then forced her way back on again as the doors were closing. She couldn't see him anywhere. She stayed on board for the next three stations, knowing the child couldn't have got off even if he had wanted to because it had been an Express service. By the time the train reached Tsing Yi she began to lose hope. It had been almost 20 minutes since she'd seen him and she had no idea where he might be going. He could have got off at Kowloon unseen or still be on the train up ahead out to the airport on Lantau Island. How did he know she would be at Hong Kong Station? She didn't know herself until she was walking down from Central. How could she have not seen someone watching her all that time? She was furious with herself.

While she waited for the next Airport train from Tsing Yi, she took Inspector Wong's business card out of her purse and dialled the number. Someone else answered his phone explaining that the detective was momentarily away from his desk. Birgitte asked them to get Inspector Wong to contact her immediately.

After a fruitless search of the platform at the airport, she caught a connecting service back to Tsim Sha Tsui and ran to the police station. To her frustration there was another desk sergeant on duty whom she hadn't encountered. She was doing her best to explain her situation when she saw Inspector Wong at the back of the station. She called out to him. He waved her through and directed her to his office.

"It happened again," she said. "Did you get my message?"

He shook his head and sat down across from her. "You were approached by another child?"

"At Hong Kong Station."

"How old?"

"Seven or eight, Chinese. Dressed in..." She tried to think. "The train was crowded. He was wearing a dark baseball cap, stripy blue t-shirt and bone pants, I think."

Inspector Wong took notes as she spoke. "What time?"

"4.07pm. I was waiting for a train to Lai King."

"Can you remember which platform and where on that platform you were standing?"

"Platform 3." She thought for a moment. "I must have been on the Island side of the platform because the train was heading north. It would have been about the third carriage from the end."

He nodded for her to continue.

"An Airport Express pulled up a few minutes before my train was due. As the passengers were getting on, I heard a young boy's voice say, very clearly: 'Will you save me?'," she said. "By the time I looked down to see who had spoken to me the child had slipped through the crowd and was on the train. I could only see the top of his head at that point. And then the doors closed."

Birgitte pulled out her metro map and opened it over his desk because she couldn't confidently remember all the station names. "I caught the next train but it was all stops to... Tung Chung... there. I got off to check at Kowloon and then... Tsing Yi, and then changed trains for the

Airport but by that point half an hour had passed. He could have been anywhere."

"And there's no guarantee your connecting train stopped at the same platform as the Express."

Birgitte's shoulders slumped with the realisation.

"And the child didn't say anything else?"

"No."

"How did he look? Frightened? Agitated? Under duress in any way?"

"None of those things. It almost looked like a meaningless chore."

"Did he sound like the other two children, as if he was reciting the line?"

She thought for a moment. "He did. Someone had to have been watching me all afternoon, to know where I was going. I literally didn't think to go to Hong Kong Station until the last minute."

"And you didn't recognise anyone else on the platform who may have been with him?"

She shook her head. "It was very busy. Can you get access to security footage of the platform at Hong Kong Station?"

"I can ask. You said the boy was wearing a baseball cap?"

"He was."

"Then he may be difficult to identify. The cameras are usually in the ceiling."

"But if you can see him pass me then you can work back and see where he comes in and who he may have been with."

Inspector Wong looked at her, thinking. His face was expressionless and his demeanour was one of stillness and calm.

Birgitte was getting frustrated. "The last two children were dead within 48 hours of approaching me, Inspector.

If we don't act fast on this, we could have another body on our hands."

He reached for the phone then paused.

Birgitte asked, "What is the problem, Inspector?"

"You must understand how this looks from the outside. You are the only one who says there is any connection between two seemingly accidental deaths. I have to be able to convince my superiors to put resources into this..."

"And if you don't, and another child dies?"

He picked up the phone and held it in his hands for a few moments then dialled. Birgitte watched as he spoke tersely in Cantonese to someone on the other end. When he hung up he said, "I've organised one of my staff to deal with the MTR to see if we can access the footage of you getting on the train. And we'll take it from there."

"Thank you," she said. "What should I do now?"

"There is little you can do," he said.

"I don't believe this. Inspector, someone is taunting me and using innocent children to do it. There has to be something we can do to get on the front foot."

"Detective Vestergaard, please understand, I am taking your concerns seriously, but at this stage there is very little we can do. I've also asked my staff to look into any recent reports of missing children, but I don't expect it will help."

"Were the other two children reported missing before they died?"

The inspector paused before answering. "They had both pretended to be sick to stay away from school the day before they died. Neither of them were being properly supervised."

"So they could have had time to approach me without their parents' knowledge."

"That is a possibility that I'm looking at," he said. "But bear in mind, they weren't reported missing. So if this child approached you, there is a good chance that his parents don't even know what he is up to."

Birgitte folded up her map and put it in her handbag. As she stood up she said, "Whoever is doing this is very smart and very organised."

"Keep your eyes open and call me if you see anything. I will let you know when we hear back from the MTR."

She thanked him and left his office, feeling disempowered. Despite filing another statement there was nothing she could do to help a child she knew was in danger.

Cripps stared across the road into the mango grove that marked the front of the Conran Hotel. From his vantage point in a small cafe he could see the mechanic he had been watching earlier. The young man was now wearing jeans and black t-shirt, sitting on a bench in the shade of the trees, watching the lobby of the hotel as intently as Cripps was watching him. Occasionally the mechanic looked at his phone, possibly checking the time or perhaps waiting for a text or a call, some sort of signal to either move or continue waiting. Cripps' nerves were jumping. He hadn't smoked a cigarette for more than two hours. All he could think about was that six months of research, which had seen him traipsing across three countries, and in effect his entire career were well and truly on the line. If he thought about it too much, he'd run across the street and demand answers from the man with the limp directly, but then all would be lost. He continued to bite his nails and wait.

The previous afternoon Cripps had sat in the cafe in Kowloon Tong until the mechanic had locked up the garage, with the intention of following him where ever he went. He watched the him hobble down an alleyway that ran down the left-hand side of the garage. Several minutes later Cripps cursed as he saw the mechanic driving an old model Jaguar up the street. Cripps ran out to hail a cab but there were none to be found. So this morning he returned to the garage. Fortunately, the mechanic worked Saturdays. Only this time, when he had locked up in the afternoon, he left on foot. Cripps followed him to the train station. He had no idea what the guy was doing but it was imperative to get a sense of his movements.

Cripps had followed him into a shopping centre on Nathan Road, where he entered a shoe store and bought a pair of sneakers. Cripps almost lost him in the crowd but then spotted him moments later and was disgusted with what he saw. The mechanic had approached a young Chinese boy wearing a striped blue t-shirt and bone pants. He held out the shoe box to the boy, who raised his hands to grab the shoes. The mechanic pulled the box away and shook his head. No amount of research had prepared Cripps for this. He was grateful when he saw the boy walk away with a look of resignation on his face, but then he realised he couldn't follow both of them as the mechanic walked towards the escalator with the box and the boy headed in the opposite direction. Cripps couldn't be certain, because it was more important to follow the mechanic, but he thought he saw the boy approach a young Chinese woman by the elevators – too young to be his mother, possibly a nanny or an older sister. Cripps had to let the boy go. He followed the mechanic out of the shopping centre and into a coffee shop further up Nathan Road. About an hour later the mechanic had made his way to the front of the Conran Hotel.

The mechanic was now standing. He had moved deeper within the grove, shielding himself from view of people in the lobby. He was also looking more intently. Cripps followed the mechanic's line of sight to the drive-in entrance of the hotel. He had to check back and forth several times but eventually he was sure of who the young man was waiting for. A European woman, dark hair, attractive in an athletic way, but obviously distracted, was walking towards the entrance of the hotel. She wore a white collared shirt and bone trousers that hugged her figure. When she reached the glass doors of the entrance, she paused to look at the other guests coming and going from the lobby. The mechanic ducked back behind the trunk he was leaning against. Cripps got the feeling she knew she was being watched. She turned and entered the lobby. Cripps looked back to the grove. The mechanic was gone. Had he somehow got into the hotel? Shit, thought Cripps, was the woman in danger?

Cripps paid for his coffee and crossed the street. He walked over to the grove but there was no sign of the mechanic. He couldn't have entered the hotel without Cripps seeing him. He must have been satisfied at seeing the woman and left it at that. Cripps wondered if he should head back to the garage to see if the guy had gone back to work or if the boy was there – that was a long shot. Cripps was now more interested in the woman the mechanic had been waiting for. He entered the lobby, wondering how he would approach her without looking like some sort of stalker. He caught a glimpse of her back as she stepped into an elevator. He was too far away to catch it. He looked about the lobby. There was a casual seating area of upholstered armchairs in front of a women's boutique. He took a seat by the window. His day of waiting and watching wasn't over yet and just his luck – it was a no-smoking area.

Birgitte punished herself for an hour and half in the gym. The burning in her muscles and the lengthy repetitions gave her something else to focus on, but the image of the boy on the train continued to taunt her. She was angry with Inspector Wong who seemed to be only paying her lip service. His tendency to consider every obstacle before making a decision was infuriating to say the least. If he acknowledged the first two children had the opportunity to approach her then that should have been enough make a connection between their deaths. She'd give Sven a call later in the evening to see if he could put her in touch with Harold Leung's replacement. She didn't like to go over people's heads, and hated it if anyone did it to her, but she was convinced there was a child's life at risk, so it was justified. Surely there was someone higher up who could get Inspector Wong to act with greater expediency, or better still, find someone who could. Did she really want a detective whose nickname was 'Grandfather' working with her on this? But as her workout wound down she reminded herself more calmly – this was not her case. She had to respect the Hong Kong way of doing things, even if it felt more bureaucratic than she would like. The inspector was anything if not thorough.

By the time she had showered and dressed it was early evening. She decided to get some dinner in one of the restaurants nearby.

As she emerged from the elevator bay and entered the lobby she noticed a pasty white man in his early 50s watching her from an armchair near the window. Her shoulders tensed as he got up from his chair awkwardly, as if his joints were stiff from sitting too long. Birgitte considered turning back to the front desk to avoid any interaction but the man was already approaching her. He swept his lank hair back from his face in an effort to be presentable, but only succeeded in looking like an ageing pool-hall hustler. Birgitte didn't like the vibe he was giving off so she tried to move past him, but he stepped in her way until she had to stop.

"Excuse me, Miss," he said in a thick English accent. "I'm Merrick Cripps from the National Agenda, Britain. Can I talk with you a moment?"

"I'm running late for a meeting," she said, moving around him. "Leave your details at the front desk and if I get a chance, I will contact you."

She proceeded to walk through the main glass doors. He chased after her. "We need to talk."

Out on the street she hailed a taxi. One pulled up from a rank that lined the grove.

Cripps called out to her as she opened the door. "There was a man watching you from the trees over there, this afternoon. I have no idea what he wants or whether or not you even know him, but I do know that if he's watching you then you may be in danger."

Birgitte could feel her lungs constrict slightly. She turned to face him. "How do I know you're not the one hurting those children?"

Cripps stared at her bewildered. He knew she was going to try to brush him off, but he did not expect to hear something like that. "I'm just a journalist following a story. It led me here to you."

"If you are a journalist then I have no interest in talking to you."

"I don't think you have a choice."

The cabbie called out to her. She looked inside the taxi, then closed the door. The cab pulled away.

The journalist didn't look excited or triumphant, just partially relieved.

Birgitte said, "Anything we discuss is off the record, understand?"

CHAPTER SIX

After showing her his press card, Cripps had suggested they talk in a bar nearby. She clearly didn't trust his motives but he was right, she had no choice but to listen to what he had to say. He led her to a dingy hole-in-the-wall off Nathan Road.

Marty's Bar was dimly lit and quiet inside, the other patrons drank alone, staring dolefully into their drinks or watching the sport on the TV. The air was chill and there was a slight odour of stale beer. The elderly barman gave Cripps a familiar nod as they passed. He led Birgitte down the back to a secluded booth where they wouldn't be disturbed, then he went back to the bar.

A few minutes later he settled in across from her with pint of lager, pushing a glass of house white across the table to Birgitte.

"They only had sav blanc."

She thanked him and watched as he pulled a packet of crisps from his pocket and ripped open the foil.

"I'm starving. Want one?"

"No, thank you."

Judging by his skin and eyes she figured heavy drinker, life-long smoker, probably lived on takeaways. She sat back and settled into the posture she reserved for conducting police interviews – her hands on the table in front of her, fingers comfortably intertwined. It gave nothing away of her thought processes and encouraged the interviewee to do most of the talking, if only to fill the void she created by her stillness.

"So Birgitte, is it?" he said hesitantly. "Have I said that right?"

She nodded.

"Swedish?"

"Danish."

"What brings you to Hong Kong?"

Birgitte stared him down, she had no time for his ham-fisted attempts to put her at ease. "Mr Cripps, you have exactly two minutes to tell me what you know about the man you said was following me, or I leave and go straight to the local police."

"Easy now," he said. "I'm doing you a favour, Love. You didn't even know this guy existed until I pointed it out to you. You should be thanking me. I'm only concerned for your safety."

"Really?" she said. "You're not looking for a story? What makes you think I'm in danger?"

"This guy, the one watching you – he's something else." He paused to consider the gravity of his own subject. He didn't want to come across as dramatic but it was difficult considering what he knew. "He's a breed apart. He's done things most people wouldn't even think to do."

"How do I know 'this guy' even exists? I didn't see anyone watching me." The thought that the killer may have been so close disturbed her deeply. "What's to say you're not making this up?"

"When I saw you arrive this afternoon you looked like you knew you were being followed. You tell me?"

She looked away as Cripps sucked the chips from his teeth and took a swig of his beer.

Eventually he said, "Listen, I get that this must seem pretty strange and more than a little dramatic. If I had the time to approach you more professionally, I would have. It was a spur of the moment thing. You see, I've been following this guy on and off for years, and if my research is correct, he's a very dangerous man, and if he's taking a special interest in you, I want to know why."

Birgitte didn't respond. Cripps nodded at this. It was the best he was going to get given the circumstances. He sighed and decided to give her the lot – it was the only chance he had of getting her on board.

"I was covering the war in Afghanistan in the late 2000s for The Independent, a British newspaper," he said. "Most of the action for our forces was up in Helmand Province, particularly around a city called Sangin. We'd set up a makeshift base a few clicks out of town, virtually in the middle of the desert. Officially the plan was to work with the local tribes to build up some sort of regional security force, win hearts and minds, and all that. The truth was we were struggling to keep a fingernail grip on the area, but the brass were well keen to hang on."

Cripps spoke as if the British Armed Forces were his favoured football team. There was a sense of ownership which entailed the right to criticise management and the coaching staff for poor performance on the field. Birgitte found it typical of British men she had met. It was a curious form of patriotism.

"While I was down in the south, covering another province," he continued, "I got wind of a shooting at that base up outside Sangin. Some shepherd kid had wandered in one morning, grabbed a service revolver and tried to execute a private as he came in from the shower block. You hear of it occasionally – locals running amok, turning on the Western soldiers. But I'd also been hearing rumours about some unfortunate goings on in that particular base, so I went up to have a look."

"What sort of goings on?" Birgitte interrupted.

"The Yanks had had similar trouble on some of their bases apparently," Cripps said, holding his beer with both hands. "In their efforts to get the tribesmen on board they had to turn a blind eye to some local practices, which was a bit hard for younger, less war-hardened lads to stomach."

"What sort of practices?" Birgitte was getting frustrated with his delivery. She wondered if his articles were as long winded.

"*Bacha bazi*," he replied.

95

"What's that?"

"'Boy play' is the direct translation. The tribesmen would have their way with the young boys in the region as a matter of course. Some of the soldiers complained to their superiors, but apparently the upper brass was telling them to turn a blind eye – we were there for international security not to police local matters."

Birgitte didn't say anything, which seemed to surprise him.

"By the time I'd got to the base, the soldier who had been shot, a Private Ian Horace, had already been shipped back to England. He was alive but he'd copped a nasty bullet to the groin. I started asking around and a few of the other privates confirmed it off the record – there were definitely cases of boy play in the area and a few instances of it on the actual base. But no one was willing to discuss it openly. They'd been given orders to keep their mouths shut about the whole thing.

"As far I could gather Horace was shot because he knew about the abuse. The kid apparently expected him to do something to make it stop and when he didn't, the kid lashed out. The brass unofficially confirmed the story but wouldn't go on the record. The official line was the boy had been radicalised by the Taliban."

"What happened to him?"

"Killed on the spot," Cripps said. "Not wise to pull a gun in a barracks full of jumpy soldiers apparently."

His attempt at humour fell flat.

"I don't understand what this has to do with me."

"I'm getting to that," he said, licking salt from his fingers. "Anyway, I though it odd that this Private Horace would be shipped out so quickly. I asked his platoon mates about him as a person, and the general gist was that he was a very good mechanic and a reliable soldier but outside of that he wasn't exactly popular. They kept saying there was a 'darkness' to him. Of course, if you spend any time with these young guys that's not out of the ordinary. A lot of them come from rough neighbourhoods and given a few months in a hell hole like Afghanistan they've all seen too much – it's bound to make you a bit 'difficult'. But I got the impression from his platoon, Horace was a bit of an unknown quantity, kept to himself, didn't go out of his way to make friends."

"Do you think he was involved with the tribesmen?"

"Well, that's the thing. The guy gets shot by a child who has probably been abused – although there was no way of verifying it because the kid was dead, and the general line on the base is that Horace got shot for not stopping the abuse. His platoon mates didn't want to entertain any other ideas and obviously the brass needed to put some sort of palatable spin on it, hence the Taliban line." He looked at Birgitte to make sure she was following the subtext. "I wasn't convinced – it was all too neat and the right questions weren't being asked. I had some leave coming up so when I went back to England, I tried to track this Private Horace down to see if I could get an interview."

The door to the bar opened. Cripps quickly looked over his shoulder and paused until he was satisfied it was just another patron wanting a drink. He continued. "I eventually found him in this bedsit in Bermondsey in South London, not far from where I was living at the time. He was recovering from his wounds. His girlfriend, Janis Pollack, was helping him recuperate. He refused to be interviewed. Or more accurately she refused for him. Told me to fuck off in no uncertain terms. I didn't get to talk to him at all." He gathered up the remains of the chips with his finger tips and shoved them in his mouth. "I didn't like it. So I started doing some homework. Turns out our Ian used to work as a mechanic in Walsell up in the West Midlands when he first left school as a teenager back in the late 90s. Apparently, he met this Janis bird there, when they were both working for a bus company up that way. He fixed the coaches and she did the books. Nobody had much to do with him from what I could learn, but she was smitten, found his 'darkness' quite the turn-on. Any way they hooked up and it wasn't long before stories began floating around – rumours mind you, I haven't been able to verify any of it, yet."

"What sort of rumours?"

"There was talk that they're into all manner of kinky shit. Young girls in the area, you know, homeless kids on the edge of being hookers, were getting roped in by Janis for threesomes – anything to keep her man happy. There was also talk that she was turning tricks on the side. And then it got weird, from what I could tell.

"Around that time some younger kids, 11 or 12 year olds, went missing from the area – girls as well as boys – three or four of them over an 18-month period. Police started sniffing about but couldn't find anything – no bodies and no proof the kids hadn't just fucked off to London or where ever. However, I have it on good authority that Ian was pulled in for questioning at one point. Nothing came of it. It was assumed the kids had just run off to escape unhappy homes and that was the end of it. But Horace and his lady disappeared shortly after, as well, and the next thing you know, he pops up in Afghanistan on the wrong end of his own service revolver."

Birgitte hadn't moved. She was absorbing the details, committing them all to memory.

Cripps went to light a cigarette and realised he wasn't allowed. "So the war continues, I go back to it. I couldn't find anything concrete to pursue on Horace so I had to let it go. I filed a bunch of stories about the fighting then, thanks to the fucking internet, I lose my job on The Independent.

"I headed back to England, started freelancing for a bunch of start-up websites that didn't like paying their writers. All the while I've got this niggle in the back of my head about Ian Horace. I'm still in touch with some of the people in Walsell who knew him back in the day, so occasionally I'd fish around for more information in my own time to get fresh snippets about what was going on back then. I got the sense that he and Janis had fallen in with some like-minded people, visitors from London and the Continent, possibly a paedophile ring.

"Eventually I reckoned I had enough to pursue the story. If I could prove he was an active paedo in the West Midlands, and the police had hauled him in for questioning over missing children (who still haven't been found, mind you), it meant the military had a case to answer. How did a guy like that get in the army? And were they still willing to believe that he wasn't a part of the abuse on the base. At the time I didn't have enough material to speak to a prosecutor, just for an in-depth article that could at least kick off an investigation.

"I spoke to an old friend of mine who'd just started up as an editor on a new website, told him all I'd learned, and we decided to confront Horace in Bermondsey with the accusations to see how he'd react, and what do you know? He'd disappeared again. I couldn't find any trace of him or his lady in England. Alarm bells are ringing – it's starting to look like a story I really want to write and the editor is well keen for me to pursue it. He even reckons there could be a book in it if the cover-up goes far enough, particularly if the kids can be found. So he gives me a green light, even promises a bit of cash and I'm off and running.

"After no end of mucking about and pulling favours I can't repay, I tracked his Janis here, to Hong Kong. Apparently she'd got a job bookkeeping a few days a week for an international school somewhere in Kowloon Tong, which is concerning enough in itself, but my editor wasn't able to cover my flight. I figured with the way the media is going, I've got one big story left in me or I'm just another irrelevant old fart who used to be a journalist. So I sold my car and bought the ticket myself. It was a hell of a gamble because there were no guarantees that Ian and Janis are even still together."

Cripps had finished his beer. He climbed out of the booth. "Give me a minute. You want another drink?"

Birgitte shook her head. She hadn't touched her wine.

She watched him as he ordered his beer, his bony frame looking lost inside his clothing. For all the damage he'd done to his body, he appeared to be a committed investigative journalist who followed his leads tenaciously.

He came back with another lager.

"When I arrived here last Thursday I didn't even know which international school Ms Pollack was working in, but there are only a handful and I didn't want to spook her by phoning, so I've spent the past week staking out each one until I spotted her – yesterday.

"So I followed her, hoping to find out where she was living. But she walks straight to a garage a few blocks away called Mason's that looks after antique British cars – Jags from the 80s and the like. And what do you know, that bastard Ian Horace is working as a mechanic again. What the hell he's doing in Hong Kong of all places I have no idea."

"How could he afford to come out and set himself up?"

"He's on a military pension, but I don't reckon that would cover it."

"And you're sure it's him?"

"Positive. He's now sporting one hell of a limp thanks to that shepherd boy."

He knocked off half his pint in a single mouthful. "Kill my mother for a cigarette. Do you mind if I duck out for a bit?"

100

"I'd prefer you to keep talking."

He looked at her resentfully. The beer was loosening him up but the nicotine cravings were making him anxious. It was quite the rollercoaster he'd built for himself.

He sighed heavily and returned to his story. "I lost them last night, so this morning I went back to Mason's Garage and this is where it gets interesting. I followed Horace back into the main part of Kowloon to a shopping mall around the corner here. He buys a pair of sneakers then offers them to a young Chinese kid, about nine or 10 years old, which got my skin crawling, like he might be grooming the boy or something, but then he didn't hand the shoes over. The kid walked off and I followed Horace to the Conran, where I watched him watching you as you arrived in the evening. He was sitting out there for two hours waiting for you. But as soon as you arrived, he took off."

Birgitte could feel her heart beating. "The child. What was the child wearing?"

He stared at her blankly, surprised she wasn't more alarmed by the news that someone like Horace had been stalking her. "I wasn't paying that much attention," he said. "A striped shirt and some cream pants, I think."

"Was he wearing anything on his head?"

"No."

"Are you sure?" she asked urgently.

"Sure I'm sure."

"Was the child with his parents?"

"No, but he did go off with a young Chinese girl, not much older than a teenager, might have been his sister."

Christ, Birgitte thought, Cripps has seen the child and, possibly, the killer. There was still a chance they could save the boy.

"I need to make a phone call," she said, sliding out of the booth.

"Hang on," he said sliding out after her. "What happened to quid pro quo. He's after you for a reason. What the hell do you know that you're not telling me? And what about the children you said were getting hurt? What the hell was that all about?"

"I don't have time to explain."

Cripps grabbed her upper arm. "Make time."

Within three swift moves, Cripps was on the floor clutching at his solar plexus, coughing for air. Birgitte leaned down close so he wouldn't miss a syllable. "Don't ever touch me again."

Through desperate wheezing he managed to splutter. "I am trying to help you."

Birgitte stood over him, trying to think. "If you want to help, come to the police station and repeat everything you've just said."

Cripps was reluctant to get up. "What for?"

"Because, that child you say you saw?"

"Yeah?"

"He could be dead by tomorrow if you don't."

She walked out into the night air, preparing herself for the obstacles that Inspector Wong would undoubtedly drop in her path.

Cripps got up and drained his beer then followed her out onto the street, intrigued by what she'd said. He lit a cigarette and listened as she talked into her phone.

"... but he saw the boy... he can verify the boy exists... and he can prove that someone has been watching me."

Cripps leaned against a pole and rubbed his chest, still bewildered by how quickly she'd dropped him to the floor. Birgitte quickly turned to him. "Which shopping mall did you see the child in?"

"Off Nathan Road. It's round the back of the Conran. There's a Hermes store out the front. Horace bought the shoes from a New Balance store on the fourth floor."

She relayed all this to the inspector. "Are you able to pull this Ian Horace guy in for questioning? ... He was spotted trying to give the boy a pair of sneakers on the same day the boy approached me. What more evidence do you need?" She poked Cripps who was trying to re-light his cigarette. "How do you spell his name?"

"H-O-R-A-C-E."

"Where is his garage?"

"It's on Grampiani Road in Kowloon Tong over near the Walled City. It's called Mason's Garage."

Birgitte relayed this to the inspector then mentioned that Horace's girlfriend worked at the Ming Ra Primary School as a bookkeeper. "Can you move on this? .... I know tomorrow is Sunday and the garage won't be open but there is a child whose life is at risk." She stared up the street, listening. "Okay... thank you, Inspector. Please call me if you hear anything. Anything at all."

She disconnected the call.

"He said we'll have to go to the station and make another statement. He's going to make some calls to track down where Ian Horace is living, see if they can pull him in for questioning. But he doesn't like our chances because as far as the local police are concerned a crime hasn't been committed yet."

She looked up the street for any passing taxis.

Cripps said, "What is it that you think he's done?"

Birgitte turned suddenly, causing him to flinch. She pointed her finger into his chest. "I shouldn't be telling you any of this but right now I need all the help I can get. I want your assurances that this part stays off the record."

He hesitated.

"Cripps, I can go to the station and report you for stalking, if you like."

"I wasn't even following you."

"Who do you think the local police will believe?"

"Jesus. You don't play nice, do you?"

103

"Judging by the way you grabbed my arm back there, neither do you."

He rubbed his chest. "I won't be doing that again, I assure you."

Birgitte weighed up her options and realised she needed his help. "Since I arrived here a week ago two Chinese children have approached me at different times. Each of them asked me in plain English if I could save them. The first was a boy who came up to me in Central. The second was a girl who called out to me in the Museum of History in Kowloon. The boy fell from a 12-storey apartment block a few days later, the girl was pulled out of Victoria Harbour a few days after that.

"Now I'm pretty sure the boy you saw with Horace this morning is the same one who approached me on a train this afternoon. If we don't find this child soon, I'm afraid he is going to be killed like the others."

"Jesus," Cripps said almost inaudibly. He was baffled by all of this. For the past few years he'd been on the trail of alleged paedophile, with evidence that suggested the upper echelons of the British military were indirectly complicit in his behaviour. But what this Danish woman had just told him was something different all together. He struggled to accept that the man he'd been following all this time would bother to taunt a complete stranger with cryptic murders. Cripps had always seen Horace as a creepy pleasure-seeker, a narcissist who didn't care who he hurt in order to get his rocks off – not someone who would risk losing all that to scare a woman on holidays. He couldn't help wondering if the two stories were even connected. Perhaps Horace hadn't been waiting for this woman after all. Whatever she was dealing with was completely separate. But still, the boy he had seen with Horace earlier that day had possibly approached this woman a few hours later – but she could have been mistaken. He didn't know what to think.

As she hailed an approaching taxi, Birgitte's head was also in a spin. She appreciated the fact Cripps believed her, but then realised it was in his own best interests – his story was getting more interesting by the hour. So far Inspector Wong had been reluctant because there wasn't enough evidence to prove a crime had been committed. Sadly, it could only be the death of a third child that could convince him otherwise, and she was determined to not let that happen. The taxi pulled up and they both got in. She told the driver to take them to Tsim Sha Tsui Police Station.

Forty five minutes later, having each filled out statements with the desk sergeant on duty, they stepped out into the night air.

"Seriously?" Cripps said, completely flabbergasted. "You failed to mention you were a homicide detective with the Danish National Police until now?"

Birgitte turned to him and said, "Then maybe you can appreciate why I don't want to be talking to the media about any of this."

"It adds a whole other dimension."

"I'm not some character in your story, Mr Cripps," she said. "And don't forget, children are the victims here."

"Still," he said, realising that any doubts he had about the two conflicting stories were rapidly evaporating, "there has to be reason Horace is targeting you. Surely, you've considered that."

She stared out into the street.

"Well, have you?" he persisted.

"Yes, I have." She had no intention of telling him about her texts to Sven.

Cripps lit a cigarette. When the nicotine began to do its work, he apologised. "This must be pretty overwhelming for you. I'm not trying to make it worse. I'm just trying to get a story down for my editor."

She ignored his justifications and tried to think of what they should be doing next.

Cripps exhaled a plume of smoke through his nostrils and stared at Birgitte. "So you've never heard of Ian Horace? Never arrested any of his family members? Said something unfortunate in the press about British mechanics?"

She managed a feeble smile. "I honestly have no idea what this has to do with me." She couldn't bring herself to mention either of the high-profile cases she'd worked on in the past. No doubt his own research would reveal the names Zachary de Graff and Max Anders without too much trouble. Christ, she thought, the guy is going to get a book out of this and I'm going to end up back in a padded room with my hands strapped behind my back. "I have to get some sleep. I'll call you in the morning if I hear anything. How do I get a hold of you?"

He wrote down the name of his hotel and his local mobile number on the back of his business card and handed it to her.

Birgitte watched him set off across the street and seriously questioned her own judgement in working with a journalist.

When she got back to her room at the Conran she turned on her laptop, drew out his business card and began a search. The first few pages were recent feature articles he'd written for all different sorts of websites on a range of topics, from politics within the European football league, to the impact of policy changes on welfare in Britain's north. She found some of his war correspondence for The Independent. It was dry and factual, capturing the day-to-day developments of the campaigns in the south of Afghanistan, as he had mentioned in the bar. Where there was space, he would place the fighting within the context of international relations, reserving his sharpest criticism for the Tory government in opposition.

She inserted Ian Horace's name into search field – there was one article that mentioned the shooting on the base in Sangin, within a broader story about the recent fighting in the region. Private Horace was listed as wounded. The article ran the official line that the boy who shot him was under the influence of the Taliban. Unfortunately, there was no image of Horace attached.

She went back to the search results on Merrick Cripps and clicked onto the next page. About half way down she came across an article that wasn't by the British journalist, but about him. It was a follow-up piece about a court case in which a Merrick Cripps had been charged with perjury for naming a secret witness in regards to another court case, in effect accusing a high-profile businessman of involvement in an intricate paedophile ring. When questioned on the stand, Cripps had failed to provide adequate evidence to back-up his accusation. The judge said that the journalist was grossly irresponsible and had arrogantly used his position in the media to launch a smear campaign against a respected company director. He handed down a suspended sentence and put Cripps on a good behaviour bond. The article was dated after his time in Afghanistan but before the more general articles about sport and local politics.

Birgitte sat back in her armchair. It appeared that Mr Cripps had suffered a fall from grace and was only just beginning to redeem himself. It didn't sit well with her – how could she trust a man with a history of not backing up his accusations with evidence? He clearly had it in for this Ian Horace person, but what if he was wrong? She cast her mind back to his choice of words: "I'd been hearing rumours", "stories began floating around", "there was talk". He couldn't substantiate any of his claims.

Birgitte had dealt with similar journalists in the past – in their desperation to support wild theories, they didn't hesitate to distort what little they knew to present loaded arguments against their accused. It didn't matter if they were right or not. The truth got lost in the telling. As long as their readers came on board, the ends justified the means.

She went to bed thinking about how certain elements in the Danish media had predetermined her own motives in the Max Anders case. There was no convincing them otherwise. According to their portrayals, she was a cold, ambitious detective without children of her own – a woman who lacked the empathy of a mother, and it had impacted her judgment at a crucial moment in a horrific case. Three children had perished due to her shortcomings as a detective and as a woman.

It had been a long night with little sleep. Birgitte had wrestled continually with the implications of working with an unknown journalist on a case she was struggling to understand herself. Every alternative she considered crumbled under closer scrutiny. No matter which way she looked at it, she had to make it work as best she could.

She eventually crawled out of bed at about 9am and made her way up to the Executive Lounge for a late breakfast. Being a Sunday the floor was busy with weekend tourists. She was sipping her coffee and browsing an international paper when her phone rang. It was Inspector Wong. She listened carefully, her heart sinking.

A few minutes later she said, "I'm at the hotel, the Conran in Kowloon... 11am? I'll be here. Should I contact the journalist who said he saw the boy at the shopping mall? Okay. See you then, and thank you for contacting me."

She disconnected the call and quickly rifled through her bag to find Cripp's card. She dialled the number he'd scrawled on the back.

"Mr Cripps? It's Birgitte Vestergaard... I'm fine... Listen, the body of a small boy was found this morning on a train line in the outer suburbs. He'd been hit by a train." She lowered her voice so the other hotel guests enjoying their breakfast around her wouldn't be disturbed. "Yes, he's dead. It might not even be the boy who you saw, but it doesn't look good. Inspector Wong wants to ask us some questions. Can you come to the Conran Hotel by 11am? ... I'll see you then. And remember, Mr Cripps, all of this has to stay out of the papers. It's an ongoing investigation. Do I have your word? ... Mr Cripps?..."

He'd already disconnected.

Birgitte spent the next hour pacing about her hotel room, going over every aspect of what had happened so far. There had to have been something she'd missed. She was wary of what Cripps had told her the previous evening. None of his claims could be verified, but if even half of what he had said was true then she was dealing with a deeply troubled man who had developed a fixation on her. She thought of all the cases she worked on or read about where unstable men became obsessed with particular women – it rarely ended well for the women. She could only hope she could ascertain his motives through his MO, then she could do something to stop him.

The thought that another child may have lost his life in some way because of her was devastating. She tried to contain her personal feelings so it wouldn't cloud her judgement. She was frustrated that more hadn't been done since she initially flagged her concerns with the Hong Kong Police but appreciated there was little they could do given the circumstances.

At 10.45am she went down to the lobby. Cripps was already there, looking frail and out of sorts. She suggested they grab a coffee while they waited for the inspector, but Cripps shook his head. She had considered asking him about the perjury case in Britain but decided it could wait. He seemed quite distracted. She wondered, with all his war correspondence, how many child murders had he encountered.

She said, "You need to detach yourself as best you can, Mr Cripps. This may not even be related to your story."

He looked at her with incredulity.

"And if it is," she continued, "you'll need to do your best to keep it professional. It's not easy, believe me, but it's very important."

She was reassuring herself as much as him.

Inspector Wong entered the lobby carrying his leather folder under one arm. She studied his face as he approached, but it gave little away. She couldn't tell if he was masking his wounded pride for not acting more quickly when she had initially raised her concerns, or if he was beyond that and was simply preoccupied with the minutiae of the case. She wasn't looking for any sort of apology. A third child was dead. She was just grateful she had the inspector's complete attention.

"Where can we talk that is private?" he said.

"My room," she replied.

She introduced Cripps to the inspector as they approached the elevator bay. A few minutes later they were in her room, sitting around the writing desk.

"What I'm about to show you is confidential," Inspector Wong said, staring at Cripps. "What you see does not leave this room."

"Hey, I can keep my mouth shut."

The inspector opened one of the folders and pulled out a small stack of photographs.

There was something desolate about the images of dead children that always hit Birgitte hard and these images were no different. The first was taken from a deserted outdoor platform in what looked like an industrial zone of the mainland. The only splash of colour in the bleak grey setting was the bright green t-shirt and blue jeans crumpled between the tracks. Birgitte passed the photo to Cripps. The next shot was medium range, the body framed by the tracks. It could have been the body of a sleeping child lying on his belly, the small hands curled, a slightly cocked leg. She almost expected it to twitch with waking dreams. But the damage done to the child's head by the weight and force of the train destroyed any illusions. She passed the photo to Cripps. The other shots were closer still, but nothing more could be gained. As Birgitte allowed her process of detachment to clear her mind, Cripps leapt up from this seat and ran into her bathroom.

Inspector Wong turned to Birgitte. "Do you recognise what the boy is wearing?"

"No. But he's about the right size."

"There aren't any features that will allow you to say for certain that this was the boy who spoke to you?"

She went through the photos again, more carefully. Cripps appeared in the door way, wiping his mouth and the tears from his eyes. "Sorry."

"It's okay," Birgitte said. "It's natural. The images are horrific. Get yourself a drink from the mini-bar if it helps."

He didn't hesitate. He poured a scotch with shaking hands into a wine glass and knocked it back in one, then he opened another.

Inspector Wong turned to him. "Do you recognise the boy?"

Cripps struggled to speak. "What's there to fucking recognise?"

"The clothes," Birgitte said calmly. "Do you recognise the clothes?"

He shook his head and sat heavily into an armchair, clutching the wine glass.

"Mr Cripps," Inspector Wong said, turning his chair to face the journalist, "I need you to tell me everything you told Detective Vestergaard yesterday. I've read your statement but I'd like to hear it from you first hand."

It served as a helpful distraction for Cripps to explain once again how he came across Ian Horace. As he spoke, he slowly got this nerve back, but Birgitte could tell the story was slightly different. His tone had changed. Hearing a rumour about children going missing wasn't the same as seeing the corpse of a child who had met a violent death within only the past few hours. There was a tinge of anger and revulsion every time he mentioned Horace's name.

Inspector Wong took notes and peered at Cripps' statement as he had done when he first met Birgitte. She was impressed with how thorough the detective was being. When Cripps had finished, she asked, "Inspector Wong, what can you tell us about the boy?"

"Not much. I was hoping you could recognise his clothing." He sat back in his seat. "He was hit at about 6.10 this morning at Sheung Shui Station."

"Where's that?" asked Birgitte.

"It's on the MTR up in the New Territories, about 40 minutes out of Kowloon, up near the border with Shenzen. He was on the southbound platform, for trains heading back into the city. The driver said he didn't even see the boy until it was too late. He kind of leapt out from behind that wall." He pointed to one of the photos that showed the platform. "He didn't have a chance."

"Were there any witnesses?"

"No. The platform staff were up the other end. They didn't even see him arrive. Just after dawn on a Sunday morning. No one was around."

"Is there any security footage?"

"We're looking into it. The station doesn't get as much traffic as the metro around here. That's why I was hoping you'd recognise what he was wearing. We can't even contact the family because we don't know who he is. We're waiting to see if any parents report their child missing."

Birgitte surprised herself when she asked, "Could it just be an accident?"

"It's a possibility. Prior to meeting you and hearing Mr Cripps' story, I would have said as much."

Cripps stood up with a curious look on his face. "The sneakers."

Inspector Wong looked at him. "What sneakers?"

"Does he have new sneakers on? I don't want to look at those photos again, so just tell me. Is the kid wearing new sneakers?"

Birgitte and Inspector Wong both stood up and splayed the photos out on the desk. The child was wearing bright new sneakers. Birgitte flipped one of the photos over and used the blank side to cover the child's body. "Merrick, this is just the shoes alone. Can you take another look, please?"

He hesitated then stepped towards the desk. He stared at the photo for a long while, then said, "I can't say. All I know is that Horace offered the boy I saw a new pair of sneakers and this kid is wearing a pair."

"It's a long shot," said Birgitte, "but it could be a connection."

"I had one of my officers do a search for the name Ian Horace, and so far nothing has come up in terms of residential addresses or a driver's licence. I'll go back and use the information about the garage." He checked his notes. "Mason's Garage on Grampiani Road. But even if I can verify that this Mr Horace is in Hong Kong, I don't

113

know if it's enough to pull him in for questioning. We could be mistaken on all of this."

"Is it too late to see if the first two children, the ones who approached me, were sexually assaulted? It would be worth investigating with this child as well. From what Merrick has found out he may have form as a paedophile. If we could get some DNA it could expedite this investigation considerably."

"I'll see what I can do. But you need to understand, given the nature of their deaths, I will have to tread carefully. I can't afford to alarm the families involved or allow the media to get hold of any of this." He looked specifically at Cripps, who no longer had the energy to defend his profession.

Birgitte thanked him and escorted both men back down to the lobby.

Inspector Wong shook their hands and excused himself, setting off towards the main entrance.

Cripps said, "Christ, I need a cigarette."

She followed him out to the mango grove at the front of the hotel, trying to picture where Horace might have been standing when he was watching her the day before. Would security cameras have picked him up? She suddenly had an aching desire to know what this man looked like. She prided herself on her ability to read faces, which is what made these crimes so frustrating. She felt she was working blind. She made a mental note to ask the inspector about this the next time they spoke.

Cripps wrestled with the packaging of his cigarettes then got one lit. He stared into the middle distance, willing the nicotine to calm his nerves.

"Do you have children of your own?" Birgitte asked.

"Just the one, a boy. Daniel. Good kid. Don't get to see him much since his mother took off with him."

"I'm sorry."

"You?"

114

"No." She didn't feel the need to explain her marital situation to a man she barely knew.

"Those bloody photos." He shook his head in disbelief then muttered, "Fucking animal. And those, fucking, fucking bastards."

"Who?"

"The fucking brass in Afghanistan. We should have stopped this before it started. We were there to do a job, and part of that job was protecting the people. If we can't do that, we're no better than the fucking Taliban."

Birgitte struggled to keep up.

"What are we if we go into those places and behave like animals." He turned to Birgitte. "And don't get me started on the Metropolitan Police. If they knew he had something to do with those kids going missing in the West Midlands, why didn't they do more to stop it? By fucking Christ, I'm going to out the lot of them."

"You do know you can't report any of this."

"What? I'm a fucking journalist. 'Reporting this' is exactly what I do."

"If you start writing about this for your website – any website – it could damage the investigation, put more children at risk."

"He wouldn't have an investigation if it wasn't for me," he retorted without thinking.

"Mr Cripps, I can appreciate how much work you've put into this and right now you are the only journalist who is across the story, but you have to appreciate how your behaviour could impact on the actual case. You're a witness to a possible abduction."

Birgitte watched as Cripps paced about.

"You have no idea how much pressure I am under to deliver something to my editor," he said. "If I can't pull together some sort of story soon, I'm finished."

Birgitte listened, knowing full well that Cripp's apparent selfishness was a defence mechanism. He needed to explain himself. What he'd experienced upstairs had shaken him considerably.

He turned to her, his eyes slightly yellow at the edges. "I'm a 56-year-old investigative reporter, Detective. When my career started out, I worked with a pad and a pen and phoned my stories into a news desk. I'm now answering to a 26-year-old features editor who's never conducted a fucking interview in his life, but he knows more about the internet and phone apps than I could ever hope to understand. This story is my last shot at maintaining anything that resembles relevance in the marketplace."

She thought about his perjury trial and understood the pressure he was under. "Then I guess you need to play it smart, Mr Cripps," she replied coolly. "If this killer is trying to contact me then surely you need to keep me onside."

He realised what she was saying.

Birgitte gave him a reassuring look. "So you'll hold off for now?"

He stared through the trees, trying to find a way out but couldn't. Reluctantly he nodded. "What if he contacts you? I mean, would it be better if we stuck together? Safer, I mean?"

"Mr Cripps, I'm a detective with the Danish National Police. But thank you for your concern." She couldn't help but smile at him. "It was my safety you were concerned about?"

"Yeah. Don't worry about me, Love. I can handle myself."

She offered her hand and said, "I'm afraid we'll have to leave it there for the time being. I'll call you as soon as I hear anything from Inspector Wong."

Cripps left Birgitte and headed straight for Marty's Bar. It would take more than a few drinks to eradicate the images of the dead child that were now emblazoned on his mind's eye.

CHAPTER SEVEN

There was a peculiar barrenness to Sheung Shui Station at dawn, even for a Monday. It was a still, warm morning. The few exterior lights from distant factories had already shut down, casting the surrounding industrial area in a dull grey wash that obscured all detail. Inspector Wong stood midway along Platform Two, his broad face puffy with sleep, his dark hair slightly askew. He wanted to see the crime scene at a similar time to when the event occurred. The first southbound train wasn't due for another few minutes. He'd passed only two staff since arriving, one sat in her office sipping a coffee, the other was busy with a faulty bench at the opposite end of the fourth platform. There were some early commuters waiting along each of the platforms but so far he had only counted seven. On a Sunday that number would have be even lower. In fact, there had been no witnesses, outside of the driver, within 200 metres of the incident.

He slowly made his way towards the end of the platform. According to the driver's statement, which the inspector had drawn from his leather folder, he had no chance to apply the brake any harder. He saw the little body disappear beneath his window and that was it. The train didn't even shudder. He was horrified by how smoothly it had happened. He knew colleagues who had had similar experiences with suicides but this was a child. It was different. He had three kids of his own. The inspector gleaned the rest of the statement but there was no reference to the driver seeing anyone else on the platform.

The inspector wasn't surprised by what he found at the far end. The photos had suggested as much. There was a supporting wall that ran across the platform between both the northbound and the south bound lines. It formed a narrow passageway with the utility building that marked the platform's furthest point. He walked the short length of the passage, turned and walked back to the edge of Platform Two. He could see the train approaching across the wide expanse of tracks to the north. He looked back up the passageway. Again, two points of exit – cross to the northbound line and walk around the supporting wall or move towards the other line. In this instance there was obviously room for the boy to move back along the platform as the supporting wall stopped two metres short of the edge. But it was a more enclosed space than the alley near Hung Hom, even more so than the corridor in Maestri Tower. If the opposite end of the passageway was blocked by someone and the threat was imminent, the boy may have felt compelled to leap to safety.

The inspector turned as if following the movements of a child frightened for his life as the southbound train hit the station with surprising speed. The force of its arrival sent a gush of air against his face, blowing his hair back. In the time it took for his fringe to settle a young boy's life had been destroyed.

He tried to think of any other reason why an eight-year old boy would be somewhere so remote at dawn on a Sunday, and nothing came to mind. He had the same feeling about the other two victims – they had to have been lured. He thought about what the British journalist Merrick Cripps had told him the previous day. The mechanic was definitely a person of interest, and it bothered him that there was no listing of the name Ian Horace on the most obvious databases.

The inspector set off back along the platform towards the stairs leading up to the station. As soon as his colleagues arrived at work, he'd get them to pull up what they could find about Mason's Garage, and to verify key aspects of both the journalist's and the Danish detective's statements, particularly in regards to the Saturday.

Birgitte sat at the back of the cafe using the same mirror Cripps had used several days ago to peer into Mason's Garage. She had decided she needed to see Horace for herself, to get a sense of who she was dealing with. She still wasn't absolutely convinced he was the man they were looking for. There was a chance Cripps was mistaken or that his story didn't overlap so neatly with her own.

She had arrived in Kowloon Tong just after 9am. It was now close to 10am, and despite the garage being open, there had been no sign of the mechanic. She ordered another coffee from the manager, who was working the till, and continued to wait.

It was hard to believe she had been in Hong Kong for almost a fortnight. She only had a bit over a week left of annual leave. She had wanted to contact Sven to explain what had been happening, but she'd barely had a chance since she spoke to him on the previous Thursday. The truth was she didn't want the situation to affect her chances at promotion. Of course, she could trust Sven not to say anything but if she requested more time, unpaid, that would take some explaining. And what was she hoping to achieve, anyway? The bottom line was she felt partially responsible for the deaths of those three children. Now that she was sure she was being targeted and the killings were the act of one person, she was determined to get on the front foot.

Birgitte thanked the waitress who brought out her second coffee. When she looked back across Grampiani Street, she didn't expect to see anything other than an empty garage, but there on the pavement just out the front was a young girl who was staring into the cafe directly at Birgitte. Had she come from inside the garage or had she already been on the street? The girl was seven or eight years old, wearing a t-shirt, dark pants and sneakers. Her face was devoid of expression but there was no doubt as to who she was looking at.

Birgitte carefully slipped out from behind her table and walked to the front of the cafe. The child's eyes began to show alarm. Birgitte stopped. For a moment they stared at one another, neither of them moving, then the girl slowly began to shake her head. It was a warning not to come any closer. Birgitte peered behind the girl into the garage but there was still nobody there. She turned to see if any of the cafe staff were watching what was playing out but the waitress was out the back and the manager was bending down behind the counter putting away a stack of plates. When Birgitte looked back across the street she realised the girl had turned and was now running away from her, down the alleyway by the side of the garage. Birgitte set off across the street after her, trying to wrestle her phone from her bag to call Inspector Wong. The girl turned left at the end of the alley, but when Birgitte reached the junction she saw that it split off in two different directions a few metres on – both narrow laneways cluttered with garbage bins and stacked refuse. She looked frantically up each alley but couldn't tell which way the girl had gone until she heard a bin being knocked over on the alley to the right. Birgitte hoped it wasn't a stray dog. She ran as fast as she could then spotted the girl as she ducked into a doorway. Birgitte followed her down a dark side passage between two tall buildings. The girl turned left at the end then, within a matter of a seconds, took several more sharp turns. Birgitte was sure they were now running back towards Grampiani Street. The girl was too quick. She disappeared from view. Birgitte had to stop occasionally to listen for the sound of slamming doors, or creaking fences. She tried to call out for her to stop, but it was pointless. After five minutes of running blind, peering down alleys and into doorways, Birgitte fell back to a steady jog then stopped to call Inspector Wong.

She told him she had been in pursuit of a possible fourth victim and he said he was on his way with a few officers for back-up. Birgitte negotiated her way back along the alleyways to Grampiani Street, emerging 50 metres up from Mason's Garage. There was still no sign of the girl so she squatted down on her haunches and waited, looking up and down the street for anything unusual.

Eventually she heard approaching sirens. Two unmarked cars pulled up outside the garage. Inspector Wong got out of the front car, with a female plain-clothes officer. Two male uniformed officers got out of the second car. Birgitte didn't waste any time.

"It was an Asian girl, seven or eight, 140cm tall, dark hair in a pony tail, green shirt and dark blue pants, with white sneakers. She ran down the side of the garage and I followed her as far as I could. That was 20 minutes ago. She could be anywhere by now."

The female officer, a tall hard-faced woman in her late 20s, looked at Inspector Wong, who motioned for her to check down the alley way. As the officer turned towards her, Birgitte said, "Down there, she turned left at the end but then took the path on the right. Left at the end of that one, through a door... or was it right? It got hazy. I had no idea where she was going."

The officer nodded and set off at a pace down the alleyway.

"Did she say anything?" asked Inspector Wong.

"No, she just shook her head, like I should stay away from her."

"But she didn't ask you to save her? Or anything like that?"

"No, not this time."

One of the male officers looked perturbed.

Inspector Wong told him to go and ask the cafe manager if he'd seen anything, then he turned back to Birgitte. "Is this the garage where you think Ian Horace works?"

Birgitte nodded. He gave it a once over from where he was standing then turned back to Birgitte. "What are you doing here, Detective?" His tone was slightly impatient.

"I needed to see him for myself."

He stepped towards her. "You do realise we were about to pull him in for questioning – based on information you provided?"

"I appreciate that..." she began to say, but he cut her off.

"This doesn't look good," he said, "you being here for no reason."

He shook his head and walked across to the entrance to the alleyway.

Birgitte said, "I have every reason to be here if those children are being killed because of me."

He didn't respond. He peered up the alley, then wrote a few notes in his pad.

"She looked so frightened," added Birgitte.

Inspector Wong walked back to Birgitte. "Do you think she was running from you or from somebody else?"

"I couldn't tell."

Something caught their eye in the back of the garage, a movement. A tall white man in dirty coveralls rolled down to his waist was standing by a work bench. His bare torso was pale and wiry and covered in amateur tattoos, the sort associated with hardened criminals; his dark hair combed back from his face, giving him a severe appearance.

Birgitte felt cold, like a shadow had moved over her soul. It was the man's eyes – even from this distance they were black and impenetrable but piercing – it reminded her of animals in the wild: furtive, unpredictable. His face was too small for his body, his features sharp. Slowly, he wiped his hands on a dirty rag, staring at the two detectives as if they were some novelty act he hadn't asked for.

"Are you Ian Hurley?" the inspector called out, shooting Birgitte a quick glance.

123

"Who wants to know?" the mechanic said, his voice low and controlled.

"I'm Inspector Wong with the Hong Kong Police."

The mechanic nodded slowly. The inspector didn't move. "Mr Hurley, I was hoping to ask you a few questions."

"About what?"

"About a young girl who was seen out the front of this garage about 20 minutes ago."

He continued to stare at the officers then directed his gaze at Birgitte. "Don't know what you're talking about, Inspector."

Birgitte entered the garage before the inspector could reach his hand out to stop her. The interior was poorly lit; her eyes struggled to adjust but she didn't shift her gaze from the tattooed man. Over the years she'd dealt with numerous men accused of sexual offences, and believed she could profile them confidently, but she'd never encountered anyone like this. The man she was looking at exuded a hypnotic combination of malice and sensuality that was genuinely unnerving. She knew immediately the child she had seen earlier was in serious trouble.

"Where is the girl?" she asked.

"What girl?"

She turned back to Inspector Wong who had followed her to the line of the property but no further. The second uniformed officer stood behind him. The two men were now silhouettes against the light, accentuating her proximity to the mechanic.

"There was a girl standing right there 20 minutes ago," she said, pointing to the street. "Where is she now?"

"I have no idea what you're banging on about, Love. I've been out back doing paperwork for the past hour."

Birgitte took a deep breath. "So you haven't seen a young girl, about seven or eight, anywhere near your garage this morning?"

"Need to get your head checked, Love," the man said, with a distinct note of mockery.

Birgitte tried to control the anger in her voice. "I don't know why you're doing what you're doing, but I will find out. And when I do, you are going to wish you never heard of me."

Hurley tossed the rag on a work bench and moved towards her, his bare shoulder dipping with a steady rhythm, like a car's piston. His unusual gait was disarming. Birgitte didn't react as he stepped right up into her face.

Inspector Wong took this as reasonable provocation and entered the property. He moved swiftly across the concrete and positioned himself between Birgitte and the mechanic. The uniformed officer came in behind him.

Hurley considered the inspector sourly, scoffed, then took a step back.

"Did you see a girl waiting outside your shop, or not?" Inspector Wong asked firmly.

He didn't respond.

"Would you be willing to come down the station to answer some questions?"

"Do I have a choice?" Hurley asked, turning his back on the small group. His shoulders were littered with symbols and phrases in dark ink.

"It would be advisable if you came with us," Inspector Wong said. "It shouldn't take long."

Hurley slowly pulled up his coveralls, slipped his hands through the sleeves and buttoned up the front, staring at Birgitte with contempt. She ignored him, instead peering around the garage from where she stood, searching for any signs that a child or children had been held there against their will. It was a messy workshop but there was nothing that would suggest a crime had been committed on the premises. The inspector nodded for the officer to escort Hurley back out onto the street.

The mechanic pulled down the shutter doors and took his own time applying the locks. Inspector Wong waited patiently then directed him to the second car, where the other constable was waiting. Hurley got into the back of the car. As the inspector closed the door, the female officer who had run down the alley, reappeared on the street at a trot.

"Anything?" he called out to her.

"No sign of her, Goong."

She noticed the white guy in the back of the car, looked at her colleagues and quickly sensed that something serious had taken place in her absence. She looked at Birgitte who stood off to one side, her face impenetrable.

Inspector Wong said, "Okay. I'll go back with Mr Hurley. You call in for some back-up and start canvassing the neighbourhood for a girl matching Detective Vestergaard's description – two blocks. Call me if you get anything." He turned to Birgitte. "I'm not happy to find you out here, Detective Vestergaard."

"Is this the same man that Merrick Cripps has been following?" she asked.

"The only British person who works at this garage is Ian Hurley, and we still can't find any record of an Ian Horace in Hong Kong. For your sake, I hope your journalist friend has his facts straight."

"Will you let me know how you get on?"

"I'll see what he has to say for himself." It was a non-committal answer that left Birgitte wondering if she'd just burned the only real bridge she had in Hong Kong. The second car pulled back into the street and headed back towards Tsim Sha Tsui.

Birgitte caught a cab back to Kowloon. She didn't want to be cooped up in her hotel room so she walked down to the harbour's edge. She took a seat on a bench and looked across the water to Hong Kong Island, but all she could see was the man who called himself Ian Hurley – his black eyes, his pinched features and the way he moved when he walked. She had to stop herself from automatically assuming he must be the killer without further evidence, but his behaviour was so full of malice and contempt it was hard not to. If what Cripps had told her was true, he was once called Ian Horace – a paedophile who may have already killed several children in England. But was Inspector Wong right: could Merrick Cripps' information be trusted?

Every 10 minutes or so she checked her phone for texts. She hated not being in control of the investigation. It made her realise how important it would be if she took the promotion to be able to let other people follow leads. She also realised how her behaviour must have looked to the local detective. If someone behaved like that with her in Copenhagen, she'd have come down on them like a concrete block. She would just have to trust that Inspector Wong knew what he was doing. She looked at her phone again. Nothing. She got up and decided to walk along the promenade just to give herself something to do.

After two hours of walking back and forth and sitting in cafes, Birgitte checked her phone one last time. Still nothing. It was almost 3pm. They must know something by now. Even if it was just an idea that they were on the right trail. What bothered her most was the thought the child she saw could be in serious danger. There was a chance she wasn't – her behaviour didn't marry up with what Birgitte had experienced so far, but could they afford to assume she was okay? Birgitte couldn't stomach the thought of another child losing her life in a ridiculous game designed to attract her attention. She hailed an approaching cab and told the driver to take her to Tsim Sha Tsui Police Station.

Fifteen minutes later, as she approached the front desk, she spotted Inspector Wong emerging from an interview room. He looked tired. He saw Birgitte and motioned her into his office. The desk sergeant waved her through. Birgitte thanked him and headed for Inspector Wong's office, closing the door behind her.

"Any sign of the child?"

Inspector Wong shook his head. He sat down at his desk heavily. He looked deflated. "He's barely saying anything."

"He's not answering your questions?"

"Quite the opposite. He's very forthcoming but he's not saying anything of any help."

"Have you asked him if he goes by the name of Ian Horace?"

"I need to verify his current identity first. If he came into Hong Kong as Ian Hurley then he could be operating on a false passport which raises a lot of other questions. I don't want to show my hand too early."

Birgitte resisted the urge to press Inspector Wong on this or question his methods. He was clearly frustrated.

"He has confirmed some of what Mr Cripps told me yesterday. He says he's been in Hong Kong for just over three years, on a renewed General Employment Policy Visa, working at Mason's Garage the whole time. And that he knows nothing about any missing kids, dead or otherwise."

The inspector checked his computer, probably for any emails that might have required his immediate attention. Satisfied, he turned back to Birgitte. "He admitted to being in the shopping mall the other day, and even to buying a pair of sneakers, but denied talking to a Chinese boy. Then he corrected himself and said that a child approached him to ask him where the toilets were and he told him. He also admits to being outside the Conran Hotel but he said he was just sitting down because his leg was giving him trouble."

"Did you ask him how he got his injury?"

"He said it was a motorbike accident in the mid 2000s. Still gives him trouble on certain days. So basically he's got a plausible explanation for everything. When I asked him about his whereabouts at the times of the three earlier deaths, he provided alibis to each one." Before Birgitte could challenge this, he continued. "He said he was with his girlfriend – a Janis Pollack, but since then they've had a fight and as far as he knows, she has flown back to England."

"Convenient," was all Birgitte could muster. "Did you ask for a DNA sample?"

"I did and he said he'd be more than happy to – almost challenged me to do it."

"That's something. Any word back on the victims in regards to possible sexual assault?"

"Not yet."

There was a knock on the door. The female officer who had come out to Kowloon Tong that morning poked her head in. "Goong, that search you had me do on the pest-inspection company at Maestri Towers? Nothing. There isn't a company registered under that name or anything even close to it. And I haven't heard back from the Museum of History yet. We're still chasing the security footage. I might have something tomorrow. And there's a lawyer at the front desk. Says he represents Ian Hurley."

Birgitte and Inspector Wong exchanged glances then peered through the venetian blinds. Sure enough a tall Caucasian gentleman in a pin stripe suit was standing at the front desk, looking every part the expensive lawyer.

"You better wait outside," Inspector Wong told Birgitte.

She took a seat in the waiting area while the lawyer, who was well bred in an Oxbridge kind of way and in his early 30s, was led into the interview room. Twenty minutes later Ian Hurley emerged with a subtle smug smile on his lips. His lawyer walked beside him and Inspector Wong followed them to the front desk.

Hurley saw Birgitte. As his lawyer once more assessed the statement he had provided, the mechanic limped smoothly into Birgitte's personal space. His dark eyes passed over the length of her body, lingering on her breasts and throat. "Such a waste."

Birgitte gritted her teeth and stared him down.

"Do you think they screamed much?" he asked in barely a whisper.

"Who?"

"The children. Before they died."

Birgitte flashed a glance at Inspector Wong but he was behind the lawyer and couldn't see the altercation.

"I'm talking to you," Hurley said sharply. His breath was sour and sharp. "Do you think they begged for their lives?"

"Which children are you referring to?"

"The Svedbo children, of course. Who else would I be talking about?" He smiled at her with his mouth but his eyes were pure malice. "You haven't let any other children die lately, have you?"

His lawyer turned from the front desk. "Are you ready to go, Mr Hurley?"

The mechanic nodded, not taking his eyes off Birgitte.

The lawyer said, "My driver can give you a lift back to the garage, if you like."

"Much appreciated."

Inspector Wong spoke up so everyone could hear. "We may need to call you in again, Mr Hurley, so please notify us if you intend to leave Hong Kong."

"Is my client under suspicion, Detective?"

"At this stage, no, but until I can verify his version of events, I'd like to be able to question him again – to clear up any anomalies."

"Be that as it may, Detective, if he's not under immediate suspicion, then he's not obliged to notify you

130

of anything. Just as he is not obliged to provide you with a DNA sample."

"It would simply make our ruling him out of the investigation easier."

"That's not the way I see it. There are correct procedures for doing things, in regards to civil liberties, as I'm sure you are aware. I expect them to be followed to the letter."

With that the two men left the station. Birgitte sat back down, holding her hands together to conceal how much they were shaking. That son of a bitch, she thought to herself. He knew about about Max Anders. What else did he know? Why the hell was he taunting her?

"Are you okay?" Inspector Wong asked.

"He's being protected by someone," she said flatly, trying to control the tremor in her voice. "A mechanic couldn't possibly afford a lawyer of that calibre. And why the hell did counsel show up when you're only questioning him? It's overkill to say the least."

"He hadn't even made a phone call – that guy just showed up automatically."

"We need to find that child, Inspector."

"The canvassing of the surrounding buildings hasn't turned up anything. I'll get you to provide a detailed description to our sketch artist. We can float it with the officers in that area and see if we can come up with something."

Birgitte nodded.

"And, Detective," the inspector added, "in future, I'd appreciate it if you let me do the actual police work. Judging by what I saw of Mr Stanthorpe, we can't afford to step a foot out of place."

"I understand." He had every reason to reprimand her and she was grateful he did it in such a measured way. She was about to apologise when the female officer who had come into the inspector's office earlier approached them.

She introduced herself as Probationary Inspector Lindy Kwok. Inspector Wong explained that PI Kwok was working with him while she prepared for her examinations to become a full inspector. The young woman was direct in her manner, almost cold. Birgitte recognised a younger version of herself in the PI. She was overcompensating for being a woman in the police force. Birgitte quietly hoped she'd loosen up a little when she passed her exams, probably with distinctions.

The young officer led Birgitte into an office then left her to find the sketch artist. Birgitte spent the next hour giving a physical description of the girl she saw that morning. The whole time if felt slightly pointless, as if they were merely going through the motions of an investigation while a child's life was at risk. By the time she left in the early evening she felt thoroughly disheartened.

"Well, no one told me I shouldn't be following him," said Cripps blithely. He took another sizeable mouthful of his pint. Normally he'd be happy to be sitting in a pub like The Archer, preferably if it was in South London, but as he was still stuck in Hong Kong, the simulacra of an English pub in Wan Chai would have to do. Frankly, he thought to himself, the Danish detective could be a bit more appreciative of his efforts.

Birgitte stared at him in disbelief. "Why didn't you tell me Hurley was here when you phoned earlier?"

"You mean Horace? Would you have come out?"

She peered over the journalist's rounded shoulders and through the noisy crowd of drunken tourists and expats, trying to see Hurley, without him seeing her. "Of course not," she said. "Inspector Wong was angry enough with me for going out to Mason's Garage this morning."

"Well, I didn't know that, did I?"

Birgitte gave up her search and hunched down behind Cripps. "Is he still there?"

Cripps nodded. "He hasn't finished his pint yet."

"And he didn't see me walk in?"

"Not a chance."

They were standing at one end of the bar, tucked against the back wall. Cripps might have been right, she thought. The football was playing on several screens – a European match that was holding most people's attention. Occasionally a collective shout would rise up over the surly tones of 90s Britpop blasting from the sound system. The journalist's attention was split evenly, one eye on Hurley, one eye on the game.

He had phoned Birgitte just after 10pm, asking if there had been any developments. She'd told him about her trip out to Kowloon Tong, seeing the girl and how the inspector had referred to the man in the garage as Ian Hurley. Cripps had cursed and wondered out loud how the hell he could afford a fake passport. Birgitte mentioned Hurley being hauled in for questioning. Cripps was as bothered as she was when he heard about the lawyer who had turned up unannounced. The same question was buzzing across the wireless airwaves between them – where was he getting the money for any of this?

He had told Birgitte that she should come out to Wan Chai straight away but wouldn't say why. His tone had sounded urgent. So far his information had been invaluable, despite being unsubstantiated, so she got dressed in a black collared shirt, dark trousers and pair of comfortable shoes. She caught a train over to Hong Kong Island. On the way Cripps had texted twice to change the meeting place. The last text said; "The Archer Hotel. Use side-street entrance off main street." She had arrived in good time, genuinely curious why Cripps was being so evasive. That was until he pointed out, quite proudly, that

133

the man he called Ian Horace was sitting not 10 metres away, having a beer and watching the game like everyone else. Birgitte didn't know whether to strangle Cripps on the spot or buy him a drink.

She quickly tried to weigh up the situation. Part of her knew the best plan of action would be to leave immediately, get on a train and go back to the hotel. She could tell Inspector Wong about it the next day. As long as Hurley didn't see her leave, no damage would have been done. But now she was here, and Hurley hadn't seen her, it was an opportunity to see if he was meeting with anyone else. Furthermore, if Hurley was in the pub on his own, it meant he wasn't hurting the child. She discreetly surveyed the room. There were no mirrors, which limited her ability to watch but increased her chances of remaining unseen. With Cripps serving as her eyes she keep tabs on him a while longer. The situation wasn't ideal but with a child's life at risk she felt she was doing the right thing.

Cripps suddenly said, "Looks like he's getting ready to leave."

"Okay. I want you to follow him at a reasonable distance. I'll fall back and follow you. I can't afford to let him see me. Keep an eye on your phone. I'll text you if I run into trouble and you do the same. And for Christ sake, don't check if I'm behind you. I'll be there. Got it?"

"Got it."

Hurley drained his pint and stood up. He looked casually about the room at nothing in particular then limped out onto the street. Two older white women approached him. They were both drunk. They said something to him and he managed a loose grin but shrugged them both off and headed across the street. They called after him but he ignored them. As Cripps stepped out of the bar the same two women, Brits on holiday from the north of England, tried a similar line on him, only this time it was done out of nastiness. Cripps didn't smile but he did tell them both to fuck off in a tone that wiped the smiles from their faces.

Hurley disappeared around the opposite corner. Cripps jogged awkwardly across the street then settled into a casual walking pace until he reached the lights. He turned left. Hurley was several metres ahead. The heavy-set madams who worked this part of Wan Chai called out to him as he passed but he showed no interest so they didn't bother harassing him. When they saw Cripps they thought they were on a winner. They grabbed his upper arm, patted his arse, one woman even pulled a teenager in a bikini out of a doorway. Cripps struggled to get past them.

Birgitte watched from the opposite side of the street. She was a good 30 metres further back. She was worried that Cripps would lose sight of Hurley and considered cutting in front of him but the journalist managed to extricate himself from the women's grasps and continued up the street at a good pace. The mechanic was oblivious to their presence.

At the next corner Hurley turned left. Cripps followed. Birgitte hung back because she felt she was getting too close. But when she came round the corner she found Cripps standing alone in the street, looking very agitated. There was no sign of Hurley.

"What's wrong? Where did he go?"

Cripps was shaking his head and looked across the street anxiously. "Fuck," he cursed into the night air.

"What is it? Where the hell is Hurley?"

"He went in there," Cripps said, pointing to a doorway on the opposite side of the street where a large white bouncer stood with his feet hip-distance apart as if on military patrol. A sign overhead said The White Stag in neon lights.

"So get in there and find him," Birgitte said, slightly exasperated.

"I can't."

"Why not?"

"The bouncer knows me. I've been there before. He won't let me in."

Birgitte stared at him. "I don't believe this."

"I'm sorry but there is not a snowball's chance that I'm getting past that prick on the door."

"We can't lose him." She looked up and down the street, trying to think. "What's it like inside?"

"Dark but there are a lot of mirrors, from memory. It's a night club. Shouldn't be too crowded at this time of night so you'll have stay on the edges. It's an underground bar, plenty of pylons to hide behind. If you're careful, you might be able to stay on him without being seen, but it's a hell of a gamble. Should we just wait out here?"

"I need to see if he's meeting with anyone. I'm sure someone is protecting him."

"Are you certain you want to go in alone?"

"It's not ideal," she said, looking up and down the street in the hope of coming up with a better alternative. "Not without back-up but..."

Cripps waited as she considered the potential ramifications.

"... I keep thinking of that girl outside his garage. I'll be careful. First sign of trouble, I'll come out."

"Okay, then. I'll grab a beer in here and watch the entrance from the window if you like," Cripps said, motioning to the saloon bar behind them.

"Keep your phone on. If you see anything that's not right, anything at all, call me."

Cripps nodded. She waited as he went inside, ordered a beer and took a seat in the window.

Birgitte crossed the street and caught the tail end of a group of drunken 50-year-old men sauntering into the nightclub. The bouncer ignored her as she entered. A flight of stairs led down into a dark cavernous space dimly lit with neon strip lighting in the floor. It already felt seedy. The guys ahead were jostling one another like teenagers. They'd obviously heard Wan Chai was a paradise for single men over 40.

Her eyes struggled to adjust to the darkness. She was in a large underground room, a bar ran down the left-hand wall, there were tables and chairs set up along the far side that swept around to the dance floor to her right, which was lined with dark mirrors. She spotted an emergency exit door tucked into the opposite wall and wondered if it was alarmed. As Cripps had said there were plenty of pylons. It was like a large basement storeroom. She scanned the crowd for Hurley, and to her surprise she spotted him on the dance floor, draped in a young Filipino girl whose denim skirt had ridden up high enough to reveal cheap underwear. Hurley had his arm around her waist and was moving mostly with his shoulders and hips, adjusting the weight between his feet so as to minimise his disability. It gave him a snake like appearance which the girl mimicked with her own body. They were oblivious to anyone else in the club.

Birgitte moved quickly to the bar, ordered a mineral water and made her way into the back where she could sit hopefully unnoticed. The place reminded her of the bars in Istedgade, a suburb of Vesterbro, where she had conducted raids as a young officer. It was no real surprise to her that a guy like Cripps would be familiar with this particular establishment. Still, she didn't like being in here with Hurley on her own.

The bar was actually quite crowded. There was an even mix of middle-aged white guys and young Asian girls – poverty had driven them to the bigger cities in the hope of meeting someone who could support their families back home or at least give themselves enough to live on. Most of them looked bored or sad. A few of the prettier ones were skilled at giving the impression they were having the time of their lives. There were now also a bunch of backpackers who were too drunk to get in anywhere else, making the most of the cheap booze and loud music to wrap up their night in the city. Out-of-date R'n'B hits were being blasted through hidden speakers and the drinks were flowing steadily. Occasionally Hurley would disappear from view and Birgitte would have to stand up or move tables to keep an eye on him, but for the most part he kept to one corner of the dance floor. The sensuality of his dancing had attracted the attention of two other girls, who had tired of the lumbering drunkenness of the older men. All three girls were competing for his attention by moving themselves against him. Between songs he gave them cash to buy drinks. Within half an hour they were all quite drunk. Birgitte timed her trips to the bar carefully so as not to be seen, but by 11.30pm the place was so crowded she could no longer keep to one table. She had to move around the club constantly.

It was the first time she'd been in a nightclub since arriving in Hong Kong and hadn't been approached by anyone. The men looked at her like she was some sort of desperate imposter – a jealous wife looking to spoil her husband's fun. The men avoided her eyes and almost hid behind the Filipino girls who were half their age and barely legal. At one point two young girls tried to draw Birgitte on to the dance floor for some sort of three-way show but she firmly declined and pushed her way to the back of the room again. It was getting very hot and after several drinks she had to risk going to the toilet. She prayed Cripps was watching the entrance from across the street. If Hurley decided to leave via the fire exit, there was little they could do about it. Thankfully, when she came back out she managed to find the mechanic. She checked her watch. It was past midnight. Her legs were getting tired from standing up for most of the night. She wondered how much longer she could continue her surveillance.

The men were getting more raucous, slipping in their spilt drinks, groping the girls more overtly. It was like being stuck on a cheap cruise boat in rough seas. She had no choice but to move with the crowd as it leaned one a way or the other. Then without warning, she realised Ian Hurley was staring at her from across the dance floor. He had a grin across the lower half of his face but his eyes were dark with loathing. She quickly reached into her handbag to find her phone but her hands felt strange and she was suddenly very disoriented. The lights began to strobe rhythmically, plunging the crowd into darkness for seconds at a time. Each time the stark white light exploded into the room, everyone had moved position. Faces leered at her drunkenly. Then darkness. More faces, distorted, revolting. Then Ian Hurley directly in front of her. He was no longer grinning.

CHAPTER EIGHT

Everything was white again. The walls, the ceiling, the bed sheets. White but unfamiliar. Birgitte struggled to open her eyes for any length of time as if her subconscious was willing her away from the light. Her mouth was dry and her throat ached. She desperately wanted a drink of water. She tried to call out but her voice sounded strange, distant.

A Chinese woman appeared by her side. She wore a nurse's outfit, but she seemed more interested in the monitors behind the bed than the fact that Birgitte needed a glass of water. Birgitte tried to turn her head but it felt heavy. The nurse left the room and Birgitte succumbed to her need for darkness.

When she woke again the first thing she realised was that her hands were strapped by her side, which caused her to panic. As she pulled against the straps, the monitor behind her began to beep faster and faster. She called out to the nurse. One came but she was different, older, but just as serious. The nurse checked the monitors then took a syringe and injected fluid into an IV drip that was already in her arm. Her heart beat slowed and she fell back into darkness once again.

The third time she awoke Inspector Wong was standing by her bed, staring down at her. She felt reassured, safe.

"Can you remember anything?" he asked bluntly, no sympathy in his voice.

Birgitte tried to think but she couldn't get a firm grasp on any of the images swirling on the periphery of her mind.

She shook her head with frustration. She tried to swallow but the pain in her throat was excruciating so she gave up. In a raspy voice she said, "I was in Wan Chai with Cripps. A bar. Underground. The White Stag, I think.

Cripps couldn't get in or wouldn't come in. It was crowded."

"Why were you there?"

"I was following Ian Hurley."

The inspector didn't say anything.

"Cripps phoned. He didn't say he was following Hurley. I had no idea..." The excuse sounded as feeble as she knew it would. "I should have left as soon as I realised Hurley was there." She looked down at the straps. "What happened?" The alarm in her voice was beginning to rise. "Peter, why am I strapped down?"

"What was the last thing you can remember?"

She looked at the inspector in desperation. "I was in the bar, like I said. I was watching Hurley – he was dancing with a few young Filipino girls. Then he saw me..."

The image of him grinning at her jolted through her body. And then it was gone. "I can't remember anything after that."

"What time do you think that was?"

"After midnight, probably approaching 1am."

The inspector stared at her. She couldn't tell if he was using the information she had provided to calculate a schedule or if he was testing her to see if she was telling the truth.

"Was it only you and Cripps?"

"Yes, but he wasn't in the club. He said he couldn't get in. He had to wait in the bar across the street." She licked her lips but her tongue was as dry as the rest of her mouth. She desperately wanted some water but now wasn't the time to ask for favours. "Have you spoken to him?"

"No, but we will."

"I shouldn't have gone in alone."

"And you said you saw Hurley inside the club?"

She nodded and pulled against the restraints. She was beginning to get angry at being confined. "Why am I strapped?"

He ignored her. "Was he drinking?"

She struggled some more then gave up. It was no good. She was stuck and would just have to answer all of Peter's questions. "He was drinking beers," she said. "Bottled beers. He'd had a pint at a pub further up the street but I don't know how much before that. He wasn't fall down drunk. He seemed quite lucid."

"Had you been drinking?"

"Not at all." She resented his implication. "I was on mineral waters."

"And you bought your own drinks."

"Of course."

"How many did you have?"

"I don't know. Three or four small bottles. It got very hot in there."

"So it was crowded?"

"By midnight I could barely move."

"And you definitely weren't drinking?"

"I told you, I was only drinking mineral waters. What the hell is going on? Please, Peter," she pleaded, "why am I strapped down?"

A young Indian doctor with soft, clean features and kind eyes came into her room and checked the chart hanging on the end of the bed.

"Inspector," he said, acknowledging Peter. He looked at Birgitte. "So you're awake. How are you feeling?"

"Awful, like my head is wrapped in cotton wool, and my throat is killing me." She looked about the room. "And I can't remember how I got here. I don't even know where I am."

"You're at the Queen Elizabeth Hospital in Kowloon. I'm Dr Pali, by the way. I've been looking after you since you arrived."

142

"When was that?"

"A bit after 7am this morning."

"What happened?"

"Hard to say." He came around the side of the bed opposite to the inspector. "You'd consumed the better part of a bottle of vodka. We had to pump your stomach, which would explain the sore throat."

"But I didn't..." She looked down at her hands and could feel the tears beginning to well in her eyes.

Dr Pali said, "The straps are for your own safety and ours. You were very agitated when you came in. You started swinging at my staff when they tried to put the tube in your throat."

He looked across at the inspector as he said this. Birgitte struggled to accept his explanation. Dr Pali looked back at her and said, "We have been running some tests, blood and urine etc to ensure there wasn't anything else in your system."

"Anything yet?" asked Inspector Wong.

"Still waiting."

"What tests?" asked Birgitte, still trying to comprehend how she drank a bottle of vodka without remembering anything at all. "What else are you looking for?"

"We're not sure. You were in a state of shock when you came in. Did you take any drugs last night?"

"No. I wasn't even drinking."

The doctor looked at her incredulously. "Yes, you were. So I will ask again. Did you take any drugs last night? It's important that you tell the truth."

"This doesn't make sense. I can't remember anything after midnight, but I know I wasn't drinking in that club." When she raised her voice her throat hurt even more. She winced and fell back against her pillows.

The doctor considered what she was saying. "If there is Rohypnol in your system, or some generic equivalent, it will come up in the tests. Your drink could have been spiked. It might explain the lack of memory."

"I was drugged?"

"We see the occasional case of it over the weekends, but usually with university students in night clubs."

At first she felt stupid then she began to panic as there were obviously several hours she couldn't account for. She suddenly felt overwhelmed. She couldn't breathe. Her hands flapped about uselessly at her sides. "What happened? What did he do?"

Dr Pali reached over and put a hand on her shoulder. "You need to stay calm. I can't give you anymore sedatives."

She took a deep breath and tried to still her nerves.

Peter asked, "Did Hurley know you were following him?"

"I don't think so. Until... the end. He looked straight at me across the dance floor. Then things became weird very fast."

Dr Pali interrupted. "I have to be going. I'll be back as soon as I have the results of your tests. Try to get some rest."

The inspector thanked the doctor as he left the room.

When they were alone Birgitte asked, "What happened, Peter?"

He took a deep breath. "You were found this morning just after 6am, in an alley in Sham Shui Po. You were unconscious..."

"And?"

"...there was a dead child in your arms, Birgitte. A girl aged about seven or eight."

Birgitte couldn't comprehend what she had just heard. "The girl from...."

"We don't know. We are still waiting to identify her."

Birgitte went to cover her face but couldn't. Her head lolled around on the pillow in anguish. She took several

144

deep breathes then looked up at the inspector. "You don't think…"

"We couldn't be certain until you came to."

"But I couldn't…"

"We don't know that."

"Do you think I could? Why would I hurt the child I'm trying to save?"

"At this stage what I think isn't important. You were found with a dead child in your arms and we haven't been able to question you until now." He looked at his watch. "It's 11am and my superiors are pressing me for answers because the media are smelling a story. And you're telling me you have no memory of what happened since 1am."

"I don't know what else to say."

"You could have passed out trying to save the child. But there are several inspectors who attended the scene who say you could have just as easily been involved in her death. We just don't know."

"My bag? Do you have my bag?"

Peter went to the cabinet by her bed and pulled out her bag.

Birgitte said, "Is my phone in there? Check if there are any messages from Cripps."

He drew out Birgitte's phone. She gave him the password and walked him through the menu to collect any voice or text messages.

"There are several messages from Cripps asking where you are," he said, looking down at the phone. "The last one was at 3.30am."

"When the club closed they may have opened the fire exits at the back of the dance floor. I wouldn't have come out onto the main street so Cripps wouldn't have seen me leave."

"Could you have left earlier?"

"I guess so, as long as the door wasn't alarmed. I honestly don't remember."

"So you may have left somewhere between 1am and 3.30am."

"Then what about Hurley? And where's Cripps?"

He held up his hand and made a phone call, talking rapidly in Cantonese. She recognised the mention of Hurley and Cripps's names and the name of the hotel where Cripps was staying.

When he hung up Birgitte asked, "How did the little girl die?"

"We don't know as yet. I'm expecting a call from the coroner."

"Christ, what is happening?"

She closed her eyes and tried to retrace her steps from the moment she arrived in Wan Chai. Her memory brought up faces in the street, passing cars, shop fronts, signage – none of it important, but there must have been something she missed at the time.

Several minutes later Inspector Wong took another call, listening intently. When he hung up he said, "That was the coroner. The girl died from asphyxiation. He says there was significant bruising around her throat, suggestive of a man's hands. There were also bite marks and deep scratches on her hands and legs. He thinks she was possibly attacked by a dog or some sort of animal before she died. He'll confirm that aspect later today. They're still waiting on the toxicology report."

"Does Hurley have a dog?"

"We don't know. There wasn't one at the garage as far as we could see, but we didn't know to check. We were only pulling him in for questioning."

His phone rang again. He answered in clipped sentences in Cantonese then hung up. "My boss is coming up. You'll have to tell him what you told me."

A few minutes later, an elderly Chinese man in a dark suit and white shirt entered the room. He nodded to Inspector Wong then looked at Birgitte. He was slightly

146

overweight for his height, a suggestion that he was once heavy set. His hair was cropped short and neatly combed as if he may have to go on camera at any point. His face was expressionless, his eyes almost black.

"So," he said, "you are Detective Vestergaard. Danish National Police."

She nodded.

"I'm Chief Inspector Wan Li. The media are waiting outside the hospital now. They don't know who you are, yet, but they know you were found with the body of the child this morning and they obviously want a story. Problem is – I don't know your story." He crossed his arms over his large chest. "Inspector Wong has suggested you are on some sort of private case here in Hong Kong, which hasn't been authorised by me."

Peter went to clarify the point when his superior held up a fat hand to stop him. He continued staring at Birgitte. "I need to know what the hell you are doing in Hong Kong and why you woke up this morning with a dead child in your arms?"

Birgitte couldn't get a clear read on him and her throat ached when she spoke so she kept her response as concise as possible.

She ran through everything that had happened since the first child had approached her in Central, making it very clear she had provided written statements at the Tsim Sha Tsui Police Station every time there was a development. She told him about meeting Merrick Cripps in the lobby of the Conran on the Saturday night, and did her best to relay everything he had told her about the man called Ian Horace and his time in the West Midlands and Afghanistan. When she reached the point where Peter became involved she highlighted the thoroughness of his approach to the investigation. She admitted she had behaved brashly by going to Mason's Garage without telling him, and that following Hurley through Wan Chai was a mistake that shouldn't reflect on him in any way. The chief inspector listened, occasionally looking over at Inspector Wong, who had remained stone-faced throughout.

Eventually he said, "I'll need to speak to your superior officer in Denmark."

"Of course," said Birgitte. "I was going to call him myself." She felt like a teenager who'd failed to measure up in a test of responsibility. She should have called him days ago and kept him in the loop with every development.

"Does he know anything about what is going on here?"

She shook her head. "His name is Sven Augerson, Commissioner Sven Augerson. He'll back me up in regards to my position with the Danish National Police." She was no longer too sure how much he'd back her up beyond that.

Dr Pali came back into the room. He introduced himself to Chief Inspector Li then turned to Birgitte. "Flunitrazepam."

"What's that?" she asked.

"The generic version of Rohypnol. You were definitely drugged last night, which would explain your loss of memory."

"And even under the influence of a drug like that, could it make me do anything I don't want to do?"

"As you probably know, it's used as a date-rape drug because it is a very strong sedative. So it's not that the girls want to have sex, they just can't defend themselves from a man if they don't want sex – and then they have no memory of the act so they feel too ashamed to say anything.

"So no, I don't believe you would have done anything out of the ordinary beyond being incredibly drunk. So drunk in fact I'd be surprised if you had any motor skills at all. If you were drugged between 1am and 3.30pm and found by 6am, you consumed close to 750ml of vodka in three hours."

Peter said, "The coroner rang earlier. He said the cause of death was asphyxiation and the bruising on her throat indicates large hands, most likely that of an adult male."

They looked at Birgitte's hands strapped by her side. They weren't petite but no one could mistake them for a man's hands.

For the first time Chief Inspector Li showed some emotion. He rubbed his face furiously with his hand. "I have no idea how I'm going to explain this to the crowd downstairs but for the time being, she's free to go."

Dr Pali cut in. "She'll be free to go when I've finished treating her."

"Of course, Doctor. Sorry."

Peter was already undoing the straps on her wrists.

"We'll obviously need a full statement about last night," Li said staring down at Birgitte. "And from this point forward, Detective Vestergaard, you don't do a thing without speaking to Inspector Wong or myself first. Understand?"

She nodded and thanked him.

He turned at the door. "Keep an officer on guard here until she leaves, and let me know when she's released."

"Yes, Sir," said Inspector Wong.

"Meet me downstairs in 15 minutes. We have to work out how we're going to approach this Hurley character."

Dr Pali moved to the side of the bed. "Normally, if a kid comes in here to get their stomach pumped, I would have sent them home by now, but given the drugs in your system and the fact that I'm still waiting on a few results, I'd like you to stay a little longer. Is that okay?"

"Thank you," she said. "And Doctor?"

"Yes?"

"Is there any way of checking if I was... assaulted in any way, while I was under the influence."

"I'll have the appropriate staff come in this afternoon."

He pressed her hand warmly then left the room.

The inspector was staring at the door frame.

"Peter?" said Birgitte. "I'm so sorry... for all of this. I had no idea how it was going to play out."

He didn't say anything, which Birgitte found hurtful but understandable. He nodded then left the room without another word.

Birgitte reached across to the cabinet and grabbed her phone. She checked all the messages then called Cripps but it went to voicemail. She left a message telling him she was in hospital and she should call immediately. She still felt very groggy.

Then she drifted back to sleep.

Birgitte managed to eat a light meal for dinner. She was grateful she'd had the sense to ask whether Hurley could have molested her or worse. A kindly nurse had run some basic tests during the afternoon and from the face of it they were both sure she hadn't been sexually assaulted.

Birgitte was preparing to nod off again when the doorway to her room filled with the formidable bulk of Sir Albert Canningvale. He looked genuinely concerned. "Are you taking visitors?"

She nodded.

He stepped into the room with a surprising lightness, drawing a chair carefully up beside her bed. His face was soft and open. "Are you okay?"

"Just shaken up and still a bit groggy. Rohypnol isn't for me, apparently. How did you know...."

"I have contacts at most of the embassies. When a European woman is found with a dead girl in her arms it passes through the official channels like a brush fire. It didn't take me long to find out it was you."

"I'm sorry if this causing trouble."

"Not at all. I'm just glad you're okay."

She suddenly looked at him with apprehension.

He smiled warmly. "I haven't contacted Jan or Loll, so stop worrying."

She sighed with relief.

"If you need legal counsel, let me know. I have a stable of lawyers at my fingertips."

"Do you think I'll need it?"

"From what I've heard this afternoon, you are no longer a suspect, but until the police know exactly what happened, it's best to have a lawyer on hand. Here's hoping you won't need one. I'll leave my card over there just in case."

He drew out another business card and placed into the cabinet by her bed. She recalled when he gave her his card at Government House, and his behaviour on the balcony when he thought no one inside could see him. She wasn't entirely sure she could trust him but his concern for her seemed genuine.

He stood up, towering over the bed. "I'll let you get some more rest. Please don't hesitate to call me at any time."

She thanked him and watched him leave. An hour later Dr Pali came back in.

"The nurse said you were able to get up and use the bathroom earlier."

"I did."

"You feel okay?"

"I won't be drinking vodka anytime soon."

"The pump got rid of most of it but you'll probably feel a little under the weather through tomorrow. I gave you a vitamin B shot for good measure. You're right to leave, but I suggest you keep your fluids up as best you can."

"Are the drugs out of my system."

"It can stay there for up to 72 hours but the main effect lasts for two to four hours."

She sat up slowly and eased herself off the bed as Dr Pali left the room. She noticed a parcel on the armchair by the side table. It contained a pair of dark trousers, a nondescript blouse and a pair of flat shoes. There was a note from Peter:

"Your clothes are in evidence. PI Kwok bought these so you can get back to your hotel."

Birgitte got dressed, gathered her things and signed herself out.

Down in the reception area, several journalists were leaning against walls, looking bored. She didn't know what the chief inspector had told them, but they didn't consider her someone of interest as she headed for the main doors. She wanted to get to the police station to talk to Peter again.

When the doors opened she saw Cripps walking at a pace across the emergency entrance. He looked tired and frustrated, but then relieved when he saw Birgitte. "Thank god, you're okay."

She couldn't help wondering if his concern was more her wellbeing or his story. "Where have you been?" she asked.

"Well, I spent most of my afternoon at Tsim Sha Tsui Police Station being grilled by a bunch of inspectors about last night. They want all my files on Hurley," he said with exasperation.

"What happened last night?"

"You tell me?"

"You didn't see me leave?"

He shook his head. "I stood outside til closing and I never saw you come out. I texted you repeatedly but you never answered. And when I tried to call you, your phone was off. Check your phone."

"I have. And you were outside the whole time?"

"I stayed at the window of the bar as best I could until it closed at about 1am. Then I waited on the corner across the street."

The call log on her phone verified what he'd said. "Sometime after midnight he slipped something in my drink probably using one of the girls he was dancing with. I have no memory after that."

"I'm sorry. I had no idea you were in so much trouble."

"It's not your fault. He chose that bar because he knew you couldn't come in. He lured me in there so I'd be alone."

"He's been watching me too?" he said with surprise. "That fucker. The girl they found with you – was she the one you saw outside the garage?"

"I'm heading to the station now to have a look. What will you be doing?"

"I'm still trying to chase up a few leads from Horace's time in the West Midlands. The time difference between here and England is causing a few problems."

"Can you keep me posted?"

"Sure. And again, I'm sorry about last night."

"It was my fault," she said. "I shouldn't have gone in alone."

Cripps watched her leave. He tried to think what else Horace may have seen since he'd arrived in Hong Kong. The thought of being watched by a guy he thought he'd been following unseen for a number of years unnerved him. And given the photos of the third victim he saw the other day he was beginning to wonder if he was out of his depth. Was his investigation really worth it? Was his own life now in danger?

He fumbled with his cigarettes and decided he needed another drink.

It was after 8pm when Birgitte arrived at Tsim Sha Tsui Police Station. Peter was still in his office. He was talking on the phone.

"I know... not much longer... I will... and I am sorry."

He put the phone down. "My wife. I was supposed to go to a dinner with her colleagues. I forgot all about it. How are you feeling?"

"Better," she lied. She still felt like she had an awful hangover and her throat hadn't eased up at all. "Thanks for the clothes."

He nodded. "You can thank PI Kwok when you see her."

"Any news on the girl?"

He opened a manila folder and slid it across his desk as she took a seat opposite. Birgitte studied the photos carefully. The girl was lying on the ground, having been lifted from Birgitte's arms. She could see the bruising around her throat but it was the bite marks and scratches that were more shocking.

"It's her. The girl I saw outside Mason's Garage. You said the bites weren't post-mortem?"

"Correct. Judging by the damage done to her hands, she was trying to protect her face."

"And she definitely died of asphyxiation?"

"Yes. And the same drug – the generic Rohypnol – was in her system."

Peter stood up and walked around the desk. He took the photos from Birgitte and pinned them to the board beside the others.

"What did your boss tell the media?"

"Not much. He dismissed any rumours that a 'European woman' was involved – said he couldn't say anymore, ongoing investigation, all that. He's quite good at that sort of thing."

"What are his thoughts on all this?"

154

"He agrees Hurley is the way to go, but he's checking with Legal on the warrant situation."

"You can't be serious?"

"A lot of what we are working on is based on your witness statements. You saw the girl yesterday and you said you were drugged by Ian Hurley last night but that doesn't put Hurley with the girl."

"She was out the front of his garage."

"Not inside."

"Why did she run?"

Neither of them had an answer to this.

Peter said, "It will happen. We just have to be thorough. If we don't get it right at this point, we could lose him."

"What about the dog angle? Were you able to find out if Hurley owns one?"

"Not yet."

"Has anyone been to his house? Looked over the fence?"

"We've run into a problem there."

She looked at him querulously.

"On all his official documents he's listed his address as a place in Lok Fu in the north of Kowloon, but it's a vacant shopfront – been empty for years."

"So you have no idea where he lives?"

"Correct. And there have been no sightings of him since you saw him last night in Wan Chai."

"What about the girlfriend, Janis Pollack?"

"She also provided the same false address to her employer – the Ming Ra Primary School in Kowloon Tong where she works as a bookkeeper."

"Were any of the deceased children from the school?"

"No. And she hasn't been in to work for the last few days apparently."

"Could he have killed her?"

"At this stage we have no idea."

"Have you contacted his lawyer and said you need to speak to him again?"

"We have but he says he's having trouble reaching his client. He could be just making excuses. He seems to revel in being difficult."

"What about searching the garage?" She shook her head, answering her own question. "Not without a warrant."

Peter said, "What I was able to do was contact each of the families of the deceased children to ask if they had dogs, or if their neighbours or friends had dogs."

Birgitte couldn't quite see the connection.

"None of them did but each of them mentioned that their children had recently begged them for a puppy. There were variations in their stories but it sounds like all of the children had seen a cute little dog at some point in the days leading up to their deaths and they were keen to get permission from their parents to have one for themselves. It might not mean anything, but I thought it was worth pursuing. Anyway, it's getting late, even for me. And you must be exhausted." He turned off his computer and put his jacket on. "Do you need me to drive you back to the hotel?"

"I'll be fine, thanks. It's only a few blocks. Just before I go, was there any news on the security footage from the Museum of History?"

He paused behind his desk. "PI Kwok has gone through what they sent us from the Tuesday morning. The camera in the Opium Wars gallery wasn't working and the rest of the footage is pretty grainy, and the rooms were crowded with children. Lindy did her best but we can't prove Jenny Lieuw was there or not."

"Damn."

"It's frustrating to say the least." He guided her to the front of the station. "I'll call you as soon as I get word on the warrant. I'm sorry I can't do any more right now. If I don't get to this dinner, I won't hear the end of it."

156

"In the morning, would you mind taking me back to where I was found with the girl?"

He looked at her, unsure of whether it was a good idea.

"It might jog my memory."

He nodded. "I'll call you first thing."

He stepped into the elevator that would take him down to the car park.

Birgitte said, "Please tell your wife it was my fault you were delayed."

As the doors closed, he replied, "I intend to."

She couldn't tell if he was joking.

Birgitte walked out into the humid night air. She checked her watch and quickly calculated the time in Copenhagen; it would be just after 3pm. If she was lucky she might catch Sven at the office.

Her phone rang. It was Cripps.

She could hear the excitement in his voice. "I've just heard back from a woman in Walsell, in the West Midlands, who used to work with Horace at the bus company I told you about."

"And?"

"She was the only one I couldn't get a hold of when I looked into Horace's past the first time. She was going through a divorce at the time, she said, didn't have the energy to deal with my questions." He paused. Birgitte could hear him drawing on his cigarette and exhaling. "Well, thank god I contacted her again."

"What did she say?"

"She said that Janis doted on him, was almost hypnotised by him. I'm reading this from her email: 'There were rumours they were into some wild business, that Janis may have worked as a prostitute from their home. Then there was talk of her pulling in teenagers for Ian to have sex with.'"

"But you already knew all that."

"I know. I know, but just listen. The last line of her email says: 'You want to talk to Talia Mackland. She was only 13 at the time but I'm pretty sure she got roped into a night with the pair of them. I'm sure she'd have some stories for you.' Then she gave me her number."

"Have you called her?"

"I left a message half an hour ago. There's a seven-hour difference between here and England."

"Good work. Let me know if you hear from her."

"We're going to get this bastard, Birgitte. I can feel it. And then I'm going to get the bastards who allowed him to get away with it for so long."

Birgitte disconnected the call. It was a promising development, but her throat ached and she was still concerned about what may have happened to her while she was under the influence of the Flunitrazepam. She just wanted to get back to her hotel room and take a very long shower.

Cripps put his phone in his pocket and stepped out of the foyer of Hanjin Mansions, enjoying the rare feeling of elation that came when things went his way. The bright lights and busy traffic on Nathan Road suddenly held new appeal – Hong Kong was an exciting place to be. He pulled out his cigarettes and even offered one to a middle-aged Indian hawker who had tired of yelling about cheap watches. He looked at the journalists warily, took the cigarette and waited for him to light it. They smoked in silence as the city grinded, bleated and whined around them.

Cripps was genuinely grateful that Birgitte was okay. He felt partially responsible for her abduction but didn't know what else he could have done to prevent it. Deep down he knew if he wasn't the sort of guy who goes to pick-up bars in places like Wan Chai, things may have been different; he could have done something to protect

158

her. The realisation threatened to dampen his mood so he tried to put it to one side but the fact that another child was dead and Ian Fucking Horace was still doing whatever the hell he pleased ate at his peace of mind like a corrosive liquid. The only thing he could do at this stage was make sure the monster was held responsible for everyone he'd ever hurt.

Several cigarettes later he walked back into the hotel. As he stepped out of the elevator on the 14th floor, he heard his phone receive a text.

It was Talia Mackland, returning his call from Walsell. She said she wanted him to outline in an email exactly what he wanted to know and how he intended to use the information. The address was attached at the bottom.

He ran into his room, closed the door and fired up his laptop. If this Ms Mackland could verify first-hand that Horace was a paedophile, he could go back to the military commanders who had turned a blind eye to the abuse in Sangin with some actual leverage and then turn his attention to the police in the West Midlands. He shot off a detailed letter outlining his intentions.

He stared at the screen for what felt like an hour, praying for her to respond. He checked his watch. It was after 11pm. He was about to give up when an email popped into his inbox. It was short and riddled with poorly constructed sentences and bad spelling. The crux of it was she knew Ian Horace but wasn't comfortable talking to the media about how she knew him.

For the next hour or so they corresponded haltingly. It was a dance Cripps was used to, having dealt with many reluctant witnesses on other articles. He needed to be patient but also apply just the right amount of carrot and stick. He was empathetic with her concerns about dredging up the past, but had she considered how many other children Horace may have assaulted over the years? Was she aware that he was now in Hong Kong, possibly hurting little children here? Did she have children of her own? She didn't mention any but admitted she'd love to see 'that bastard get what he deserved'. She couldn't talk for much longer because she was writing from an off-licence round the corner from her apartment. Cripps decided to go for the money shot. He told her there was a good chance Horace could be made to pay for what he did, if someone was brave enough to tell their story. There was a certain empowerment in that, surely.

At this point he realised he may have pushed too hard. She didn't respond. He waited half an hour then sent a follow-up email, suggesting if she had had access to a laptop she could talk via video link to a female police officer he knew in Hong Kong, who was familiar with the case. Detective Birgitte Vestergaard was with the Danish Police so there was nothing Talia could say that about her childhood that could get her into any trouble. There was still no response. He threw his shoe across the room in frustration.

"Fuck it," he said. He turned off the light and lay back on his bed. The lights from the city outside filled his room. He lay awake like this for hours.

CHAPTER NINE

There was no escaping the sound of traffic in Hong Kong, Birgitte mused as she entered the alleyway where she and the fourth victim were found the previous morning. It was several streets from a main road but she could hear the whine of truck engines and car horns and changing gears. The alley ran between two low-rise apartment blocks she guessed were built in the 1930s. From overhead she could hear noises emanating from kitchens – people preparing breakfast. This part of Sham Shui Po was densely populated but with less high-rise development than Kowloon. The air was still and humid and it was only 8am. It was going to be a hot day. The smell of garbage juice and cats' urine was only going to get worse. Birgitte paused midway along the alley. It would have been quiet enough in the predawn hours to dump two bodies, and soon busy enough that they would be found without delay. The killer wanted the bodies found as quickly as possible. She continued on, occasionally recalling her video conversation with Sven the previous evening. After detailing everything that had happened since she'd arrived in Hong Kong, she'd brought up the issue of the promotion.

"I was beginning to think you'd forgotten you'd even applied for the role," he had said.

"I've been a little distracted with developments here. Please don't take that as a lack of interest on my part."

"Of course not."

"Is there any news?" she had asked hesitantly.

"Not as yet. I've spoken to a few of the board members on the quiet and there is considerable support for your application. They're meeting again this Friday. We may have an answer by then."

She had thanked Sven for all his support and promised to keep him informed of any developments of her situation in Hong Kong. He told her to stay safe before disconnecting the call.

Peter and his young protégée Lindy Kwok were waiting in their car on Ki Lung Street. Birgitte had asked to be alone when she explored the crime scene. Not that it looked like one. All the police tape that had marked the area the previous day had been removed. Birgitte was surprised at the speed and efficiency of the Hong Kong forensic teams. Yet it saddened her that there was nothing there to mark the passing of a young life. Just the usual detritus of a rarely used side street. It wasn't that life was any cheaper here, it just seemed to always be moving.

Lindy had said that the residents in each of the blocks had all been questioned as to whether they had heard anything in the early hours of the previous morning. They hadn't. Birgitte stopped at the far end and turned to look back where she had come from, doing her best to recall what may have happened the night before last. She closed her eyes and pictured the alley in her mind, trying to imagine how it might be lit during the night, in the hope that it would spark an image she could build on. Anything.

But there was nothing. She had lost several crucial hours – a window of her memory that possibly opened onto Hurley's whereabouts, or at the very least could give some indication of his MO. For a moment she wondered if subconsciously her mind was protecting her from what she might remember. Did she really want to know what happened in those missing hours? Could she deal with the truth if it was revealed to her?

She didn't have a choice.

"Detective Vestergaard." It was Lindy, she was calling out from the entrance to the alley.

Birgitte started to walk back to the car.

"We just had a call," the young woman yelled. "We need to go. Now."

Birgitte broke into a run. Peter already had the engine running as she approached. As she climbed in the back and shut the door, the air outside erupted with the slow whoop of his siren. The PI turned from the passenger seat. "A girl was abducted from outside an elite school about an hour ago."

"Hurley?"

"We don't know. She was snatched about 100 metres from the front gate, pulled into a dark sedan."

"Witnesses?"

"A child who was further up the street. She didn't see who did it. There were bushes in the way apparently."

Peter drove at breakneck speed with the professionalism of a rally driver. They cut through the narrow urban streets, onto a busy main road, heading north. The rundown buildings and masses of electricity wires soon gave way to wooded hills as they skirted the edge of a vast national park. Twenty five minutes later they pulled into the main gate of the Fenlow International School.

It was chaos. The street leading into the exclusive property was blocked with cars belonging to alarmed parents. Peter parked where he could. Over the rooves of cars they could see police vehicles and media vans parked at odd angles all over the front lawn. They ran through the gathering crowd. As they approached the front entrance of the Victorian building, Peter grabbed Birgitte's arm to hold her back. He said, "Stay out here. It will only raise questions from the media."

She stopped. "You're right."

"We'll find out what's going on."

Peter and Lindy disappeared through the crowd.

Birgitte found a discreet place behind a tree on the front lawn. She watched the madness unfold as the sky filled with the sound of helicopters. The same circus she had seen in Copenhagen and Sydney. She tried to think: why would Hurley abduct a child so brazenly. It was one thing to dump a child where it will be found long after he was out of the area, but to risk being seen in the middle of the day? It didn't make sense. Perhaps it wasn't Hurley. The Fenlow International School was an elite institution, one of the most expensive in the country, as Lindy had explained along the way. It was attended by the children of international dignitaries, multinational CEO's and even a few white-collar criminals. It didn't marry up with Hurley's behaviour to date. The first four victims were from poor to middle-class neighbourhoods. This could have been an unrelated kidnapping for ransom.

More parents and journalists were running towards the main building as a row of uniformed officers formed a human cordon at the front door. Birgitte could see that it was about to descend into a shouting match. She tried to concentrate. If it was a case of extortion, she reasoned, there would be contact from the kidnappers within a few hours, demanding a ridiculous amount of money. Birgitte found herself hoping this was the case, because if it was Hurley, his behaviour was becoming increasingly erratic.

She saw Peter and Lindy pushing their way through the crowd on the front steps. Journalists thrust microphones in their faces and tried to follow them with cameras, but as soon as they realised the two officers had nothing to give them, they turned their gaze back to the front of the school.

Birgitte crossed the lawn to meet them on the way back to the car.

"The girl's name is Catherine Yi," said Peter, "her father is Anthony Yi, founder and CEO of one of Asia's largest toy manufacturers. He's based in Beijing but she is schooled here. Outside of that we know very little."

"No contact with the kidnappers yet?"

"No, but we have now got a warrant to search Mason's Garage. Given the circumstances, my boss was able to present a stronger argument to the magistrate." He

164

handed his car keys to Lindy. "Take Detective Vestergaard in my car." He looked at her directly. "You are not to touch anything. Understand? Just look. If you find anything that might help, tell Lindy and she will call me immediately."

"What will you be doing?"

"I have to stay here. At this stage we don't even know if the crimes are connected."

Birgitte and Lindy ran back to Peter's car.

It took 15 minutes with the siren blaring for the PI to negotiate her way through the incoming traffic. When they got clear she worked the back streets across the city to Kowloon Tong. There was a team of plain clothes detectives waiting outside Mason's Garage. The roller doors were down and locked. There was no sign of Ian Hurley or anyone else, which was odd in itself given it was a Wednesday.

Lindy briefed them on the warrant, introducing Birgitte without going into too much detail on her involvement in the case. She nodded to one of the officers who had drawn a pair of bolt cutters from the boot of his car. He busted the locks and pulled up the roller doors. Lindy directed two officers to search the back of the property, two to work the right-hand side of the garage then the kitchen and lunch room, while she and Birgitte handled the left and would then move into the office. The teams broke off and began to examine every aspect of the building.

It was a messy garage with rusting tools left lying about. There were two old-model Jaguars raised up on hydraulic lifts, engine parts were scattered around the floor in no discernible order. Hurley wasn't meticulous by any stretch of the imagination, thought Birgitte – the thought jarred with her impression of the crimes. Then she reasoned that if he knew his engines as well as his former platoon mates said, then he probably didn't need to be too tidy. There

165

was possibly some order to the chaos that only he understood.

"What are your thoughts on the child abduction," Birgitte asked the PI.

"Could be extortion."

"That's the official line. Do you have any thoughts of your own?"

The officer was pleased to be asked. "No ransom note yet, which seems odd. And believe it or not, there are far richer kids at that school to target. If your motive was solely money."

"Do you think it was random?"

"If not random, then not entirely planned. They may have picked the school, but not given much thought as to who they were grabbing."

"Why do you say 'they'?"

"One car. She was pulled into it through the side door. Someone had to be driving."

"And why that school?"

"Chances are any of those children come from high-profile families. It's as if the kidnappers are looking for media attention."

Birgitte considered what Lindy was saying. If it was Hurley, it seemed very rash, but it also opened up the idea of him having an accomplice.

Satisfied they had searched the garage thoroughly, Lindy reminded the other two officers to check the kitchen and lunch room while she and Birgitte would search the office.

It was a small pre-fabricated room that looked onto the main garage. Again it was messy, paperwork was scattered everywhere. There was a filing cabinet but it was open and overflowing with duplicate copies of job orders. Obviously his wife, the bookkeeper, didn't come into his office very often.

Birgitte grabbed a short pile of paperwork on top of the desk. She took a moment to assess each sheet – invoices, orders, bills. Then she came across a small order for steel fencing to an address in Shek Lei. "Inspector?"

"Yes." Lindy came over.

"Does this address mean anything to you?"

"Shek Lei. It's in Kwai Chung, part of the New Territories – a run-down area, public housing."

"Does it strike you as strange that he'd be sending an order for steel fencing out there?"

She shrugged. "I'm not a mechanic."

"Do you know what OLSL stands for?"

She shook her head and continued searching the piles of paperwork behind the desk. Birgitte committed the address to memory and moved on. They didn't really have time to questioning every sheet of paper they came across.

After three hours of investigation they had to admit they had nothing connecting Ian Hurley to any of the deceased children and there was no sign that a dog had been kept on the premises.

Birgitte listened with growing frustration as Lindy relayed their results to Peter over the phone.

"What now?" Birgitte asked when Lindy hung up.

"There's nothing more we can do here. I was going to head back to the station. Do you need a lift?"

"No, I'll be fine." As Birgitte went to thank Lindy for letting her tag along, the PI politely held up her hand to answer her mobile. She looked at Birgitte as she listened to whoever was on the other end. When she disconnected the call she said, "Our Lady of the Shining Light."

"Sorry?"

"It's an abandoned Catholic School in Shek Lei, on the edges of Kam Shan Country Park."

Birgitte still didn't understand.

"OLSL? You asked me earlier, so I called it in to find out what it meant."

Birgitte was impressed. "What do you know about it?"

"It was a popular school in the 1970s but it was closed down in the early 2000s and it's gone to ruin. The property is tangled up in a court case between the Catholic Church and some developers apparently."

"So why would Ian Hurley have an order for steel fencing sent to an abandoned school?"

"It's worth taking a look. I'll call Goong and let him know what we're doing."

An hour later, Lindy and Birgitte drove through the rundown streets of Shek Lei up into the leafier hills on the edge of Kam Shan Country Park. Birgitte had spent the drive telling Lindy the background to the investigation as it pertained to her. Lindy had asked intelligent questions, which suggested she would possibly make a good detective, or she'd at least pass her exams. Birgitte knew well enough the real test for Lindy would be on the ground once she was promoted. At one point the young PI had said, "It must be difficult being targeted by someone like Hurley. I don't know how I'd cope."

"The more cases you work on the more you have to deal with people like Hurley, and worse. Occasionally, some of them make it personal. It's your job to see past that." She looked across at Lindy. "And you'd be surprised with what you can deal with when you have no choice."

"You could leave Hong Kong," she had suggested.

"Four children have been murdered and possibly a fifth has been abducted because I'm here. Leaving doesn't make that go away. There is more chance of us catching the killer and bringing some peace of mind to the families if I'm here."

"Do you think he wants to kill you?"

"He wants to taunt me first."

They turned right on to a private road that ran up through the trees past a faded but ornate sign that announced: "Our Lady of the Shining Light est. 1972."

Within 200 metres they came to a stop. The former school for Catholic girls was a sprawling complex of imperious buildings in a Georgian style tucked among dense woodland, overrun with weeds, as if the national park was reclaiming its own land. The entire property was enclosed in a cyclone fence and the front gate was sealed with a large chain.

Birgitte and Lindy got out of the car and approached the gate.

"The chain's old but the padlock looks pretty new," Birgitte noted.

Lindy peered through the mesh, looking for signs of activity in the main building but all was silent. Birgitte walked along the fence line to the right until she found a section of the mesh that had been turned up, probably by curious teenagers. She looked back at Lindy.

"I can't follow you in there," the PI called out flatly. It was a statement of fact not a warning to hold back.

Birgitte nodded then crawled through the gap. "I won't be long. I'll call you if I need you."

She followed a narrow path through the knee-high weeds. The school yard was deserted and most of the surrounding windows had been smashed. The main building, in dark brick with a gabled slate roof, was five stories high – an overt statement of British values writ in bricks and mortar. She found a door that had been pulled off its hinges. It was dark inside, and thankfully cooler, but there was enough sunlight for her to make her way along the corridors without a torch. She peered into several classrooms. The few desks and chairs that were left had been thrown into piles against the walls. There were other suggestions of the building's former use – fading posters for teaching numeracy and literacy, chalk boards, drawings of farmyard animals over a doorway to brighten an otherwise dour interior. In some rooms the vines from outside had found their way into the window frames blocking the light, adding a vegetative odour that was thick and cloying.

Birgitte checked two of the other floors and found nothing to suggest that anyone would be using it for the delivery of industrial supplies. It didn't make any sense. Then she remembered – this would have been a boarding school. There had to be dormitories somewhere on the property. She descended the main staircase and walked along the corridor back out to the courtyard. She noticed a walkway in the far corner that cut through to the back of the school. The surrounding yard was overrun with palms and ferns that had sprawled down the hill from the neighbouring park. She found a path through the greenery that looked recently used. It entered into a thick woodland. In a few minutes the trees cleared to a vast grassy opening. There was a three-storey boarding house in red brick built in the same style as the main block, only here the diamond-paned windows provided an air of domestic respectability. She thought of Sir Albert Canningvale as she crossed the wild grass.

The main doors of the boarding house were timber with glass. She tried to peer through but they were too dirty. She gave one side a push and it opened to reveal a grand staircase which swept up from a black-and-white tiled forecourt. The walls were lined with dark oak. It looked heavy and oppressive. It was much darker in here than in the classrooms, shielded as it was by the woodland. The lower floors housed the kitchen and dining rooms, and offices for the senior masters and nuns. Anything of value had long been stripped away.

Birgitte climbed the grand stairwell and decided to follow it around to the left. It swept around until it reached a walkway that was directly over the forecourt. She walked along a long wide hallway, imagining the sounds of hundreds of school girls moving from room to room. They were mostly dormitories – rusting bed frames that couldn't be salvaged had been left. Many of the diamond panes in the windows had been smashed from the outside. The stones were scattered across the floor. Cheap thrills for bored teenagers.

From somewhere deeper inside the eastern wing Birgitte heard a noise. She stopped and listened but all was silent again. She opened a door to another dormitory, more of the same. Then she heard the noise again. It sounded like a low, guttural growling, and sporadic scraping as if something was being dragged across the floor. She peered back down the corridor and froze – at the far end she saw a silhouette of a person in a doorway. The corridor erupted with the viscous barking of an angry dog. Birgitte ducked back into the room, and turned her phone to silent so it wouldn't give her away. There were several bed frames. She found a metal bar from one of the beds and picked it up. It was the best she could do to protect herself. She moved through the dormitory to the door at the opposite end, which also opened onto the main corridor. She gently pulled it open and leaned into the hallway. The silhouette had vanished and the building was silent again. Birgitte continued to make her way along the floor, entering each dormitory at the first door and emerging at the other end so she wouldn't have to expose herself walking straight down the main corridor.

When she reached the far end, she realised it wasn't a doorway to a dormitory but to another stairwell. She ascended it to the second floor, which had a similar floor plan to the first. She moved swiftly from one dormitory to the next, crossing back and forth across the main corridor. As she went, she could hear the distant sound of scraping again. It reminded her of the Svedbo children's last hours, and despite her best efforts, she could feel her heart beat rising with every step. Whoever was in there with her, with their dog, had followed her onto the same floor.

171

She cleared three more dormitories before she came across a door marked "Showers". Pulling it open slowly, she crouched down and crept into the shower block. Wooden benches with hooks for clothes and towels lined the room. Birgitte figured there must have been lockers here in the past but they had obviously been stripped out. She scanned the room for the doorway to the actual showers and that was when she heard it – a low whimpering sound. She had to resist the temptation to run towards it. It was too dangerous to do anything rash. It occurred to her that the owner of the dog may not have seen her in the darkness. The dog had sensed her presence but she may still be able to move around undetected. The scraping returned much louder than before. The dog must have been pulling hard against the lead to stalk its quarry. It was on the other side of the door. Birgitte saw a built-in cupboard in the far corner. She moved quickly, pulling open the door and stepping inside without seeing what else might be in there with her. She didn't have time. She pulled the door to until it was completely dark.

The dog barked once. And she could hear the rattling of the collar as it pulled against the lead. Its nails scraped against the linoleum floor. Footsteps – an adult. The whimpering got louder and became sobs. The crying of a very frightened child. The scraping faded until she sensed the dog and the owner were now in the shower block with the child. Birgitte held her breath as she carefully pushed open the cupboard door enough to see through the crack. She saw into the next room, the corner of a metal cage and a table littered with medication and syringes. Tiny fingers appeared through the top of the cage as the dog began barking violently. The child was pressed into the far corner screaming with fear.

"Shut it," Hurley yelled at the dog. "For fuck's sake. You're making my fucken ears bleed."

The dog stopped barking but continued growling at the girl in the cage.

"Enough with your snivelling as well, ya little bitch."

Hurley limped into view as he peeled a syringe out of its packaging. He was wearing a dirty grey t-shirt and jeans. He pierced the lid of a vial and drew out a measure of yellow fluid. He rested the syringe on the table and reached for a bunch of keys hanging from his belt.

Birgitte was about to come out of the cupboard swinging the bar when she heard a voice from within the boarding house calling her name. It was Lindy. Damn it, she thought. What the hell made her want to come inside?

Hurley bent down to the girl in the cage and muttered something indecipherable. The girl held her breath and tried not to make a sound. Hurley slipped out of the room quietly with the dog. As Birgitte stepped out of the cupboard she could hear Lindy's footsteps running up the main staircase. She continued to yell out Birgitte's name.

Birgitte moved quietly into the shower block. The girl in the cage suddenly turned and stared at her wildly. She was about eight years old and she looked sick with fear. It was the student who had been abducted from the Fenlow International School. She was still wearing her white blouse and dark blue skirt from the day before. The terrified child stared at Birgitte uncertain whether she was there to save her or make her living hell even worse. Birgitte held her finger to her lips and prayed the child would understand. Out in the corridor she could hear the dog barking viciously. Lindy screamed in pain and there were loud banging noises, scuffling and more barking.

Birgitte ran out into the corridor, carrying the metal pipe. Lindy was on the floor at the top of the stairs. Ian Hurley was sitting on her chest trying to stick the syringe in her neck and a large Rottweiler was tearing at her leg. Birgitte took a running swing and hit Hurley hard in the back of the head. The dog let go and stepped back on its haunches, growling. Lindy was writhing in pain completely confused.

Hurley got up on one elbow and felt blood dripping from his skull. He looked angry but dazed. He gave the dog an abrupt command. It paused, turned, then ran down the stairs. He looked up at Birgitte, appraising her for the first time. He grinned, tossing the syringe to one side, and slowly got up on one knee to steady himself.

Birgitte shifted her weight from one foot to the other with the metal pipe over her shoulder, ready to take another swing. If she didn't time it right, he could dodge it entirely or, worse still, grab the bar from her hands. Lindy was rolling around on the floor behind Hurley, clutching her leg where the dog had bit her. She was moaning with pain.

Hurley slowly got to his feet but stayed in a crouched position, his arms out like a wrestler, his weight mostly on his good leg. Birgitte took in the wiriness of his frame and the glint of contempt in his eye. She could already tell he was underestimating her. He was a highly trained former British soldier, obviously fit, very strong and probably psychotic. She hoped the blow to his head had given him concussion. She needed every advantage she could manage. Her self-defence training kicked in naturally. She felt balanced, centred and ready to fight.

Hurley lunged. She leapt back along the corridor, maintaining the distance between them. It was a feint to see how she'd react. He lunged again, this time with greater intent. She moved to the left and as he receded slightly, she took a swing. The metal bar made a loud resonant bong as it hit Hurley's left wrist. He grimaced but didn't yell. She was sure it must have broken something. He shook his head and laughed at her, shifting to his left in an attempt to swing her round to limit her movement, making the narrowness of the corridor work in his favour. She sensed what he was trying to do so she

174

leapt to her right, reversing their position, except now Lindy was somewhere on the floor behind her. She didn't want to trip over her if Hurley came on the attack. But what she hadn't realised was that Hurley wasn't just trying to limit her movement. He'd spotted a shard of glass on the linoleum. He took a rag from his pocket with his right hand and quickly picked up the glass and wrapped it around the base so that the long jagged tip extended several inches from his hand. Birgitte was concerned that the odds were now tilting back in his favour but noticed that his left hand was hanging by his side, virtually useless.

Hurley moved in closer. Birgitte stood her ground. He held the glass out in front of him. He lunged with the shard. She swung at it but missed. His hand came back, sweeping under her elbow. She felt searing hot pain across her abdomen, which made her scream. She danced back so he couldn't cut her again but tripped over Lindy's leg. She fell and landed awkwardly, the bar rattling away from her hand. She scuttled backwards using her palms and heels as Hurley jumped over Lindy. In a flash of instinct Birgitte went on the attack, thrusting her heel out so it hit the base of Hurley's good knee just as he was about to put all his weight on that leg. He pitched forward with a look of shock and pain. Birgitte rolled to the left so he wouldn't fall on top of her. In an instant she was up but the metal bar was too far away to be of any use. She would have to stay on the defensive. In some ways, given her training, she felt more confident without the bar. She knew how to defend herself from a knife attack. Having her own weapon only added a layer of complexity she didn't need.

Hurley got up and placed his weight on his left leg. She'd clearly damaged his right knee. He was breathing heavily through his nose and was struggling with his own rage. The fall had also shifted the glass in his hand. Blood ran down his arm. He had cut his own palm.

"She was right," he said. "Should have listened. You are a feisty one."

Birgitte had no idea what he was talking about. He moved toward her with the shard out front. "I'm going to cut that pretty face of yours so bad you're going to wish you never heard of me."

He came at her with everything, slashing the glass back and forth. Birgitte leapt back again and again, then came at him after he swiped to the left, bringing her elbow up into his nose. He'd expected her to block the glass not strike at him. The crunch of his bone surprised them both. He fell back against the wall, wiping the blood from his top lip with his forearm. She was wearing him down and he knew it.

She reached down and picked up the metal bar, now ready to go on the offensive. She took an almighty swing at his head, screaming like a banshee as she brought the bar down. He lifted up his injured left hand to protect himself but the force of the blow knocked him to the ground. She came at him again, full of blind rage. The images of the dead children flooding her consciousness. He cowered in a huddle as she rained down blow after blow on his back. He made a last-ditch attempt to go on the offensive, lashing out with the glass at ankle height. He slashed her across the left shin. The pain was immediate but she was so full of adrenalin she barely felt it. She brought the bar crashing down on his right wrist. The glass shot across the corridor out of reach. She stepped back. He managed to get up on his knees. He was covered in blood and his eyes were glazed. He spat at her, "I'm going to fucking kill you, you rotten fucking bitch."

And with that she stepped forward and took one final swing. The bar hit him up under the chin sending his head back with a resounding crash on the corridor floor. He didn't move again.

176

Birgitte stood over him with bar poised over her shoulder, breathing heavily. Ever so slowly she stepped back. She dropped the bar and checked her stomach. The glass had cut clean through her shirt and across her abdomen. It was going to need a lot of stitches but she'd live. She checked her shin. It was also bleeding heavily but looked worse than it was. She had been incredibly lucky. She ran to Lindy. She was gripping her leg and shaking her head. "I wanted to warn you," she said through her tears. "I saw Hurley in one of the windows so I jumped the fence."

"I found the girl from Fenlow. Will you be okay for a minute?"

Lindy looked warily at Hurley lying on the floor, unmoving. She nodded.

Birgitte grabbed the keys from Hurley's belt and ran to the shower block.

"Catherine? Catherine Yi?"

The girl looked at her wildly, untrusting but desperate. Birgitte undid the cage door and beckoned her to come out. The girl was too traumatised. She only pressed herself deeper into the corner.

"It's going to be okay," Birgitte said softly. "The bad man and the dog are gone."

The child saw the blood seeping through Birgitte's shirt. She shook her head violently.

"I'm okay," Birgitte said. "It looks worse than it is. You can stay there if you like. You're safe now."

There was nothing more she could do so she left child and went back to Lindy, who had propped herself up against the corridor wall. Hurley still hadn't moved. She checked his pulse; he was alive.

She turned her phone back on and dialled the emergency number. She explained that she had found the abducted girl from the Fenlow International School and there were three people in need of ambulances. She gave the address

177

of Our Lady of the Shining Light then slid down the wall next to Lindy with her hand over her stomach.

When the child was eventually coaxed out of the cage by a young female police officer, she was wrapped in a blanket and guided along the corridor, down the stairs and out the front of the boarding house. Two helicopters hovered overhead, with camera crews leaning out trying to get a shot of Catherine Yi, heir to a toy manufacturing empire, preferably running into her parents' arms, but they were to have no such luck. She was placed in a wheel chair, which was then pushed quickly through the woodland and into the schoolyard.

The lock on the fence had been broken, allowing several more police cars and four ambulances to pull up close to the main building. Hurley had been strapped to a gurney and loaded into one of the ambulances, which backed its way through the melee, its siren blaring, escorted by three police cars.

Peter was standing to one side giving his superior officers a brief overview of what had happened. Chief Inspector Li was among them. Peter spotted Birgitte and Lindy as they came back through the schoolyard, and excused himself from the group. Lindy had her arm around Birgitte's shoulder to take the weight off her wounded leg, and Birgitte had a hand across her own stomach and was limping slightly as well.

Peter approached them. "You should have called before you went in."

"I was just having a look around," Birgitte said. "I didn't expect him to be here. And for the record, PI Kwok tried to stop me. She only came in when she saw Hurley through one of the windows."

Peter waved over two paramedics. "You'll need to be examined."

178

Birgitte undid her blouse. The bleeding across her abdomen had slowed but the cut was deep in the centre.

Peter said, "You were lucky. Another quarter of an inch..."

He stepped back to let the paramedics assess her. "Hurley was about to inject the girl with some drug and then probably dump the body somewhere public," he said. "Once we've had him checked out at a hospital, we'll get him in to lock-up and begin interviewing him. We'll need you to both make detailed statements this afternoon. Think you'll be up to it?"

Birgitte looked about the school yard. "Where's the dog?"

"What dog?"

"Hurley's dog, a Rottweiler."

"We didn't see one as we arrived. Probably took off because of the sirens."

They looked at one another and both thought of the fourth victim staged in Birgitte's arms. Peter said, "I'll get a team out looking for it immediately." But before he set off he turned to Lindy. "You and I aren't done." He strode across the school yard to a group of officers.

Lindy looked crestfallen and was in shock. Birgitte pressed her shoulder. "He'll be fine. He's more worried for you than angry. I'll back you up."

"Thank you for what you did in there," she muttered.

"It could have gone either way. If you came in a minute later, it would have been you saving me."

"I didn't even think to draw my gun."

"Be grateful he didn't get a hold of it."

"I froze when the dog came at me."

"It's okay. It happens."

The paramedics guided the two officers to the back of the waiting ambulance. With the child now safe, there was an air of triumph shared by most of the emergency crews, but Birgitte didn't feel so confident. They had caught

Hurley and there was no way he could talk his way out of being charged with abduction, even with an expensive lawyer, but something wasn't sitting right, she just didn't know what it was.

CHAPTER TEN

Peter Wong emerged from the interview room stone faced. For two hours he'd been working on Hurley and getting nowhere. Stanthorpe continually advised his client not to answer questions or gave a nod when he was confident the answer would mean nothing at all. Hurley had sat through it all saying next to nothing, his nose was covered in plaster and his head was bandaged. His blackened eyes were dark with anger.

He had remained under armed guard at the Queen Victoria Hospital until he was released into police custody late the previous evening. The media had been waiting on the street and stormed the transport vehicle with cameras as it pulled out of the hospital grounds, journalists screaming questions through the back windows. Then he was transferred to the holding cells in Tsim Sha Tsui Police Station. When Peter had him brought up to the interview room he had struggled to walk without help. Stanthorpe started the official recording by announcing his client intended to sue the police for brutality and that Detective Vestergaard should be charged with assault – which had set the tone for the rest of the morning.

The inspector went into the kitchenette off the main corridor, made two coffees and carried them into his office. Birgitte was sitting at his desk, researching on his computer.

"It doesn't make sense," she said as he placed the two cups on his desk and slumped in the chair opposite. He waved his hand for her to stay seated when she went to get up.

"What doesn't?"

"His behaviour. There was a distinct pattern," she said, motioning to the white board against the far wall on which were stuck photos of each of the victims and their crime scenes. "Three children, none of whom can speak

181

English, trained to recite a single line to a foreigner. Each of them then turns up dead in apparent accidents. It was a specific MO."

Peter listened as best he could, but he looked preoccupied.

Birgitte continued, talking to herself as much to him. "There was a methodical pattern – a sense of control. The purpose of which was to taunt me. Whoever was doing it must have known I would get close to them sooner rather than later."

He sat up, now visibly perturbed by what he was hearing. "Are you now suggesting Hurley may not have killed those first three children?"

"Not exactly, although we should keep that idea on the table," she said. "You've said yourself we don't have enough evidence to link him to the murders, only the abduction. No evidence – no leverage – less chance of a confession. As long as he doesn't say anything to incriminate himself, he's looking at limited jail time. So instead of trying to fit Hurley into a box of our own making, it would be better for us to work out the MO behind the killings, regardless of who committed them – find the patterns and look for the deviations. The more we know about the murders the more you'll have to work with in the interview room."

The inspector nodded slowly.

"How long have we got?"

"We have 24 hours. By mid-afternoon tomorrow we'll have to charge him with something."

"There was a distinct pattern," she said, "then it suddenly changed. Why?"

"You got too close. Perhaps that fourth victim, the child you saw outside Mason's Garage would have been forced to approach you if the opportunity had presented itself. You may have interrupted the MO. She got frightened and ran, and Hurley is able to deny everything because no one actually saw her on his property. It was a close call."

"Have we been able to ID her yet?"

"Cindy Chan. Lived in Teun Mun in the New Territories, up in the north west. I spoke to her parents this morning. I couldn't get much information. Like the others, she'd taken a sick day from school and there was no one home to mind her. When they realised she was gone in the evening, they just thought she'd must be playing with friends. They gave the impression she was a fairly independent but responsible child. Didn't really sense she was missing until much later that night."

Birgitte considered what he was telling her, then said, "So why was I drugged and staged with her body? Did the killer actually think I would be blamed for her murder? Were they trying to scare me off? I get that I may have interrupted them but it still doesn't make sense. It lacks the methodology of the first three crimes. And the abduction of the fifth child – Catherine Yi? Brazen to the point of stupidity."

"If you hadn't questioned the fencing order at Mason's Garage, we may not have found her in time. It wouldn't have looked so stupid then."

Birgitte shook her head, perplexed. "She goes to an elite international school. It's safe to say she speaks English. Another factor that suggests the existing MO was being ignored."

Peter was staring at the map of the greater Kowloon area which was marked with pins where the bodies were found. They had found no correlation. But something was bothering him. He went to his files and drew out another map of the same area and quickly taped it across one of the window that looked out over the department. He ran round his desk as Birgitte stood up to let him access his computer. He opened a file, cut and paste copy from several documents and hit print. He took the printout from the printer behind his desk and returned to the map with a packet of coloured sticky tabs.

Birgitte watched him. She knew better than to ask questions while a senior detective was developing a theory. Five minutes later the map was littered with tabs in two different colours. He stepped back and stared at it intently. "Okay. The red tabs are where each of the victims lived. The green tabs are the schools they attended."

Birgitte could see the five sets of tabs as pairs because none of them overlapped. "What are we looking for?"

Peter sighed, not yet convinced by his own ideas. "It's what you said about the MO. These kids had to have been approached at some point. I interviewed all the families and they have nothing in common: they don't live in the same suburbs, don't use the same tutors, don't holiday in the same places, but there is something that connects them all. Let's treat Cindy Chan and Catherine Yi as anomalies because that is how it played out – the deviation in the MO." He removed the last four tabs. "Now let's look more closely at the first three, bearing in mind that each family mentioned their children had recently become obsessed with the idea of getting a puppy."

Birgitte moved behind him, staring at the map. "Parks," she muttered, tracing her finger between each of the three sets. She stepped back and took in the photos of the victims. "Ming Gao, the boy who approached me in Central, lived in the south-east of... where's that?" she asked pointing at the map. "Sham Shui Po?"

He nodded. "He walked through Fa Hui Park to get to school."

"Jenny Lieuw, in the Museum of History..."

"Lived in Hung Hom. She walked through Hutchison Park to get to her school down here."

"And the third, the one on the train?"

"The third child was Yu Chen. He lived here," Peter said, pointing to a red tab at the top of the map. "Sheung Shui, and he would have had to cross Northern District Park."

They both sat down without saying anything, their minds furiously trying to process the information in tandem. Eventually Peter turned to Birgitte. "I'll get Lindy to organise a team. We can check each of the parks, retrace the kids' steps, see if it leads to anything."

"Do you mind if I tag along?"

"You'll have to keep a low profile, if you can. Chief Inspector Li is getting a headache from management. Some of them don't like the idea of a..."

"A foreigner?"

"... a detective from outside of Hong Kong getting involved."

She nodded and wondered if she would have been willing to let an outsider join one of her investigations in Copenhagen.

Peter checked his watch and stood up. "I better get back to the interview."

"Can I make a suggestion?"

"Sure."

"Hold off on the information about the parks. It's the only angle we have that he doesn't know about."

PI Kwok sent two officers to each of the three parks in the afternoon. Peter had given instructions to consider how the MO may have played out by getting each team of officers to retrace the steps of the children as they would have cut through each park at the beginning and end of a school day and to take photos along the way. Were there any buildings overlooking the parks? Vantage points of any sort? When each team had finished walking back and forth across the park, they were to rotate between each one until every officer had walked in the footsteps of each victim, then they would meet up in the afternoon and compare notes. Birgitte decided to concentrate on Fa Hui Park in Sham Shui Po where Ming Gao, the first victim, lived.

After consulting the statements provided by the parents and checking their stories against the map, it was relatively straightforward to determine the path the boy took in the mornings and afternoons. He lived on the north-west side of the park and his school was in the south east, and the MTR train line that ran overland between Mong Kok East and Kowloon Tong formed the eastern boundary of the park which meant he had to make a beeline for the pedestrian tunnel in the southern-most corner on Boundary Street. What was interesting to note was that there was also a school within the confines of park – at the northern end, which meant the area would have been crawling with children several times a day.

She arrived on the north-western edge of the park with Lindy and two plain-clothes officers but moved away from them as they proceeded to retrace Ming Gao's steps. She wanted to get a sense of the place as the killer would have seen it. She moved around the periphery which was lined with a thick bed of mature trees. In the centre of the park was a paved communal area with community gardens, and further south were several netball courts. She moved through the trees, watching the walkers and the joggers, the elderly women doing tai chi, the local workers looking to escape the office for half an hour. There were plenty of visitors walking their dogs. Given the lack of living space in the city, most of the dogs were tiny – shitzus, poodles, terriers, King Charles cavaliers – it was as if the only dogs bred in this part of Hong Kong were designed to fit into Louis Vuitton handbags.

At the northern end she found the school just as the final bell chimed. Suddenly that end of the park was filled with children and their parents and nannies. It was difficult to see if anyone was lingering who shouldn't be. Birgitte crossed to the eastern side. Every few minutes a train would fly past on its way north to Kowloon Tong or going the other way to Mong Kok East.

After an hour of scoping the site from different angles she found Lindy and her two officers moving back towards their starting point. Lindy called out to her, "We're heading across to Hutchison Park. Do you want to come along?"

"I think I'll stay a while longer."

"The other team should be here within the hour."

"Okay. Good luck." Birgitte watched the three officers return to their car. When they had driven off, she took a seat on a bench and began to process everything that had happened since she'd arrived in Hong Kong two weeks earlier. She suddenly realised she hadn't thought about her promotion or Tomas having a child for several days. Maybe this was her idea of a holiday. She decided that she would ring her mother that night, just to let her know she was still in Hong Kong and everything was okay.

Somewhere behind her, beyond a copse of bushes, she could hear kids cooing over a puppy, then delighted squeals. A young woman called out something in Cantonese. To Birgitte's left a tiny dark puppy broke through the bushes and went gambolling across the lawn in front of her. She didn't think anything of it until the woman came through the foliage chasing after the little scamp. She was in her early 20s wearing a faded grey t-shirt, a short tartan skirt over ripped panty hose and sneakers. She would have been very attractive if she didn't wear such dark make up and hadn't shaved the side of her head.

When the young woman caught up to the puppy the ferocity of her behaviour alarmed Birgitte immediately. She grabbed the puppy by the scruff of its neck, lifted it up to her face then whacked it repeatedly on the nose.

The poor little dog flinched and wriggled. It fell from her grasp but was too cowed to move. Birgitte was reminded of Catherine Yi cowering in the cage the previous day. The young woman stood over the puppy yelling at it to go back where they were before. All the puppy could do was wet itself. She snatched it up again like a rag doll and headed back to the line of bushes but then stopped, disappointed. The children who had been fussing over the puppy earlier were gone. The young woman turned back and set off across the park, oblivious to Birgitte's presence. The whole scene was very unfortunate, but what compelled Birgitte to follow her was the type of puppy she was abusing. It was a Rottweiler.

Birgitte kept a comfortable distance between them as the young woman neared the far side of the park. She was about to phone Peter when she noticed a dark sedan driving up the street. It slowed and pulled into the kerb as the woman with the puppy approached. Before Birgitte could get close enough to see the make of the car or note the license plate number, the young woman had got into the passenger side with the puppy, and it pulled away. She didn't even get to see who was driving. It may have amounted to nothing but there was something unsettling in the young woman's behaviour.

There were times when Merrick Cripps had to wonder if he'd been cursed at birth. The reflection in the glass said it all. He was staring at a middle-aged man slumped over a pint of beer in the front window of an otherwise empty bar – it didn't really matter if it was in Kowloon, Sangin or London. It was one of those moments where his lot in life just made sense. He'd bet everything on this trip and now it seemed his one winning ticket, which had been fluttering out of reach for months, was just a worthless piece of paper.

The day before had gone smoothly enough for the most part. He had spent it in a cafe on Nathan Road, working on rough drafts for the early part of his article – the years when Horace was in Walsell – while continually checking his email for news from England. At one point he was distracted by the TV on the far wall over the entrance to the kitchen. There was breaking local news of a child abduction outside an elite school in the New Territories. He immediately thought of Horace but then dismissed the idea because it looked more like a case of attempted extortion. If it had anything to do with the mechanic, the kid would have been found dead already in what would have looked like an accident. Cripps kept a vague eye on the story during day, purely out of professional interest.

By mid-afternoon he was satisfied with what he'd accomplished with his article and was wondering whether it was time to go and grab a beer. There was still nothing from the Mackland woman, which had begun to irritate him. Then he looked up at the TV. The abducted child had been found safe and a man was in custody. A good ending considering the circumstances. As he packed up his laptop, he wondered how the families of the four victims would feel knowing some children could be saved, just not theirs. He drained the last of his coffee, watching the aerial footage of what looked like an abandoned English estate littered with ambulances and police cars. Then he moved towards the TV as if being pulled by a rope. There was Birgitte talking to Inspector Wong. What the hell were they doing there? And Christ, there was Horace, strapped to a gurney and under police guard – they'd fucking got him!

Cripps had paced about the cafe wildly, not knowing what to do first. He couldn't believe it – Horace was behind that abduction. What the fuck?! He grabbed his phone and rang Birgitte but he only got her voice mail. He rang Inspector Wong and got the same. His heart was pounding. This was it. They fucking had him. He rang his editor in England and left a message explaining what was happening. He felt so good about Horace's arrest, he even demanded an increase in his agreed payment to cover his costs. Then he legged it to Tsim Sha Tsui Police Station in the hope of catching the inspector at the office. He had to move fast because the local media were already across the story. It would only be a matter of hours before the English press would pick up on the fact the crime was committed by a British citizen.

And that was when things had begun to unravel.

The desk sergeant at the station had refused to let the inspector know he was there. He told Cripps that all media enquiries had to be directed through Press Office. Cripps wasn't interested in that. He needed to be mainlined into the head of the investigation. Frustrated, he left the station and continued to call Birgitte, but she wasn't returning his calls either. Fucking typical, he had thought, they were both all over him when they had no idea who they were dealing with, now they were out of reach. He ran back to the Conran Hotel and enquired with the front desk as to whether Detective Vestergaard was up in her room. The uptight young receptionist didn't like his attitude and refused to answer his questions. He couldn't believe it. The biggest story of his career was taking off and he was shut out from the two most important sources. He went back to his own hotel and wrote them both terse texts demanding they return his calls immediately.

A few hours later, when he still hadn't heard from them, he resigned himself to not knowing anything further that night. It might not have been as bad as it seemed. The important thing was Horace was behind bars and his own story would be secure because no one else knew anything about Horace's past in the West Midlands or Afghanistan.

He decided to have a few drinks to celebrate. That was at 6pm last night.

This morning he'd woken up in a hovel somewhere in the back streets of Wan Chai – a double mattress on the floor, sheets pinned up over the windows. The Filipino woman with the birth mark was lying beside him, snoring through her hair. He couldn't stir her, so he had got dressed and was about to leave when she suddenly began whining from the bed in broken English about how he had promised to help her with some money. She was in desperate need. He couldn't deal with her moaning, but didn't know if she was telling the truth or if this was the same line she'd hit the other guy with two weeks back. Cripps opened his wallet and handed her the contents, which she took with a look of contempt before falling back on her pillow. As he had left her darkened room, he'd hoped the sex had been good because he couldn't remember a bloody thing.

In the street outside he had checked his phone. The battery was dead. It took him an hour to get back to Hanjin Mansion only to find that once the phone was charging there had still been no response from Birgitte or the inspector. On the upside his editor had obviously seen the news overnight and had agreed to wire him enough money to cover his expenses so long as he filed something that afternoon. Cripps wrote back that it was too soon to reveal Horace's history – the police still thought they were dealing with someone called Hurley – but he'd do his best.

He spent the rest of the day writing a 1000-word piece on the abduction and arrest, with details gleaned mostly from the local media. He hoped to get a quote from Inspector Wong before filing.

By 2pm Birgitte had finally returned his call but said she couldn't talk until later that day. They had agreed to meet at the Conran Hotel at 5pm.

They had sat in the lobby as Birgitte ran through what had happened to the school girl from Fenlow and Hurley's subsequent arrest. But when she explained Inspector Wong would only be able to charge Hurley with abduction and assault of a police officer, Cripps couldn't believe what he was hearing, and he said as much. Wong needed to be hitting Hurley with questions about his time in Afghanistan or at the very least those years in the early to mid 2000s in the West Midlands. They needed to make the connection between his life as Ian Horace and his new identity as Ian Hurley. If they could prove that then they'd have more chance of pressuring him into a deal.

Birgitte had argued that it wasn't about proving what Hurley had been doing back then. It was about finding evidence to prove beyond doubt that he had killed those four children in Hong Kong, and they had more chance of finding that evidence if they could work out the MO behind the murders. If that didn't support Cripps' story, then too bad. He resented her implication that he was only interested in backing up his own article. As far has he was concerned, it was all interconnected. If they could prove he'd been a paedophile for years, then it would be easier to link him to the deaths of the children – "there's your motive!" he had yelled at her in frustration.

And that was when she broke the news to him that knocked him sideways.

Apparently, in the afternoon, during the second interview with Hurley, the inspector had mentioned in passing the children may have been sexually assaulted, and with DNA testing it wouldn't be difficult to prove a link between the killer and each of the victims. He was obviously hoping to see how Hurley would react, but the mechanic just shook his head as if the police were idiots. The inspector asked him what made him so sure this wasn't an issue. Hurley finally responded through gritted teeth that he hadn't been able to get it up since his motorbike accident back in the late 2000s – irreparable nerve damage, he said, obviously referring to the shooting outside of Sangin. He was impotent and had been for years.

"Even if you do find a wad of jizz in those kids," he had said, "it won't have nothing to do with me. Couldn't blow my load if I wanted to."

Birgitte had said the Hong Kong Police were still chasing up the British military to officially determine if Ian Hurley was in fact Ian Horace and whether the shooting destroyed his capacity for sexual performance. If it was true, killing children to cover up sex abuse was no longer a viable motive.

Cripps was crestfallen.

For several years he had been chasing a paedophile who hadn't even been able to get a hard-on since the journalist had first got wind of his alleged crimes. The shot in the groin by the shepherd boy was no different to Hurley being chemically castrated, the very punishment Cripps and many others had been hoping for. The journalist had laughed dryly as the irony took the air from his lungs. Then he struggled to calculate the implications this would have on his story, and his career.

Birgitte could see how difficult it was for him to comprehend.

"I'm sorry," she had said. "I really am. But right now, the most important thing is to work out the MO behind the first three murders. If we can do that, we have a better chance of finding a link between them and Ian Hurley."

"You have Hurley for the abduction," Cripps said without conviction. "Why don't you just work backwards from that?"

"Until we can find forensic evidence placing the other children at the abandoned school or in Mason's Garage, then we can't link him to any of their deaths."

Cripps stared at her in disbelief.

"Seriously," Birgitte said firmly, "we need evidence. So far they have nothing that would stand up in court."

A blind rage began to swirl within the journalist. All his efforts were going to hell and there was nothing he could do about it.

"Fuck this," Cripps had yelled, causing several other guests in the lobby to look over. "You wouldn't even know about Hurley if it wasn't for me. And now you lot are fucking everything up."

"I understand why you're angry. I'm just as frustrated, but if we cut corners now, it will ruin everything. Please, you have to trust Inspector Wong – he's handling a difficult case exceptionally well. You'll get your story. You just have to be patient."

"Explain that to my editor."

He had stormed off without another word.

And now here he was sitting on his fourth pint, staring at his own miserable reflection in the front window of an empty bar. It didn't matter how hard he tried, he realised, it always went to shit. He was sure Horace had a history of paedophilia in England, and he was also confident that, as 'Hurley', Horace was behind the murders in Hong Kong, but couldn't prove either one. And now the only link he had between the two periods – the man's predilection for children – was not only gone; it had never been there in the first place. The abduction story would be yesterday's news in no time. It might have been the beer talking, but he just didn't see the point in going on any further. Horace would be the one that got away. Every investigative journalist had a similar story that marred their legacy. No doubt this would plague him on lonely nights until long after he'd given up the game, but he just didn't care anymore. Maybe his ex-wife was right, he wasn't the journalist he'd always believed himself to be.

He pulled out his phone and proceeded to look up flights to Heathrow. There were a few spare seats on a

194

direct service leaving the next morning. He counted the hours – he could be back in his apartment in Stoke Newington by the weekend. If he pulled a few favours he might get some casual work generating digital content for a sport site at 50 pence a word, and in 20 years he might have enough to buy another car. Christ, how was he going to be able to explain to his boy why he couldn't pick him up anymore? Guess they'd both have to get used to catching public transport – just another thing the boy's mother would ride him about.

Then his phone blurted angrily in his hand. Now what, he wondered, tempted to ignore it.

It was an email from Talia Mackland which stated, "I'll only talk to the Danish woman. 11am my time today."

His beer-addled brain struggled to compute the significance of her statement, then it hit him between the eyes. He quickly checked his watch. He had two hours to get a hold of Birgitte and convince her to make the call. Perhaps, it wasn't over yet.

At 8.05pm Birgitte was sitting at the writing desk in her hotel room staring at her laptop. The video connection wasn't great but as long as the audio was clear it would be okay. Despite Cripps' drunken persistence, she still wasn't convinced this was going to help the investigation. She'd discussed the idea with Peter who had received confirmation that afternoon that none of the victims had been sexually assaulted. As far as he was concerned, the paedophile angle was moot. Still, as Birgitte suggested, Cripps had done a lot to further their lines of inquiry, so it was only fair to meet him halfway. Peter had agreed and told her to keep him up to date if there was anything that could help them. Now she glanced over at the journalist as he sat in an armchair by the window keeping silent and out of view of the laptop's camera. Unable to smoke inside, he bit at his nails. She hoped something may come of this even just for his sake.

On the screen was a pixelated image of a young woman sitting in a bedsit apartment of a housing estate in Walsall, in the West Midlands. Talia Mackland had a wide face, not unattractive, but hardened. Her hair was bleached blonde. She was obviously nervous, not comfortable talking to the police, even from another country, but Birgitte was being very reassuring. Talia was chain smoking and constantly getting up to walk around. Birgitte had to ask her several times to talk into the computer's microphone and repeat what she had just said.

"Like I said, he's a sick bastard that one," she said shaking her head. "He liked 'em young. I mean I was 13 when I met him, and no virgin mind you, but if he could have had me younger, he would have."

"How did you meet?"

"His girlfriend."

"Janis Pollack?"

"Yeah. Her. We got chatting one morning, can't remember where, some apartment, mutual friend at the time. She was all right, I guess, when I first met her. Nothing suspicious like. We were all using at the time and I said I was hard up for cash. I'd been kicked out of home and I was moving from one place to the next. She suggested I come over her place and meet her boyfriend. They might be able to help me out for a bit. I wasn't in any state to argue.

"Anyway. Went round to their place, which wasn't far away, just another grubby house. And there was this Ian Horace guy. He didn't think much of me to start with. Didn't have much to say, but I could tell she doted on him, made a right fuss like of him. He just sat round like Lord fucken Muck. I remember being a bit hurt. I looked a lot better then than I do now. I was trying to get him to like me.

196

"Anyway, it was later in the day when we'd all had a few tall boys and it started to get a bit merry. He loosened up a bit and Janis started saying stuff like 'he likes you'. I brushed it off but I was kinda pleased. He was real dark but well sexy like. He looked dangerous, and at that age that was a right turn on. So we started fooling around and Janis just sat and watched. Then we moved into their bedroom and that's where it got weird. I was too whacked out to care. If they wanted to film shit that was their business. I didn't give a fuck, as long as they were giving me smack and a place to crash for the night, I was willing to do just about anything. And fuck me, if this guy wasn't into just about anything. I could barely walk when he was done."

She looked away from the camera. "Grateful I was smacked out, to be honest. I try not to think of those days too much anymore. Hard enough to stay clean without reliving all that shit. I hope this is fucking helping you lot because I'm going to come crashing down when we're done. I've been real good these last few weeks. I shouldn't even be thinking about this shit."

Birgitte continued to reassure her. She'd dealt with plenty of addicts in her time, active and recovering, and she was comfortable in her approach.

The woman lit another cigarette then realised that her last one was still burning in the ashtray by the computer. She stubbed the new one out and finished the last one.

"Makes me think if he wasn't fiddled with himself as a kid, you know. Not that I feel sorry for the bastard, but if that was what got him off, what seemed normal like."

She wiped her eyes. "Fucken smack. I never would have done half the shit I done without it. Bastards like them kept feeding that shit to me day after day."

"How long were you there for?"

She shook her head. "Days.... weeks maybe... I saw a lot of shit... bad shit... They let me stay and just carried on as if I wasn't there. More people came to the house, you know... other kids my age, and younger. Adults, men mostly would come in and I'd do the rounds. He'd grown tired of me but Janis was happy to shop me out to their mates. I was sleeping out on the living-room floor with a couple of others. Janis kept bringing them in. I knew some of them but others were from out of the area. Every day, different faces. Fucking surreal. He was one sick puppy."

The mention of the word seemed to prompt new memories. "She was the one you had to watch out for."

"What do you mean?"

"I mean he was sick, but she was the one behind it all. She might have worshipped him, but she was also the one driving him on like. I don't reckon he'd have done half the stuff he did to me without her egging him on. He was spiteful but he needed prompting. They were both delusional, but she was worse."

"How do mean delusional?"

"Thought they were going to be famous. Everyone would know who they were. That their fucked-up view of the world was the truth and everyone else was living a lie. He used to bang on for hours and she'd agree with everything he said as if it was fucking gospel. I was too young to know what the fuck they were talking about but I could tell they were off their fucking rockers. And her always with that fucking evil dog."

"Sorry?" said Birgitte quickly, "The line cut out. Did you say she had a dog?"

"One of those angry-looking dark dogs from them Omen films. A rotter... A roller-wheeler..."

"A Rottweiler?"

"Yeah, she bred them out the back of her place. Controlled them like she controlled him. Again, if I wasn't off my head for most of those years, I would have run for the fucking hills to get away from it."

198

"What prompted you to leave?"

"They kicked me out. Got bored, I guess. I remember being hurt at the time. I didn't want to go back on the streets but it was more the rejection. Like I'd done something wrong to get on their bad side. Like I said, I was young, didn't know any better; blamed myself. Hit the smack harder then it all became a distant memory. Wasn't till that journalist got in touch the other day that I thought about it really. It was a real dark period of my life like. I'm doing good now. I just want to stay on track, you know?"

"Do you mind if I ask one more question?"

"Sure. Why the fuck not," she said with a mirthless laugh.

"Why didn't you tell anyone about this? You were a child being forced into sexual service for money."

"Yeah, I was a child. Didn't know any better. But she also threatened to hunt me down and feed me to her dogs, before I left, and I believed her."

CHAPTER ELEVEN

Peter listened carefully as Birgitte relayed what Talia Mackland had told her the previous evening and what she had seen in Fa Hui Park earlier that day. They were sitting in his office. It was just after 10am on Friday. Occasionally he looked over at the map on the wall, the one marked for the parks, quietly processing the new information with what they already knew. The three teams that had retraced the victims' steps hadn't come up with anything new, but he was satisfied they were on the right track. When Birgitte was finished, she asked, "So what do you think?"

"It certainly provides a fresh outlook on his MO."

"Someone else was driving that car when he abducted the private school girl. It might have been his girlfriend, Janis. Could she still be procuring children for him? She has a history of breeding Rottweilers. She might be taking the puppies to parks and getting children interested."

Peter dismissed the angle. "None of the children spoke English. The first four, anyway."

"Could she speak Cantonese?"

"She and Ian haven't been here that long. I'd be very surprised if she could speak Cantonese well enough to convince children, complete strangers, to learn a line of English then recite it to a foreign adult."

"What if there was someone else?"

He looked at her with incredulity. "We've gone from Ian Hurley, to his girlfriend, and now you think someone else is involved. Should we be looking for a cult, Detective?"

"Hear me out, what if they know someone here who can speak Cantonese and English. Someone who can facilitate their needs and is willing to do so."

Peter didn't look convinced.

"Janis has a history of befriending troubled teenagers to serve her purposes, maybe she's done the same here."

"I think we need to stick to Ian. I've got Lindy speaking to Immigration to see if we can access his passport details. If it is a fake, then we can charge him with entering the country illegally."

Birgitte stared at the photo of Ian Hurley pinned to the wall above the five victims. Part of her mind wanted to pursue how he could have secured a fake passport in the first place. Convincing counterfeit documents cost a fortune and aren't just available to anyone. But she was also beginning to get an image of Janis in her mind, which began to dominate her thought processes.

It was classic co-dependent relationship, she realised. Ian was a giant to Janis. She adored him from the outset. She wanted other people to see what she saw in him, wanted him to be bigger. She not only gave him what he wanted but did everything to make him grow in her eyes. She fed his desires, procuring children for his pleasure. How depraved could she make him? If they had killed those missing children in the Walsell, it would explain his eagerness to enlist, to get out of the country.

But when he was shot in Afghanistan, everything changed. If he couldn't get it up, she would have suddenly served no purpose in his life. She wouldn't have been able to please him. Did she feel like she was losing him?

"Have you heard back from the British military?" she asked.

"Not yet."

"If he couldn't perform sexually when he came back from the war, then Janis couldn't keep him happy in her usual way."

"How do you mean?"

"Her role in his life prior to that incident was to fuel his desires, however deviant. If he couldn't be aroused, then she no longer served any purpose."

"What's your point?"

"It might be her behaviour that is escalating, not his."

201

"I don't follow."

"She is terrified of losing him, of losing the illusion of him as the giant in her life; it gives her life meaning. Without sexual gratification as a reason for pleasing him, she has had to find something else. She might be killing children in his name to make them both famous so that he stays with her." She stood up. "We need to find the girl from the park; the girl with puppy."

"Where did you see her yesterday?"

"In Fa Hui Park."

"And she didn't see you?"

Birgitte shook her head.

"If we're lucky she might be at the same park today." He checked his watch. "I'll speak to Chief Inspector Li and see if I can pull a team together for this afternoon. Schools finish at around 3pm."

"How long have we got before you have to charge Hurley?"

He checked his watch. "We brought him in at around 5pm on Wednesday – so about three and half hours."

"It's cutting it fine, but it might just give you something more to work with."

It was a clear, warm afternoon. Unbeknown to the many people relaxing across Fa Hui Park, there were six undercover police officers moving among them, working in pairs as part of a hastily organised operation. One pair posed as joggers, another as a young couple, the third operated separately but within 100 metres of one another as two workers on their way home. This time their brief was to find a young Chinese woman with a Rottweiler puppy who may get out of, or into, a dark sedan with tinted windows. They were operating under instructions from Peter, who sat in his car with Birigtte on Tat Chee Avenue, which formed the north-west perimeter of the park. Each of the teams stayed in touch using ear pieces

202

and wire microphones. After the first hour there was no sign of anyone resembling the woman Birgitte had seen the previous day or the car she had left in.

Birgitte anxiously watched the teams moving back and forth across the park from the passenger seat of Peter's car. She was frustrated Chief Inspector Li was unable to provide more resources. The park covered only three hectares, but at times the officers were well beyond visible distance of one another. Apparently, his superiors were not convinced that Ian Hurley had done anything more than abduct a wealthy man's daughter, and as that was where the media attention was focused, they had little interest in pursuing other angles. Li had reasoned with them at length then accepted that Peter would have to make do with what he was provided.

Birgitte was grateful she was allowed to participate as an observer as she was the only one who could provide positive identification on the young woman she saw the day before. They sat in silence, listening to the updates from the three teams. She checked her watch – it was 3.03pm. Schools were getting out. She pointed to the north-eastern corner of the park, near the school. Peter followed her gaze. His teams were too spread out to cover that area. She gave Peter a concerned look. He peered back out across the crowded park and told her to stay within his line of sight. He didn't have an extra earpieces and wire microphones. She got out of the car and told him if she saw anything, she'd call.

She stuck to the tree line along the street to start with, then crossed the far corner with a loose plan of criss-crossing back and forth across the park. She spotted several young Chinese women, some with puppies, but they were just out enjoying themselves. School children began to appear deeper into the park. They came through in small groups of three or four, a few in pairs, and several were alone. A handful stopped to hang out, dumping their bags and falling into loose circles. Balls were kicked around. Games of chase. Birgitte watched them all carefully, paying particular attention to the children who were on their own.

She quickly realised that by getting out of the car she wasn't privy to what the other teams were doing, which was isolating. She could only hope Peter would contact her if anything happened.

About 45 minutes later, as she crossed that section of the park for the umpteenth time, she saw a person in the far distance crouching down in front of a child in a pale blue uniform, between them was a dark puppy. It was too far to be certain. She headed straight for the cover of trees and started to jog toward the pair. By the time she was 200 metres away she recognised the woman's hairstyle – the shaved side of her head and was sure it was the young woman from the day before. The child looking at the puppy was a girl of around 10 years old. The woman encouraged the girl to pick up the puppy. The child didn't need to be asked twice.

Birgitte continued to use the trees as cover. She called Peter: "I have her, far north-western corner, near the school. Black t-shirt, denim skirt, white sneakers. She has the puppy, and is talking with a child."

"On our way. Don't engage."

As she looked up the girl handed the puppy back to the woman and was waving goodbye. The woman held the puppy's paw and waved it at the girl who giggled before turning to head back towards the school. She watched as the woman put the puppy on the grass and began walking towards the northern end of Tat Chee Avenue – she was heading to the dark sedan Birgitte had seen the first time. Christ, she thought, had this woman already offered the child a puppy? Was she in danger? Or should she not worry about the girl and chase the woman in the hope of confirming that Janis Pollack was behind the wheel? At

204

the very least should she get the number plate of the sedan before it pulls away? She saw the child enter the school grounds as the woman opened the back door of the car. She remembered the Svedbo children, and against her intuition, she ran after the child, phoning Peter as she ran.

"I have to follow the girl," she said between breathes. "They may have organised to meet again. The woman is on the far end of Tat Chee Avenue getting into the sedan – same car as last time – it's facing south."

Peter relayed the information to his team who were now running across the park from different directions.

Birgitte caught up to the young girl and followed her through the school out the main gates onto Dianthus Road. Every so often Birgitte turned to look over her shoulder back through the trees, expecting to see police cars trapping the sedan at the far end of the street. Nothing. A few minutes later, Peter called to say they had driven up and down Tat Chee Avenue but there was no sight of the sedan.

Damn it, thought Birgitte. She suggested one of his female officers catch her up and interview the child. Within 20 minutes, the little girl was talking to Lindy. She was frightened by all the fuss and didn't know what she had done wrong. Lindy reassured her and told her they just wanted to speak to the woman with the puppy dog. The girl looked nervous. It was the first time she had ever seen her, she promised. She just wanted to pet the pretty puppy. When she was asked if the woman offered to give her one, she pretended she hadn't, but Lindy gave her a look that suggested she needed to tell the truth. The girl said the woman had told her she could have a puppy of her own. She was going to bring that puppy to the park on Sunday. But it was a secret. Lindy thanked her for being so helpful and told she had done the right thing. After conferring with Peter, Lindy drove the girl home so she could make a formal statement with her parents present.

Birgitte walked back through the school to the gate that opened on to the park.

"You didn't see the car at all?" Birgitte asked Peter as he approached her.

He shook his head.

"She was parked there," she said pointing to an empty space between two cars 20 metres away.

"Did she see you?"

"No, but there is no guarantee the driver didn't."

"They must have turned right further down before we had a chance to get up the street. And you didn't get any details?"

"I should have chased the woman. At least got a licence plate."

"The child is safe – that is the most important thing."

"I know. I'm just furious. It's the second time I've seen the car and I still don't know who is driving it." She looked around the park. "Why are they coming back here? The first three children were approached in different locations. They are breaking their own MO again."

Peter nodded his head towards the school. "If it is them, and they are getting desperate, targeting a park with a school would make sense."

"It's a hell of a risk in terms of parents and witnesses," Birgitte thought out loud.

"They are desperate," said Peter. "Ian is locked up."

"So why keep going?"

"Maybe she thinks if the murders continue loosely along the same pattern, Ian can't be blamed because he has an alibi for any deaths that take place after his arrest. He'll only go down for the abduction."

"Which suggests they don't know we are across their MO."

The three teams headed back to the cars on Tat Chee Avenue. Peter phoned Chief Inspector Li and explained the situation. Given the development with the child, he agreed to another operation in the park for Sunday. They could work out the arrangements when he got back to the office.

He turned to Birgitte. "Don't be too hard on yourself. The girl is okay."

She nodded.

"I have to get back to the station to charge Hurley," Peter said. "I'll speak to the magistrate too. See if bail can be denied. If he's here on a fake passport, he's definitely a flight risk."

"Good idea."

"Do you want a lift back to the hotel?"

"No thanks. A long walk will clear my head."

They shook hands. As Peter went to get into his car, he said, "By the way, I'm making lunch for my family tomorrow. My wife thought you may want to join us. Nothing fancy; just my relatives around a table at my place out at Lam Tin. We do it every second weekend."

Birgitte was surprised by the invitation. She hadn't given a thought to Peter's personal life. "Of course, that's very generous of you. What time?"

"I'll text you the details."

Birgitte walked back across the south-eastern corner of the park and through the pedestrian tunnel. Along the way she thought of the boy Ming Gao who was possibly approached in this park just over two weeks ago. The poor child had had no idea the danger he was in when he noticed the woman with the puppy. This realisation provided some perspective on her performance. Despite her annoyance at not being able to verify whether Janis Pollack was involved, Birgitte began to feel better about her choice to protect the young girl.

It was just after 5pm when she got back to her hotel room. She didn't have the energy to go to the gym. She took a long hot shower to wash away the day. When she got dressed again, she noticed a text had come in from Cripps, asking if they could meet up that evening. He obviously wanted an update on the case. She texted him back that she would meet him at Milly's, a bar tucked in the narrow streets between the Conran and Kowloon Park, at 7pm.

Birgitte ate an early dinner at the same northern Chinese restaurant she was in on Tuesday. By the time she arrived at Milly's, she felt quite flat. She was just tired, she reasoned with herself. It had been an exhausting week.

Cripps was sitting in the window, halfway through a pint. Probably his third, she mused as he nodded in her direction. She stepped into the bar and ordered a glass of shiraz. She noticed Cripps looked tired also. The skin beneath his eyes was sagging even more than usual and what little lustre his eyes possessed had faded further.

He raised his glass. "To your health," he said, as if it was a concept he'd given up on for himself years ago.

She took a seat beside him.

"Any word on Hurley?" he asked.

She shook her head. "We spent most of the afternoon following leads on the MO."

He looked at her expectantly but Birgitte wasn't keen to divulge too much about the park angle until they had more information. "I can't say much at this stage. How about you?"

"I've been putting pressure on the Metropolitan Police in the West Midlands to find out if there has been any news on the children reported missing from Walsell back in the mid 2000s. If those kids are still alive, they'd be in their 20s by now. There must be some record of them somewhere on the system – credit cards, employment records, anything."

"Do you think they're still alive?"

He shrugged. "Hard to say. Kids from poor neighbourhoods go missing all the time, without being really missing. Of course, some of them turn up dead in alleyways years later with a syringe in their arm or hanging from a tree in a park." He took a long pull from his beer then wiped his mouth. "My gut says they were killed by Ian and Janis, but without any bodies or witnesses it's near impossible to prove."

"I meant to thank you for encouraging Talia Mackland to talk to me. She provided some real insight into Janis Pollack that I think will be a significant help to the case."

"Really? That's great. I've asked her to let me know if she remembers the names of any of the other kids from back then. If we can find more witnesses to the abuse who are willing to step forward, it will help build a picture of exactly what was happening. They might even remember who else was involved – she did mention men coming up from London and from across the Channel. How's the girl who was abducted on Wednesday?"

"She's still getting counselling, but she'll be okay."

He shuffled on his seat and peered out the window. "Any chance I could interview her?"

"Seriously? After what she's been through?" Birgitte shook her head and looked at the journalist with disbelief. "He was going to kill her. Do you have any idea what that has done to that poor girl's mind? She's only nine years old."

"It's my job, Detective," he said, raising his palms in his own defence. "It was hard enough filing a story without a quote from Inspector Wong."

"Sorry?" Birgitte said. "You filed a story on this case?"

"I had to," he said bluntly. "My editor saw footage of the abduction – it's huge news in England that a British citizen has been accused of the crime. I'm already across the story. I couldn't not file a story."

"But you promised not to say anything."

"That was before the guy I've been following for years decided to snaffle a kid in broad daylight."

Birgitte exhaled in exasperation. "How the hell are we supposed to find out what really happened if you go opening your mouth all the time?"

"It's one article, and the local media are already across the story. I didn't mention anything about Ian Hurley being Ian Horace – I just gave my version of the abduction for the website. You can read it if you want."

"It's already gone live?"

"Of course, I filed it yesterday. It's getting some good hits too apparently."

"I can't believe you would do this, after all you've seen – the photos of the boy on the train line, what the hell is wrong with you?" She stood up, too frustrated to sit still. "Children are being brutally murdered, and all you can do is think of yourself."

"Ease up, Luv. I'm doing my job. I'm putting my career on the line to catch this bastard."

She leaned into him, making no effort to disguise her disgust. "And your efforts could just as easily see him get away with it."

Cripps didn't like the stance she was taking. He climbed down from his stool so they both stood glaring at one another. "That's utter fucking bollocks," he said between his teeth. He began pointing his finger at her angrily. "I gave you Horace and I gave you Talia Mackland. If it wasn't for me, there would still be kids coming up to you in the street."

Birgitte looked away, her mind galloping. "I knew I couldn't trust you. What I read about you was right. You're a desperate little man trying to redeem yourself in the public's eye."

"What the fuck are you talking about?" he said.

She turned to him so fast he flinched. "That story you wrote about the businessman in London. You published his details when there was no evidence he was a paedophile. How ridiculously unprofessional."

He laughed bitterly in her face. "You have no idea what you're talking about. There was evidence all over the place. The judge was protecting him because they were a part of the same network. And everyone knew it. I had to take the fall for that, but everyone at The Independent knew I was on to something."

She laughed dryly. "You can't admit you did the wrong thing?"

"I don't know what you're getting all high and mighty about. Don't think for a minute I haven't read up on you. Three children died because you were determined to catch a killer and make a name for yourself."

"I was acquitted of any wrongdoing at the inquest."

"Still having trouble sleeping at night? The conscience is a rabid beast, Detective. Believe me." He returned to his beer confident his arrow had found its mark.

"I don't need to listen to this." She grabbed her bag. "If you publish one more story without telling me first, I'll cut you off completely, and I'll convince Inspector Wong to do the same. See what sort of scoop you have then."

She strode out the door. He called out after her. "You'll be back. You don't have a case without me."

He sat back down heavily. Stupid bint, he thought. Who the fuck does she think she is? Fucking hypocrite. He had to file that story. And it was a bloody good piece – more than 300 hits by the afternoon. He was writing better than he'd done in years. There was nothing Birgitte Vestergaard could do to take that away from him.

He drained his beer. The barman eyed him warily when he approached and ordered another pint. "What?" he said, staring about the empty bar. "Am I disturbing your other patrons?"

The barman pulled him another beer. Cripps returned to his seat and continued to stew.

Several minutes later he was so deep in his own musings he hadn't noticed a woman had sat down beside him. She was drinking a glass of white wine and staring out at the street. When he realised he wasn't alone he turned towards her. She had a very pale wide face, dark ginger hair, worn short, but it was her eyes that intrigued him – they were just a fraction too far apart – catlike. She didn't smile. She simply stared back at him as if he was only of vague interest. She looked familiar, but he couldn't place her.

He was about to get up and leave the bar when, against his better judgement, he asked "First time in Hong Kong?"

"No, Mr Cripps. It's not. I've lived here a while now." Her accent was dry, brittle, Northern.

"How do you know my name?" He stared at her, trying to recall where he had seen her before.

"I know a lot about you, Mr Cripps," she said. This time a subtle smile played on her lips which were thin and quite bloodless.

She reached out a pallid hand. "My name is Janis. Janis Pollack. We've met once before."

Birgitte went straight back to her hotel room and turned on her laptop. She was furious with herself for losing her temper, and very disappointed in Cripps. He'd promised to do the right thing. But then what did she expect? She knew from the outset he couldn't be trusted. While the laptop warmed up, she paced about the room, debating whether to call Peter or not. It was hard to gauge what impact it could have on the investigation. She rifled through her bag for Cripps' card but there no mention of the website he worked for, so she did a search of his name.

She eventually found his article and sat down at her desk to read it. It was written as an on-the-ground report of the abduction, something other British journalists couldn't do from London. She kept expecting to see a triumphant paragraph about what Cripps knew of Hurley's history – but there was nothing. It was a dry, factual account of the day's events. The only criticism she could have given was that it lacked a quote from an authoritative source, which is exactly what Cripps had admitted when he first told her about it. She read it again. Then a third time. There was nothing in the article that could jeopardise the case against Ian Hurley. She felt like a fool. She had completely overreacted – not without cause but, still. She had accused him of being an unprofessional journalist when everything he'd done to date had suggested the complete opposite. She resented what he'd said about the Svedbo case, but it was only fair that he would come back at her just as strongly as she had accused him. They were both proud, ambitious people, who were plagued by their own choices over the years. His jab at their conscience being a rabid beast had cut so close to the bone only because he had lived it.

She sat back on her bed and tried to think. There was nothing she could do except apologise. She picked up her phone and dialled his number. As she listened to the dial tone, she hoped they would both be able to laugh about it at some point. His phone went to voice mail. She balked at leaving a message. It didn't seem the right way to handle the situation. She'd try again later. She lay back on her pillows and tried to process all the conversations and images swirling around in her mind. She felt utterly overwhelmed and exhausted. Her eyes closed without her even realising it and within a matter of minutes she drifted into a much-needed deep sleep.

Cripps had never felt so alone. He knew he'd reached his end and none of it mattered anymore – his ex-wife, his boy. He could feel the ties binding his hands together behind his back but couldn't see a thing. There was a dark cloth bag over his head that made it difficult to breathe. His legs felt weak. He desperately didn't want to mess his pants but wasn't sure if he could control himself. The fear was coursing through his body like electricity. He knew he was going to die.

He began to sniffle and mutter incoherently. He wanted to say he was sorry to Birgitte. He honestly wanted to help her bring Ian Horace to justice. He had gone with Janis Pollack willingly in the hope that he could get some information off the record that might help the Danish detective build a case against her and her boyfriend. Now he was about to die and Birgitte would never know.

Pollack had appeared so calm and in control when she had introduced herself at Milly's. He had kicked himself for not recognising her sooner. She told him she wanted to set the record straight about her partner, Ian.

"Ian Horace?" he had asked.

"Don't be glib, Mr Cripps, or this won't go so smoothly."

He didn't know how to play it, but he knew he was about to have the scoop of his career. Janis eyed him carefully. "First and foremost, turn off your phone."

He pulled it out of his pocket.

"Are you carrying a digital recorder?"

He shook his head. She moved in closer anyway. She was wearing a thin blouse and loose skirt that sat neatly on her hips. He could just make out the shape of her beneath her clothes and the view wasn't unpleasant. She lightly pressed herself against one of his knees. There was a way about her that stirred him. She was confident with men, knew how to disarm them. Not just men, but men like him. He only ever felt this way around the women he'd paid for sex — it unnerved and aroused him at the same time, which he found intoxicating. She ran his hands inside his jacket, across his torso, down his abdomen, brushing his crotch with her fingertips until she traced a line around the pockets of his trousers.

Her cat-like eyes had adopted a playful gleam that seemed to say, "I hope we can be friends... secret friends."

He smiled at her awkwardly, wanting to take the initiative. "Phones off. No recorder. Where can we talk?"

"My place or yours?"

He thought of his room in Hanjin Mansion. "Yours would be better."

"I know. Shall we go?"

He downed his pint in one and followed her out into the street. She moved with a self-conscious grace that caused her skirt to sway gently. In the gaudy neon lights she came across colder and harsher than she had in the bar. She wasn't conventionally attractive by any means, but she was alluring. He found himself being surprised that someone like Ian Horace could hold onto a woman like Janis Pollack.

Within a few minutes they were in the back of a taxi heading north through the city, along Nathan Road. She had leaned forward between the front seats and given the driver directions in a voice that was barely audible to Cripps. His better judgement was beginning to raise objections to allowing himself to be so easily led. His phone was off and he had no idea where he was going. If this Pollack woman had any idea of what her boyfriend had been up to these past few weeks, Cripps could be putting himself in serious danger. He reassured himself that Ian Horace was in jail. What harm could she do? Even if she tried to attack him, he figured he was strong enough to get the better of her. For a moment he remembered Birgitte knocking him to the ground the night they met, but he told himself Janis Pollack was just a bookkeeper, not a highly trained police officer.

She hadn't said anything in the cab. She just crossed her legs high and peered out the window. Occasionally he looked across at her, genuinely conflicted. He tried to work out what questions he needed to ask her of their time in the West Midlands, what she knew about Sangin, and was she involved in the abductions in Hong Kong or was Ian Horace working alone. The picture he had in his mind of the people who committed those crimes didn't marry with the image of the woman beside him.

About 40 minutes later they had pulled up on a quiet back street, somewhere on the edge of the city. She paid the driver cash and motioned for Cripps to get out. The streets were dark, there was less neon advertising, less retail, more wholesale business closed for the night behind sliding metal doors. It felt like a lower-class neighbourhood. Cripps stared up at a corner block, no more than five stories high. The ground floor was boarded up.

"This way," Janis said, stepping over the refuse in the street. Again he found himself admiring the line of her calves. She approached a side door, unlocked it then held it back for her guest. A narrow stairway led up away from the street. If he knew then what was about to happen he would have turned and ran as fast as his legs would carry him.

Suddenly he felt the chair move. He hadn't heard anyone come into the room. He screamed as the hood was yanked from his face. Janis was standing right in front of him, leaning in so close their noses were almost touching. He could smell her skin and it repulsed him.

"Don't be frightened, Mr Cripps. You've got off lightly."

He looked about the room wildly, trying to avoid eye contact. He had no idea where he was in the building or if he'd been moved somewhere else while unconscious – a

216

bare room, a steel bench, a sink. He couldn't process the details fast enough. Some distant inner part of him still believed he might survive and he needed to remember everything he saw, but then he realised Janis was completely nude. She was leaning forward with her hands behind her back. It didn't make any sense.

"Why are you naked?" he asked repeatedly, his voice rushing on sharp, shallow breathes like a mantra. "Why are you naked? Why are you naked?"

His panic immediately erased any doubt as to his own fate. He tried to look away, as if denying her nakedness would somehow prevent him from being implicated in her intentions. But even as he stared up at the ceiling, all he could see in his mind's eye was her slender frame, her full drooping breasts, the slight paunch of her stomach and the dark matted crop of her pubis.

He suddenly remembered a jab in the side of his neck when he was in the living room earlier in the night – a sharp, nasty pain that was followed by dull aching pressure. He couldn't get his memories in order. She had told him everything. He knew everything about them both – the children in Walsell, the *bacha bazi* outside Sangin, the children in Hong Kong. Everything. And for that he would surely die.

"I won't say anything, I promise," he blurted automatically.

"Come now, Mr Cripps. We both know that's not true. You're a liar from way back, probably always have been."

"I won't."

"I've said too much already," she said coyly. Her green eyes held him again as they had in the bar earlier that night. "My fault. I needed to offload. And you're such a good listener."

She stood to her full height. He noticed her skin was glistening with sweat.

217

"I won't tell anyone what you told me," he whimpered. "We can just forget it ever happened."

"But you will tell. Telling stories is what you do, Mr Cripps. It's why you came with me tonight. It's why you've been following my Ian since he returned from the war. Chasing wounded veterans – shame on you."

"I just wanted the truth to come out," he tried to say, but the fear was causing his lips to warble uncontrollably. He was gasping for air through his own sobs. He felt wretched and pathetic, like when he was beaten up as a child in the school playground.

"Oh, the truth will come out," she said calmly, setting her feet shoulder-width apart. "Our story will be told ... It just won't be told by you."

With one artful move she leaned forward and swept the blade of a carpet knife across the journalist's bare throat. His eyes widened involuntarily. He watched in horror as a thin spray of his own blood spread out across Janis Pollack's face. She looked ecstatic, her own eyes closed, savouring the sensation of his warmth spattering across her cheeks.

His body began to shake as he desperately tried to breathe through his mouth. The air in his lungs passed no further than the gaping wound in his throat, causing his severed arteries to bubble and gush. It felt that he'd been chasing the reservoir of air in his lungs forever. As his consciousness receded his body continued to fight.

Soon enough his legs stilled and his head tipped back even further, then lolled at a garish angle. The blade had cut through to the spine. Janis stood up and breathed in deeply through her nose. The smell of his blood was magnificent. She opened her eyes and sighed. It was over all too quickly. There was a tinge of guilt at not being able to share the killing with Ian, which threatened to spoil her pleasure of the act. She quickly reasoned he was with her in spirit. When the moment was right, she would share the happening with him in the finest detail.

There was much work to be done between now and then. She moved quickly and efficiently, silencing her mind until each of the necessary tasks had been completed.

Two hours later, having showered and dressed, she left the room satisfied. It was time to check on her babies.

The high-pitched mewing of a kennel full of puppies greeted her at the door, before she had even turned on the light. The crying became louder as she walked down the stairs. Her silhouette sent the puppies into paroxysms of loneliness and need. In the mire of the windowless room she could see tiny pairs of eyes peering at her expectantly. She flicked on the light and waited for the fluorescent bulbs to flicker to life.

It was a long narrow room with a cement floor, whitewashed walls and ceiling. Cages of simple construction ran the length on both sides – cyclone fencing and steel piping welded at the corners. Ian had whipped it up in less than a week. The bottom of each cage was lined with straw and blankets. And with two to three Rottweiler pups to a cage, the room stank of faeces and fear. There was a fridge at the bottom of the stairs that held their food supply. On the other side a hose connected to a tap. Each week, the dogs were all moved into one cage and the rest were flushed out and the straw replaced.

Janis stepped down into the room and walked between the cages, still on a high from the evening's activities.

"Hello, my babies," she said, trailing her hands along the wire mesh. The puppies ran to the front of their cages to lick her fingers, continuing to whimper and bark as she passed.

At the far end of the room were two special cages, each holding a full-grown Rottweiller. The larger one was a male. It sat on its haunches, its body tense, eyes flickering with aggression. Janis nodded to Nero. "There's a good lad."

In the other a tired looking female with a bloated stomach lay on its side, too pregnant to get up. It didn't look well.

"Patience, Snowflake," Janis said, "you'll be free of that lot soon enough."

She stared at the swollen belly. The darkness in the back of her eyes grew in increments. There was a noise upstairs of furniture being moved. Xi Xi was home. Janis took a deep breath and felt the darkness recede. She climbed back up the stairs, flicked off the light and closed the door, oblivious to the desperate cries of her many charges.

The apartment was a converted restaurant in the outlying suburbs in the New Territories. It was on the first floor of a five-storey block. The other floors were empty. Ian and Janis had taken it despite the agent explaining that it would all be demolished as soon as a buyer could be found for the site. It was perfect for their needs Janis had said.

As a corner block two walls were lined with windows that opened out at angles onto the street below. Through the darkness a young Chinese woman appeared at the door to the kitchen carrying a glass of water. She was wearing a large t-shirt of Ian's that hung down over her thighs, her thick black hair fell over her face, tangled from sleep, but for the patch that was shaved over her left ear. She must have come in while Janis was cleaning up downstairs. She walked past the dining table – a timber setting recycled from the original restaurant counter, surrounded by mismatching chairs, around the back of the second-hand couch which faced onto a large flat screen TV, and through a purple silk sheet that hung from the ceiling to the queen-sized ensemble bed. She took a

220

mouthful of water, rested the glass on a bedside table and crawled back under the covers.

Janis watched her from the door until she settled back into sleep. She noted the sizeable wad of cash that had been left on the sideboard near the silk dress and heels Xi Xi had worn earlier in the evening. The meeting with the banker had obviously gone well. Her charge was developing a keen sense for return business.

Janis went into the kitchen and washed her hands with soap. She felt sad. Even with Xi Xi now living there full time, the place felt devoid of personality. Christ, she missed Ian. She could almost sense him coming in through the door, walking to the fridge and making himself a sandwich. If he'd noticed her, he would have sat at the island bench eating his sandwich and watching her with those dark penetrating eyes she'd always adored. Then he'd get up, and approach her slowly. She'd be at the sink doing something domestic and he would take her in his arms from behind, pressing her gently against the cold steel of the bench. He'd lift her dress slowly but then the hunger would overwhelm him and he would tear at her panties and scratch at her skin. The pain of him would be exquisite.

The thought flushed her cheeks. She dried her hands and pushed through the kitchen door into the main apartment. She slipped out of her clothes and crawled into bed beside Xi Xi. She curled up beside the young woman, using a single finger to lift the hair away from her face. Xi Xi opened one eye to see Janis gazing at her longingly.

"Are you awake?" she whispered to Xi Xi.

She slowly sat up and went to pull the t-shirt over her head but Janis held out her hand for her to stop. "Leave it on. I want to be able to smell you both."

Xi Xi lowered herself over Janis and began to kiss her neck and breasts. Janis closed her eyes. The scent of grease and sweat from the unwashed t-shirt filled her nostrils, the touch of Xi Xi's lips across her belly stirred her from within. As Xi Xi pleasured her in the ways Janis loved most, Janis thought of Ian – her Ian before the war – strong, animalistic, daring, hungry. When her passions were fully aroused she screamed out: "Now!"

Xi Xi slipped off the bed and opened a draw, from which she pulled a large black phallus with well-worn leather straps hanging from the base. She attached the device and returned to Janis who embraced her.

"Take me, Darling. Take me."

Xi Xi gently penetrated her lover then steadily began to ride her with the rhythmic pulse of a quivering animal. Janis moaned and clutched at her, wanting more and more of him. She wept with loneliness for him as she came.

Xi Xi fell back on the bed, covered in sweat, breathing heavily. She lazily undid the straps, rested the phallus on the bedside table and fell back into a deep sleep.

Janis curled over in the foetal position, trying to savour the memory of Ian inside of her. As the wonderful sensation slowly faded, it was replaced with a familiar bitterness like sour milk in her stomach. She wouldn't be sleeping tonight after all. She stared across the apartment and thought of what else needed to be done in the days ahead.

CHAPTER TWELVE

It took just under an hour by Metro to reach Lam Tin. Birgitte stepped out of the subway station and tried to get her bearings. She was now in the east of Hong Kong looking back towards Victoria Harbour. It was slightly disorienting. Being a Saturday, the streets were crowded but there was a relaxed feel to this part of the harbour. The clouds that had threatened to break during her run earlier in the morning had cleared by 10am so she wore a loose skirt and a light shirt. She felt dressy enough to meet the inspector's family and casual enough to be comfortable. It was now just after 1pm.

Peter had texted her directions from the station so she had no trouble finding his apartment block, which was a short walk uphill.

When she pressed the intercom for his apartment at the front gate, a young child's voice squealed out of the speaker. "Helloooo?"

She introduced herself. The gate opened without another word from the intercom. She caught the elevator to the eighth floor. As she walked along the narrow corridor, she could hear muffled voices from behind the furthest door. She was about to knock when the door opened. A Chinese woman in her early 30s stood with a full bag of garbage in one hand. She was wearing dishwashing gloves and an apron. Behind her was a chaotic scene of children and other Chinese faces moving about with plates of food.

"Excuse me," the woman with the bag of garbage smiled and said. "I have to get rid of this. Go in. Uncle Peter is in the kitchen."

She slipped past Birgitte towards the maintenance room along the corridor. Birgitte walked into the dining area of a surprisingly spacious apartment. It was tiled throughout and sparsely decorated. A little girl in a pretty white dress wandered up to her, stopped and stared.

"Hello," Birgitte said.

The girl spun around and ran through the apartment. A plump woman in her 70s emerged from what looked like a study. She called out to the child, "Celina, that's no way to greet our guest."

The woman approached Birgitte. She had a warm face and clear eyes. "I'm Lin, Peter's aunt. Please put your bag down. We're almost ready to eat." She turned and called into the kitchen. "Peter, our guest is here."

Two more children appeared either side of Birgitte – a girl and a boy, both slightly older than Celina. They stared up at her as she slipped her bag from her shoulder and placed it against the wall.

"Where are you from?" the boy asked.

"I'm from Denmark. Do you know where that is?"

He shook his head. His sister punched his arm. "It's in Europe, dummy." Then she turned and screamed as loud as she could, "Uncle Peter, she's here!"

The inspector emerged from the kitchen wearing an apron, with a mixing bowl in one hand. He was mashing minced pork with the other. He looked down at the little girl. "Thank you, Jo."

"I'm not Jo," she squealed with laughter. "You're so silly. He's Jo."

Her brother glared at her. "He's just teasing you, stupid."

"Don't call me stupid, dummy."

"That's enough, you two. Go and break my television again. I've only just fixed it."

They ran off into the living area. He turned to Birgitte. "I'm sorry I can't shake your hand," he said. "But welcome to our home."

Birgitte noticed an unfamiliar brightness to the inspector's demeanour which she put down to his being with his family. It was lovely to see the lighter side of a man she had had difficulty reading.

The woman who had passed Birgitte at the front door came back in. Peter introduced her as his niece, Maggie – the three kids were hers; her husband was away on business. The elderly lady was his Aunt Lin. Her husband, Van, was asleep on the couch in the living room. "He's only pretending," said Peter, "so he doesn't have to help in the kitchen or play with the kids. Would you like some tea?"

"Sure. Is there anything I can do to help?"

He shook his head. 'It's all under control. I just have to finish up in here. Give yourself a tour. Michelle will be out in a minute"

Birgitte walked through the living room past the sleeping uncle and the kids who were playing video games on the TV, out to the balcony.

The view back along Victoria Harbour from Lam Tin was hard to get used to. When Birgitte had taken a ferry cruise around the harbour on that first Sunday with her father, she had noticed how much the mass of apartment blocks resembled white cliffs. Now she was among those cliffs looking west. The balcony provided a clear view across Kowloon Bay to Hung Hom and then Tsim Sha Tsui on the mainland, and across the eastern end of Victoria Harbour to Quarry Bay on Hong Kong Island. She wondered if living this far out gave the inspector some distance from his work at the end of a troubling week.

She looked back through the balcony door and noticed another women appear from the main bedroom. She was possibly in her mid 50s but could pass for much younger. She wore her hair in a simple pony tail but looked elegant in bone slacks and a white blouse. Her face softened when she spotted Birgitte.

"I'm Michelle, Peter's wife. I'm so glad you could join us for lunch."

They shook hands. Birgitte was taken at once by her sincerity. "I'm very pleased to be here. You have a lovely home."

"It's a bit chaotic," she said, laughing. "Peter has is family over every fortnight. We thought you might like to meet a few of them."

"Will your family be joining us too?"

"They're mostly in Shenzen. And if you think this is too noisy, be grateful they aren't coming."

"Tea's ready," someone called out from inside.

"I better see if Peter needs a hand," Michelle said.

Birgitte stepped back in and took a seat at the dining table. Maggie had taken off the dishwashing gloves and apron and poured the tea into six tiny cups, offering one to Birgitte. She took the cup and held it in her palms, enjoying the warmth. Maggie and Lin sat across from her, both smiling.

"So," Birgitte said, "is Peter the only cook in the family?"

"We all love to cook," said Maggie, "but Uncle Peter likes to think he's the only one."

Peter poked his head out the kitchen. "I heard that. Play nice."

"It smells wonderful," said Birgitte.

"He's making gong bao chicken," Maggie said.

"And pork and chive dumplings," Lin added, then she turned to her husband who was still in the living room. "Van, get up."

The old man opened his eyes but he made no effort to move.

Peter called out, "It's Aunty Lin's recipe for the chicken."

Lin leaned in towards Birgitte. "It's my recipe but he does it different. He always has to do things his way."

226

Michelle smiled knowingly at the remark as she brought out a large salad bowl and placed it in the centre of the table.

Birgitte said, "Peter told me you teach nursing, or you used to?"

"I'm more on the administrative side now," she said. "I manage a department within a nursing school."

"Is that a new position?"

"Two weeks last Friday."

"Congratulations."

She laughed. "I'm not so sure if 'congratulations' is the right word for it. It's a new challenge. Peter said you are a senior detective in Copenhagen."

"I am. Homicide mostly."

Van appeared at the far end of the table. He settled into his seat and sipped his tea.

The women continued to chat while Peter began to cook the dumplings. Maggie told Birgitte she and her children lived further up the hill and that Lin and Van lived one suburb over. Her mother, Peter's older sister lived in Guangzhou.

"If Peter and I can get some time off over Christmas," said Michelle, "we'll drive up and stay with her for a while."

Birgitte liked the thought of Peter getting away with his wife to visit family. It suggested, if only for a moment, there was life outside of police work.

Eventually, Peter came out of the kitchen holding a large frying pan with both hands. It was filled with dumplings, which he scraped on to a large plate.

The children leapt up from the living room floor and began carrying dishes from the kitchen to the dining table. Uncle Van went to serve himself until his wife gave him a withering look. She took it upon herself to serve Birgitte, ensuring she got the best pieces from each dish.

Everyone took their seats and settled into the meal. Birgitte was impressed by the quality of Peter's cooking and said as much. She turned to Lin. "I must try your version one day."

Lin proceeded to share humorous stories of Peter as a young man, when he first joined the police and moved out of home. Back then his cooking wasn't so great.

Michelle said, "I often wish I met Lin before I met Peter – I might have chosen more wisely."

He shook his head slowly and looked at Celina. "I'd still be single."

She giggled at her great uncle.

"How did you meet?" Birgitte asked Michelle.

"Well, before I was a nurse, I did a short stint as a paramedic. During my first week after training I was called out to a terrible accident in the New Territories – two trucks." She motioned with her hands so as not to alarm the children. "It was all very chaotic as you could imagine. To be honest, I was quite terrified, but I focussed on the task at hand and got to work on one of the drivers.

"There were people everywhere. It was very hard to concentrate. Then I heard this voice over all the chaos – a firm, commanding voice telling people to 'get back'. Then it was quiet, and I was able to work properly.

"When we had the driver on the gurney, I looked up for the first time and saw this strapping young man in uniform consoling an elderly woman who was distraught. I knew it was him. Somehow, I knew his face matched the voice I had heard earlier. He just looked so incredibly calm and kind."

Peter cut in. "I convinced her she was a witness and that I needed her details for a statement. True story."

"Needless to say, I wasn't a paramedic very long," she said, ruffling Jo's hair. "And your great uncle was no longer single."

Jo rolled his eyes. "Do we have to hear this story with every lunch?"

"It gets better with every telling," said Peter. "In the first version I was just milkman passing by. Now I'm the hero!"

He shifted the conversation on to Birgitte. She reluctantly obliged with stories of her own family, her childhood as the daughter of a diplomat. She played down Jan's prominence in Danish foreign affairs and spoke warmly of her mother's academic achievements and the role she played in bringing normalcy to an otherwise unconventional life – she admitted it was a dull story compared to how Peter and Michelle had met.

Birgitte made a conscious choice to not mention Tomas and they were polite enough not to ask whether she was married. It still felt strange to leave such an important aspect of her life unmentioned, but it was more out of respect for their hospitality than any desire to hide the truth.

After they all shared another pot of tea, and ate squares of coconut jelly, Peter stood up and began to clear the plates. It was almost 4pm. Maggie gathered up her children who each shook Birgitte's hand before filing out the door. Uncle Van, who was yet to say a word, did the same. Aunt Lin gave her a hug and so did Maggie.

Michelle asked if she could be excused as she had paperwork that was due Monday. She disappeared into the study and closed the door.

The apartment felt empty and quiet. Peter continued clearing the table. Birgitte went to help.

"No. Please. I'll leave it till later." He ushered her away from the kitchen towards two armchairs that faced onto the balcony. "Usually, when they leave, I pour myself a drink. Would you like one? There is plenty more tea in the pot if you'd prefer that."

"What are you having?"

"Single malt."

"That would be lovely."

"How do you take it?"

"With a splash of water, thanks."

"Same."

He walked into the kitchen. Birgitte took a seat and when he emerged he was carrying two expensive crystal glasses with a generous shot of golden-honeyed scotch in the bottom of each.

She took a sip. "Wow. It's good."

"I don't share it with my Uncle Van – I wouldn't get any myself." He raised his glass. "To families. May they always know when it's time to go home."

"To families." She thought of Jan and Loll. "My parents would have loved the lunch you put on. It was wonderful."

"You mentioned your father was here, a few weeks ago."

"Yes, just for a few days, before all the madness, thankfully. He was supposed to have come with my mother following their holiday to China but she had to go back to Copenhagen to look after my aunt."

"Well, if they ever come to Hong Kong together, I'd be happy to cook for them."

"Is this an average Saturday for you?"

"Pretty much. I sometimes play cards with my neighbours up on the 10th floor later of an afternoon."

"I have to say, I'm pleasantly surprised at how crowded your life is outside of work."

"Keeps me sane."

"Do you ever socialise with your colleagues?"

He shook his head. "It's better that way."

"How is Lindy progressing with her training?"

"She's very smart, won't have any trouble with the exams, unless her nerves get the better of her, but she needs to get out more, get a better understanding of people. The exams will get her the title, but it won't protect her on the job."

"I think she may surprise you," she said with a knowing look. "She says you're a very good mentor."

"I think the saying is: Do as I say, not as I do."

"So you're not one to take a compliment."

"She's a good student and I believe she's learning more from me than if she was lumped with one of my colleagues. Not everyone is so keen to see women like PI Kwok do as well as they deserve."

"Ever been tempted to go into management – to change the culture of the institution?"

He shrugged. "My opportunity came and went."

"Do you regret not going further?" She wanted to tell him about the promotion she had applied for in Copenhagen. She wanted his advice, but she wasn't too sure if it was impudent to ask for it.

"I do my job well," he said, taking a sip of his drink. "It's enough."

"I'm surprised. You strike me as the type who could do good things in management."

"Hong Kong hasn't been in British hands for some time now."

"What do you mean?"

"We answer to different masters."

"I'm sorry – I forgot about the handover."

"We all have our own ways of coping."

"What's yours?" she asked, expecting him to perhaps raise his scotch glass.

He looked at his drink then placed on the side table. "One moment," he said, standing up. He went into the bedroom and came out a minute later carrying a bedraggled child's toy – a bunny rabbit that had been loved near to extinction. He placed it on the side table next to his scotch.

"One of your niece's?"

231

He shook his head.

"Several years ago I was part of a team that focused on organised crime in the construction industry – racketeering, extortion, that sort of thing. We'd been tracking one group with strong links to mainland China, when an informant of mine suggested we take a closer look at a brothel in Wan Chai. I wasn't interested in locking up some low-level madam servicing the US navy on R 'n' R. I was ambitious – always chasing the bigger fish. And at the time I was up for promotion – what would have been the first serious step in my career. But this particular informant was valuable so, in the interests of good business, I secured a warrant and took a handful of officers down to premises one night.

"We came in through the reception area quite hard – clients and girls running everywhere, the usual chaos. The madam was this nasty woman from mainland China, who just laughed as if she had nothing to fear. She knew the clients and the girls were too frightened to say anything, but just as we were about to wrap up, one of the girls made a break for it. But she didn't run for the front door. She took off down the main corridor. The madam suddenly looked very nervous and tried to distract our attention. I followed the girl to the last room on the end of the floor but she was nowhere to be seen. That's when I noticed some of the panelling was slightly askew. I pulled it back. It was a false wall, concealing an access point into the building next door. It was a whole other brothel, only this one housed about 15 underage girls, some in their early teens, some younger. 'Housed' is too nice a word – they were basically chained up. They looked so frightened. Turns out they were from a state-run orphanage in Guangzhou. Some bureaucrat had been turning a solid profit for many years selling these poor kids into slavery.

232

"I called for back-up and a bunch of ambulances. A team arrived about 15 minutes later. And we did a thorough search of both buildings, treating them as one establishment. It was huge. As the children were being led into ambulances, I did one more sweep of place to see what else I could find. I was in one of the very back rooms when I heard scuffling under some blankets. I pulled up the sheets and this girl, probably 12 or so shot out and ran through the place like a rabbit. For the life of me I couldn't catch her. I called for some of the female officers to help, in the hope of calming her down but somehow she escaped. I still don't know how. Anyway, I went back into the room where I first saw her and realised she'd left behind this." He picked up the bedraggled looking bunny. "I didn't know what else to do. This poor frightened child was so traumatised she couldn't tell we were there to help her."

Birgitte listened. She could see the case still affected him deeply. He nursed his scotch and stared at the rabbit doll.

"Among all the ledgers we collected, we found a coded client list, which we couldn't make head or tail of. And within a matter of days the madam who ran the brothel was released without charge. She fled back to China. The girls were sent back into state care on the mainland, to god knows what fate, and I was told by my superiors at the time to focus my attention elsewhere. I couldn't believe it, and I said as much. Obviously there were people on that client list with a lot of sway with the Hong Kong Police, or at least the Ministry, perhaps higher. When I continued to push in that direction, sensing something was rotten, one of the senior inspectors who was due to retire pulled me aside and told me the Party were not happy, and that if I didn't let it go I could find myself out of a job. 'The Party'? It took several minutes to realise what he was talking about. 'The Party'," he scoffed, shaking his head. "I used to worry that they had bugged my apartment. Now I don't really care.

"Needless to say, that promotion I was hoping for was no longer on offer and I spent the next two years shuffling papers on tax evaders. It's taken me a long time to get back on track. I guess I keep the toy to remind me of what's more important. It's my way of coping."

"Did you ever come across the girl again?"

"No. I kept an eye out of course. Asked around. She'd be in her early 20s by now, if she's still alive."

"I hope you didn't think I was questioning your ability as a detective."

"Not at all."

"I think it's admirable that you keep a reminder like that," she said nodding to the rabbit doll. "I think more detectives should follow your lead."

She checked her watch. "It's getting late. I better be going. Are you sure I can't help tidy up?"

"I'm certain. It was good of you to join us." They stood up. "I will get a team ready for tomorrow and let you know when we're organised."

"Is there anything else I can do to help?" she asked as she put her bag over her shoulder and headed towards the front door.

"Try to switch off from the case if you can – you're supposed to be on holidays."

Michelle emerged from the office. She kissed Birgitte on the cheek. "I hope we didn't bore you."

"It was wonderful. Thank you so much."

"It was a good break for Peter too. This case is getting to him. I'm very glad you're here to help."

Birgitte kissed Peter's cheek and squeezed his hand, grateful to see a side to him that further confirmed her belief in him as a detective and a man.

Back down on the street the afternoon sun had sunk behind the city. She walked back down to Lam Tin

Station. On the train she thought more about what he had said. It wasn't right that someone of his calibre had been held back because corrupt leaders were threatened by his tenacity and professionalism, not least his compassion. She was surprised he wasn't more damaged by bitterness and resentment. She could think of several officers in Copenhagen who had turned to drink and worse.

It suddenly occurred to her that she hadn't contacted Sven about her own promotion. He had said the board were meeting on Friday, which was yesterday. For the rest of the journey she tried to not entertain thoughts either way about the outcome.

Back in her hotel room, she opened her laptop then the video-conferencing software. She clicked on Sven's details and waited.

When he answered he was sitting at his kitchen table in a thick white jumper.

"How's the weather there?" he asked.

"Sultry. There?"

He swung his laptop round so she could see the rain lashing the bi-fold doors that would normally be open out onto the deck in summer. It looked like a dark and miserable November morning in Copenhagen. She envied him being curled up indoors, listening to the rain.

"How's work?" she asked. "And where are you at with the girl we found in Skovlunde?"

"Busy. It was the uncle." He went on to explain the details of the case. Birgitte felt a pang of regret at not being there to see it through. They talked shop for 20 minutes or so, but it was obvious why Birgitte had called so Sven cut her off at one point and said, "They knocked you back."

She didn't say anything.

"Their official line is that you are not ready," he said, keeping his tone neutral, as if reciting a text. "They feel although your work in the field is exceptional, you still have a tendency to behave impetuously under stress. There were other candidates who had proved themselves more reliable."

Birgitte managed a nervous smile.

Sven said, "Personally, I think they've made a mistake, but it's not my choice to make. I'm sorry. I know it meant a lot to you."

Her smile had faded. She looked over the top of her computer, at nothing in particular, simply processing the news. She cleared her throat. "Well, that's that then."

"There will be other opportunities, Birgitte. You have to be patient."

She resisted the temptation to snap back that she wouldn't want to be impetuous, but she knew it wasn't Sven's fault. "I have to go," she said. "Thanks for the news. Keep me up to date on Skovlunde."

She disconnected the call before he could reply.

Xi Xi was sitting on the living room floor playing with one of the puppies. It scampered about on the rug, tearing at a short length of coloured rope. Xi Xi would grab the rope and the puppy would pull with all its might. She'd yank it back and forth, jerking the dog's neck as it refused to let go, then she would drop it and watch the pup shaking the rope like a bird with a worm, desperately trying to animate the toy so it could be destroyed again and again.

When Xi Xi heard the latch on the door turn, her eyes widened with fear. She swept the puppy up into her arms and ran for the door that led down to the kennels. She knew she wasn't supposed to let any of the puppies into the apartment but she had been so bored and was sure Janis wouldn't be home for hours. As she stepped carefully down the stairwell, she took her hand from the puppy's mouth, confident she'd slipped away unnoticed. The puppy thought it was game. It tried to chew on Xi Xi's fingers. Play time was over so she slapped the puppy hard on the nose. It wriggled in her grasp but had nowhere to go. Confused, it went soft in her arms, submissive – all its rage at the many punishments it had received in its short lifetime would be channelled at a later date. Until then it allowed itself to be carried back to its cage, listening to the whimpers and yapping of the other pups. Once inside it didn't bother to turn as it usually did as Xi Xi locked the cage door behind it.

Xi Xi turned off the light and ran back up the stairs. She looked about but the apartment was empty. Her heart was still beating fast with apprehension. The kitchen door flew open and Janis appeared with a bowl of ice-cream, her wide cat's eyes didn't register at first, but Xi Xi's entire body had flinched with the noise.

"Oh," said Janis coolly, "you're here."

Xi Xi could already sense that Janis was in one of her unpredictable dark moods. She didn't move. "I was sleeping before."

"Of course you were." Her voice was flat. She walked to the couch, tucking her legs up under her with the bowl in her lap. "Did you want some ice-cream?"

"No, thank you."

Janis reached across to the coffee table and found the remote for the TV. She turned it on. A live studio game-show was on. Janis was content with that. The volume was low but the apartment filled with the distant ocean's roar of an excited crowd as fresh-faced teenagers competed for points in an oversized obstacle course. Janis paid it no mind, instead savouring each mouthful of ice-cream.

Xi Xi didn't know which way to go. She suddenly wanted to leave. She knew it wasn't safe but going now could have incited the same wrath from Janis as staying. She went to the sideboard and began to wipe it down with a cloth even though it was already spotless. Behind her the gentle clacking of the spoon against the bowl was a sign that things might still be okay.

"Stop your fussing," Janis called out almost playfully.

Xi Xi's hand, which held the cloth, froze mid swipe.

"Come here. I want to talk to you."

Xi Xi crossed the floor and walked tentatively around the side of the couch. Janis was looking up at her. "Sit," she said, patting the couch beside her.

Xi Xi sat down.

"Closer, Darling. I'm not going to bite." But her smile was thin and her eyes flickered with a familiar glimmer. She rested the empty bowl on the coffee table.

Xi Xi's shoulders slumped as she picked at the hem of her dress.

"Stop fidgeting," Janis snapped. The words were softened with laughter that could have been released from a tin can. "You're always fidgeting. You'll make me nervous... and I've had such an awful day that I can't afford to be nervous. You know that."

"You want some tea?" Xi Xi asked, her voice barely audible over the sound of the studio audience who were laughing hysterically at something the compare had said.

Janis ran her fingers through Xi Xi's hair very gently. "No, Sweetheart. I don't want tea. I just want to sit quietly. My mind's been a buzz and I just want it to be still. You know what that's like, don't you?"

Xi Xi nodded plaintively. Janis pulled her in close to her and Xi Xi allowed herself to be held.

"I miss him so much. It's a physical ache. Do you understand?"

Xi Xi rested her head on Janis' breast and began to stroke her thigh the way she liked. And for the first time since her owner had come home she felt the stiffness in her own body fade.

"It's going to be okay, Sweetheart," Janis said. "Ian is going to come home and it's going to be okay."

Xi Xi could feel Janis' hand tighten in her hair. She had grabbed a clump and was now pulling her head back at an awkward angle. Xi Xi knew better than to scream.

"But until then," Janis spat, "we need to keep it together." Janis stood up still clutching Xi Xi by the hair. She dragged her off the couch to the living room where she had been playing with the puppy. Xi Xi didn't need to see the rope toy to know she'd left it in plain sight. Before she could thrust her hands out to protect herself, Xi Xi's face was being pressed into the rug with a brute force that had always surprised her. Janis wasn't a large woman but she possessed a rage that made her as strong as a tiger.

The resounding thud of her head being whacked against the concrete floor made her vision flicker with blackness. Janis was screaming something about order and happiness. The studio audience was laughing and calling out for more. Then she was being dragged to the bedroom. She knew what was coming next but no amount of trying would dissociate her mind from her body. She struggled to think of those rare moments in her childhood when she had experienced something akin to joy.

She landed on the bed and refused to open her eyes. Somewhere in her mind was an image that would allow her to survive what was about to come. She whimpered as it continued to elude her. She feared the pain but she feared the suffering without solace even more.

She slowly turned, praying to herself that her owner would suddenly change her mind as she had once or twice in the past but it was too late. Janis stood over her on the bed, her wide eyes blazing with a dragon's rage. The black phallus protruded from her waist like a sinister blade. And the last thing Xi Xi could picture before 'Ian' ripped off her dress and pinned her to the bed was the bedraggled face of the stuffed bunny she once held as a child. She closed her eyes and held the bunny close in her mind as the studio audience screamed for more.

CHAPTER THIRTEEN

A tall elderly European man stood with his hands behind his back, his shoulders slightly stooped, peering out at the ferries cutting across Victoria Harbour to Hong Kong Island. There was something to the angle of his head or perhaps the frailty of his body that reminded Birgitte of her father.

She was sitting on a bench seat near the Star Ferry Pier. It was mid morning on Sunday. She thought of Jan and their time together the previous fortnight. Had they got any closer in his old age? Or had the gulf that had always existed between them merely been bridged by a temporary fog of familiarity – forced together on an impromptu holiday by her mother? What would he have thought of her being knocked back for such an important promotion? She knew he wouldn't have blamed her directly. His criticism of her tended to take a more circuitous route. He would have highlighted the limited reasoning of the senior police in Copenhagen – a backhanded compliment that they couldn't see what was in front of them – then he would have suggested that to intentionally put your career in the hands of such people was a failing in itself. He would have patted her hand, as he did her mother when he felt she had fallen short of the mark in some way, and then reminded her that pride could blind the finest minds from seeing what was right in front of them.

She didn't like to think she had made a mistake putting herself forward for the promotion. Was it too soon? Possibly, in the eyes of outsiders. But Sven knew she was up to the task. Still, the rejection hurt more than she thought it would.

She checked her watch. 10.45am. Peter and his team would be across Fa Hui Park, waiting for the arrival of the young Chinese woman and her Rottweiler puppy. She and

Peter had discussed whether her own presence would have been a help or a hindrance. They erred on the side of caution. If Janis had been in the car at Fa Hui Park on Friday and had seen Birgitte following the young woman, then spotting her again this morning could ruin everything. Birgitte had given the team as detailed a description of the Chinese woman as she could.

The other complication was their unwillingness to use the child as bait. So they were basically hoping to spot the woman before she realised the rendezvous had fallen through. Peter had reasoned, it was safe to assume some of the kids she may have approached in the past hadn't turn up as planned for any number of reasons, responsible parenting being the obvious one. If the woman went on to meet up with Janis Pollack, then Birgitte and Peter's theory would be proved correct and they could pull both of them in for questioning, perhaps get a warrant for Janis' home, where ever that was.

According to the child, the proposed meeting had been set for 10.30am. It was now 10.50am. Birgitte's phone bleated. It was Peter. Nothing as yet. She could only imagine the tension that would exist between the three teams working across the site, analysing every face in the area, searching windows and vantage points. Were the watchers being watched? By 11.15am Peter texted to say the operation was over. No one had turned up or made their presence known. The three teams were being dispersed. He asked her to meet him at the office the following morning. She said she was sorry it hadn't gone differently, then put her phone back in her bag. She knew how frustrating it must be as a lead detective in such a complex case. She thought about what Peter had told her the previous day and really felt for him. He was an exceptional detective who deserved to be more advanced in his career. Rising through the ranks in Copenhagen obviously required certain skills which she was no longer sure she possessed, but answering to a slowly evolving Communist regime must have presented a completely different set of challenges.

She decided to head back to her room to write an apology to Sven for hanging up on him the day before. It had been childish and disrespectful of her. It wasn't Sven's fault she had been knocked back. As she turned to go she almost fell over a young Chinese girl who was staring up at her.

"Put your phone under the bench and get in the taxi." Her voice was calm but direct. She was pointing to a taxi that was waiting on Salisbury Road. Birgitte looked at the cab then back at the child, her heart beginning to pound. She looked about quickly but all she could see were tourists going about their day. She went to ask the girl if she could point to the person who had given her these instructions, but she cut her off. "There isn't much time. Put your phone under the bench and get in the taxi."

Birgitte drew her phone out of her bag, crouched down and slipped it behind a leg of the bench seat. She knew she was being watched and didn't have time to text Peter for help. The child pointed at the waiting taxi again. Birgitte approached and got in the back seat. The driver, an elderly Chinese man with a stern look on his face, pulled the car out from the curb without acknowledging his new passenger. She looked back through the rear window. The child hadn't moved. The cab swung round onto Nathan Road heading north. She asked the driver in English if he knew who was paying for the fare. He shook his head with miscomprehension. There was no point in talking to him any further. She tried to calculate her options and the possible outcomes but she soon realised she had little choice but to acquiesce in the demands of a stranger. The child's life was already at risk. She berated herself for not thinking faster on her feet. She should have grabbed the child and ran to the nearest police station.

But what if there was another child being held elsewhere and the girl was just the messenger? It was hopeless. And there was no way of signalling Peter. As far has he was concerned they wouldn't be in touch for another 24 hours.

Thirty-five minutes later the taxi pulled up on a busy narrow street in a rundown neighbourhood somewhere in the New Territories. After a while all the streets had begun to look the same to Birgitte. The driver grunted something in Cantonese. Birgitte figured he was telling her to get out, the ride was already paid for.

She watched him drive off and turn right at the next corner.

The street she was on was busy with local pedestrian traffic, people going about their day oblivious to the insanity that was playing out in their midst. She looked into the windows and doors of the surrounding businesses but saw nothing out of the ordinary. She cast her eyes upwards, scanning the first-floor windows. There, in a corner block across the street, she saw a white woman with ginger hair looking down at her. The woman was wearing a white silk bathrobe, barely pulled across her chest. There was something vaguely familiar about her face but it was hard to tell at this distance. Birgitte looked away, checked a few more windows then looked back. The woman waved to her playfully with her fingers. Birgitte realised she was staring at Janis Pollack, and worse still, she recognised her as the woman from the Central Ferry Pier, who had also bumped into her on Hollywood Road the following Saturday. Oh Christ, she thought, Janis had been following her each time. She was the reason the children knew where to find her. The realisation made her feel vulnerable, then incredibly angry.

She looked down at street level and saw a doorway. She crossed the street and pressed the buzzer by the door frame. The latch clicked open and the door was unlocked.

Birgitte peered up the dimly lit stairway. Janis was waiting for her at the top of the stairs. She looked imperious at this angle, a jaded Hollywood starlet stirred from a restless sleep. Birgitte climbed the stairs clutching her handbag. She was unarmed but figured Janis may not know this. She steadied her breathing. She had to stay calm, push her emotional responses out of the way. It was imperative she remained clinical and on guard.

Janis ran her fingers through her hair, lifting the silk against her bare skin. Birgitte could see she was naked underneath. There was a confidence to her demeanour that was disarming. It was as if she had nothing to worry about. Birgitte reached the landing. The two women were the same height, but Janis was longer in the legs. Janis leaned in and kissed Birgitte on the cheek before she had a chance to pull away. The woman possessed a curious odour that rankled her nostrils.

"Thank you for being so sensible," she said almost quietly. Her accent was British, but very different to Cripps', more like Talia Mackland. She stepped back and raised one hand in a gesture of welcome.

Birgitte looked about the converted apartment. None of it suggested a mind that was unravelling or that any struggle had ever taken place there.

"Where's the child?"

"She's safe. For the time being." Janis stepped across the polished concrete to a door against the far wall. "You'll have to bear with me, I didn't get a chance to feed my babies earlier. They'll tear one another apart if I don't get something down to them soon."

Birgitte followed her into the large industrial kitchen, unsure of what to do.

All of the steel benches were bare except for where Janis had been cutting up dark chunks of meat on a bloodied chopping board. She returned to the task, using a large carving knife to scrap a pile of flesh into a blue plastic bucket at her feet. "They love their protein."

She reached into a plastic crate on the bench and drew out another slab of meat which she proceeded to cut into smaller pieces.

Birgitte studied Janis carefully, eager to get her measure as quickly as possible. She was mid 30s, but looked older. Like Ian, there were curious anomalies to her features which were quite compelling. Her face was gaunt but wide, her cheeks high, and her eyes, which were a striking green, were just a little too far apart. In an absent gesture between strokes of the knife she brushed her fingers against her lips, leaving a bloody smear that jarred against the paleness of her complexion.

"All done," she said brightly as if working on a cooking show. She bent down, picked up the bucket and approached Birgitte. "You're much more beautiful up close."

"Why are you doing this?"

She didn't answer. "Come along. They're dying to meet you."

She held open the kitchen door. Birgitte glanced at the knife on the bench. It was too far away to be of any use. She stepped out into the apartment. Janis moved behind her to another door which opened on to a fire stairwell. They walked down together to the ground floor, through a door that revealed a corridor. Janis walked to the end and opened a third door. She turned on the light and was greeted by the deafening noise of an overcrowded kennel. Birgitte followed her down the stairs into the narrow room lined with steel cages. She thought of the girl she found in the abandoned dormitory and felt a shudder of disgust.

Janis walked between the cages flicking handfuls of meat through the mesh, sometimes taunting the dogs so they leapt up to grab the meat from her fingers. Soon enough the room fell silent as the dogs settled down to eat. At the far end Birgitte noticed the two adult Rottweilers. The pregnant one didn't bother with her food.

"Beautiful, aren't they?" she said rinsing the empty bucket out under a tap then washing her hands. "That's Snowflake – another batch on the way in a matter of weeks. I can barely keep up."

She dried her hands on an old pink towel and walked back to the bottom of the stairs. "After you."

Birgitte ascended the stairs with Janis close behind.

When they were back in the apartment Birgitte said, "You saw me in the park on Friday."

"Of course."

"So there was no rendezvous today."

"No child; no rendezvous," Janis said. She held up a hand for her to wait where she was before disappearing back into the kitchen. She returned a few moments later carrying two glasses of white wine. "I have to say, I've admired you for a long time." She handed one of the glasses to Birgitte then leaned back against a long side board which ran along the wall adjoining the kitchen. "You've been such a good sport. We couldn't have asked for better. Ian wasn't convinced at first. But it didn't take long."

"Why me?" Birgitte asked, trying to keep her voice steady.

"Pure luck, so please, don't blame yourself. The game would have continued with or without you. Your presence just added an element, ramped up the excitement."

Birgitte stared at her unable to decipher what she meant and genuinely disturbed by how close she had been to the killer all along. Again she took a quick look around the apartment for any signs that would help her determine the sort of person she was dealing with. She knew she needed to stay calm in order to work the room like a crime scene. There were no photos of Janis and Ian, no artworks on the wall. It was as if they were living a temporary existence or had no personal hobbies outside of the dogs they bred.

Janis smiled warmly at her curiosity. "When I realised you were in Hong Kong I couldn't believe it. Ian and I have been following all the greats – and Max Anders is one of the best."

The mention of the child killer's name jarred her. Janis obviously enjoyed the reaction but carried on as if it meant nothing. "To work with the woman who caught him was simply irresistible." She sipped her wine slowly, then said, "I'm going to write to him, you know, to see if he wants to compare notes."

"This is all just a game to you? Killing little children?"

"We don't kill them, Sweetheart," she said defensively. "We don't touch the little darlings. Never laid a finger on them."

Birgitte thought for a moment. "The dogs."

Janis smiled. "Fear is a terrific motivator, Birgitte. Do you mind if I call you Birgitte? Or should I call you Detective?"

Birgitte ignored the question.

"To be honest, we were never too sure how each one would play out," she continued, staring into her glass, "but they didn't disappoint. The first one crawled out that window in a flash. Gravity did the rest."

"It's still murder," Birgitte said bluntly.

"You should have seen Ian's face. He was almost disappointed it happened so fast. Then he burst out laughing and couldn't stop for ages. It was the happiest I'd seen him in years." Janis rested the glass on the side board and folded her arms beneath her breasts. "Do you know what it means to make someone so happy?"

When Birgitte didn't answer she looked away. "To think he was a going to try to move on without me."

Birgitte placed her wine glass on another wooden console that backed onto an old sofa. She had no

248

intention of drinking any of it but didn't want her reluctance to look too obvious. Janis had picked up her own glass and took another sip. "It's true," she said, with a tinge of sadness. "He left me back in England. Flew out here on his own. But I knew better. I knew he wouldn't be half the man he could be without my help. He sees that now, of course. If I think back – we've achieved great things together. Not wanting to sound American – but that's the power of love."

She smiled at the gaucheness of her own words.

"The child outside the garage?" asked Birgitte "What happened?"

"You, Sweetheart. For a moment there, you were more than we could handle. It certainly raised the stakes. You turned up before we were ready. That's not entirely true. My Ian was getting impatient, greedy even, bless him. He enjoyed the first three happenings so much he wanted to be in control of the fourth. I couldn't disappoint him but unfortunately, what he possesses in vigour he lacks in finesse. It was no bother, mind you. I thought my solution to the problem was quite inspired."

"Did you really think I'd be blamed for the death of the girl?"

"Not at all. You've missed the point entirely. We were just playing with you."

Birgitte decided it was time to take an angle. "The abduction at Fenlow," she said, "it also lacked your finesse."

Janis laughed. It sounded thin and brittle like cheap wind chimes. "Admittedly, Ian got a bit ahead of himself. He wanted the happenings to be more hands on. My fault, I gave him a taste of it with that fourth girl."

"I thought you said you didn't murder the children."

"Plans change, Birgitte."

"So what now?"

"We carry on. Ian will unfortunately do time for the abduction. And I will have to wait for him. But he can't be done for the murders."

"I thought the idea was to win your boyfriend back. Surely having him in jail isn't a victory."

"He's still mine. He's not going anywhere."

"And your game?"

"The game, Sweetheart, has been exhilarating."

She drained the last of her wine. They both turned as the front door opened. A tall Chinese woman entered the apartment using her own key. It was the woman from Fa Hui Park. She was wearing a body-hugging top and a tiny mini skirt and heels. She looked every bit the mid-level escort. She put her keys on the sideboard, eyeing Birgitte carefully.

Janis said, "Darling, this is the woman I've been telling you about."

The young woman moved across the room and kissed Janis on the lips. She noticed the blood and wiped her own lips nervously then moved behind Janis like a child behind her mother.

"Don't be shy, Xi Xi. This is Detective Birgitte Vestergaard." She stepped back so that the young woman was unprotected and said, "Detective, this is another of my triumphs – Xi Xi."

She ran her hands through the woman's hair. "I've feed the dogs. Could you whip down and make sure they're okay."

Xi Xi moved across the room, not looking at Birgitte. She quickly slipped out of her clothes, pulled on a t-shirt and shorts then left through the door by the kitchen, slamming it behind her. She clearly didn't like the way Janis was behaving in front of Birgitte.

"Apologies. She's a petulant little thing. Gets jealous over the slightest things."

"You used her to approach the children."

250

"She likes the game as much as we do."

"Does she know the outcome?"

"She's really not more than a child herself," Janis said with a wicked grin. "A naughty little child at times. It's what our clients love most about her – she dances delightfully between innocence and corruption."

Janis noted the slight confusion on Birgitte's face. "She doesn't live here rent free, Sweetheart. When I found her, the most she could do was give a passable blow job and fake an orgasm. You can't fake love if you don't know love, can you? Now, thanks to me, she's one of the most sought-after girls in the high-end market. That's my doing, Sweetheart. I made her." Her voice had thickened with malice. "And I made Ian. I am their reason for being. And they both fucking know it. Neither of them will leave me any time soon."

"So that's what this is all about," said Birgitte "your insecurities."

Janis flashed a look of hatred which alarmed and informed the detective. "Don't psychobabble me, you trumped up little bitch. I'm providing for you as much as I'm providing for them."

"How do you figure that?"

"When people realise what Ian and I have achieved over the years – this will go down as your biggest case."

"What is it exactly that you've achieved? Scaring a few children into fatal situations is hardly an accomplishment. Anyone can scare a child."

"They could, Detective, but they don't. Ian and I live on the other side of your moral boundaries. We celebrate our union by exploring the unacceptable. And let me tell you, it's the most exhilarating experience you'll never have."

"And he would have achieved nothing without you?"

"I opened his mind to the possibilities. The desire was always there. I simply had to unlock his imagination."

"How many children in the West Midlands?"

251

Janis smiled proudly. "You've been talking to our friend Mr Cripps."

Birgitte didn't like her tone. It was too triumphant. "What do you know of him?"

"He's a grubby little a perve with a nasty case of yellow fever."

"He knew about your activities in Walsell."

"I know. I'll give him that much. But he had delusions of grandeur, was convinced that our story was going to be the making of him."

"Had? What have you done with him?"

"Five, is the answer you were looking for."

"What?"

"Five. The number of children in the West Midlands. If you'd ever met any of them you'd know they were better off dead. None of them were showing much promise. We did them a favour. Of course, Mr Cripps didn't see it that way."

"Where is he?"

"He struck me as a lonely man. Do you think if he ever knew real love, he would have bothered chasing people like me and Ian? Still, I must say I was surprised how much my babies loved him."

It was an odd thing to say – Birgitte couldn't picture Cripps as a dog lover much less a man who would play with the dogs of someone he reviled so much. She thought of Janis washing out the bucket downstairs and suddenly realised Cripps' fate, then immediately became aware of her own. She was alone in an apartment with a serial killer who put Max Anders in the shade. Janis's eyes flickered as Birgitte's demeanour altered ever so slightly. It had given her a rush of pleasure to watch a famous detective finally enter the world she had created for all of them.

Birgitte wondered how long it would take before Peter even knew she was in trouble.

The inspector was sitting across from Ian Hurley in a bare interview room deep within Stanley Prison. Since being charged, Hurley had been denied bail and was transferred from the Temporary Holding Area in Tsim Sha Tsui Police Station to the notorious prison on the far side of Hong Kong Island.

Hurley looked calm, his face was still bruised and swollen but all the bandages had been removed. He sat with his hands cuffed to a metal table. His loose drab prison garb gave him the curious appearance of a man who had discovered spiritual awareness, willingly rejecting all his worldly possessions rather than his access to them being denied by the state. A tall, thin, armed guard in two shades of khaki and a blue baseball hat stood at ease by the door.

Peter knew it was a matter of patience and persistence, but he was running out of time. The family of the second victim, Jenny Lieuw, had confirmed the silver-plated bracelet he had found in the alley in Hung Hom definitely belonged to their daughter. The fact that it was lying, broken, so far from the harbour's edge raised immediate concerns. They said that Jenny loved the bracelet and wouldn't have removed it and she certainly wouldn't have left it broken on the ground. They were convinced their daughter hadn't died in an accident and when Peter couldn't provide any further information they went straight to the media for help. The city awoke to blanket coverage across all media platforms that there was a child killer stalking innocent victims across Hong Kong. Commentators were demanding answers as to why it had taken so long to connect the deaths of four children, did they have a suspect, and was any of this related to the British man arrested for abduction of Catherine Yi earlier in the week. The police switchboard was inundated with calls. Chief Inspector Li was furious that Peter had taken so long to chase up the bracelet angle because it was proving so costly, but he had to accept that given how much had happened in the past few days it was understandable that such a minor detail could be overlooked. His own superiors weren't so forgiving. They were all now under considerable pressure. The atmosphere in the office for a Sunday was tense. Peter had spent the morning chasing authorisation for an interview request with Hurley through the Department of Justice. As soon as it was granted he'd jumped in his car and driven across the harbour to the other side of Hong Kong Island.

Much to his surprise, Peter discovered on arrival that Hurley had declined his right to a lawyer being present. Without Stanthorpe there to block questions, the interview could be far more fruitful, but he also knew Hurley wasn't about to just blurt out everything he'd done. Peter knew he had to come at his subject from multiple angles, testing weaknesses in his story, finding out which topics riled him and which ones made him swagger. All the while building a picture of the man in his own head. He needed to lure Hurley into a position in which he was more likely to incriminate himself.

Previous interviews had shown Hurley was undoubtedly a challenge. He was naturally reserved, comfortable with long silences and felt no need to portray himself in any particular way in the hope of influencing other peoples' perceptions. But Peter had the impression there was a ground spring of rage beneath the steady exterior.

In fact, he could hear it now in the man's voice when questioned about Janis.

"I told you," he said between gritted teeth. "We had a fight and she fucked off. I haven't spoken to her in weeks."

"What day did she leave?"

"I can't remember, a few weeks back."

254

"Is she still in Hong Kong?"

"How the fuck would I know and why would I care?"

"Was it her idea to come to Hong Kong?"

"No. I came by myself."

"She came before or after?"

"After."

"Why Hong Kong?"

"I heard the weather was balmy."

"Did you have work lined up?"

"A friend of a friend told me he knew someone who was looking for a mechanic who could specialise in British cars."

"Do you have this friends name?"

"John Smith."

Peter didn't bother writing it down. "Why did Janis follow you here?"

"You'd have to ask her."

"The address you provided on official documents was false."

He shrugged.

"Where are you living?"

"At the garage.

"Is Janis living at the garage?"

"I told you she fucked off."

"Was she living with you at the garage?"

"Sure."

"There was no evidence of either of you living at the garage when we searched the property."

"I keep a clean house."

"Does the owner of Mason's Garage know you are living there?"

"He lives overseas."

"We know." He didn't let on they'd had trouble contacting him. "When was the last time you spoke with him?"

"When he hired me?"

"He doesn't check on you?"

"Business is good. He doesn't need to. As long as the numbers add up, he keeps to himself. And that's the way I like it."

"Why did you abduct Catherine Yi from the Fenlow International School for Girls?"

"I don't know what you're talking about." He had stuck to the same line whether his lawyer was present or not.

"You were found at Our Lady of the Shining Light by PI Kwok with the girl in a cage. You're hardly in a position to deny you abducted her."

"Like I've already said," he replied with a tired grin, "I happened to be in the neighbourhood when she found me."

"Who was driving the car when to you took her off the street?"

"Jimmy Saville," he said with a leer.

"Was Janis driving the car?"

He shook his head with disgust. The questions were beginning to grate on his nerves.

Peter changed tack. "The dog."

"What dog?"

"The dog that attacked PI Kwok, did it belong to you or Janis?"

"I can't recall any dog."

"Does Janis own a dog?"

"You'd have to ask her."

"You can't recall whether she owned a large Rottweiler?"

"She might have."

"How would you describe your relationship with Janis?"

"Over."

"But when you were together?"

He shrugged. "She was alright, kept my motor running."

"You said in a previous interview you couldn't achieve an erection due to your injuries." He checked his notes. "A motorbike accident, I believe."

"That's right."

"So how does she keep your motor running?"

"It's just a figure of speech."

"So you didn't have a sexual relationship with your girlfriend?"

"I kept her happy."

"Can't have been easy... for her."

"Like I said, I kept her happy."

"She must be a very patient woman."

He smirked at this. "You have no idea."

"What makes you say that?"

Again he shook his head and looked away.

Peter stood up and officially terminated the interview.

"I'll be back shortly to continue."

"Suit yourself."

He motioned to the guard who opened the interview room door for him. He walked through the facility to an outdoor area reserved for staff of the prison. Over the clanging of metal doors and the distant hollering of bored prisoners, he could hear the South China Sea pushing against the rocky coastline of the island. He pulled out his phone and called Birgitte's number. He only got her voice mail, which struck him as odd. He'd left three messages already. He knew she didn't expect to talk again until the next morning but he was surprised that she wouldn't be answering at all. He tried the journalist Cripps' number to see if he'd seen the Danish detective in the last few hours. It went straight to voice mail as well. Something didn't feel right. He rang the Conran Hotel and explained that he needed to get a hold of Detective Vestergaard. He was put through to a manager who explained she was seen leaving earlier that morning at around 9.30am and hadn't come back since. He had last spoken to her at around 11am. It was now close to 5pm.

Something wasn't right.

He quickly returned to the room where Hurley was sitting silently, and officially recommenced the interview. Hurley tipped his head forward to rub his eyes then settled back into his chair.

"Your passport," the inspector said.

"What about it?"

"It says your name is Ian Hurley."

"So?"

"We know your name is Ian Horace. Which means you're travelling on false documents. Who provided the false passport?"

Hurley stared at him. The change of pace was unsettling. "It's legit. I got it back in England. You'll have to talk to them."

"We are. We are also talking to the British military about your time in Afghanistan, particularly in and around Sangin. And we are talking to the Metropolitan Police in the West Midlands."

"What for?" Ian tried to appear nonchalant but Peter could tell he was rattled.

"We are making enquiries about your time in Walsell."

"Wouldn't think you'd find any records of an Ian Hurley living in that shit hole."

"It won't be difficult to prove you are Ian Horace, and once we do, I assure you there will be considerable interest in what you've been up to that extends way beyond the recent abduction."

"So let's say you convince yourselves I'm this Ian Horace. What the fuck does that have do with the price of sardines?"

"Patterns of behaviour, Mr Hurley."

Hurley shuffled in his seat but didn't say anything.

258

"We know that Janis Pollack lived in Walsell and that she bred Rottweilers. We know that she was in a long-term relationship with a man who went by the name of Ian Horace. We know he was questioned by Metropolitan Police into the disappearance of several children around the Walsell area. During that time they were suspected of being part of a paedophile ring. Nothing could be proved mind you. Shall I continue?"

"Do what you fucking like."

"We know that this Ian Horace served 16 months with the British Armed Forces, spent several months in Afghanistan, was shot by a shepherd boy and shipped back to England. We know the boy was a victim of child abuse that is apparently rampant in the local community. There is no evidence that this Ian Horace abused the boy himself but it certainly looks like they had some sort of relationship. We know that Ian Hurley turned up in Hong Kong three years ago and that Janis Pollack arrived a few months later. According to official documents you both provided the same false address. Now, are you beginning to see how this will play out when we prove you are Ian Horace, a man who has had brushes with investigations into paedophilia in two other countries outside Hong Kong?"

"Enlighten me."

"Janis is the link, Mr Hurley. She was with you in Walsell, she nursed you when you got back from Afghanistan and she's been with you in Hong Kong. Janis breeds Rottweilers. The fourth child, the one found with Detective Vestergaard had been bitten repeatedly by a dog, probably a Rottweiler. The fifth victim was found with you at Our Lady of the Shining Light Girls School with a Rottweiler. Whether you deny having one or not, two police officers place you at the scene with such a dog in your possession."

"I don't know nothing about no murders."

Peter could feel himself getting frustrated by Hurley's flat denials in the face of so much damning evidence. It was a risk to bring up the information he had about England and Afghanistan. Legally, he was only supposed to be questioning him about the abduction, but he had a creeping suspicion that Birgitte was in danger. He didn't have time for legality. If Hurley had chosen to waive his right to a lawyer, Peter was going to make the most of it.

"Mr Hurley, we know you have been working with Janis Pollack to procure local children. You may not be able to abuse them sexually," he corrected himself, "probably because you can't abuse them sexually, you have been luring them to perform other duties. We know that you use the promise of a free Rottweiler puppy to get them to approach Detective Vestergaard." His voice was getting angrier and louder. "And we know these children have died in apparent accidents that would suggest they have been frightened into dangerous, fatal situations, probably by someone holding a large, ferocious animal, such as a Rottweiler. We know you have killed at least four children in the past two weeks," he was now yelling in Hurley's face. "We know everything about you."

"Yet here we are," Ian responded coolly. "No closer to charging me with anything but the obvious. You know nothing." He was grinning with malice at the inspector. "I virtually handed myself in. You can't lay claim to any victory there."

"And what can you lay claim to, Mr Hurley? Your girlfriend seems to be the one doing all the organising. Would you have been able to do any of this without her?"

Ian scoffed at the question but Peter could see it bothered him. "She must be something, your Janis. The way she plays you so professionally."

Ian ignored him.

"What happened, Mr Hurley, did you start making decisions for yourself. Is that how you justify 'virtually handing yourself in'? If you stuck to your girlfriend's plan, you'd still be out and about."

"And you'd still be looking for me with your head up your arse."

It was his first admission. Peter went on the front foot. "Has she always tidied up your mess for you?"

"You don't know what you're talking about."

"Really? It seems pretty obvious to me," he said, deciding to pursue Birgitte's theory. "You're nothing without her. She has made you who you are. But she's the real killer. You're just the guy who she entertains. No?"

"You have no idea who you're messing with."

"Tell me. Is she really such a force to be reckoned with?"

Ian shook his head. "I just wish she was here to listen to this nonsense."

"She'll be here soon enough. Sounds like it should be her we're after and not you. I tend not to waste my time with the little fish, Mr Hurley."

"Oh fuck off," he screamed at the inspector. "I don't need her. I came here on my own, under my own fucking steam. She wants you to believe I can't do anything without her, but I've done plenty. I didn't ask her to come here!"

"But she did." Peter felt a surge of adrenalin as he realised he had hammered his first wedge between Ian and Janis. "And here you are. Locked up in a cell and she's out there doing whatever she pleases. What if she never came to Hong Kong? Do you ever think about that? Would you even thought about abducting someone? From what we've learned about your past – those days were over the moment you got shot in Afghanistan. That's right Mr Hurley, we're not accepting your motorbike story, and the British military are providing evidence to that effect as we speak."

261

The realisation blackened his demeanour. "You don't know... you... you know nothing about me... "

"You can't satisfy women. You can't indulge your own desires. That must be hard for you. To be frank, I'm surprised you're still here."

"Guess I'm lucky."

"How so?"

"I've got the love of a good woman to keep me on track."

"I thought you said she'd 'fucked off'."

"Well, she has but who knows... we might sort it out."

Peter knew he'd caught him in another lie. "It sounds to me like she is the one who keeps you on track and leads you astray. You must feel a little lost without her."

"I'm doing fine without her."

"Locked up in a cell with at least a five-year sentence hanging over your head." He let that sink in. "Do you think she blames you for the predicament you're in."

"How the fuck would I know?"

"It seems that your impulsiveness got you arrested. If you'd stuck to her plan you might still be outside. Has she always had to reign you in?"

Ian didn't answer.

"Sounds to me like she knows when to push you on and when to hold you back."

"That's half the fun of having a good woman, Inspector. They bring out the best in us, don't you think?"

"Do you think she'll be loyal to you, when we catch her? You know her better that we do, obviously. Does she strike you as a survivor? In my experience with women, when they feel trapped they come out clawing and whoever is in their way is at risk of getting hurt. Does that sound familiar, Mr Hurley?"

Ian smiled. "I wouldn't want to be on the wrong side of her."

"Do you think that's where you'll be if we catch her? Think about it, if the only thing standing between her and a life in prison is you, do you really think she'll continue protecting you?"

He snarled at the inspector. "She doesn't protect me. I'm my own man."

Peter nodded down to the man's crotch. "Well, almost."

Ian lunged at the inspector but the cuffs held him back. Peter didn't flinch. The guard moved toward the prisoner but Peter held up his hand. "Why did you join the army, Mr Hurley? Did Janis convince you to get out of the country because the Metropolitan Police in the West Midlands were getting too close?"

Ian looked away, now wary about what he was saying.

Peter continued. "Just think, if you hadn't gone to Afghanistan you wouldn't have been shot. Her advice isn't always so sound is it? Is that why you came to Hong Kong without her? You realised that all the bad things happening in your life began with her. You wanted a fresh start, a chance to find out who you really are, without Janis constantly goading you on. But she turned up again, didn't she? Couldn't let you go. The killings were her idea weren't they? You just wanted to get on with your life but she got under your skin again, didn't she? She knows you need a rush every now and then to keep your head screwed on straight – and thanks to her, in effect, sex is no longer an option. She had to find something else. So she found you the ultimate rush – killing children in apparent accidents."

Ian was glaring at him, breathing heavily through his nose like a bull preparing to charge.

Peter knew he was on to something. "Must have been a thrill at first, yes? Watching a child die, knowing there was no direct evidence linking you to his death. Did you feel powerful?"

"You have no idea."

Peter leaned back and grinned. It was time to change tack again. "I had a friend at school who had a bad girlfriend. We were in our final year. She was something else, not conventionally pretty but she had a way about her that made good men behave irrationally. Even my teachers got nervous around her. She took a liking to my friend and he felt 10 foot tall. He would have done anything for her and he told her as much. You know what she did? She told him to prove it. She started goading him with silly tasks, just small things at first, standing up to teachers, stealing school equipment – each completed task was rewarded with more of her, but it was never as much as he'd hoped. So he kept trying to impress her. She showed him a side of himself he never knew existed. It was intoxicating. Until he got expelled for arson. He could have gone to jail. And if she had her way, he would have walked in there under his own steam, deluding himself she'd be outside waiting for him, remaining faithful. Turns out she was the one who gave him up. First sign of pressure from the police and she blamed him for the fire and several other crimes he knew nothing about." Peter laughed at his own recollection, then stared at Ian. "Did you have any idea what you were capable of before you met Janis?"

He didn't answer. He didn't need to; Peter could tell he had hit his mark. "How many doors to your soul did she open? Did it ever occur to you some doors are best kept closed. Once you step through them it is very difficult to find your way back, particularly if the only familiar sight is your girlfriend tempting you to keep making the wrong choices. It sounds to me like you almost got clear of her when you came to Hong Kong, and all she's done is lure you through more doors. I actually feel sorry for you."

"Save your fucking pity," he growled, his voice low and guttural. "I am what I am. Always fucking have been, since as long as I can remember. I've seen things you'll never have to see. I grew up on the other side of those doors. I live in the darkness beyond a thousand fucking doors and you will never reach me."

Peter was stunned by what he was hearing but did his best to conceal it.

Ian looked about the interview room, but he wasn't really there anymore. His mind was somewhere else deep in his own past. His lips began to move. He muttered incoherently. Spittle formed in the corners of his mouth. The veins in his neck bulged and wriggled as his muscles tensed and his fists clenched. He pulled steadily against his cuffs and began to growl like a dog through his teeth. He began to howl. The howl turned into a scream of blind rage and pain that filled the room. A lifetime of horror had come back through his psyche like a fork of lightening.

Half an hour later Peter driving at speed away from the prison. He got on his radio to PI Kwok. "We have an address for Janis Pollack. It's in the New Territories."

Her voice crackled through the speakers. "He talked?"

"He wept like a baby. Birgitte was right – it's Janis who is behind it all. And now we have her. Get the team together immediately. I haven't been able to get a hold of Birgitte all day. I think she may be in trouble."

CHAPTER FOURTEEN

As the streetlights flickered on outside, the interior of Janis' apartment appeared even darker. Janis moved about the living area, turning on lamps, filling the large room with elongated shadows. Her silk robe made a gentle swishing sound as she walked.

Birgitte was still standing by the console at the back of the sofa. She knew Janis had brought her here to kill her. It was merely a question of when and how. If Xi Xi was a part of the plan, Birgitte would struggle to defend herself from two of them at once, but something about the young woman's behaviour had suggested she was naive to Janis's intentions.

Birgitte looked at the front door. She could attempt to escape but knew Janis would expect as much and that would put her at risk. It could also ruin her only chance of detaining Janis herself. Birgitte could put an end to all of this tonight, if she played it smart.

"You're not unlike him," she said.

"Unlike who, Sweetheart?" Janis moved back into the light that fell short of Birgitte's feet, her complexion glowed a sickly yellow, the smear of blood on her lips a dirty brown.

"Anders," replied Birgitte.

"Really? That's generous of you, Detective. I wouldn't have thought you held him in such high regard."

She went to take Birgitte's glass but noticed it hadn't been touched. Rather than make a point of it she turned and collected her own.

"He's quite remarkable in some respects," Birgitte continued. "Apparently there's a queue of PhD students wanting to write theses on him."

Janis paused at the kitchen door with her glass in her hand. "Does he indulge them?"

"No. He's not interested."

266

Janis considered this then pushed through the kitchen door with her shoulder. Again Birgitte looked at the front door. All she needed to do was get to a phone and Peter would hit the building within the hour with every officer he could muster. But anything could happen within that hour. Losing Janis Pollack at this point was not an option.

Janis reappeared with the bottle of white in one hand and her half-filled glass in the other.

"I don't know," she mused, answering a question in her own head. "I kind of like the idea of teaching the kiddies a thing or two. Letting them peek behind the curtain." She raised the bottle to Birgitte, who shook her head politely. Janis shrugged and placed it on the sideboard by her glass.

"He wanted people to see what he was capable of," Birgitte said. "Wanted them to understand that his particular form of power was a rare and beautiful thing. It should be respected, admired."

"You talked to him much, did you?"

"I interviewed him several times before the trial."

"And he was willing to indulge you with the innermost workings of his mind?" she asked with a note of scepticism in her voice.

"I caught him, didn't I? Believe it or not, he actually respected me for that."

"Caught him? And how did you catch him, Detective? Remind me. That's right, you let three children perish under the floor boards of a house so you could parade your trophy in front of the waiting media. I think you have more in common with him than I do. Do you ever think about that?"

There was no point mentioning the inquest. Janis had clearly followed every aspect of the case.

"I made my choice, and I've lived with the consequences. So does Max Anders."

"Bully for you, Sweetheart," she said flatly, clearly bored by Birgitte's attempts to appeal to her ego. "You do realise you are now a part of something much bigger than him, don't you?"

Birgitte didn't answer.

"Anders was notorious in Denmark, but only freaks like me bother to read about him from outside of Scandinavia. What I've created spans three continents."

"Your parents must be so proud."

She laughed at this. "My parents are still sitting in their horrid little workers' cottage, sipping tea in the afternoon and complaining about austerity measures. They think I'm in my bedroom playing with dolls. No, my parents have no comprehension of who I am or what I'm capable of." She ran her fingers through her hair in frustration at the memory. "They thought Ian was a 'sweet thing', 'a little dark, mind you, Love', as my mother would say. We could have dragged a child's corpse into their kitchen and all they'd say was "doesn't talk much, does he?'."

She inhaled deeply through her nostrils as if clearing the thought from her mind. The side door opened and Xi Xi came back into the apartment. She looked sullen and unsure of herself.

"Thought we'd lost you, Pet," Janis said facetiously. "The babies all good?"

She nodded, then walked into the kitchen.

"She doesn't know, does she?" asked Birgitte, suddenly realising her chances looked better than before.

Janis stared at her, considering her answer. "Xi Xi has been a crucial element of our little game, Detective. We couldn't have accomplished half so much without her."

"But she doesn't know you've killed the children."

"She performs best on limited information."

"She's been luring the children into your web and has had no idea what you intended to do with them. What did you tell her?"

"What can I say? She's a child herself. Games don't have to make sense to children as long as they feel included.

They're even more engaged when they think there will be a reward at the end."

When Xi Xi came out of the kitchen with a glass of milk and piece of toast on a plate, she sensed the two women had been talking about her.

The dark-haired woman was looking at her like she felt sorry for her. She didn't like that. She glared at Janis, who looked away.

"Go and eat on the bed. We're talking," Janis said abruptly.

Xi Xi pulled a face at her benefactor, only because she was looking elsewhere, and moved towards the bed at the far side of the apartment.

"Xi Xi," Birgitte said warmly.

The young woman stopped and turned.

"Do as your told, Xi Xi," snapped Janis, "or you'll get what for."

She winced at the threat but didn't move.

"Did you talk to a young girl today down near the Promenade of Stars?"

Xi Xi looked at Janis for guidance. She didn't know whether she was supposed to answer.

"A pretty young girl, about 10 years old. Do you know where she is?"

Before Xi Xi could answer Janis said, "Detective Vestergaard is a police officer Xi Xi. You know what police officers do?"

Xi Xi suddenly looked nervous. She moved behind the bed and realised she'd backed herself into a corner. Janis kept at her. "They take you away, don't they? This police officer wants to take you away." Janis moved towards her. "Away from here. And away from me."

Xi Xi glared at Birgitte with genuine resentment, unsure if this stranger had the power or intent to do what Janis was accusing her of. She didn't look like she was here to take her away.

"I'm not going to hurt you, Xi Xi," Birgitte said. "I just want to know where the little girl has gone."

"I let her go," she said nervously.

Janis looked ropable.

Xi Xi started breathing heavily. "I let her go. You didn't tell me to keep her."

"It's okay, Sweetheart," Janis said, moving in behind her. "You did well." She put her arms around the young woman's waist and held her, whispering in her ear to console her.

"Where are the other children, Xi Xi?" asked Birgitte, with a tone of genuine curiosity. "The other children you spoke to, did you let them go?"

"Enough," said Janis.

"Or did you lead them to Janis, here?"

Xi Xi covered her face with her hands, horribly confused.

Birgitte said, "Where are they now, Xi Xi? Have they just disappeared?"

"I don't know." She turned and looked at Janis. "Where are they? Where did they go? Did they like their puppies? Which ones did you give them?" She couldn't comprehend the direction the conversation was taking. "All the puppies are downstairs. Which ones did they take?"

"Other ones, Sweetheart, don't worry about it."

"You have other puppies?" She looked back at Birgitte.

"Janis took the children, Xi Xi."

Xi Xi's eyes widened then the lights in apartment suddenly stretched and warped as Janis picked up a bedside lamp and drove the base into the young woman's temple. She collapsed to the floor at her feet. Janis held the bloody lamp in her hands, shining the light up under her chin like a kid with a torch telling horror stories round a campfire. "You fucking cunt," she screamed at Birgitte. "You fucking horrid little cunt."

270

Birgitte grabbed her wine glass and smashed it across the console leaving the jagged stem jutting from her hand. She moved back and steadied herself, waiting for the onslaught.

Janis dropped the lamp and moved around the bed slowly, watching the shard in Birgitte's hand carefully. "I had such hopes for you and me," she said. "We could have achieved so much more than this."

To Birgitte's surprise she kept coming towards her unarmed. Birgitte backed up a little, but Janis kept coming, offering her wrists. "You want to do this, don't you? Bring an end to it all?"

Birgitte moved the broken glass back to minimise the risk of cutting her. It was counter intuitive. She knew Janis was a threat to her safety, but she couldn't attack an unarmed person with a potentially lethal weapon.

Janis walked straight up to her and embraced her, holding her tight to her body, pushing her back against the opposite console until she was unable to move. She whispered in her ear, "Do it. Thrust it into me. I want to feel you inside of me. Do it."

She pulled Birgitte's hair back so she could look into her eyes. Birgitte stared back at her, repulsed by the forced intimacy. There was a damp, sour smell to Janis' skin and breath which made Birgitte gag. She could feel the woman's bare leg pressed up between her thighs. One of her hands was running down the length of Birgitte's spine. Birgitte's body was tense and unrelenting. The stem of the glass broke in her hand. She dropped it to the floor and pushed Janis' face away, smearing the woman's cheek with her own blood. That sight of the wound aroused Janis even more. She was wild, her eyes brilliant with a carnal rage.

Birgitte realised that Janis was physically much stronger than she had originally assumed. Pressed against the console, she struggled to get a footing which meant she

271

couldn't use her own weight to push Janis back. She could feel one of Janis's hands under her right thigh. She lifted the detective up onto the console, spreading Birgitte's legs with the force of her body. She then grabbed Birgitte's lower back and pulled her towards her so her back was at an awkward angle. Clearly Birgitte wasn't the first person Janis had overpowered.

Janis was panting heavily with the exertion, the acrid smell of her breath soiling the air between them. She grabbed Birgitte's wrist and lifted her hand to the light. The wound from the broken glass was deep; it needed several stitches. Birgitte grit her teeth and suppressed a scream as Janis pulled the hand towards herself and began to smear the detective's blood across her own breasts, staring at the pattern of dark smears. She was in a trance-like state, but had done nothing to relinquish her hold. Birgitte remembered her self-defence training – there was no point opposing an immovable force, it would simply drain her of much-needed energy. She closed her eyes and allowed her body go limp in Janis's grip. She fell into the woman's arms, her muscles softening. Janis sensed the change and pulled her in closer. Birgitte didn't know how far she was willing to acquiesce to create a window of opportunity. She could feel Janis' fingers undoing her shirt, her clammy hand inside her bra. Then they both heard a muffled bleating from across the room.

Janis froze. She looked over shoulder. The bleating continued. It was a phone somewhere in the apartment. She stepped back from Birgitte, slightly dazed at being ripped back into reality.

"Stay," she said, holding up one finger. She moved across the room to the living area and began searching the couch and surrounding areas wildly. Birgitte pressed her hand to her stomach to stem the bleeding.

Janis found a handbag. The bleating grew louder. She rifled through it till she drew out the phone. She looked at

272

it oddly as if it was doing something a phone shouldn't do. She held it to her ear. The bleating stopped. She listened intently, glaring at Birgitte, then slowly lowered the phone and killed the connection.

"I guess we won't have time to get to know one another after all."

Peter was baffled and more than a little frustrated. Someone had answered the call but then just hung up. He was standing with his team in a one-bedroom apartment in Kwai Fong. The place was vacant, as if it had never been used – no furniture, no appliances, no signs of life, except for a mobile phone connected to a charger plugged into the far wall of the living room. On a post-it note was a number. His officers had secured the rooms in a matter of minutes. He had looked down at the phone, considering his options, then decided to make the call. It was the only way to find out what it all meant. And now he regretted his decision.

He turned to Lindy. "Trace that number immediately."

The probationary inspector grabbed her own phone and began patching through the details to a desk in the head office.

Peter paced about the room trying to think. It had all been an act – Ian's breakdown, the incoherent weeping, the willingness to divulge his girlfriend's whereabouts. The inspector had just sent a signal to someone, most probably Janis Pollack. And the only reason the signal was called for was because Peter had played his hand. In his desperation to break Ian Hurley, he had told the mechanic exactly what the police knew. A net had been drawn tight enough to enclose him but not so tight as to prevent his accomplice escaping if she was given fair warning.

He quickly made a call to the relevant authorities to be on the lookout for a white British woman travelling as Janis Pollack. It would be passed onto immigration desks at airports and border controls. He looked over at Lindy who was still on hold. Where the hell was Birgitte? Did she have any idea what was playing out? He called out to Lindy, "Get them to trace Birgitte's mobile as well."

Janis stood in the living room talking to herself. "It's not ideal. None of it's ideal. That's why we made the plan." She looked over at Birgitte, who hadn't moved from the console. "Such a pity. I wanted more from you... Still, I should be grateful." She turned and looked at Xi Xi lying prone on the floor by the bed. She closed her eyes momentarily and shook her head with disappointment. "Stupid. Stupid. Stupid." Her voice was becoming shrill. "I wanted more from all of you." She took a deep breath. "Stick to the plan."

Birgitte watched Janis as she collected herself. The call had obviously disturbed her. She considered making a break for the kitchen to grab the knife. But with only one hand she was limited in her ability to go on the offensive.

"Right," announced Janis, as if talking to a group of Girl Guides, "I need you to understand what will happen if you don't do everything I say. There is a child, in a room, somewhere... the details are not important at this point. But if you don't do as I say, that child will die, horribly. Are we clear so far?"

Birgitte nodded.

"I need you to go down to the kennels and stay there. I have so many things I need to do and I just can't have you sitting there watching me."

"My hand," Birgitte said calmly. "I'm losing a lot of blood. I need something to protect my hand."

"Yes, yes of course. Your hand. I almost forgot. Don't move." She ran into the bathroom and came back out with a bandage which she tossed to Birgitte. "I look a fright, don't I?"

274

Her robe was still open and the blood on her face and breasts and dried in dark smears. "Can't go out looking like this. First things first. Go down to the kennels."

Birgitte finished wrapping her hand as best she could. Janis held open the door. As Birgitte moved past her, Janis reached out and touched her hair. Birgitte paused.

"It could have been different. You and me. But I have to think of Ian now. You understand, don't you?"

Birgitte descended the stairs. At the bottom she stopped and turned. Janis was watching her with a yearning in her eyes. "That's it, Darling. Go through the door. It will lock behind you."

As Birgitte opened the door the narrow room erupted with barking. She turned on the light and stepped inside. The door swung shut automatically behind her. She couldn't hear the door at the top of the stairs closing but she knew Janis had gone back into the apartment. She slumped to her knees, grateful to be alive but overwhelmed by the afternoon's events. Her hand throbbed and she couldn't stop thinking about what Janis had said. Was there a child whose life was at risk? Janis' tone hadn't been convincing. It was as if she was just saying it, because she knew how Birgitte would react. And what could she do now? The puppies leapt at the sides of the cages, their tails wagging. In the corner Snowflake panted heavily, only hours away from giving birth to a new litter. Nero glared at her from the corner.

Janis showered quickly, washing the blood from her skin. She was almost sad to see it drain away, the final traces of what could have been. But there was no point having a plan if they didn't stick to it. And god knew, at this stage, her life depended on sticking to the plan.

She dressed quickly, a plain dark skirt, a neat shirt and flat shoes. Nothing that would catch attention. She stepped over Xi Xi as she went to her bedside table. She drew out her passport, a wad of cash and new phone. She crouched down, and ran her fingers through Xi Xi's hair. "Silly girl. I could have helped you become more than this."

She gave the room a once over from the front door, her bag slung over her shoulder. So this was it. It was time to move on, again. Ian would be okay, she told herself. He was strong enough to do his time. And she would wait for him, from wherever she landed. It was a pity to leave her babies behind, but she knew they would be looked after, or at the very least, put down humanely.

Out on the street she hailed a passing cab. It pulled over. She opened the back door and leaned in.

"Heathrow Airport?"

The driver, a tired young Chinese man, was in no mood for silly tourists. He didn't even bother answering. He simply accelerated, driving away, the back door closing automatically. Janis smiled as the cab rounded a bend, carrying the phone which had bleated earlier in the foot-well of the back seat. The police would find the apartment soon enough, but would waste valuable time and resources chasing her phone. Satisfied, she made her way quickly to the nearest main road and hailed another cab.

"We've got a location!" Lindy yelled out to all the officers in the apartment. "It's moving south along Nathan Rd.

"Let's go." Peter led the group out of the room back down to the cars. Two officers stayed behind wait for a forensics team to arrive.

Lindy stayed on the line feeding updates to her boss as he drove wildly through the New Territories back towards Kowloon, the siren blaring overhead.

"It's stopped. In a back street off Nathan Road, East Tsim Sha Tsui."

Peter accelerated and almost lost control coming round a corner.

"It's moving again."

Shit, he thought. What the hell are they doing?

20 minutes later they were parked in front of Peninsula Hotel dealing with a very confused taxi driver and his irate American passengers who just wanted to go back to their room. Lindy found the phone in the back of the cab and realised her mistake. Before she could apologise, Peter said, "Where was the call actually made from, Lindy?"

It was another hour before the door to the kennel beneath Janis' apartment was opened. Inspector Wong stood at the top of the stairs genuinely relieved that Birgitte was alive. Xi Xi had regained consciousness and was being tended by paramedics out on the street.

Birgitte was led to another ambulance. She had asked after Janis but Peter didn't have any news. So far there had been no reports of a British woman matching her description leaving the country. Birgitte mentioned there may be a child being held somewhere but she didn't have any information. The inspector approached Xi Xi who looked dazed and bedraggled on the back tray of an ambulance. He spoke to her softly in Cantonese. She refused to answer at first but then began to shake her head in response to his questions. She talked hesitantly then became upset and started to scream. The paramedics struggled to treat her head wound. The inspector held out his hand which he placed firmly on her shoulder until she settled again. When her head was dressed she looked at the inspector and fell into his arms, crying like a child.

Birgitte was sitting in Peter's office with Peter, Lindy and Chief Inspector Li. It had been a long day. Her hand was wrapped in a proper bandage and held in a splint. She had received seven stitches to her palm at Queen Victoria Hospital, and had been kept in overnight for observation. The sedatives had put her out that evening but didn't quell the images of Janis Pollack and Max Anders laughing at her as she struggled to pry up the floorboards on

Velstrom St, her fingers had morphed into Rottweiler's claws and she no longer trusted her own motives. It was a vile dream that had lingered with her all morning.

As Peter tried to explain Xi Xi's involvement, Birgitte's mind raced with alternative scenarios from the day before where she might have been able to stop Janis from escaping. Had she failed in her duty as a police officer? Should she have done more? And of greater concern, was another child's life at risk because of her own actions? She took a deep breath, closed her eyes and did her best to bring herself back into the room.

Xi Xi was down in the holding cells, so far without legal representation. Peter had questioned her once that morning and it seemed, at the face of it, she didn't have any idea what had happened to any of the children she had approached. She had admitted to working for Janis as a prostitute, servicing mid- to high-end clients, and to helping her raise the dogs. In return she had been living at Janis's apartment in the New Territories for the past few months for reduced rent. It wasn't a permanent arrangement, but from what Peter had been able to gather, there hadn't been anything permanent in Xi Xi's life prior to meeting Janis through another client a little more than a year ago. Most importantly, the young woman was able to verify Janis and Ian's MO – using the puppies to lure children into talking to Birgitte. This physically connected them with each of the first four victims, making it far easier for Peter to at least build a solid murder case against Ian.

The British Metropolitan Police and the British military had provided information that proved beyond doubt that Ian Hurley was in fact Ian Horace. This raised the question of how he got the false passport to leave England anonymously and then enter Hong Kong, and how he could afford such a high-calibre lawyer. The solicitor Guy Stanthorpe was called in for questioning but was adamant he had been providing his services pro bono and that he knew of Ian through a mutual acquaintance he had no intention of naming. None of which now mattered, as far as he was concerned, because his client had just fired him.

Birgitte then spent an hour or so running through everything that had happened to her since the previous morning, providing a detailed statement, which Lindy took down. Occasionally the chief inspector would interrupt to ask a question, but for the most part Birgitte spoke freely and at length. When she was finished they were all astonished she'd come out alive and were baffled by Janis' behaviour. The fate of Merrick Cripps was difficult for them to comprehend. They were all exhausted and dissatisfied with how the events had played out.

After several moments of silence, Birgitte asked, "What's going to happen to the girl?"

"Xi Xi?" replied Peter. "I provided her a list of possible lawyers but she didn't know what to do with it. I can't tell if she has the emotional maturity to understand what's been going on."

"Is she over 18?"

"She's 22, but she's stunted in her development — limited formal education, I'm guessing, and who knows what living arrangements in terms of adult role models. I think she's been in sexual servitude for most of her life. She's a key part of the case so we have to look after her and tread carefully."

"I might know someone who can help," Birgitte said. "I'll give him a call after this. Any word on Janis?"

"Not yet. She either got out of the country before any warning could be put through or she's holed up somewhere, biding her time."

"I'm sorry I couldn't stop her."

"Not at all," the chief inspector said. "It's more important you got out in one piece. She'll turn up somewhere. And when she does, she'll be held to account."

Peter asked, "Was there anything in what she said that would suggest where she was going?"

Birgitte shook her head.

"Well, no other kids have been reported missing, so here's hoping her threat was a hollow one."

"What about the dogs?" asked Lindy.

"They've been impounded and will be put down apparently," Peter said. "Seems like a waste but that's the way these things are handled. The larger male will be kept alive while we look for evidence of it being used in the fourth murder."

"The media are waiting outside," said the Chief Inspector, "I've organised a press conference for 3.30pm. I suggest you head out the back at 3.32pm."

"What will you tell them?"

"I can give them some background on Mr Horace and hopefully it will jog some memories – someone might come forward with information on Janis. The British Police are very keen to look more closely at the events in the West Midlands in the early 2000s. They're going to see if they can shoot through some images of Janis when she was working as a prostitute, to help with the search." He stood up. "Thanks for everything, Detective. I'm glad you're okay." He left the room.

"Where could she be going?" Birgitte asked no one in particular.

"I'll go back to Stanley Prison to question Ian again. But given his performance yesterday, I'm going to struggle to believe anything he says from this point forward."

"Don't be too hard on yourself; you were only trying to put an end to this madness."

"I walked straight into it, and she escaped as a result."

Lindy interjected, "I should have pushed for the GPS location of the phone when it was answered instead of telling Peter to chase that taxi."

"If anyone should be blaming themselves," Birgitte said, putting up her hand. "But there's no point dwelling on it. Given who we've been dealing with, it all could have turned out much worse." She stood up and checked her watch. "It's almost 3.30pm. Lindy can you get me out of here?"

"Sure."

She turned to Peter. "I'm going to see if I can organise a lawyer for Xi Xi. I'll give you a call in the morning."

"Okay."

"And thanks, to both of you. I could still be locked in that kennel if it wasn't for your persistence."

It had seemed like they'd been driving uphill slowly through the trees for an age. The taxi dropped Birgitte at the end of a long, wide winding drive. She stood in the shadows of a large palm, watching the taxi do an awkward three-point turn then disappear slowly round the first bend. Through the foliage she could see a dimly lit path, which she followed to a large pair of dark timber doors.

Halcyon Towers, which had only finished construction in the last 24 months, comprised 30 luxury apartments, each boasting 270 degree views across Victoria Harbour to the mainland. Birgitte found the buzzer for the penthouse and pressed it. An elderly woman's voice greeted her through the intercom.

"Can I help you?"

"Birgitte Vestergaard. Sir Albert is expecting me."

The lock on the heavy doors was released. Birgitte pushed the door with her one good hand and it glided open.

The foyer of the tower was modernist in design, softened by subtle Balinese references and over-sized indoor plants. The elevator took her automatically to the penthouse. When the metal doors slid back she felt like she was on the top of The Peak. All of Hong Kong glittered in a sea of blackness.

The apartment was tastefully decorated; restrained but warm. Considerable thought and expense had been given to the lines and blocks of colour – original American paintings from the 50s and 60s were balanced with enormous rugs of contemporary Middle Eastern design. Like so many apartments in Hong Kong the floors were tiled white throughout. It could have been the lobby of a world-class gallery.

"Thank you, Mina," Sir Albert's voice came booming from another room, "as always you've been a marvellous help. I can take it from here. You get yourself home. I'm sure your kids are waiting for you." The statuesque former officer was dressed in dark suit pants and a white business shirt. He guided his diminutive Filipino maid towards the front door. He gave Birgitte a friendly wink as he held the door open for the elderly lady.

"You've gone above and beyond, Mina. So please, take tomorrow off."

She tried to protest, obviously for fear she might be losing a day's work. But Sir Albert reassured her by giving her a considerable cash tip from his wallet. She thanked him profusely. When the door finally closed, he said, "The routine never gets tired. She only has to go down two floors." He gave Birgitte a wide warm grin. "But the strata fees here are exorbitant. I should know; I set them."

He gave Birgitte a polite kiss on the cheek and led her into the apartment.

"How's the arm," he said, acknowledging the sling over Birgitte's shoulder.

"It's fine. Thank you."

"I was just having a scotch. Would you care for one?"

She nodded.

"It's quite warm out tonight, why don't we take a seat on the balcony."

She stepped out through the sliding glass doors and experienced a slight sensation of vertigo. The railing was all glass, giving the impression she was standing on the edge of a cliff. With only one hand to hold the railing her balance wasn't so great. The spectacular view quickly preoccupied her mind. It was a truly a remarkable city. She tried to get a sense of the different suburbs she had visited over the past two weeks but the skyscrapers on the Kowloon foreshore made it difficult to see as far as Sham Shui Po or across to the New Territories. She looked east towards Lam Tin and wondered if she could see Peter's apartment. But she couldn't. For a moment it occurred to her the benefit of such wealth was it its ability to blind you from other people's lives.

"There's a table setting a bit further along," said Sir Albert as he stepped out on the balcony carrying two crystal glasses of scotch. Birgitte took her drink and thanked him. He led the way to a two-seat table that would be the ideal spot to enjoy breakfast.

"So," he said, sitting down across for her, "you need a solicitor for a young local girl. Is that correct?"

"From what we can tell, she's spent most of her life working as a prostitute for various people, organisations. Most recently she came under the influence of a British woman and her husband who have been living here for three years."

"The couple who put you in hospital last week? And damaged your hand, I assume."

"Correct."

"I've been following it on the news and to be frank it's all anyone wants to talk about. The girl is a key witness?"

"Yes," replied Birgitte, "she'll be put into protective custody – it's imperative she testifies. We also need a lawyer who can shield her from the fallout."

"Was she a part of the abductions?"

"Unknowingly, would you believe." Birgitte took a sip of her scotch. It was incredibly smooth. She hoped it would lessen the throbbing of her hand. "She's really just a child in a young woman's body. She never would have been caught up in any of this if she hadn't been a child prostitute in the first place."

"I have a few firms in mind," he said, staring out at the harbour. "I'll make some calls in the morning and see who would be most suited."

"We'd really appreciate it. Obviously she can't afford to pay. I don't know if the Hong Kong Police or the legal system cover these sorts of things."

"It's fine," he said, dismissing her concern with a large hand. "It's a high-profile case. Plenty of opportunity for branding in the media. I could almost start a bidding war."

Birgitte was surprised by his cynicism.

He realised his faux pas. "It's the way the industry works, I'm afraid. But I promise we'll get the best team for the job. Hopefully, we can get a suspended sentence and she can start again. Have you spoken to your parents?"

"Not yet. I'll call them later tonight. I'm sure they've seen the footage on the news and are worried sick."

The conversation drifted to more palatable matters: Sir Albert's spectacular new apartment, the property market, state of the Hong Kong economy in general. The former commander was confident on most topics, providing insights into Hong Kong's place in greater China. He asked her about her police work, whether she had children, what the future held for someone like her within the Danish National Police. He even asked if she'd considered becoming a security consultant. Big money, apparently, he said with an inviting smile. She said she'd think about it.

When Sir Albert finished his drink, he said, "Top up?"

"If you're having one."

He walked back inside then returned with a half-empty bottle of Islay scotch and small carafe of water. The second round was poured more liberally than the first.

She enjoyed talking to him, but there was a sense that he was applying the same disarming charm he had used on his maid earlier, only on a more sophisticated level. She'd never had a chance to ask Jan about his time with Sir Albert when they were in London. Now, she wished she knew a little bit more about him. She also noticed he was occasionally slurring his words, which made her wonder how long he'd been drinking before she'd arrived. She intentionally pulled back on her on intake, encouraging him to fill his glass whenever it got low.

He became nostalgic for his time working in the diplomatic service. Birgitte listened to several well-worn anecdotes designed to sum up the reality of international relations – the reality being British superiority over the developing nations they had exploited in the past. It was all delivered in good humour but she could see the scotch had loosened his tongue as well as the mask he wore so effortlessly. As he talked she thought back to the night she met him at Government House – the string quartet playing Sibelius at the entrance, the interior of the Living Room, the crowd of guests as they milled about sipping Champagne and admiring the artworks. She remembered the elderly Chinese diplomats with stunning young women on their arms, very young women. The glimpse of a face moving through the crowd, which meant nothing at the time, now taunted her as she struggled to determine its possible significance. She dismissed it momentarily; she was incredibly tired and so much had happened, but more images of that evening began rushing through her mind. Images which hadn't made sense at the time were suddenly falling into place.

Birgitte reached into her bag for her phone. While Canningvale stared into his glass, lost in memories of his own, she accessed the digital recording app, then asked, "That night we met, at Government House."

"For a second time," he interrupted.

"Sorry?"

"I knew you as a child, remember?"

"Yes, of course. That night at Government House, I noticed you talking to someone on the balcony late in the evening, just before we left."

He tried to recall. "I spoke to a lot of people that night. It seemed like a dreadful episode of This Is Your Life at one point."

She nodded and smiled. "This conversation in particular seemed to upset you."

He rubbed his face with a large hand at the memory. "Yes, I remember now. It was nothing. A minor misunderstanding. Fixed with a phone call."

He looked warily at Birgitte, who decided to change direction. "I noticed some of the elderly gentlemen there were accompanied by very pretty young women. I remember thinking to myself that they'd brought their daughters."

Sir Albert chuckled boyishly at this. "I think you've been round long enough, Birgitte, to know that some gentlemen require company at these events. They aren't as fortunate as, say your father, who has such a beautiful wife to join him at the endless string of dinners and cocktail parties. You wouldn't begrudge a lonely old man a bit of company, would you?"

"Not at all, Sir Albert, I spent a couple of years in Vice in Copenhagen earlier on in my career. I hold quite a liberal attitude on such matters."

He shrugged as if to say, "Well, there you go."

"What bothers me, however, was one of the girls in particular."

286

"Really?" He poured himself a triple measure and didn't even think to offer her any.

"If I'm not mistaken, the girl who I'm asking you to help defend was actually at that party, working." She waited for the information to sink in. The elderly businessman stared out into the blackness, trying to find solace in the pretty lights of the city.

"I didn't know why she looked so familiar when I first encountered her in a park last week," Birgitte continued. "I didn't have any reason to think I'd seen her before, and I certainly wouldn't have known to pick her from a crowd of guests at a formal event at Government House. But I'm confident, when questioned, she'll confirm she was there." She put down her glass. "The thing is, Sir Albert, the girl, whose name is Xi Xi, was the sole employee of the British woman behind the murders of four children here in Hong Kong. Which makes me wonder who organised for her and several other prostitutes to be at your function."

Sir Albert steadied himself on the chair, holding both arm rests as if the balcony was threatening to collapse.

"It was Janis Pollack you were talking to on the terrace that night, wasn't it?" Birgitte asked bluntly. "She provided the services of Xi Xi for one of your guests?"

The businessman slumped in his seat, shaking his head. "She wasn't supposed to be there. She shouldn't have even been allowed on the property. But she managed to sweet talk one of my staffers at the front gate. For such a rancid cow, she seems to have a way of getting what she wants."

"Why was she there?"

"She wanted the money upfront. Christ, if you think my maid is fleecing me, she's got nothing on those two. I paid her of course, just to get rid of her, and made a promise to never use the girl's service's again, but the Minister for

Trade had an awful crush on the girl. He had literally begged me to get a hold of her."

"Which you had to do through Janis."

He nodded. "Insufferable bitch. Threatened to cause a scene if I didn't pay her on the spot."

"And you then rang Ian?"

"She was getting out of control. It was beyond a joke. He had to pull her in to line. But all he did was laugh at me. You have no idea how that made me feel. All those years... my little Bunty, laughing at me like I'm some old fool." He knocked his scotch back and poured another just as large. His voice was now thick with bitterness. "To think of all I've done for him."

Birgitte steadied her breathing and tried to look empathetic. She couldn't believe what she was hearing. "It can't have been easy."

"The favours I've had to pull over the years, I can tell you. He talks about Afghanistan as if he was handpicked for some special mission. It was all I could do to stop his incessant complaining. And then the silly little prick goes and gets himself shot. Christ, all he had to do was fix the fucking trucks. My life would have been a whole lot easier if that kid had aimed a little higher." He shook his head and stared into the blackness, his lips wet with spittle and scotch. "But it was that fucking Janis who was constantly ruining everything. He's wanted to be rid of her for years, to run a mile. That's what he told me. I believed him. Poor little Bunty, he never could think for himself."

Birgitte couldn't reconcile her image of Ian Horace the paedophile and child killer with Sir Albert's pet name. The businessman was leaning forward with his elbows on his knees staring down between his feet. "I could have got him here safely, but he was adamant, Janis had to have her own passport. I pleaded with him to come here and start again. I know people. I know so many people. He could have just disappeared, but no, he had to look after that fucking wench. He promised me she was going to travel somewhere else. That's the only reason I did it."

"The false passports."

"But not only did she not travel somewhere else, but she followed him here, to me, and on her own bloody passport. How could she be so fucking stupid. She brought all that mess, all that West Midlands nonsense with her to my doorstep." He stood up unsteadily. "But that was always the problem. She was never one of us, not really. She brought it out in Bunty, bless him. It was always there mind you, but she brought it out in him. But she didn't know what she was dealing with, what was really inside him. She couldn't control that. No one can. I should know."

He tipped the bottle to his glass before realising it was empty. He staggered past her into the apartment. She followed him inside, carrying both their glasses. He found another bottle and fell back into his oversized sofa, almost sending the bottle through the glass coffee table.

"How long have you known... Bunty?"

He looked nostalgically at his own hands. "Forever," he mumbled. "He was the prettiest little thing you've ever seen." He tried to get up. "I'm sure I've got some photos here somewhere." He fell back down again. "Silly of me. You don't want to see photos of my special Bunty." He stared about himself as if his surroundings were slightly unfamiliar. "I thought I'd lost him you know. These little creatures tend to drift in and out of your life. But Bunty was special. I discovered him at a party in Walsell back in the early 90s. Can't remember who brought him into my life but I'm eternally grateful." He raised his glass awkwardly, splashing scotch over his pants. "Then he was taken away, or I moved away, I can't remember, I moved around a lot in those days. Anyway he turned up at another party – what must have been 15 years later. There he was, my beautiful Bunty, and his rancid hag, fucking

Janis Pollack. He was as surprised as I was. I didn't know how he'd react, but it was fine. Better than fine, in fact. The years just fell away between us. Until, of course he started coming to me with his troubles."

He looked imploringly at Birgitte, no longer aware of who he was talking to, she was just an anonymous audience member privy to one of his many monologues. "What was I supposed to do? Turn my back on him?"

"The children in Walsell in the mid 2000s?"

Sir Albert sighed heavily, struggling to concentrate. "It had got out of hand. Or that's what he said. The police were poking around. He was confident they wouldn't find anything but he needed to get away for a while. He made a such a dashing young soldier. I was devastated when I got the news about the shooting, honest, but still, I've been to Afghanistan, there are certain pools you don't go swimming in, even I know that."

Birgitte struggled to process everything she'd just heard. Sir Albert had set Ian Horace on the path to abuse from childhood, Janis had released that little genie in her own special way and his former abuser had used his position of power and influence to protect them both. It was insanity. But it was how networks worked, favours pulled, new connections made, those in the know can reinvent themselves in other countries.

"Janis's passport..." Birgitte said, speaking the words as she formed them in her mind. "She didn't use it coming into Hong Kong."

Sir Albert shook his head, barely following her line of thinking.

"What name was the new passport under?"

"What? I need another drink." He stared at the bottle but was unable to move. His eyelids drooped as he began to slip into unconsciousness.

Birgitte leapt over the coffee table and slapped his face lightly several times. "What name is she travelling under?"

His head lolled. She grabbed the carafe of water and tipped it over his head. He spluttered, wild eyed. "What the hell?"

"What name is Janis travelling under?"

"Janis? Janis who?"

"Janis Pollack," she screamed. "You gave her a new identity in England. What was the name on the passport?"

"I don't know. Hanson. Hammersmith. Hanley."

She reached her arm back past her shoulder and brought her good hand down against the old man's face. The slap shocked him to his senses. "Harrison," he blurted. "The name on the passport was Janis Harrison."

She pulled her new phone from her pocket and stopped recording, then she phoned Peter.

"She's travelling as Janis Harrison. Get the Immigration Department to search for any mention of that name – Janis Harrison... I'll tell you later. You need to come up to Halcyon Towers, an apartment block on The Peak. I'm here with Sir Albert Canningvale, a British businessman. He knew Ian and Janis and knew all about their past. Hell, he's the reason for a lot of Ian's past." She didn't know how much to tell Peter over the phone. "He's blind drunk but you'll need to take him in for questioning. I think he's a part of a very complex, long-standing international paedophile ring."

When she hung up she checked on Sir Albert. He was snoring heavily. She looked around the apartment but couldn't find anything incriminating connecting him to Ian or Janis. She didn't know if the recording on her phone was admissible in a Hong Kong court but it could go some way to forcing him into a deal to implicate any other members of the ring, not to mention holding Ian and Janis to account for their crimes in England and Hong Kong.

Peter arrived with Lindy and two other officers just after 9pm. When Sir Albert woke up he was initially confused

291

by the sudden influx of police into his apartment, then some part of him accepted it as a fate that had been waiting for him for decades. They helped him to his feet, handcuffed him and led him to the front door. Birgitte stood there waiting as they brought him past. He looked smaller now, cheaper. She suddenly remembered him from her family's time in a London – it was a vague image of a large corpulent figure who inspired revulsion in her and her friends. "Cunning Whale" indeed.

"I wouldn't look so smug, Missy," he said at the door. "Ask you father about the Ember Room. We've all got secrets. They make us who we are."

Peter shoved him through the door as Birgitte felt the blood rush to her feet. What the hell was he talking about? Oh Christ, what did her father know? How close were those two men? She couldn't consider the possibility. It was a nightmare that was only getting worse.

CHAPTER FIFTEEN

As Birigtte packed her bag on her final morning in Hong Kong, her mind was in overdrive. She couldn't stop thinking about what Canningvale had said the night before. What did any of this have to do with her father? She was sure to raise it with him as soon as she got back to Copenhagen. If only to ease her mind, but darker thoughts plagued her subconscious. What if...?

She moved about the hotel room, gathering her toiletries from the bathroom and her earrings from the bedside table. Within a matter of minutes she was ready to go. It was hard to believe she'd only been in Hong Kong for a couple of weeks. Merrick Cripps was dead. Ian Horace was in jail. Xi Xi was in custody and would now have to rely on the beneficence of the state for her legal defence. And Janis Pollack was still on the run. It didn't seem right to be leaving, but she had worked on enough unsolved cases to know that the wheels would keep turning even if she had to move on.

She gave the room a final once over then closed the door behind her.

Peter and Lindy were waiting for her in the lobby. He took Birgitte's bags as she went to reception to check-out. A few minutes later she exited the Conran Hotel for the last time, the sultry air hitting her as the doors slid open. She paused to double-check she had her passport and airline ticket.

Peter closed the boot and got in the front. Lindy sat in the back, leaving the passenger side free for Birgitte. She climbed in and put her belt on. She didn't know what to say to her temporary colleagues so she didn't say anything at all.

Peter pulled the car out into the traffic.

They drove out to the airport on Lantau Island in silence. What more could she have done, Birigtte wondered. She had proved her theory about the MO, and Janis had admitted to the killings (even though she had escaped), Xi Xi was willing to testify. Ian Horace was looking at life in prison and the same could be expected for Janis.

Sir Albert Canningvale was already providing swathes of information through his lawyer Guy Stanthorpe, in the hope of securing a plea deal of some sort. He had admitted to raping Ian Horace as a child (although these were not his words), then joining him 15 years later in a paedophile ring that was operating in the West Midlands. He was not only responsible for getting Horace fast-tracked into the military, but had used his connections to get him out again before an enquiry could be launched into the shooting outside of Sangin. When Ian had complained about his life on his return to England, it was Canningvale who convinced him to leave Janis and join him in Hong Kong. He provided the false passport and set him up at Mason's Garage. Canningvale still blamed Janis for everything.

The last sighting of her was on the border near Guangzhou. She had slipped into China on the Sunday night as Janis Harrison, then promptly disappeared. The Chinese government were dragging their heels with further information, clearly embarrassed at having let such a high-profile child killer slip through their defences unnoticed.

As they reached the turn off for the airport, Birgitte wondered out loud whether Janis would have any connections in China, through the broader networks she'd been dealing with for so many years. Peter said it was hard to say, but he would put it to Canningvale and see if they could come up with some names worth pursuing. They were all quietly hoping that she would make some sort of mistake, anything to give herself away to the authorities in whatever country she was hiding in. But secretly, Birgitte was concerned if Janis got out of Asia and back into Europe their chances of finding her would decrease considerably.

Peter pulled his car into a free parking spot near the departure terminal. He and Lindy helped Birgitte with her bags.

"How did you go with Xi Xi this morning?" she asked.

"She's still very traumatised. The only people in her world who she could rely on have abandoned her, and she's also realised they had manipulated her into doing horrible things. It's been a pattern for most of her life by the looks of it. I gave her the bunny I showed you the other day to cheer her up and she just started crying uncontrollably. It's going to take some time for her to recover."

"Will she be charged?"

"Not if I can help it. As long as she can testify against Ian and provide as much information as she can about Janis and Canningvale, then I think she deserves to be given a clean slate. But it's not up to me. I can only put a case to the magistrate."

"What will she do?"

"I don't know."

Birgitte could see that the subject was bothering Peter so she turned to Lindy. "So, when will we be calling you Inspector Kwok?"

The PI pushed her glasses back on her nose. "My exam is next Monday."

"How have you had time to study?"

"I don't run on much sleep," she said with a nervous smile.

Peter said, "I'll help her study in the coming days. I reckon she's learned more about police work in the two weeks you've been here than when she was back in the academy."

Lindy laughed, "I guess I should thank you, Birgitte."

"No, I should be thanking you. We made that Rottweiler connection together, remember?"

She looked down at her leg. "How could I forget."

"And you helped find Janis' apartment."

She smiled. She knew it wasn't true but it felt good to have the confidence of two detectives she respected so greatly.

They entered the terminal, joining the crowds heading for the check-in counter. "How's Chief Inspector Li coping with the media."

"I think deep down, he's loving it," Peter said without a smile, but a note of humour in his voice. "He's obviously not happy that Janis escaped but the case has certainly put his department on the radar. He's made a lot of international connections which will only serve him well."

"What about you?" she asked.

Peter shrugged. "I don't expect anything to change."

Lindy's face darkened slightly at this. "It's not right, Goong."

"You pass your exams and I'll be happy. You don't need to worry about me."

"Well, I should check in," Birgitte said nodding to the counter for SAS. "Thanks for giving me a hand with my bags." She turned to Peter. "And please thank Michelle again for inviting me to lunch."

"It was our pleasure," Peter said. For a moment he seemed lost for words. "It's been... interesting working with you. Obviously you'll hear from us in regards to the trial."

"I hope to hear from you before that, Inspector. I want to know that Janis Pollack has been found and arrested." She shook both of their hands. "Please, I'll be fine from here. Once my luggage is checked-in, I can handle my bag without any trouble."

Peter held her hand in both of his. "You did well. The children's families will be grateful that Ian Horace will answer for what he did."

"I wish I could have done more."

With that she turned and headed for the check-in counter. As she stood in the queue she watched them both walk out of the terminal. Peter Wong was a good man. She could only hope his efforts would be rewarded while he was still young enough to contribute to the police at a higher level.

She checked-in her luggage, got her boarding pass and made her way slowly towards Gate 22. As much as it had been an incredible two weeks in Hong Kong, she was truly glad to be heading home. She was due back at work on the Thursday and really just wanted to immerse herself in her caseload, in the hope of forgetting all about the promotion.

An hour and a half later, as the Boeing Airbus banked over the islands, Birgitte closed her eyes and fell into a deep sleep.

As planned, the next few weeks back in Copenhagen were a heady mix of long hours, bleak settings and the minutia of several unsolved cases running concurrently. Winter had arrived, with chill December winds blowing in from across the Baltic. It only took a few hours working in bracing horizontal rain for Birgitte to forget about the cloying humidity of Kowloon.

Ian Horace's trial in Hong Kong was scheduled for the new year. Occasionally Birgitte fielded video calls from Peter and Chief Inspector Li, in order to clarify certain aspects of the investigation, but for the most part, Peter would send her updates via email. There were still no sightings of Janis Pollack.

On a more personal note, Birgitte had spent her first Sunday afternoon back in Denmark talking to Tomas. She suggested it was time to proceed with the divorce and thankfully, but not without regret, he agreed. He had already decided to do his best to make it work with the new woman in his life. Birgitte knew he was quietly looking forward to being a father and appreciated his candour on the matter. She wasn't ready for kids herself and didn't want to be drawn into his new journey in any way at all. The idea of the divorce was to get clear of her past as efficiently as possible so she could move forward with her own life. She was satisfied that her feelings about Tomas fell into the same category as her feelings about her weeks in Australia. It was time to move on, not dwell on the past.

It was hard to believe it was almost Christmas. Loll had suggested a few days up in Skagen for old time's sake. They couldn't get their favourite cottage on such short notice but a friend of a friend who had four-bedroom house a few kilometres south of the fishing village would be in America over the break and they were more than welcome to make use of it in their absence. Loll thought it would be wonderful to get the extended family together again. Birgitte wasn't so sure. She hadn't had a chance to talk with Jan about Sir Albert Canningvale. The media were too caught up with the Horace/Pollack relationship to give him much coverage, and without Cripps to bring the sordid details into the light, it seemed his story wouldn't be told. Occasionally she wondered what Cripps would have made of Canningvale's involvement but, given what the former officer had said about Jan on his arrest, she was quietly grateful that aspect of the case wasn't drawing much attention. She needed time to sort that out for herself.

It had played on her mind every night since Canningvale's arrest. She knew the best way to deal with it was to confront her father outright, demand the truth. Had he been involved in any way socially with the British businessmen? And what had happened in the Ember Room? She couldn't bear the thought of letting her mind run with the possibilities. Nor could she broach the subject with her mother. It would break Loll's heart. Birgitte had wanted to call him on several occasions, usually after a few drinks, when the stress and fatigue of her job were getting to her, but she couldn't risk Loll sensing something was wrong. So it had gone unresolved far longer than she had intended.

Before she knew it, it was December 22. She had opted for extra shifts in order to have a valid excuse not to go to Skagen but Sven had reworked their schedules so everyone on his team could get at least some time with their families.

Birgitte negotiated the long drive up to North Jutland alone.

When she arrived, Jan and Loll were busy getting the house ready for all their guests. She slipped into her role of the helpful daughter as best she could, refusing to be drawn on any of the events in Hong Kong. They knew better than to press her for information. The main thing was she was home safe and the man behind the killings was in prison awaiting trial. They were both sure his girlfriend would be caught soon enough. Loll didn't mention the promotion and Jan followed suit. It was Christmas and all they wanted was for everyone to get along over the holiday season. They were expecting 12 for lunch on Christmas day and there was a lot to be done to prepare.

It surprised her then that she would blurt out the question the next day in the kitchen. Loll had excused herself moments earlier to take a much-needed nap, which had left Jan and Birgitte alone together for the first time since they had arrived.

Jan continued folding napkins.

"Jan?" Birgitte said, "I asked you a question."

299

"I heard you."

The house was quiet. A gas fireplace gave the living room a warbling glow, sending shadows pulsing and fluttering up the white-washed timber-panelled walls. Jan put the napkins down and made his way slowly to a leather armchair. He paused at one point because he thought he heard Loll stirring from their bedroom. Birgitte watched him. Physically he looked frail as he nestled himself back into the chair, but he had been having a good morning, his mind was lucid, even sharp. He nodded to the other chair, which was angled towards the fire. Birgitte perched on the end of it, sitting up straight, her hands in her lap.

"So? How well did you know Albert Canningvale? You must know he was charged with being part of an international paedophile ring, among many other things."

"I did hear about that." Without his napkins to keep him busy, he didn't seem to know what to do with his hands, so he rubbed them together slowly for warmth. "I knew him well enough to know he had some problems."

"When we were living in London?"

He nodded slowly, staring into the flames. "I don't know whether you remember, but we were there to help negotiate an agricultural deal. It was the mid-80s, neither country was doing very well at the time and it was seen by Cabinet as an important opportunity to get Denmark on her feet. Canningvale was there as a mediator of sorts. He wasn't essential to the deal in terms of signatures or anything, but he was key in bringing the right people to the table – the people who could make it all happen. We all worked together for many months, hammering out a range of packages that would work for both sides. It was a lot of work, long hours. I wasn't really there for your mother."

Birgitte knew all this. Her father was stalling. "Canningvale mentioned The Ember Room," she said rather tersely. "He said you'd know what he was talking about."

At the mention of The Ember Room his eyes flashed across to her with slight alarm, then returned to the fire. He shook his head slowly, as if he always knew this day would come. Birgitte could feel her skin getting clammy and began to wonder if she had opened a door she should have kept closed.

"There were many functions over that period," Jan said in a measured, even voice, like a veteran politician giving a radio interview, "some aimed at loosening collars in order to better facilitate certain aspects of the deal – sticking points in the board rooms; others, just to blow off steam, a chance to be immersed in the higher end of British life. I saw the inside of more historic houses over that period than most curators at the V & A." He grinned feebly, then coughed into his hand. Birgitte stood up and poured him a scotch. He thanked her but avoided her eyes as she sat back down across from him.

"There was particular house, an estate really, about 40 minutes outside of London. It belonged to a friend of Sir Albert's. He was still just Albert then. You know the sort: sprawling grounds, sweeping drives, imposing stone edifice, haughty livery staff watching everyone with that dreadful mix of envy and contempt. We were there to smooth over a particularly difficult aspect of one of the packages, something to do with fertiliser from memory. As usual the Brits were being impossibly polite but painfully obstinate. We ate a lavish meal in the dining room, surrounded by several pre-Raphaelite paintings, working ideas back and forth over many bottles of red. However, when the meal was over we still were no closer to an understanding. A lot of the guests were getting frustrated with the proceedings. Albert stood up and suggested a splash of Port in The Ember Room. Reluctantly we all shuffled off to an oak-lined library with an open fire place about five times the size of this one. Albert told everyone about the great great grandfather of the owner who had almost set himself and the house on fire as a child when he'd scooped out a small pile of burning coals with a shovel to see them better in the light. The name had stuck and been carried down over the years. It was a beautifully appointed room – sombre and soothing. It seemed to inspire serious meditation. Anyway, I don't know what it was but within the next three hours, we'd settled our differences and signed off on one of the most challenging parts of the deal. It was then that I realised the importance of someone like Albert Canningvale. Without him the agreement would have stalled completely."

Birgitte was listening with interest but getting irritated with how long it was taking for Jan to get to the point. If her mother woke up, she may not get another chance to question him so freely. Jan leaned back in the chair, crossing one long leg over the other, obviously resigned to revealing everything he knew but quietly determined to do it as his own pace.

"I remember taking my gold pen – do you remember the one the Prime Minister had given me a few years earlier? I took it with me to all the important meetings – almost a good luck charm."

Birgitte remembered it well. She had spent most of her awkward early teenage years resenting everything the pen represented. She had screamed at him childishly once that he loved the pen more than he loved her mother.

"We were so relieved to have come to an agreement I allowed my pen to be used for all the signatures. It was passed around the room, admired by each person who used it. I didn't want to brag where it came from so I just said it was a graduation present. Still, they all lingered over it. Then we all relaxed and the Port began to flow. Cigars were lit. You know how those things proceed. I was poured into a limousine a few hours later and sent back to our place in Kensington. It wasn't until the next morning that I realised I'd left my pen behind. I'd last seen it resting on the mantle over the fireplace. It sounds foolish now but I was mortified. I couldn't believe I'd been so wrapped up in the moment as to leave it lying around in a stranger's house.

"Anyway I tried to call Albert, but couldn't get a hold of him, or any of the people whose contact details I had, so I got my secretary to ring the estate direct. Rather than risk putting the pen in a taxi or sending it by courier, I asked if I could come round that evening to collect it myself. Apparently the woman on the other end of the phone said it would be fine. She told my secretary the staff were off for the evening so if I wouldn't mind coming in around the side entrance. I didn't think anything of it.

"After work I had my driver take me back out to the estate and sure enough the place looked deathly quiet. I told him to wait, I would only be a minute and set off round the side of the manor house. It was very difficult to see anything but as I got closer I could hear music, old jazz by the sounds of it. I found the side door and, as the woman had told my secretary, it was unlocked – not that you'd know it from outside. The place looked impenetrable. I fumbled around in the dark, beginning to wonder if the pen was really worth all the fuss, when I found myself in the dining room. I called out if anyone was home but there was no answer. I made my way from memory towards The Ember Room. The door was closed but I could hear the music playing quiet loudly inside. I knocked but no one heard me."

They were both startled to hear the fridge door opening. It was Loll. Birgitte stood up almost too quickly. "Mother? Is everything okay?"

"I have a splitting headache, Darling. Just wanted to take an asprin with some ice water. Don't mind me."

Jan stared into the fire, ignoring his wife. Birgitte didn't move.

Loll tipped her head back and raised her glass then shuffled blearily back into the rear of the house. They waited until they heard the bedroom door close. Birgitte sat back down again, hoping her mother would have thought nothing more of their fireside chat than Jan holding court about the good old days.

Jan was mesmerised by the flames. He had uncrossed his legs and was leaning forward, with his elbows on his knees. He continued on as if Loll had never entered the room. "I knocked again, but knew no one could hear it over the sound of the music, so I opened the door. I'm not sure what I saw, even to this day."

Birgitte was ready to interject that he should damn well try to remember every detail because the future of his family depended upon it, but she bit the inside of her cheek and waited.

"There were, maybe, 15 to 20 people in the room," he said. "It was hard to tell. The only light came from the large fireplace, which set most of the room in abstract highlights and deep shadow. The music was jarring, too loud. It was incredibly disorienting. But they were all wearing masks, like the Venetians do, and most of them were undressed or wearing very little. They were all in some sort of theatrical garb, loin clothes, capes, garlands. It looked... absurd. I noticed several young men, purely by the tone of their physiques; some of them were... very young."

"What were they doing?" Birgitte's voice was cracked and brittle.

"I couldn't tell at first. It was some bacchanal fantasy they were recreating. Some were dancing, some were draped over the same ottomans we'd been sitting at the night before talking about tariffs and quotas. Only now it looked as if no one was talking, they were in some sort of drunken trance. It was hard to see, as I said, but there was a curious rhythmic pulse to it all, possibly it was the music, but it seemed as if the whole room was heaving and shifting as one.

"Then a mask appeared by the door — a hawk, I think, very ornate, gold on white. I said I was there to collect my pen. The hawk tilted his head, the way hawks do when they consider their prey. He was wearing a thick black cape over his shoulders but I could see he was naked underneath, and somewhat older than the others, possibly mid 50s. He looked back into the room. Over by the mantle a giant of a man with a minotaur's head lifted a gold pen from the mantelpiece. My pen. He handed it to a very young boy in a fox's mask who ran through the room swiftly. He handed me the pen and the hawk closed the door in my face. All the time the minotaur was looking straight at me.

"I left the estate, bewildered, confused. I knew what it was but I still didn't feel right stumbling into it — like walking in on your own parents. The woman my secretary had spoken to must have thought I was a guest for that night, otherwise I'm sure she would have made some excuse to prevent me from arriving when I did. Perhaps she was being contrary. I don't know."

"The minotaur?"

"Undoubtedly Canningvale. He was the only one who knew the pen was resting on the mantle. He didn't seem the least alarmed by my presence. I'm sure the owner was there somewhere as well, behind another mask, but most were too lost in the moment to have even noticed there was someone at the door before I was back in the car and heading off the grounds.

"The next day, there was a meeting at Whitehall — trade ministers, financiers and the like. Canningvale was there. He eyed me carefully from across the boardroom. At one point during the meeting he announced that he may have

305

to pull out of negotiations due to unforeseeable business reasons. It sent a wave of unease around the entire room. You must understand, that by this point, Canningvale was the man of the hour, but there was still a long way to go to ensure the agreement could be a success. There were billions of dollars resting on this, the economic security of both nations could either be bolstered, or falter at the gate.

"He looked directly at me as he spoke. I'll never forget it. He said: 'Certain parties, whom I'm in no position to name, are themselves in a position to alter the outcome of these proceedings. Until I can be sure of their good intentions, I'm afraid there is a risk that my presence could undermine all our hard work.' No one knew what the hell he was talking about, but me.

"I'd spent the rest of the previous night sitting awake in the living room of our apartment, unsure of what I'd seen and what I was legally responsible to do about it. Part of me knew what I'd seen was wrong, very wrong, but another wasn't entirely sure – it was dark and I'd only really been there for a moment peering through a crack in a door. The more time that passed, the more external factors began to play in my rationalising of the event. By morning I was gutted to realise there was nothing I could do. Canningvale, of course, knew this, and was waiting to see how I would handle the information. He knew me well enough, it seems. I remained silent during the meeting. And silent ever since.

"By the afternoon, he'd assured everyone the negotiations were back on track. There was nothing at all to worry about. Six months later, the agreement was ratified by both parliaments, and myself and Mr Canningvale were held up as models of progressive economic planning. It secured the rest of my career, and his.

"Thankfully, our paths didn't cross again... until, of course, I heard about the impending soiree in his honour while your mother and I were in Shanghai. You must believe me, I had no interest in going. Your mother insisted."

He slowly settled back into the wings of the armchair almost disappearing. "I wanted to say something to him even then. I don't know what... 'I know', perhaps. What good it could have done."

Birgitte shifted on her own armchair. "You could have told someone."

"There was so much at stake."

"Even afterwards?"

"To be frank, it fell from my memory. We were sent back to Copenhagen then on to Budapest, remember. I barely had time to be there for you or Loll."

"But Jan, he's been assaulting children for decades. If you'd said something... anything, back then you could have put a stop to so much misery."

"It was different back then," he snapped. Clearly annoyed with his daughter's inability to see the episode from his perspective. "A different time. I was a child of the war. We lived with the Nazis, soldiers in the street. My earliest memories are seared with an awareness of evil on a far grander scale. You know that!"

Birgitte couldn't see his point. He had always brought up his childhood during the occupation when he felt put upon. She reminded him, "You saw Canningvale abusing children in the 1980s."

"I was never certain I had."

"Oh, come on, Jan. What else could it have been?"

"A lot has changed since I was your age, and it's been changing faster still in the past decade or so. Nowadays everyone is obsessed with the individual, this ridiculously reflexive surveillance of the self. The moral landscape has changed considerably."

She shook her head. "I don't buy it, Jan."

"We simply didn't concern ourselves with what went on behind closed doors, quite literally. The bigger evil, the greater evil, was going on outside our very homes."

She didn't care for his rationalisations but had to admit, he was of a generation that were wilfully blinded by their own world view. Since the 70s the patriarchal hierarchy of Western society had steadily broken down, struggling to protect its privileges under greater scrutiny from the disenfranchised. Now only entrenched institutions like the church or the state could continue to pretend they didn't know any better back then. The moral landscape had changed, but pleading ignorance was no defence. There was a far greater onus for people to speak up about injustices on a domestic scale – there was now a moral imperative. It bred paranoia in certain quarters, but it was small price to pay for necessary change.

Birgitte couldn't help thinking of all the damage someone like Canningvale had caused, the organic nature of his crimes. His behaviour instigated the emergence of abusive impulses in others. God knew, how many others. Four children had been murdered in Hong Kong alone, possibly another five in the West Midlands of England. Talia Mackland's life was a mess; she may not have achieved much otherwise, but she never deserved to be treated so poorly as a child. There was no excusing Ian Horace's behaviour but without Canningvale and Janis Pollack, would he have ventured down that path unaided? How many other children's lives had been soiled?

It saddened her to watch her ailing father wipe tears from his eyes. She had never seen him cry. He sniffed loudly and said, "It's just like that bastard to throw grenades on his way out the door. He's spent a lifetime ruining people's lives. He obviously wanted to turn you against me, make you think the worst."

"I must say, I did for while."

He looked at her with horror.

"What was I supposed to think? A lifelong paedophile, who you used to work with, suggests that you have some shared secret dating back more than 30 years?"

"I did nothing wrong," he said bitterly. "But I should have done something more at the time." He sighed and wriggled uncomfortably in his chair. He looked emotionally drained. "I'm sorry I didn't warn you when we were in Hong Kong. I honestly didn't know what to say."

She was quietly grateful his sin was one of omission rather than anything darker. Nowadays, as he'd suggested, that was sin enough. He seemed frightened by the contemporary moral landscape, and clearly very disappointed in himself.

She thought of the inquest into her arrest of Max Anders and wondered if she was similarly guilty. Would a better person have behaved differently in the same circumstances. It was all too much. "I think I'll have a lie down myself."

Jan watched her as she stood up and pressed his hand. She looked down at him, as if seeing him whole for the first time. She didn't know what else to say so she just left him alone in front of the fire with his own memories.

CHAPTER SIXTEEN

The next morning Birgitte helped her mother in the kitchen while Jan raked the yard. Loll had told him not to bother because there was storm forecast for the afternoon but he didn't pay her any mind. Birgitte quietly suggested they might get more done with him outside, so Loll let it be.

Birgitte prepared them all a light lunch of smorrebrod with roast beef and remoulade, smoked salmon and fresh dill, as well as some liver paste for her father. They sat around the dining table building their own sandwiches. At one point Loll commented how quiet Jan was being. Normally he would have made some sort of caustic reply. Instead he offered a strained smile and said he was just enjoying his lunch. She raised her eyebrows and gave Birgitte a look as if to say "there's one for the books". He'd obviously been doing a lot of thinking through the course of the previous night.

In the afternoon, Birgitte rugged up in several layers with a thick jacket on top and drove in to town to do some last-minute shopping. Before heading back to the house she parked by the beach to take a long, solitary walk out to the most northerly point of Denmark. The sky was grey and heavy and the air was bitterly cold, but so long as the rains held off, she was content to walk along the shore looking out at the sea.

She felt more at peace with herself than she had for some time. Acceptance was a necessary step to any trauma or dramatic change. She was a soon-to-be divorced 30-something woman with a solid, albeit slightly stalled career. She didn't know what the new year would hold but she felt ready to face it with a more open outlook. It was time to sit down with Sven and have a serious chat about alternate opportunities, possible training courses. Hell, maybe even a transfer to a different part of Denmark.

Perhaps 18 months away from everything she knew was what she needed. It was something to consider at least. She looked to the south and could see the darker clouds of the forecasted storm-front steadily sweeping up the coast. It would be dark by 4pm. The breeze had picked up to a strong wind. She almost didn't hear her phone ring in her jacket pocket.

She took it out and shielded it with her hand.

"Birgitte Vestergaard... hello?.... it's a very bad line." She ran up the beach to a line of trees to get out of the wind.

"Peter? Is that you?... How are you?"

The inspector kept it short. There wasn't much to say and the line was too crackly to waste words with small talk. Ian Horace had been found dead in his cell the previous night. His head had been caved in – the result of multiple blunt-force trauma wounds. Two British prisoners, also holed up in Stanley Prison, had taken it upon themselves to mete out their own justice on a man who had taken pleasure in hurting children.

Birgitte spoke loudly into the phone, thanking the inspector and asking him to keep her up to date on any further developments in regards to Janis. The line went dead. She wasn't sure if he'd heard her or not.

She drove back to the house in a daze, her mind whirling with possibilities. Had the two prisoners been paid off? If so, by who? Canningvale could have been covering his tracks. It was hard to know what he was capable of. Did Janis know? How would she react to the news? Would she give up the chase? Or simply disappear? In Janis' own words Ian Horace had been her reason for living.

When Birgitte pulled into the yard she realised she was gripping the wheel in anger. The bastard had got off too lightly. Two other thugs had taken matters into their own hands. It wasn't right. He should have stood trial, been held accountable then spent the rest of his sorry life thinking about his choices. She got out of the car and slammed the door. The first thick drops of rain, splashed across her face. By the time she got her shopping to the front door, the rain was torrential and the wind had sprung up, throwing sheets of water in all directions. She stamped her feet and shook her head, trying to shed the rain from her clothes and hair before going inside.

After unlocking the front door and carrying the bags into the kitchen she called out at she was home. She proceeded to put away the groceries she'd bought, but noticed two half-made cups of tea were sitting on the bench. Then she realised the back door to the deck was open and rain was blowing into the living room. She called out again, baffled as to what could have drawn her parents out into the storm. When she had closed the door to the deck she walked back through the house, calling out to Loll.

Birgitte found her mother in the bedroom, face down on the floor by the window. She was bleeding from the head. A lamp was on the floor near the bedside table, its base smeared with blood. Birgitte checked Loll's pulse. There was still a feint rhythm beating through the skin. She pulled out her phone and called emergency services, telling them her elderly mother had been attacked and knocked unconscious. She was told paramedics and police were on their way.

As she ran through the house looking for her father, she remembered the back door had been open when she arrived. She ran out into the rain. The afternoon sky had darkened further with the weight of the storm-front directly overhead. The wind was getting stronger by the moment, twisting the trees that lined the front of property, threatening to uproot them and cast them against the house. The noise of the squall was deafening. She called out Jan's name and staggered up the grass embankment then down the other side, along the dirt path that quickly turned to sand. The sea was a ragged grey torment of forces rising up and collapsing on itself as the sky continued to unleash torrents of rain along the coast. She ran down through the dunes, continuing to call out for her father as she looked through the mire in either direction. From what little she could see, the beach appeared deserted. Then she spotted him.

His head and shoulders were jutting just above the waves several metres out to sea. It didn't make sense. He was staring back at the house, not moving as the waves crashed over his shoulders, at times covering his head completely. Why didn't he climb out? He was a strong swimmer, even for his advanced years. But then she realised why he couldn't. Close to the shoreline she spotted deep parallel grooves cut into the wet sand. He must have been tied to a chair that had been dragged into the sea.

She ran towards the water, screaming at him to hang on, she was going to help him. As her body careened across the sand, propelled against the wind with fear-induced adrenalin, she looked about desperately to see if there were any neighbours within view, perhaps looking out a window. But there was no one to help her.

Birgitte kicked off her shoes and leapt into the shallows, ripping her jacket off her shoulders. The water was shockingly cold – barely eight degrees, stiffening her bones and causing her to inhale involuntarily. How could her father cope being fully immersed? She looked out to him – his long face was weary with the struggle of catching his breath between the waves. He only had a matter of minutes before the rising tide or the chill of the sea would take its toll. His eyes didn't register the possibility his daughter might actually save him. When Birgitte was up to her knees she heard her name being called out behind her. She didn't want to stop to find out who it was because she just didn't have time. As she was about to dive into the waves, she heard it again.

"Birgitte." It was a familiar voice commanding her attention. She stopped and turned. There on the shoreline, soaked to the skin in a white dress was Janis Pollack. Her face was wild, imperious. She held a gun and was pointing it directly at Birgitte.

Birgitte wanted to ignore her. With the wind and the rain, there was a chance Janis would miss. But Birgitte knew already she wouldn't be able to get her father out to safety with her still standing there. She looked at the crazed woman imploringly.

Janis began to laugh.

"You knew they killed him, didn't you?" she screamed into the wind.

Birgitte nodded. The icy water was making it difficult to breathe.

"My Ian shouldn't have gone out like that."

"It was beyond my control," Birgitte yelled back. She turned to her father who was now twisting his head to keep his mouth and nostrils clear but the waves kept coming.

"It's only fair – this," Janis screamed. "You, watching someone you love dying in front of you."

"Don't, Janis."

"Or perhaps I could shoot you, and the last thing your father sees is his precious daughter dying helplessly in front of him. What would you prefer?"

"Oh Christ, Janis. Ian's gone. There's nothing you can do about it. Why make it any worse for yourself?"

"Worse for me?" she screamed. "Ian would have loved to have seen this. I'm doing this in his honour. The game continues... don't you get it?"

It was hopeless. Either way someone was going to die. She couldn't live with herself not doing more to save her father, so she stopped thinking and leapt into the waves.

Before she hit the water she could hear the shot ring out, but she was too busy swimming against the waves to care if she'd been hit.

The next few minutes were all a blur. She had struggled to turn the chair around then tipped it back to drag it into shore, but the force of the waves made it almost impossible to negotiate. At one point the chair fell back, plunging her father under the bitterly cold water. She kicked and scrabbled and tore several muscles in her own back trying to lift the chair out of the wet sand below. It wasn't until a fresh swell lifted them both and carried them a few feet closer to shore. When the waves drew back, the sea was around his waist. He was spluttering desperately to get air into his lungs and she could feel him shivering violently with the cold. Once she was clear of the bigger waves she was able to drag him up onto the beach.

Between the shore and the house she saw a young male police officer sitting in the sand, clutching his stomach with a look of shock on his face. He must have been in the area when the call went out about Birgitte's mother. He'd run down the beach and been shot by Janis before he could even draw his weapon.

Birgitte could just see Janis running south along the beach. She told Jan to hang on then ran up the sand to the young man. She grabbed his radio, announced that an officer was down, gave the address and demanded back up. She sprinted up to the house as two paramedics approached the front door. They were surprised to see a soaking wet woman standing in the living room.

"I'm a detective, homicide, Copenhagen," she said. "There is a woman, my mother, unconscious in the front bedroom. She's been hit with a lamp. Down on the beach... two men – an officer has been shot and my father who has been in the water, I think has hypothermia. I've already called for more ambulances. The assailant has run

315

down the beach. I'm going to grab some blankets for my father then go after her."

One paramedic headed for the front bedroom, while the other ran through the house and up the embankment. Birgitte followed shortly after with blankets she found in the linen closet.

When she got back to her father he was barely conscious. She wrapped the blanket around his shoulders. "The paramedics will help you," she yelled through the wind. "I have to get after her before she hurts someone else."

Jan managed to nod but he couldn't talk.

She broke into a run, trying to gauge how far ahead Janis would be. She figured she'd have at least a kilometre on her, and she may have cut up onto the street at any point. It depended on how organised she was. Did she have a car waiting somewhere?

The storm front had passed and the gusts of wind had abated but the rain continued to fall in a steady drizzle. Birgitte's lower back ached with the strain of saving her father and she had never been colder in her life. She did her best to ignore the pain and discomfort, telling herself she had to catch Janis now or she may never get a chance again.

After several minutes of running she reached a less populated stretch of coast. The houses were set back further from the beach on broader swathes of land where the bush was allowed to act as natural hedging. The houses were much large here – modernist mansions, holiday homes of the extremely wealthy. She looked up into each property as she jogged by to see if there was an obvious exit point, but there was nothing.

The light was fading fast. Birgitte stopped running. She looked back along the beach but could no longer see where she had come from. She hoped the paramedics were able to help her parents and the officer who had been shot. Part of her wanted to stay there to look after them but she simply didn't have that luxury.

A light turned on to her left. She looked up into the window and saw Janis drying herself with a towel in a living room window, as if she was enjoying a weekend away with her wealthy friends. At this distance, Birgitte couldn't tell if it was dark enough to obscure her own body from sight. She ran up the beach, over the embankment. The property was fenced in but Birgitte found where Janis had entered only minutes earlier. A side gate had been jimmied open with a large branch. Janis had used a rock to smash a floor-to-ceiling slit window to enter the house. Did she know if the owners were even away? How long had she been in Denmark, Birgitte wondered, how long in Skagen? Birgitte stepped inside carefully so as not to make a noise on the broken glass.

The mansion was all polished concrete, white walls and sharp angles. Birgitte moved upstairs silently. She could now hear Janis moving around, turning on lights, scoping out her new domain. Birgitte ducked down and crept along the corridor that led to the back of the house. When she reached the arc of light from the expansive living room she tried to peer into the kitchen to see what Janis was doing. She looked straight into the barrel of her gun.

"Up you get, Sweetheart," she said. "You must be freezing. There's a bathroom through there. From what I've seen of the wardrobe there should be something warm and fetching you can slip into."

Birgitte slowly stood up.

"Go on, you'll catch a death if you don't warm up this instant." Janis' tone was warm, matronly. Birgitte made her way passed the kitchen, along a narrow corridor that led to several bedrooms. Janis walked behind her with the gun trained on Birgitte's back. "Down the end. It's all a bit Grand Designs, don't you think? The walls are probably insulated with llama wool."

317

Birgitte found the master bedroom. The ensuite led off to the right. There was a walk-in shower. Janis' wet dress was crumpled on the floor.

Birgitte peeled off her shirt and pants and slipped out of her underwear. Janis leaned against the vanity, enjoying the view. "That's quite a scar you've got there," she said, looking at the angry red stripe across Birgitte's stomach. "My Ian do that?"

Birgitte ignored the remark and stepped into the wet area.

"It's a bit hot at first," Janis said, "but that's just because you're so cold."

Birgitte turned on the water and winced. It was like needles piercing her skin. Moments later she could feel the warmth of the water soak into her frozen bones, softening her limbs. She had no idea how she was going to disarm Janis.

When she was finished, Janis tossed her a clean towel. "Look at us, like two girls at summer camp."

She guided her back into the master bedroom, to the wardrobe. She picked out two pairs of thick trousers, some shirts and a several jumpers. "This oughta to do it."

She continued to hold the gun on Birgitte as she dressed. When Birgitte pulled the jumper over her head, Janis said, "Right, go back in the shower and wait till I'm dressed."

It was a smart move. If Birgitte did decide to make a break for it, Janis would have plenty of time to pick up her gun.

Within a matter of minutes they were both back in the living room facing onto the kitchen.

Janis found the remote for the gas fireplace then set about looking for something to drink. She came out of the pantry carrying a bottle of Cognac in one hand, the gun in the other. "This ought to do nicely to warm our insides, no? The glasses should be behind you."

Birgitte searched through the cupboards until she found two crystal balloons. "What do you think is going to happen next, Janis? You've shot a Danish police officer. This whole area is going to be crawling with police and media within the hour."

"To be honest, Sweetheart, I'm really not sure anymore." She removed the cork with her teeth and poured out two doubles. She put the bottle on the bench and picked up one of the glasses. "You see, you're all that's left. I've lost Ian. I've lost Xi Xi. The dogs. Whatever happiness I had is gone. You're my only connection to the things that make me who I am." Her flippant tone belied the reality of the situation.

Birgitte tried to offer a look of sympathy. "You're very sick, Janis. You need help. I don't know what set you on the path you've been on but you can get treatment. Don't you want all this madness to stop?"

"This madness, as you so condescendingly describe it, is who I am, Darling. And right now, you're the only future I've got."

"I'm your future?" Birgitte laughed despite herself. "Do you intend taking me hostage? Where will we go? Have you even thought any of this through?"

"I got here, didn't I?" She waved the gun out towards the sea behind her. "Halfway across the fucking globe."

Before Birgitte could ask how, she went on in a droll tone. "You may think Canningvale and his cronies are depraved, Sweetheart, but they're all the more resourceful because of it. I've got more leverage with those animals than you can imagine. I could bring down half the fucking Tory party and the BBC to boot with an email to the press and they bloody well know it."

Birgitte didn't say anything, unsure of whether Janis was just bragging.

"Don't believe me?" she said. "I had a fresh passport waiting for me in Shanghai and another in Berlin. Both from different sources. Both untraceable. Neither cost me a fucking cent."

There was a note of triumph in her voice, but it was brittle. The wretchedness in her eyes softened momentarily. "So, Darling, it would seem I've had a lot of time to think things through. And all I want is for you to understand what you mean to me."

Birgitte kept her tone even. "You don't know me."

"You don't know yourself!" Janis screamed. "You don't know what you're capable of because you've never had the guts to look. You've glimpsed into the abyss and looked away because it's all too horrible."

Birgitte had no idea what she was talking about but didn't like the rage that she was seeing – it was unpredictable.

Janis took a deep breath and lowered her tone. "I can help you discover what else is out there. I can bring you out of yourself, the self you thought you knew. You can become something other... other than this." She waved the gun up and down with contempt. "We could be so much more... more than this. Don't you see?"

Birgitte was beginning to understand how Janis had manipulated Ian and Xi Xi – two partially formed minds that were open to suggestion at low points in their lives, needy little puppy dogs who could be trained to behave violently. But what made her think she could manipulate Birgitte?

"Is your life so good?" Janis almost pleaded.

Birgitte managed to shrug but didn't say anything.

"From what I've gleaned, your career is in limbo. One more inquest and you can kiss goodbye any chance at advancement. Your husband has shacked up with another woman, yes? About to have a baby? You've been deluding yourself, Sweetheart. For what? Don't tell me you're waiting for their approval?" she scoffed, now waving her gun at the outside world. "Why wait? Do you really think they have your best interests at heart? The one thing I taught Ian and Xi Xi is you have to act in your own interests at every opportunity or this life just passes you by, always on everyone else's terms. Surely you can see that, can't you? You have to take it by the throat, Sweetheart."

Birgitte was considering whether it was worthwhile to play along with Janis' new game in the hope of seizing an opportunity overpower her, when the doorbell rang.

Janis' body tensed. She raised one finger to her lips. The was a loud banging on the front door. "Don't you fucking move," she whispered through her teeth. She turned and slipped along the corridor, and down the stairs. Birgitte quickly followed. Through one of the slit windows Birgitte caught a glimpse of a young male security guard, who may have been alerted by some sort of sensor alarm when Janis had jimmied the gate or smashed the window. There was a gun on his hip but he made no attempts to use it. He peered through a window near the front of the house, saw nothing, then casually moved further along the wall towards the sea. He'd probably spent his evening responding to several sensor alarms set off by the storm on other properties in the area. There was no sign of Janis. She must have slipped out through the broken slit window. Birgitte saw her chance. Further along the ground floor corridor was a side door to the house. She ran as fast as she could and pulled the door open as the security guard stepped past.

The sound of the door opening alarmed him. As he spun round his chest erupted with two deafening explosions. Janis stood 15 feet behind him with the pistol in both hands. The security guard looked up into the rain, utterly confused and terrified as his legs gave way. Before he could fall, Birgitte used his body for cover and managed to release his gun from his holster.

Janis realised what was happening and leapt back into the house before Birgitte could get the safety off. The security guard slumped to the ground, dead. Birgitte stepped back through the side door and crouched down. Janis had already run back up the stairs.

Birgitte turned and headed for the front of the house. Through a door she found a four-car garage. There were two SUVs parked side by side and two empty berths. In the opposite corner was another door. It opened onto a stairwell leading up to the ground floor. Birgitte paused and listened for Janis but couldn't hear a thing. She crept up the stairs. At the landing she looked down the corridor to the living room but there were no signs of her, so she continued up the stairs to the first floor. She recalled noticing a mezzanine level that looked over the kitchen and living room. The first floor held three other bedrooms and bathroom which all led onto the upstairs living area. It was a large space with oversized couches and an enormous flat-screen TV. Outside she could hear sirens passing the house; the police and more ambulances on their way to assist her parents. There was no way of alerting them to her own situation.

There was a stairway she hadn't noticed earlier, that led down to the main living room. If she took it, she would be exposed in both directions, but she was sure Janis was somewhere on the ground floor. She listened for any doors opening or closing. Janis must have arrived by car. She might make a break through the front door or back out through the slit window.

Birgitte crept down the stairwell she had ascended earlier. She couldn't cover the front door and the slit window but she could get midway between both and hope for the best. She found a storage room down towards the garage, checked it was empty then used it as cover.

"Janis?" she called out. "I know you can hear me. This needs to end. You can hear the sirens. It's over."

There was no response.

"I don't want to have to shoot you," she called out. The silence was broken with laughter. It was coming from the ground-floor living room. Birgitte crouched down and stepped carefully along the corridor, this time hugging the far wall, aiming her gun exactly where Janis had trapped her earlier. She was confident she could get a shot off before Janis could raise her arm. She was highly trained. Janis wasn't. But as she approached the living room the house filled with brilliant sweeping lights as the heavy thud of helicopter rotors filled the air. A chopper was hovering over the beach. It had been searching the area for the person who had shot the policeman further along the shoreline. The pilot had obviously spotted the branch propping the gate open and the car parked outside an otherwise deserted house.

The spotlight swept back and forth, momentarily blinding Birgitte then warping the interior in all directions. As she stood up the light came to a halt directly into the living room. Janis was standing in the front window, glass of Cognac in one hand, gun in the other. She was looking out at the helicopter. On the rail a male officer was bracing himself with a rifle.

Birgitte entered the room with her gun poised at Janis' back. She knew she couldn't shoot her from behind, even though she was armed. Birgitte stepped closer and closer, but then realised the officers in the helicopter had no idea which of the two of them had shot their colleague further along the beach. She could just make out the sniper, with his rifle raised oscillating his aim between the pair of them, unsure of who the real target should be.

Birgitte had run out of time. "Turn around, Janis."

Janis smiled at her own reflection. "Don't want another inquest, Sweetheart? But you're desperate to kill me. I guess the choice is mine then."

She drained her Cognac, dropped the glass and spun around with her weapon raised to the ceiling. Before the glass had hit the floor, Birgitte had squeezed off one round which hit Janis square in the chest and shattered the floor-to-ceiling glass behind her. The next two shoots lifted her off the ground and pushed her back through the window. A fourth shot rang out which hit Birgitte in the shoulder. She was thrown back against the island bench of the kitchen. The helicopter dipped and adjusted its position, then two more shots were fired into the house, ripping apart the sofa, which Birgitte had crawled behind. She could hear the front door being bashed in, the boots marching along the corridor. She slid the gun across the polished concrete. "Police!" she screamed in Danish over the sound of the chopper. "I'm the officer who called it in. I am unarmed. Don't shoot." She held her breath and grit her teeth. Within the next few seconds, if the officers took her as an immediate threat, she would be shot pieces.

A male officer barked at her from behind the kitchen wall. "Name!"

"Detective Birgitte Vestergaard, homicide, Copenhagen. It's my parents who were attacked up the beach."

No one moved.

"Call off the chopper," she screamed. "I've been hit. I need an ambulance."

After what seemed an interminably long time the spotlight turned away and the chopper lifted up into the night sky. The police swept through the building with assault rifles still drawn. When the commanding officer was satisfied the real threat had been eliminated, they lowered their weapons and called for another ambulance.

While they waited for more assistance, Birgitte's wound was assessed then patched on both sides to stem the bleeding. The bullet had passed straight through, shattering what felt like her collarbone on the way. The pain was making her nauseous but she said she could stand up so an officer helped her to her feet. With his assistance she shuffled to the window of the living room and peered down into the abyss. There, lying face up in a white-tiled courtyard, with ribbons of blood trailing from several points on her chest, Janis Pollack stared up at the sky. There was always going to be a path of destruction to this point. Birgitte could only hope she'd contributed in some way to mitigate the damage. She thought of Catherine Yi in the cage at the abandoned Catholic school in Shek Lei. Perhaps that was enough – to know that one child had been saved. Cripps' death wouldn't be in vain either; with time the truth about Janis, Ian and Sir Albert Canningvale would come out.

As if on cue, two more helicopters appeared in the sky – media. The police chopper had landed on the beach and the sniper, a tall man in his 30s, walked awkwardly up the embankment. He'd already been told that he'd shot the wrong person, and that that person was a homicide detective. Birgitte could see the devastation in his face.

A few minutes later he approached her in the living room. "I'm so sorry."

"It's okay," she said. "It was all very confusing. I don't blame you."

"But I should have waited."

"You took the shot because you had to."

"Will there be an inquest?"

"I won't be asking for one."

"She had her gun in the air."

"I know."

The realisation that Birgitte had shot too soon as well dawned on him. If there was going to be an inquest, they'd both have a lot to answer for. "I could say the gun was lower..."

"Just tell the truth. It's all that will be expected of you."

325

The pain in her shoulder and the loss of blood overwhelmed her. She slumped into the other officer's arms.

EPILOGUE

Christmas passed by virtually unnoticed. Birgitte's parents were still recuperating in the Aalborg University Hospital, an hour or so south of Skagen; her mother with severe concussion and a fractured skull, her father with pneumonia. The doctors were confident they would both make a full recovery, but given their ages they needed more time under observation. Birgitte's shoulder was healing well but was still taped up and her right arm was in a sling. Fortunately her collar bone wasn't shattered, but there was limited damage to the bones in her shoulder. It would take a few months of intensive physiotherapy before she could move her arm normally.

When she wasn't visiting her parents she was at the house, making the most of the peace and quiet. The Christmas festivities had been cancelled, which meant there was an abundance of food and wine and no one to share it with. She'd considered calling a friend to come and stay with her but she really just wanted to savour her own company for a few days.

Sven had called earlier in the day to suggest he put her on light duties through January, with an eye to discussing her future before the end of the month. He was still annoyed with his superiors' unwillingness to see her potential. His kind words were a much-needed salve for her wounded ego. Her time would come, he reassured her before returning to his own family lunch.

She had spent the afternoon on the couch with her laptop catching up on the regional news she'd been missing for the past few weeks. Most of the headlines were devoted to a breaking story from England. The skeletal remains of three children had been inadvertently dug up by a bull dozer in a disused lot in the West Midlands, about 20km north-east of Walsell. A large tract of land was now sealed off as forensic teams from

Scotland Yard began the bleak task of searching for at least two more bodies – Birgitte had briefed them before leaving Hong Kong on everything Janis had told her prior to disappearing. The property had belonged to a long-deceased man from Walsell. Birgitte sent an email to her contact at the Metropolitan Police to see if the owner had had any connection to Sir Albert Canningvale.

She then checked the time and opened up the video conferencing software on her laptop. The dial tone rang persistently before the screen came to life. Birgitte was pleased to see little Celina's beaming face staring into the camera.

"Who's that?" the little girl screamed in English.

"It's Birgitte. I had lunch with you a few weeks ago."

The girl waved then climbed off the chair. Peter Wong's apartment once again was crowded with family members preparing for lunch. Celina ran between her mother and Michelle into the kitchen. Peter came out, wearing an apron, squeezing balls of pork mince in his hands.

"Birgitte, how are you?"

"I'm so sorry to bother you. I didn't realise you would be preparing lunch."

He shrugged. "Just the usual vultures. How are you recovering?"

"I'm okay."

"And your parents?"

She had sent him an email outlining what had happened on Christmas Eve, including her shooting of Janis.

"They're okay too. They both should be out in a day or two. Thanks for asking. Listen, I can call back later tonight when it's more convenient."

"Not at all. Just let me wash my hands. We can go out on the balcony."

A few minutes later Peter had set his laptop up on the table outside. Birgitte could see that it was a beautiful clear day in Hong Kong. Peter slid the balcony door closed. "Is it too noisy out here? Can you hear me?"

"It's fine. Did you read about the remains of the three children dug up in the West Midlands?"

"I did. I was going to call you. How many did Janis Pollack say they'd killed?"

"Five. The footage has been harrowing but at least it will bring some closure to the families."

He nodded.

"How are things there?"

"Chaotic," he said. "And this news from England isn't going to make it any easier. A lot of British media have flown in trying to pick up on Ian and Janis's story. Chief Inspector Li is going demented with the queries."

"I can only imagine."

"There's one journalist here, a woman in her 50s, says she's a former colleague of Cripps and that he'd sent her a copy of all his notes just before he was killed. He was genuinely concerned the story wouldn't get out, so she's taken up his cause."

Birgitte was relieved to hear this. Deep down, like Cripps, she felt the Metropolitan Police in the West Midlands and the commanders of the British Armed Forces in Afghanistan during the mid to late 2000s, both had cases to answer.

"Unfortunately," Peter continued, "there is some more bad news. When this journalist tried to contact the woman from Walsell, Talia Mackland, the other day, to push her for more details, she was told by a flatmate that Ms Mackland was found dead in her room over Christmas. She'd overdosed on heroin."

Birgitte held her breath. Christ, that poor woman. She'd done everything she could to forget what had happened to her as a child, and their investigation had dug it all up again. Birgitte berated herself for not calling again to make sure she was okay, or at least she should have encouraged someone to stay in touch with her.

"I thought you would have heard," Peter said. "I'm sorry, Birgitte, if I'm the one breaking it to you."

"It's okay," she said quietly. "Just tragic. She'd been clean for two years. What's the word on Canningvale?"

"He's being extradited back to England to face historic charges of paedophilia and corruption. Once the Metropolitan Police have enough evidence on the murders in Walsell, I'm sure they'll be on the warpath to see someone punished for what happened."

Even now, Birgitte wasn't so sure that Canningvale would see the inside of a prison. He was so well connected, it seemed he could talk his way out of anything.

"I wish I didn't shoot her," she said eventually. "At least one of them should have been held accountable."

"I'm sure you did what you had to do. Will there be an inquest?"

Birgitte nodded. "In the new year. But I'm hoping no one is going to judge me too harshly for how I acted."

"Good luck with it."

"How's Lindy?"

"Inspector Kwok is doing very well, I believe" he said with a grin. "She's now part of a new team at a different station."

"I'm so pleased she passed her exams. You did well to mentor her."

"I have a new PI under me now, a young guy who thinks he knows everything."

"I'm sure he'll realise he's on to a good thing soon enough. What about the young woman, Xi Xi?"

His smile faded. "She received a suspended sentence for aiding and abetting Janis and Ian. As I mentioned in my last email, I've been doing what I can to get her the support she needs: counselling, employment training, anything that might help her get on a healthier path…" He broke off and looked out over the harbour. "She disappeared a few days ago. No one's seen her since."

"Any ideas?"

"Probably gone back to the world she knows best."

"I'm sorry, Peter. At least she won't have to go through the trauma of a trial."

"She left this behind," he said, holding up the stuffed bunny toy, "along with a note, saying I'd do a better job looking after it."

Birgitte smiled warmly at the inspector. He stared at the bunny as if it held answers he couldn't decipher, then he looked through the balcony door into the apartment. "My family are getting restless. I better get back inside before they start pulling apart the furniture."

She wished him well and promised to stay in touch before disconnecting the line.

The house suddenly felt very empty.

Birgitte stared into the open fire place, watching the flames flicker across the logs. Despite her father's shortcomings, and the unsettled nature of her own upbringing, she was incredibly grateful her childhood had never been marred by the selfish desires of damaged adults. It had occurred to her over these past few days that it was her own choice to immerse herself in the world of criminals and the people they hurt. It was a choice she made every morning when she got up to go to work. She could just as easily choose to walk away and find something else safer to do, less demanding. But turning away wasn't a part of her make-up, even if it was her father's. In that respect she was more like her mother. There was solace enough in this, she decided. The rest wasn't worth dwelling on.

She closed her eyes, lay back on the sofa and listened to the rain sweep in over Northern Jutland.

Made in the USA
Middletown, DE
27 August 2020